The Long Mars

BOOKS BY TERRY PRATCHETT

The Dark Side of the Sun

Strata

The Unadulterated Cat
(*illustrated by Gray Jolliffe*)

Good Omens (*with Neil
Gaiman*)

FOR YOUNG ADULTS

The Carpet People

Nation

The Bromilead Trilogy

Truckers

Diggers

Wings

**The Johnny Maxwell
Trilogy**

Only You Can Save
Mankind

Johnny and the Dead

Johnny and the Bomb

THE DISCWORLD® BOOKS

The Color of Magic

The Light Fantastic

Equal Rites

Mort

Sourcery

Wyrd Sisters

Pyramids

Guards! Guards!

Eric (*illustrated
by Josh Kirby*)

Moving Pictures

Reaper Man

Witches Abroad

Small Gods

A Hat Full of Sky

Wintersmith

I Shall Wear Midnight

The Illustrated Wee
Free Men (*illustrated by
Stephen Player*)

BOOKS BY STEPHEN BAXTER

Anti-Ice

The Time Ships

Traces

The Light of Other Days
(*with Arthur C. Clarke*)

Evolution

The H-Bomb Girl

NORTHLAND

Stone Spring

Bronze Summer

Iron Winter

FLOOD

Flood

Ark

TIME'S TAPESTRY

Emperor

Conqueror

Navigator

Weaver

DESTINY'S CHILDREN

Coalescent

Exultant

Transcendent

Resplendent

A TIME ODYSSEY
(WITH ARTHUR C. CLARKE)

Time's Eye

Sunstorm

Firstborn

MANIFOLD

Manifold 1: Time

Manifold 2: Space

BY TERRY PRATCHETT AND STEPHEN BAXTER

The Long Mars

Terry Pratchett and Stephen Baxter

An Imprint of HarperCollins*Publishers*

First U.S. edition published 2014.

Published simultaneously in Great Britain by Doubleday, an imprint of Transworld Publishers, a division of Random House Group, Ltd.

Art on page xi by Richard Shailer

HarperCollins books may be purchased for educational, business, or sales promotional use. For information, please e-mail the Special Markets Department at SPsales@harpercollins.com.

FIRST HARPERLUXE EDITION

HarperLuxe™ is a trademark of HarperCollins Publishers

Library of Congress Cataloging-in-Publication Data is available upon request.

ISBN: 978-0-06-232672-0

14 ID/RRD 10 9 8 7 6 5 4 3 2 1

For Lyn and Rhianna, as always
T.P.

For Sandra
S.B.

MARS GLIDER
Design © GapSpace Inc

400:1

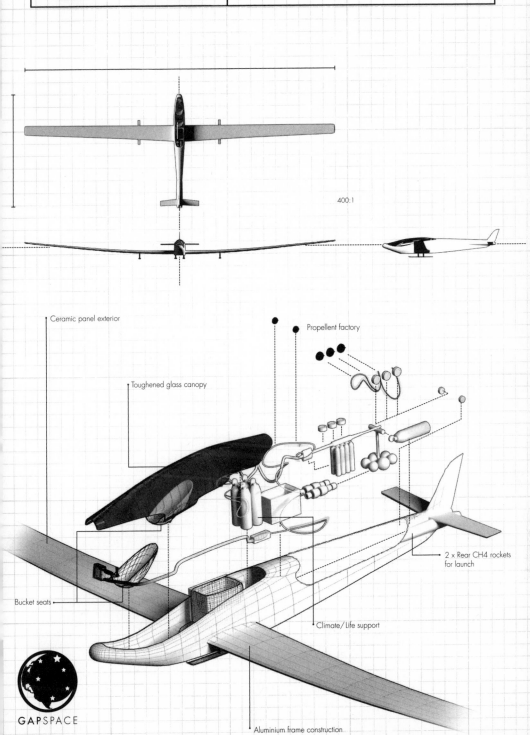

Ceramic panel exterior

Propellent factory

Toughened glass canopy

2 x Rear CH4 rockets
for launch

Bucket seats

Climate/Life support

Aluminium frame construction

GAPSPACE

1

The High Meggers:

Remote worlds, most still unpopulated, even in the year 2045, thirty years after Step Day. Up there you could be utterly alone. One soul in an entire world.

It did funny things to the mind, thought Joshua Valienté. After a few months alone you got so sensitive that you thought you could tell if another human, even just a single person, arrived to share your world. One other human, maybe on the other side of the planet. The Princess and the Pea wasn't in it. And the nights were cold and big and the starlight was all aimed at *you.*

And yet, Joshua thought, even on an empty world, under an empty sky, other people always crowded into your head. People like his estranged wife and his son, and his sometime travelling companion Sally Linsay, and all the people of the suffering Datum Earth in the aftermath of Yellowstone, five years after the eruption.

And Lobsang. Always Lobsang . . .

Given his unusual origins, Lobsang had necessarily become something of an authority on the work known in the west as the Tibetan Book of the Dead.

Perhaps its most familiar title to Tibetans was the Bardo Thodol, roughly translated as Liberation Through Hearing. This funerary text, intended to guide the consciousness through the interval between death and rebirth, had no single agreed edition. With origins in the eighth century, with time it had passed through many hands, a process that had bequeathed many different versions and interpretations.

Sometimes, as Lobsang had surveyed the state of Datum Earth, first home of mankind, in the days, months and years after the Yellowstone super-eruption of 2040, he found comfort in the sonorous language of the ancient text.

Comfort, compared with the news that had come out of Bozeman, Montana, Earth West 1, for example, only days after the eruption. News to which his closest friends had responded . . .

On any ordinary day, the community growing up in this one-step-West footprint of Bozeman must be a typical stepwise colony, Joshua thought, as he pulled on his protective coveralls one more time. A bunch of Abe Lincoln log cabins cut into a forest whose lumber was steadily being worked for export to the Datum. A corral, a small chapel. If anything this copy of Bozeman lacked facilities you'd find further out in the Long Earth, such as a hotel, bars, a town hall, a school, a clinic; this close to the Datum it was just too easy to step back home for all of that.

But this day, September 15 2040, was no ordinary day in any of the stepwise Americas. For, seven days after the big caldera had first gone up, back on Datum Earth the eruption of Yellowstone was still continuing. Bozeman, Montana, was only fifty miles or so from the ongoing blast.

And, one step from the disaster, Bozeman West 1 was transformed. Though the day was bright, the sky blue, the grass a vivid green – no volcano skies here – the town was crowded with people, jammed into the cabins and housed in hastily erected tents or just sitting on tarpaulins on the ground. People so coated with volcano ash that they were uniformly grey, their skin, hair and clothes, like they were characters from some ancient black-and-white TV show, *I Love Lucy*, cut-and-pasted digitally into the bright sunlit green of this fine fall day. Men, women and children, all coughing and retching like they had 1950s smoking habits too.

The landscape around the town, meanwhile, had been appropriated by the official types from FEMA and the National Guard, who had marked out the ground with laser beams, police crime-scene tape, even just chalk marks, to match the layouts of blocks and buildings in Datum Bozeman. Some of the outlines extended into the woods and scrubland, land as yet untamed here. The officials had numbered and labelled these blocks, and were sending stepping volunteers back to the Datum systematically, marking off computerized maps on their tablets, to ensure the whole community was cleared of people.

In a way the whole thing was a display of the basic mystery of the Long Earth, Joshua thought. It was already a quarter-century since Step Day, when he and other kids all around the world had downloaded the spec for a simple electronic gadget called a Stepper box, and turned the knob as per instructions – and *stepped*, not left or right, forward or back, but in another direction entirely. Stepped into a world of forest and swamp, at least if you started in Madison, Wisconsin, as Joshua had. A world all but identical to Earth – old Earth, Datum Earth – save there had been no people in it. Not until kids like Joshua appeared, popping out of thin air. And, Joshua had quickly found, you could take another step, and another, until you found yourself striding along a whole chain of parallel worlds, with differences from the Datum gradually increasing – but not a human in sight. The worlds of the Long Earth.

And here was the basic, harsh reality of it. Datum America was now covered by a searing blanket of volcanic ash and dust – yet here, a single step away, it was as if Yellowstone didn't exist at all.

Sally Linsay showed up, finishing a coffee from a polystyrene cup that she carefully placed in a bin for cleaning and reuse: good pioneer-type habits, Joshua thought absently. She was in a clean one-piece coverall, but the ash had got into her hair, the skin of her neck and face, even her ears, anywhere the FEMA face-masks and straps hadn't covered.

She was accompanied by a National Guardsman, just a kid, with a tablet computer. He checked their identities, the numbers on the chests of their suits, the town block they were going into this time. 'You two ready again?'

Sally began to fix her mask over her face once more, a breathing filter, steampunk goggles. 'Seven days of this already.'

Joshua reached for his own mask. 'It won't be finishing any time soon, I'm guessing.'

'So where's Helen now?'

'Back at Hell-Knows-Where.' The National Guard kid raised his eyebrows, but Joshua was talking about his home off in the High Meggers, a community more than a million steps from the Datum, where he lived with his family: Helen, his son Dan. 'Or on the way there. Safer for Dan, she says.'

'That's true enough. The Datum and the Low Earths are going to be a mess for years.'

He knew she was right. There had been minor geological events in the Low Earths, mirroring the big Datum eruption, but the 'mess' in the young worlds had been made by the vast spilling of refugees from the Datum.

Sally eyed Joshua. 'I bet Helen wasn't happy that you refused to go back with her.'

'Look, it was tough on us. But Datum America is where I grew up. I can't just abandon it.'

'So you decided to stick around and use your stepping superpowers to help the afflicted.'

'Don't give me that, Sally. You're here too. Why, you grew up in Wyoming itself—'

She was grinning. 'Yeah, but I don't have a little wife trying to draw me away. Big argument, was it? Or just one of her long sulks?'

He turned away, fixing his mask with an angry tug on the straps at the back of his head, pulling up his hood. She laughed at him, her voice muffled by her own mask. He'd known Sally for ten years now, since his own first exploratory jaunt into the deep Long Earth – only to find Sally Linsay was already out there. Nothing much about her had changed.

The National Guard kid positioned them by a strip of police tape. 'The property you'll be going into is right ahead of you. A couple of kids came out already, but we're missing three adults. Record of one phobic. Family name Brewer.'

'Gotcha,' Joshua said.

'The United States government appreciates all you're doing.'

Joshua glanced at Sally's eyes, behind her mask. This boy was no more than nineteen. Joshua was thirty-eight, Sally forty-three. Joshua resisted the temptation to ruffle the kid's blond hair. 'Sure, son.' Then he snapped on his head torch and reached for Sally's gloved hand. 'You ready?'

'Always.' She glanced down at the hand holding hers. 'You sure that fake paw of yours is up to this?'

His prosthetic left hand was a legacy of their last long journey together. 'More than the rest of me, probably.' They hunched over, knowing what was to come. 'Three, two, one—'

They stepped into hell.

Ash and pumice pounded their shoulders, their heads, the ash like diabolic snow, grey, heavy and hot, the pumice coming in frothy pebble-sized chunks. The falling rocks hammered on a car in front of them, a mound already heaped up with ash. The background noise was a steady dull roar that drowned out their speech. The sky, under Yellowstone ash and gas and smoke from a plume that by now climbed twenty miles into the air, was virtually black.

And it was *hot*, hot as a pioneer town's forge. It was hard to believe the caldera itself was all of fifty miles away. Even out as far as this, some said, the falling ash could melt again and flow as lava.

But the property they'd come to check out was right before them, as in the Guard's plan, a one-storey house with a porch that had collapsed under the weight of the ash.

Sally led the way forward, around the buried car. They had to wade through an ash fall that was feet deep in places, like a heavy, hot, hard snowfall. Its sheer weight was only the beginning of the problems the ash caused. If it got the chance the stuff would abrade your skin, turn your eyes into itching pockets of pain, and scrape your lungs to mincemeat. Give it a few months and it could kill you, even if it didn't just crush you first.

The front door seemed to be locked. Sally didn't waste time; she raised a booted leg and kicked in the door.

Wreckage clogged the room within. Joshua saw in the light of his lamp that the load of pumice and ash had long overwhelmed this wooden-framed structure, and the roof and loft space had fallen in through the ceiling. This living room was cluttered with debris, as well as with grey drifts of ash. At first glance it seemed impossible that anybody could be left alive in here. But Sally, always quick to assess a new and confusing situation, pointed at one corner where a dining table stood, square and stout and resistant, despite a thick layer of ash on its own upper surface.

They pushed their way through. Where their booted feet scraped away the debris, Joshua glimpsed a crimson carpet.

The table was shrouded with curtains. When they pulled these aside they found three adults. They were just mounds of ash-grey clothing, their heads and faces swathed with towels. But Joshua soon identified a man and a woman, middle-aged, maybe fifties, and one woman who looked much older, frailer, maybe eighty years old; slumped in a corner, she seemed to be asleep. From the toilet stink that came out of this little shelter, Joshua guessed they'd been here some time, days perhaps.

Startled by Joshua and Sally in their nuclear-alert-type masks, the middle-aged couple quailed back. But then the man pulled away a towel to reveal an ash-stained mouth, red-rimmed eyes. 'Thank God.'

'Mr Brewer? My name's Joshua. This is Sally. We've come to get you out of here.'

Brewer smiled. 'Nobody gets left behind, eh? Just like President Cowley promised.'

Joshua glanced around. 'You look like you did pretty well here. Supplies, stuff to keep the ash out of your mouths and eyes.'

The man, Brewer, forced a smile. 'Well, we did what the sensible young lady said.'

'What "sensible young lady"?'

'Came around a couple of days before the ash fall really kicked in. Wore kind of pioneer gear – never gave us her name, thought she must be from some government agency. Gave us smart advice about survival, very clear.' He glanced at the older woman. 'She also told us very clearly that the planetary alignment was nothing to do with it, and this wasn't a punishment by God, and my mother-in-law seemed to find that a comfort. Didn't take much notice of her advice at the time, but we remembered come the day. Yeah, we did OK. Although we're running out of stuff now.'

The middle-aged woman shook her head. 'But we can't leave.'

'You can't *stay*,' Sally said harshly. 'You're out of food and water, right? You'll starve to death if the ash doesn't kill you. Look, if you don't have Stepper boxes we can just pick you up and go—'

'You don't understand,' Brewer said. 'We sent away the kids, the dog. But Meryl – my mother-in-law—'

'Extreme phobic,' the woman said. 'You know what that means.'

That stepping between the worlds, even if Meryl was carried over, would invoke such a reaction in her that it could kill her, unless a cocktail of appropriate medications was quickly administered.

Brewer said, 'I'm betting you're out of phobic drugs already over there, where you're taking us.'

'And even if not,' said his wife, 'the young, the healthy will be prioritized. I won't leave my mother behind.' She glared at Sally. 'Would you?'

'My father, maybe.' Sally started to back out of the crowded space. 'Come on, Joshua, we're wasting our time.'

'No. Wait.' Joshua touched the old woman's arm. Her breath was a rattle. 'What we need to do is take her someplace where they *do* still have drugs. Somewhere away from the ash cloud zone.'

'And how the hell do we do that?'

'Through the soft places. Come on, Sally, if there was ever a time to use *your* superpower it's now. Can you do it?'

Sally expressed her irritation with a glare through her obscuring facemask. Joshua stuck it out.

Then she closed her eyes, as if sensing something, *listening*. Feeling out the soft places, the Long Earth short cuts only she and a few other adepts could use . . . Joshua's idea was that Meryl could be carried, via the soft places, to someplace other than a stepwise Bozeman, to someplace where the medications would be more freely available.

'Yes. All right. There's a place a couple of blocks from here. In two steps I can get her to New York, East 3. But, Joshua, the soft places are no easy ride, even if you aren't old and frail.'

'No choice. Let's do it.' He turned back to the Brewers to explain.

And the whole house seemed to lift.

Joshua, crouching under the table, was thrown on his back. He heard timbers crack and fail, and the hiss of the ash making still more inroads into the house.

When it settled, Brewer's eyes were wide. 'What the hell was that?'

Sally said, 'I'm guessing the caldera's collapsed.'

They all knew what that implied; after seven days everybody was an expert on supervolcanoes. When the eruption finally finished, the magma chamber would collapse inward, a chunk of Earth's crust the size of Rhode Island falling down through half a mile – a shock that would make the whole planet ring like a bell.

'Let's get out of here,' Joshua said. 'I'll lead you.'

It took only seconds for Joshua to step the Brewers out of the house, and safely over into the impossible sunshine of West 1.

And, just as Joshua stepped back into the Datum ash to help Sally with the mother, the sound from the caldera collapse arrived, following the ground waves. It was a sky-filling noise, as if all the artillery batteries in the world had opened up just beyond the horizon. A sound that would, eventually, wash around the whole planet. The old lady, propped up by Sally, her dressing gown stained grey, her head obscured by towels, whimpered and clapped her hands to her ears.

Joshua, in the middle of all this, wondered who the 'sensible young lady' in the pioneer gear had been.

The Bardo Thodol described the interval between death and rebirth in terms of bardos: intermediate states of consciousness. Some authorities identified three bardos, some six. Of these Lobsang found most intriguing the sidpa bardo, or the bardo of rebirth, which featured karmically impelled visions. Perhaps these were hallucinations, derived from the flaws of one's own soul. Or perhaps they were authentic visions of a suffering Datum Earth, and its innocent companion worlds.

Such as an image of dreamlike vessels hanging in a Kansas sky . . .

The US Navy airship USS *Benjamin Franklin* met the *Zheng He*, a ship of the Navy of the new Chinese federal government, over the West 1 footprint of Wichita, Kansas. Chen Zhong, Captain of the Chinese ship, claimed to have concerns about the role he was expected to undertake in the ongoing relief effort in Datum America, and an exasperated Admiral Hiram Davidson, representing an overstretched chain of command – well, everybody was overstretched, as the fall of this disastrous year of 2040 turned into winter – had mandated Maggie Kauffman, Captain of the *Franklin*, to take time out of her own relief efforts to meet with the man and discuss his concerns.

'As if I have the time to salve the ego of some old Communist apparatchik,' Maggie grumbled in the solitude of her sea cabin.

'But that's what he is,' said Shi-mi, curled up in her basket by Maggie's desk. 'You evidently checked him out. I could have done that for you—'

'I don't trust *you* as far as I can throw you,' Maggie murmured to the cat, without malice.

'Which is probably pretty far.' Shi-mi stood and stretched with a small, quite convincing purr.

She was a quite convincing cat, actually. Save for the green LED sparks of her eyes. And the prissy human-type personality she embodied. And the fact that she could talk. Shi-mi had been an ambiguous gift to Maggie, from one of the equally ambiguous figures who seemed to be watching her career with an unwelcome interest.

Shi-mi said now, 'Captain Chen is on his way . . .'

Maggie checked her status board. The cat was right; Chen was in the air. Chen had insisted that the two twains needn't land to exchange personnel; he was crossing in a two-person light copter which could easily be set down inside the *Franklin*, he bragged, if the US ship opened up one of its big cargo bays. These new Chinese liked nothing more than to demonstrate their technical capabilities, especially over an America still prostrate two months after the eruption. Show-offs.

Distracted, Maggie glanced out of her cabin's big picture window at this world, a Midwest sky big and blue and scattered with light clouds, the green carpet of a stepwise Kansas semi-infinite and flat beneath her – and all but unspoiled still, even on this Earth a single step away from the Datum. But more spoiled than it used to be. Before September, before Yellowstone, Wichita West 1 had been little more than a shadow of its Datum parent, scattered buildings of logs and blown concrete set out in a grid that roughly aped the Datum town plan. It had been typical of its type. Communities like this started out serving their Datum parents as sources of raw materials, sites for new industrial developments, and room for extra living space, sports and recreation, and so they necessarily followed their parents' maps.

Now, though, a couple of months after the eruption, this version of Wichita was surrounded by a refugee camp: rows of hastily erected canvas tents full of bewildered survivors, the ground littered with heaped-up drops of food and medical supplies and clothes. Twains like the *Franklin*, stepwise-capable airships, both military and commercial, hung in the sky like blimps over wartime London. It was a grim third-world scene, in the heart of a stepwise America.

Of course it could have been a lot worse. Thanks to the almost universal ability that people had to step away into a parallel world from anywhere on the

Datum, the immediate casualties of the Yellowstone eruption had been comparatively light. The refugees below had in fact been transferred from Datum camps they'd reached by conventional means, fleeing along Datum roads away from the central disaster zone, before being stepped away to cleaner parallel worlds. Datum Kansas was a relatively safe distance from the eruption site itself, which was over in Wyoming. But even this far out the ash was taking its toll, on eyes, on lungs. It induced conditions with names like 'Marie's disease', a kind of ghastly slow suffocation – horrors that were becoming too familiar to everybody, and the medical tents on the ground were surrounded by lines of exhausted people.

Lost in reflection, with worries about her own responsibilities nagging at her – as well as her own ever-present doubts about how well she could fulfil those responsibilities – Maggie was startled by a soft knock on her door. Chen, no doubt. She snapped at the cat, 'Standing orders.' Which meant: *Shut up.*

The cat calmly curled up and mimicked sleep.

Captain Chen turned out to be a short, bustling man, pompous and self-important, Maggie thought on first impression, but evidently a survivor. He'd been a party official who'd kept his position through the fall of the Communist regime, and in the *Zheng He* had in fact gone on to command a prestigious voyage of exploration into the Long Earth. She referred to this as she made him welcome.

'A voyage which you yourself, Captain Kauffman, might have emulated by now, if not for the unfortunate circumstance of the eruption,' he said as he sat down, and accepted an offer of coffee from Midshipman Santorini, who'd shown him in.

'You know about the *Armstrong II*? Well, I'm not the only one whose personal plans have been disrupted by this.'

'Quite so. And we are the fortunate ones, are we not?'

After some preliminary chatter – he said his pilot for the crossing, a Lieutenant Wu Yue-Sai, was being looked after in the *Franklin*'s galley – he got down to business. Which turned out, it seemed to Maggie, to be irritatingly ideological.

'Let me get this straight,' she said. 'You're refusing to carry ballot slips for our presidential election?'

He spread his chubby hands and smiled. He was a man who enjoyed bringing complications into the lives of others, she thought.

'What can I say? I represent the Chinese government. Who am I to intervene in US politics, even in a constructive way? What if, for example, I were to make some error – to fail to deliver the papers to one district or another, or lose a sealed ballot box? Imagine the scandal. Besides, from an outsider's point of view, to hold an election in such circumstances seems frivolous.'

She felt her temperature rising, and she was aware of the cat's eyes on her, a silent warning. 'Captain, it's November in a leap year. This is the time we hold a presidential election. It's what we do in America, supervolcano or not. I – we – do appreciate all the Chinese government is doing to help us out in this situation. But—'

'Ah, but you don't welcome my comments on your internal affairs, do you? Perhaps you'll have to get used to that, Captain Kauffman.' He gestured at the tablet on her desk. 'I'm sure your latest projections match our own, concerning the future of your country. It seems likely that twenty per cent of the continental Datum USA will eventually be abandoned altogether, a swathe spanning Denver, Salt Lake City, Cheyenne. Eighty per cent of the rest is under ash thick enough to disrupt agriculture. While the evacuation flow to the stepwise worlds has been intense, still many millions remain on the Datum, and stores of food and water are rapidly diminishing – as they are even in stepwise holding areas like this, are they not? And during this winter many will starve without gifts of, for example, Chinese rice, delivered stepwise by twain, or by freighters crossing the Datum seas. You are dependent on the rest of the world now, Captain Kauffman. Dependent. And I doubt that will change any time soon.'

She knew he was right. Her own advisers among her crew on the twain were telling her that the volcano was now having global effects, effects that were going to linger. The ash had washed out fairly quickly – though even lying on the ground it remained a problem, as Chen had said – but sulphur dioxide from the eruption was hanging around in the air as aerosol particles, creating terrific sunsets but deflecting the sun's heat. As the Datum headed into its first post-volcano winter, temperatures had plummeted fast and early, and spring next year was going to be late, if it showed up at all.

Yes, America would need Chinese rice for the foreseeable future. But Maggie could see that the challenge was going to be to stop 'friends' like China using the disaster to gain a permanent foothold in American society. Already there had been rumours that the Chinese were running tobacco into a nicotine-starved Datum America – like the Opium Wars in reverse, she thought.

Maggie Kauffman, however, worked on the principle of dealing with the practical problems before her, and letting the wider world take care of itself.

'About your ballot boxes, Captain Chen. Suppose I assign a small team of my own crew to travel with you until the election is over. They can take authority for the operation – as well as responsibility for any errors.'

He smiled broadly. 'A wise solution.' He stood up. 'And I wonder if I could send over a detachment of my own crew, in the spirit of cultural exchange. After all, our governments are already discussing sharing twain technology, for example.' He glanced around dismissively. 'Our own ships being somewhat more advanced than your own. Thank you for your time, Captain.'

When he'd gone, Maggie murmured, 'Glad that's over.'

'Quite,' said Shi-mi.

'Listen. Remind me to tell the XO to sweep this "exchange crew" from toenails to eyebrows for bugs and weapons.'

'Yes, Captain.'

'*And* smuggled cigarettes.'

'Yes, Captain.'

In the sidpa bardo, said some versions of the Bardo Thodol, the spirit was given a body superficially like the former physical shell, but endowed with miraculous powers, with all sense faculties complete, and the capability of unimpeded motion. Karmic miraculous powers.

Thus the vision of Lobsang embraced the world – all the worlds. Sister Agnes would probably ask if his soul was flying high above the ground.

And, thinking of Agnes, Lobsang looked down on an unprepossessing children's home in a stepwise copy of Madison, Wisconsin, in May 2041, half a year after the eruption . . .

As that bad first winter gave way to a desolate spring, and America entered a long period of post-Yellowstone recovery, newly re-elected President Cowley announced that the nation's capital was to be, pro tem, Madison West 5, replacing an abandoned Datum DC. And he was going to deliver a big speech to inaugurate the city into its new role from the steps of this world's version of the Capitol building, a big barn of timber and blown concrete that was a brave imitation of its long-destroyed Datum parent.

Joshua Valienté was sitting in the parlour of the Home, staring at TV images of an empty presidential podium. He was here ostensibly to visit with fifteen-year-old Paul Spencer Wagoner, an extremely bright and extremely troubled kid who Joshua had first encountered in a place called Happy Landings, many years ago. Joshua had been instrumental in getting Paul into the Home after his family broke up. But Paul was out right now, and Joshua couldn't resist tuning in to the sight of a President, in Madison.

Cowley bounced up on to the stage, all teeth and hair, under a rippling Stars and Stripes – the new holographic version of the flag, enhanced to reflect the reality of the nation's stepwise extension into the Long Earth.

'I'm amazed he's actually here,' Joshua said to Sister John.

Sister John, born Sarah Ann Coates and once, like Joshua, a resident of the Home on Allied Drive in Datum Madison, now ran this relocated institution. Her habit was as always clean and pressed. Now she smiled and said, 'Amazed at what? That the President chose Madison for the new capital? It is about the most mature city in the Low Americas.'

'Not just that. Look who's up there on the stage with him. Jim Starling, the Senator. *Douglas Black.*'

'Hmmph,' said Sister John. 'They should have invited you. As a local celebrity. As cheeseheads go, you're famous: Joshua Valienté, hero of Step Day.'

Step Day, when every kid in the world had built a Stepper box and immediately got lost in the forests of wild parallel worlds. In the vicinity of Madison it had been Joshua who had brought the lost children home – including Sarah, now Sister John.

Joshua said ruefully, 'I always kind of hope people have forgotten. Anyway they'd probably kick me off the podium because I'm so grimy. Damn ash, no matter how hard I scrub I can never get it out of my pores.'

'Still going back to the Datum on rescue missions?'

'We are going back, but there's nobody left to rescue. Now we're reclaiming stuff from the abandoned zone close to the caldera, across Wyoming, Montana, the Rocky Mountain states. It's surprising what's survived: clothing, gasoline, canned food, even animal feed. And we bring out anything technical that looks usable. Cellphone masts, for instance. Stuff we'll need for the recovery efforts in the Low Earths. Most of the workers are impressed labour from the refugee camps.' He grinned. 'They fill up their pockets with any money they find. Dollar bills.'

Sister John snorted. 'Given the way the economy's tanked and the markets have crashed, those bills would be more useful burned to keep warm.'

He made to reply, but she shushed him as Cowley began his speech.

After a routine opening, all welcome and wisecracks, Cowley summed up the situation of America and the Datum world, eight months after the eruption.

As winter turned to spring, things weren't getting any better. The global climatic effects had locked in. The monsoon rains in the Far East had failed last fall. Since then, pretty much everywhere across the world north of the latitude of Chicago – Canada, Europe, Russia, Siberia – had endured the most savage winter anybody could remember. Now a matching calamity was already unfolding below the equator as the southern-hemisphere winter arrived.

All of which meant that a new world had to be planned for.

'Well, now, we got through this first winter living off the fat of the past – of the pre-volcano days. We can't afford to do that no longer, because it's *all – used – up.*' Cowley emphasized that with hand-chops on his podium. 'And nor can we rely on food imports from our neighbours and allies, who have been more than generous so far, but who have their own problems, this cold summer. And hey, Uncle Sam feeds himself. Uncle Sam looks after his own!'

Cheers from the polite crowd gathered before the podium, and applause from the group of dignitaries behind Cowley on stage. As the camera panned across their faces Joshua noticed among Cowley's aides a very young woman – no older than late teenage – slim, dark, sober, smart enough but dressed in what Datum folk tended to call 'pioneer gear': leather skirt, jacket over what looked like a hand-me-down blouse. He recognized her; she was called Roberta Golding, from Happy Landings. He'd met her last year at a school in Valhalla, the greatest city of the High Meggers, where, in now-remote pre-Yellowstone days, he and Helen had taken their son Dan as a prospective student. She'd seemed ferociously intelligent then, and if she was working in Cowley's administration in some kind of position as senior as it appeared at such a young age then she was proving her potential.

Oddly Joshua was reminded of that family he'd helped out of Bozeman not long after the eruption had begun, and how they'd mentioned a 'sensible young lady' in 'pioneer gear' who'd come around with good advice. Could that have been Roberta herself? The description fitted. Well, as far as he was concerned, the more sensible advice humanity got at a time like this the better . . .

Joshua tuned back into the President.

With the pre-Yellowstone stores exhausted, Cowley said, now was the time to plant the crops and grow the food that would feed them all in the coming winter, and beyond. The problem with that was that the Datum growing season this year was predicted to be brutally short, thanks to the volcanic cloud. And meanwhile the infant agricultural economies on the stepwise Low Earths, none of them established longer than a quarter of a century, didn't have anything like the capacity yet to take up the challenge. Why, barely a fraction of all that stepwise land had even been cleared of virgin forest yet, on any of the new Earths.

So there would be a 'Relocation', a new programme of mass migration, organized by the National Guard, FEMA, Homelands Security, and facilitated by the Navy with their twains. Before the eruption the Datum had hosted more than three hundred million Americans. Now the target would be that no stepwise world would try to support, this first year, more than thirty million – which was about the population of the US in the middle of the nineteenth century. And that meant spreading millions of people further out stepwise, out across a band of worlds at least ten wide, East and West. *And*, meanwhile, on all the settled worlds they would be ferociously clearing land for agriculture. All of this would have to happen this summer. For sure, Joshua thought, they were going to need whatever tools and hand-me-down clothes and whatnot he and the rest of the reclamation effort could retrieve from the shattered Datum.

'It will be a movement of people to dwarf the biblical Exodus,' Cowley said. 'It will be an opening up of a new frontier that will make the expansion into the Old West look like clearing my grandmother's front yard. But we are Americans. We can do this. We can and will build a new America, fit for purpose. And I can tell you this. Just as I promised you that nobody would be left behind under the shadow of that infernal ash, so I promise you now: in the difficult seasons ahead, *nobody will go hungry . . .*' The remainder of his words were drowned out by whoops and cheers.

'Have to admit he does this well,' Joshua said.

'Yes. Even Sister Agnes says he's grown into the role. Even Lobsang.'

Joshua grunted. 'I remember Lobsang predicting a super-eruption, more than once. Blow-ups like that accounted for some of the Jokers we found out in the Long Earth, the disaster-blighted worlds. But he didn't see Yellowstone coming.'

Sister John shook her head. 'In the end he had no more insight than the geologists on whose faulty data he had to rely. And he couldn't have stopped it anyhow.'

'True.' Just as Lobsang had claimed to have been unable to avert a terrorist nuclear strike on Datum Madison itself, a decade earlier. Lobsang was evidently not omnipotent. 'But I bet that doesn't make him feel any better . . .'

In the sidpa bardo, the spirit body was not a thing of gross matter. It could pass through rock, hills, earth, houses. By the mere act of focusing his attention, the locus that was Lobsang was here, there and everywhere. But increasingly he wished to be at the side of his friends.

Friends like Nelson Azikiwe, who sat in the rectory lounge in his old parish of St John on the Water . . .

Nelson's host, the Reverend David Blessed, handed him another brimming mug of tea. Nelson was grateful for the warmth of the drink. This was August of 2042, in southern England – less than two years after the Yellowstone eruption – and outside it was *snowing*. Once again, autumn had come horribly early.

The two of them studied the third person in the room, a local woman called Eileen Connolly, as she sat before the big TV screen, watching the news report as it was repeated over and over. Three days after the assassination attempt at the Vatican, the key audio and visual clips were dully familiar. The deranged scream: '*Not those feet! Not those feet!*' The horror of the brandished weapon, a crucifix with a sharpened base. The Pope's frail white-clad figure being dragged away from the balcony. The assassin vomiting helplessly as stepping nausea belatedly cut in.

The would-be assassin was English. His name was Walter Nicholas Boyd. He'd been a staunch Catholic all his life. And what he'd done, single-handed, was to build a scaffolding in Rome East 1 to match precisely the position and height of the balcony of St Peter's, where the Pope stood to bless the crowds in the Square below. It was an obvious location for a troublemaker, but astonishingly, and unforgivably in these times of step-related acts of terror, the Vatican security people hadn't blocked it. And Walter Nicholas Boyd had climbed his scaffolding, stepped over with his sharpened wooden crucifix, and had tried to murder the Pope. The pontiff had been badly wounded, but would live.

Now, watching the reports, Eileen began to hum a tune.

David Blessed smiled, looking tired. 'That's the hymn they all sing. *And did those feet in ancient times / Walk upon England's mountains green? / And was the holy Lamb of God / On England's pleasant pastures seen? . . .*' He half-sang it himself. 'Blake's *Jerusalem*. Mr Boyd was protesting against what they are calling the Vatican's "land-grab", wasn't he?'

'He was,' Nelson said. 'In fact there's a global protest movement called "Not Those Feet". To which Eileen belongs, does she?'

Eileen, forty-four years old, a mother of two, was once one of Nelson's parishioners – and was now once more under the care of David Blessed, Nelson's predecessor, who, in his eighties now, had come out of retirement to care for the parish in these dark post-volcano days.

'She does. Which is why she's got herself into such a tangle of doubt.'

'They are difficult times for all of us, David. Do you think I could speak to her now?'

'Of course. Come. Let me refresh your tea.'

So Nelson gently questioned Eileen Connolly, taking her through her very ordinary story, her roles as a shop worker and mother – and then the divorce, but life had carried on, she had raised her children well. A very English life, more or less untroubled even by the opening up of the Long Earth. Untroubled, until the aftermath of the American volcano.

'You have to move, Eileen,' David said gently now. 'Out into the Long Earth, I mean. And you have to take your children with you. You know how it is. We all have to go. England is bust. You've seen the local farmers struggling . . .'

Nelson knew the score. In this second year without a summer, the growing season even in southern England had been ferociously short. As late as June farmers had been struggling to plant fast-growing crops, potatoes, beets, turnips, in half-frozen ground, and there had barely been time to collect a withered harvest before the frosts returned again. In the cities there was hardly

any activity save a desperate effort to save cultural treasures by stepping them away – although there would
be a globally distributed, internationally supported
'Museum of the Datum' in the stepwise worlds, the
governments promised; nothing would be lost . . .

David said, 'And it's only going to get worse, for
years and years. There's no doubt about it. Dear old
England can't support us any more. We *must* go out to
these brave new worlds.'

But Eileen would not respond.

Nelson wasn't sure he understood. 'It's not that she
can't step, is it, David? She's no kind of phobic?'

'Oh, no. I'm afraid it's theological doubts that afflict
her.'

Nelson had to smile. 'Theology? David, this is the
Church of England. We don't do theology.'

'Ah, but the Pope does, and that's what's got everybody stirred up, you see . . .'

Eileen looked calm, if faintly baffled, and she spoke
at last. 'The trouble is, you get so confused. The
priests say one thing about the Long Earth, then the
other. At first we were told it was a holy thing to go
out there, because you have to leave all your worldly
goods behind when you step. Well, almost all. It was
like taking a vow of poverty. So for instance the New
Pilgrimage Order of the Long Earth was set up to go

out and administer to the needs of the new congrega-
tions that would form out there. I read about that, and
gave them some money. That was fine. But then those
archbishops in France started saying the crosswise
worlds were all fallen places, the devil's work, because
Jesus never walked there . . .'

Nelson had read up on this in preparation for meeting Eileen. In a way it had been an extension of old
arguments about whether inhabitants of other planets could be regarded as 'saved' or not, if Christ had
been born only on Earth. Out in the Long Earth, as
far as anybody knew, no humans had evolved anywhere beyond Datum Earth. So Christ's incarnation
had surely been unique to Datum Earth. In fact the
body of Christ Himself had been uniquely composed
of atoms and molecules from the Datum. So what was
the theological status of all those other Earths? What
of the children already being born on worlds of the
Long Earth, their very bodies composed of atoms that
had nothing to do with the world of Christ? Were *they*
saved by His incarnation, or not?

To Nelson it had all been a hideous mish-mash of
misunderstood science and medieval theology. But he
knew that many Catholics, all the way up to the Vatican
itself, had been confused by such arguments. And, it
seemed, members of other Christian denominations.

Eileen said now, 'All of a sudden you started reading about these hucksters selling Holy Communion wafers from Datum Earth, which they said were the only valid ones to use because they came from the same world as Lord Jesus.'

'They *were* just hucksters,' Nelson said gently.

'Yes, but *then* suddenly the Pope says that the Long Earth was all part of God's dominion after all . . .'

Nelson had a healthy cynicism about the sudden change in the Vatican's stance towards the Long Earth. It was all about demographics. With the continuing mass exodus from much of the planet, colonies on the nearby worlds were suddenly filling up with lots of little potential Catholics. And so, just as suddenly, all those new worlds were holy after all. The Pope had taken his theological justification from Genesis 1:28: 'And God said to them, Be fruitful, and multiply, and replenish the Earth, and subdue it.' The fact that God didn't explicitly say the *Long* Earth was no problem, any more than it had been in 1492 that the Bible hadn't mentioned the Americas. But you did still need to have your priests' source of blessing deriving from the Pope, so that the Datum Vatican remained the source of all authority. Oh, and contraception was still a sin.

Some commentators marvelled at the way the two-thousand-year-old institution of the Church had survived yet another huge philosophical and economic dislocation, as it had the fall of the Roman empire that had nurtured it, and the science of Galileo, Darwin and the Big Bang cosmologists. But even some Catholics were appalled at what was called the most audacious land-grab since 1493, when Pope Alexander VI had divided the entire New World between Spain and Portugal: here was an antique ideology claiming hegemony over infinity. Hence Walter Nicholas Boyd, and his despairing cry of 'Not those feet!'

And hence poor Eileen Connolly with her utter confusion.

'I didn't like what the Pope said,' Eileen said firmly now. 'I've been out there, on treks and holidays and that, in the stepwise worlds. You've got people building farms and homes from nothing, with their bare hands. And all those animals nobody ever saw before. No, I'd say we have to be humble, not just claim that it's all ours.'

David said, 'That does sound wise, Eileen—'

'I feel angry sometimes,' Eileen said bluntly. 'Oh, just as angry as that fellow Boyd on the TV, probably. I sometimes think *this* place, Datum Earth, is so foul and messed up that it's the source of all evil. That all the innocent worlds of the Long Earth would be better off if this place could be stoppered up, somehow. Like a big old bottle.'

David said gently, 'You can see why I asked for your help, Nelson. People do get superstitious, you know, in apocalyptic times like these.' He lowered his voice. 'Over in Much Nadderby, there have been mutterings about a case of witchcraft.'

'Witchcraft!'

'Or possibly a demonic possession. A little boy who was brighter than the rest – eerily so. One tries to calm things down, of course. But now this nonsense from the Vatican!' He shook his head. 'Sometimes I feel we're so foolish we deserve all the suffering we get.'

And Nelson, who had become a close ally of Lobsang – or, as Lobsang had put it, a 'valuable long-term investment' – knew that Lobsang, at least some of the time, would agree.

'This is what I'd like you to do. Go with her, Nelson. Go out with Eileen, at least for a while. God knows *I'm* too old. But you . . . Go with her. Bless her. Bless the land she and her children settle in. Baptize them anew, if they wish. Whatever it takes to reassure her that God is with her, wherever she takes her children. And whatever the wretched Pope says.'

Nelson smiled. 'Of course.'

David stood up. 'Thank you. I'll fetch us another pot of tea.'

Lobsang longed for his friends.

At least, in the aftermath of Yellowstone, they had been drawn back to the Datum, like emergency workers rushing towards the fire. Lobsang had welcomed their company, even when, like Joshua Valienté, they seemed to have little time for him. But as the years had worn away since the eruption, and the situation stabilized, they came back less and less, they resumed their own lives, far away once more.

Sally Linsay, for instance. Who, four years after the eruption, could have been found on a parallel world some one hundred and fifty thousand steps away from Datum Earth. Although Sally Linsay was *always* very, very hard to find . . .

You could call it Sally's mission in life to be hard to find. Although in fact her life was full of missions, especially when it came to the flora and fauna of the Long Earth, about which she was quite passionate.

Which was why, in this late fall of 2044, she had come to an otherwise unremarkable settlement, in the middle of the Corn Belt, in a stepwise Idaho: a place called Four Waters City.

And why she was carefully placing the gagged and bound body of a hunter by the back door of the sheriff's office.

The guy was awake while she was doing it, his piggy eyes staring at her in alarm. He didn't know his luck, she thought. He probably didn't *feel* all that lucky, but given the kind of bad luck you sometimes got when it came to the ears of Sally Linsay that you had killed a troll – a female, a mother, *and* about to give birth . . . At least she hadn't cut off his trigger finger for him. At least he was still alive. And the itching that was agonizing him now, induced by the venomous spines of a very useful plant she'd discovered up in the High Meggers, was probably going to subside, oh, in a couple of years, no more. Plenty of time for him to reflect on his sins, she thought. Call it tough love.

And it was precisely because she *was* so hard to find that places she was known to call at – like Four Waters City, even though her visits were not frequent and certainly not regular – were so useful for getting in touch with Sally if you really, *really* needed to.

That was why the sheriff herself emerged from her office in the dawn chill, glanced down without much interest at the blubbing hunter, and called Sally over. Once back in her office she rummaged in a drawer.

Sally stayed outside the door. There were powerful aromas emanating from the office, a concentrated version of the colony's general atmosphere, which she was reluctant to breathe in too deeply. This particular community had always been a culture suffused with exotic pharmacology.

At length the sheriff handed Sally an envelope.

The envelope was handwritten. Evidently it had been sitting in that drawer, in the office, for more than a year. The letter within was handwritten too, very badly, but Sally had no trouble recognizing the hand, even if she had some difficulty actually deciphering the note. She read it silently, lips framing the words.

Then she murmured, 'You want me to go *where*? The Gap? . . . Well. After all these years. Hello, Dad.'

Friends of Lobsang's like Joshua Valienté. Camping on a hillside on a world more than two million steps West of the Datum. Escaping the ongoing five-years-on disaster zone that was the Datum and the Low Earths, fleeing into the security of one of his long sabbaticals. Utterly alone, missing his family, yet unwilling to return to his unhappy home.

Joshua Valienté, who, having celebrated New Year's Day of 2045 with nothing stronger than a little of his precious stash of coffee, woke up with a headache. He yelled into an empty sky: 'What *now*?'

2

With her final step, Sally emerged a cautious half-mile or so from the fence surrounding the GapSpace facility. Inside the fence was what looked like a heavy engineering plant, blocks, domes and towers of concrete, brick and iron, some of them wreathed with plumes of smoke, or vapour from the boil-off of cryogenic fluids.

Willis Linsay, her father, had specified a particular day for her to show up here. Well, however this latest interaction with her father turned out, here she was as requested on this January day, back in this supremely strange corner of a version of north-west England more than two million steps from the Datum. On the face of it, it was a bland British winter's day, dull, cold.

And yet infinity was a step away.

The moon was up, but it wasn't the moon she was used to. The asteroid the GapSpace nerds called Bellos had spattered *this* moon liberally with extra craters that had almost obliterated the Mare Imbrium, and Copernicus was outdone by a massive new impact that had produced rays that stretched across half the disc. Bellos had come wandering out of many stepwise skies, its trajectory a matter of cosmic chance, coming close to the local Earth, or not. Bellos had completely missed uncounted billions of Earths altogether. A few dozen, like this one, had been unlucky enough to be close enough to its path to suffer multiple impacts from stray fragments. And one Earth had been hit hard enough to be smashed completely.

Things like that must be going on all the time across the Long Earth. Who was it that said that in an infinite universe anything that could happen would have somewhere to happen in? Well, that meant that on an infinite *planet* . . . Everything that can happen must happen somewhere.

And Sally Linsay had *found* this huge wound, with Joshua Valienté and Lobsang, found this Gap in the chain of worlds. Their twain had fallen into space, into vacuum, into unfiltered sunlight that hit like a knife . . . And then they had stepped back, and survived.

The air here was cold, but Sally sucked at it until the oxygen made her drunk. She had lived through that fall into the Gap once. And now, was she really planning to go *back*?

Well, she had to. For one thing her father had challenged her. For another, people were working in there now. In the Gap, in space. And this was their base, one step short of the Gap itself.

The sea breeze was the same as she remembered, from her last visit with Monica Jansson five years ago – back in a different age, the age before Yellowstone. The big sky, the call of birds, were unchanged. Otherwise she barely recognized the place. Even the fence before her had developed from a flimsy barrier into a regular Berlin Wall, all concrete and watchtowers. No doubt the interior of the facility itself was riddled with intensive anti-stepper security.

The purpose of all this industry was evident. She could already see the profile of one rocket, elegant, classic and unmistakable. This really was a space launch facility. But it was not like Cape Canaveral, in the finer detail. There were no towering gantries, and that single rocket she spied was short, stubby, nothing like the great bulks of a shuttle or a Saturn V – surely inadequate for the task of climbing up out of Earth's deep gravity. But it didn't need to beat Earth's gravity, that was the point; that rocket would not be launched into the sky but stepwise, into the emptiness of the universe next door.

Overall, instead of being endearingly backyard-rocketship amateurish as it had been, the facility and its approaches now looked like one big engineers' playground. The Gap had become big business these last few years, she knew, as governments, universities and corporations back on the Datum had gradually woken up to the potential of the place. Now hoardings shouted the names of every major technical outfit Sally could think of, from Lockheed to IBM via the Long Earth Trading Company – and including the Black Corporation, of course. This had become probably one of the most crowded stepwise locations beyond Valhalla, the greatest city of the High Meggers.

Which was one reason she hadn't come near the place for years. And why it was hard to take a single pace forward, like she had a phobia. She reflected that Joshua Valienté would do better in this situation. Good old Joshua now seemed quite at home in moderately cramped social situations like this, while she was ever more a loner and a hardened misanthrope.

But it was her father who had summoned her here, and nothing could change *him*, for better or worse. Willis Linsay, dear old Dad: creator of the Stepping box, a gadget probably stolen out of the box from under Pandora's nose and released into an unsuspecting world. That was Dad all over, tinker, tinker. If you couldn't find him, just head towards the explosions and the wail of ambulances . . .

And as she stood there, reluctant, conflicted, uncertain, here he came, walking boldly out of the compound to meet her. How had he known she was here? Oh, of course he would know.

He was taller than she was – she had always had more of her mother's colouring and body shape – and thinner than ever, like a man built of nothing but sinews and bone. After her mother had died he'd seemed to live on nothing but brandy, potatoes and sugar, for years.

He slowed as he approached her. They stood there, wary, eyeing each other.

'So you came.'

'What do you want, Dad?'

He grinned, a slightly deranged expression she remembered too well. 'Same old Sally. Down to business, eh?'

'Is there any point me asking what you've been doing – hell, since you turned the world upside down on Step Day?'

'Pursuing projects,' he murmured. 'You know me. You either wouldn't understand or you wouldn't want to know. Suffice to say it's all for the common good.'

'In your opinion.'

'In my opinion.'

'And is there some new project that you brought me here for?'

'Here?' He glanced around at the GapSpace installation. '*Here* is only a waystation, en route to our ultimate destination.'

'And where's that?'

He said simply: 'The Long Mars.'

Sally Linsay was used to wonder. She had grown up stepping, as a child she had walked into uncounted alien worlds. But even so, as her father spoke those words, she felt the universe pivot around her.

They were met at the compound gate by a guy her father introduced as Al Raup. While his scalp was shaven, a thick black beard sprouted from his chin, giving Sally the odd impression that his head had been rotated around the axis of his stub nose and reattached upside down. He wore canvas shorts, grubby sneakers with no socks, and a black T-shirt too small for his belly with a faded slogan:

SMOKE ME A KIPPER

He might have been any age between about thirty and fifty.

He stuck out his hand. 'Call me Mr Ttt.' *Tuh-tuh-tuh.*

She ignored the hand. 'Hello, Al Raup.'

Willis raised an eyebrow. 'Now, Sal, play nice.'

'Come, let me show you around my domain . . .'

Raup swiped them through the security barriers, and they walked into the compound. Sally heard the growl of heavy vehicles, smelled brick dust and wet concrete, and saw giant cranes loom over holes in the ground. Workers wandered around in yellow hardhats. In some cases she saw 'danger: radioactivity' signs, and that was new since she'd last visited. Nuclear rockets under development maybe?

She did notice a party of trolls labouring at a concrete mixer, apparently happy enough. Sally cared little for technology, or people, compared with animals.

'So,' Raup said. 'Welcome to Cape Nerdaveral, Marsonauts!'

'You're exactly the type I remember from my last visit here,' Sally snapped at him.

'Ah, yes. When you snatched those trolls.'

'When I liberated them. Glad to see your kind hasn't gone extinct with the corporatization of this place.'

Raup waved fat fingers. 'Ah, well, we geeks were here first. We figured out the basic parameters of how to use the Gap, we started the construction of the Brick Moon and sent over a few test shots, all before anybody even noticed we were here.' His accent might have been middle American, but he had a strangulated, showy way of speaking, with looping vowels and over-precise consonants. She had an odd sense that he had already rehearsed in his head almost everything he said, in case he ever had an audience to use it on. 'We're no innocents. We filed a few patents. But in the end the corporate guys had no interest in screwing us over. Easier to buy us out; we were relatively cheap, in their terms, and we had expertise they needed.' He grinned. 'We Founders are all dollar millionaires. How cool is that?'

Sally couldn't have cared less, and dismissed his bragging.

In among the gargantuan industrial facilities she saw sprawling residential blocks, bars, a hotel, a cinema-cum-theatre, a *lot* of casinos and gaming houses, and shadier-looking establishments she guessed might be strip joints or brothels. And there was one modest chapel, she saw, built of what looked like native oak, with a small graveyard set out within a low stone wall: a reminder that space travel was a dangerous occupation even here.

'I can see you have plenty of chances to spend all those dollars.'

'Well, that's true. It's something like an Old West mining town,' Raup said. 'Or maybe an oil rig. Or even early Hollywood, if you want a more glamorous example. Actually you have to watch your step these days.'

'He means, there's organized crime,' Willis murmured. 'Always drawn to places like this. There have already been a few murders, over gambling debts and the like. One way to do it is to just drop you into the Gap without a pressure suit, and no Stepper box. *Sleeping with the stars*, they call it. That's why there's such a security presence now: policing the criminal element, and watching out for saboteurs.'

Raup said, 'But it's still a cool place to be.'

Sally just dismissed that remark.

At the heart of the complex they walked down a kind of central mall lined with office blocks, brand new, concrete gleaming white and unstained. Raup led them to a low, flashy building marked with a bronze plaque: ROBERT A. HEINLEIN AUDITORIUM. There was a crowd at the doors and Raup had to produce passes to enable them to jump the line. He said apologetically, 'We built this for Walter Cronkite-type news conferences. Our corporate masters insisted. Normally it's deserted. But you're in luck, Ms Linsay; the scuttlebutt is that the Martian rainstorms have cleared enough for the Envoy mission controllers to attempt a landing this very day. So it's a good chance to show off to you what we're doing here.'

Sally glanced at her father. 'Rainstorms? On Mars?'

'It isn't *our* Mars,' he said. 'You'll see.'

Raup led them into a central auditorium, with rows of benches before a lectern, the walls coated with big display screens. The place was full of chattering technicians and scientist types. For now the wall screens were blank, but smaller screens and tablets around the room showed grainy colour images being put through various enhancement processes. Sally glimpsed fragments of landscapes, grey-blue sky, rust-red ground.

'Wow,' Raup said, seeing the screen images, for once not sounding like he was simulating the emotions he expressed. 'Looks like they did it, they landed the Envoy. The first time we made it, to this copy of Mars.'

'Envoy?'

'A series of unmanned space probes.' Raup drew her attention to hard-copy images on the wall: trophy pictures of chunks of a planet, taken from space. 'The first couple of Envoys to Mars were flybys, and these are the pictures we got. Today's was the first actual landing, a necessary precursor to the manned missions that will follow. The very latest pictures, live from the Mars of the Gap!'

Willis snorted. 'Yeah, but they're getting the mix wrong. The sky is nowhere near that colour.'

Sally stared at her father. If these were the first landings on this Mars, how could he *know* that? But she'd long ago learned not to try to interrogate him.

Raup said, 'You understand that the probe itself is really only a test article. For now we're just proving the propulsion technology. With the Gap, you can do a *lot*. We're hauling over nuclear rocket stages – inertial confinement fusion, if you're familiar with the technology – and with those babies we're getting to Mars in *weeks*, where it used to take you seven, eight, nine *months* depending on the opposition . . .'

Sally knew or cared nothing about nuclear rocketry, but the pictures caught her attention. One showed a disc, presumably the full globe of Mars imaged from space – but it wasn't the Mars she remembered from decades of NASA pictures back on the Datum. *This* Mars was washed-out pink, with streaks of lacy cloud, and patches of steel grey that glinted in the sun: lakes, oceans, rivers. Liquid water, on Mars, visible from space. And there was green, the green of life.

'I told you,' Willis said. 'This Mars is different.'

'You understand you're seeing the Mars of the Gap universe, the universe one step over from here,' Raup said, back to his over-rehearsed way. 'The images are radioed back to the Brick Moon, our station in the Gap. We have a clever system of packet-feeding the data stepwise to our facilities here . . . *Our* Mars is a frozen desert. *This* Mars, the Gap Mars, is something like Arizona, though at a higher altitude. The Envoys confirmed the higher atmospheric pressure. On *this* Mars you could walk around on the surface with nothing more than a facemask and sun cream.

'In this particular launch window, it was unlucky for us that our twin Envoy landers arrived in the middle of the worst storm season we've seen since we started watching Gap Mars, oh, a decade or more back. Not dust storms – here you get rain, snow, hail, lightning. The controllers didn't want to risk that maelstrom, and for weeks the orbiters' cameras have sent back nothing but images of lightning flashes. But now the storms have settled out, and evidently the mission planners agreed to go for a descent attempt. We're just waiting for the images to stabilize . . .'

Now, in a stir of excitement, the technicians and scientists gathered closer around the TV monitors and tablets. The live images were clearing up, as if a snowstorm were fizzling out. Sally saw the flank of a stubby aircraft sitting on a surface of what looked like wet ruddy sand, like a beach revealed by a recently receding tide. The camera must be mounted on the aircraft itself; she could clearly see the Stars and Stripes boldly painted on its hull.

And then the camera panned away from the aircraft to reveal a glimpse of a shallow valley, with a river running, and tough-looking grey-green vegetation clumped on the banks. A living Mars.

The Poindexter types whooped and cheered.

They retired to a small coffee bar.

Sally faced her father. 'All right, Dad, enough of the space trophies and the enigmatic remarks. In no particular order—' She counted the points on her fingers. 'Tell me why you want to go to Mars. And how you're going to get there. And why under all the heavens I would want to go with you.'

He eyed her shrewdly. He was seventy years old now, and the wrinkled skin of his face looked tough as leather. 'It'll take a while to explain. Here's the headline. I want to go to this Mars, the Mars of the Gap, because it's not just Mars. It's not even just a Mars with a significantly different climate. It's a Long Mars.'

She took that in. 'You said that before. Long Mars. You mean you can *step* there?'

He nodded curtly.

'How do you *know*? . . . No, don't answer that.'

'There's something specific I'm looking for, and expecting to find. You'll see. But for now – the most important thing is, if a world is Long, then it must harbour sapience. Intelligent life.' He looked at her. 'You understand that much, don't you? The theory of the Long Earth, the interfacing of consciousness and topology—'

Her jaw had dropped. 'Hold on. Back up. You just dropped another conceptual bomb on me. *Intelligent life?* You discovered intelligent life on Mars?'

He was impatient. 'Not *on* Mars. On *a* Mars. And, not *discovered*. Deduced the necessary existence of. You always were a sloppy thinker, Sally.'

Needled, her instinct was to fight back, as it had been since she'd been old enough to need to establish her own identity. She said provocatively, 'Mellanier wouldn't agree with you. About sapience and the Long Earth, that a Long world is somehow a product of consciousness.'

He waved a hand dismissively. 'Ah, *that* fraud. As to why you might go with me to explore – well, why the hell wouldn't you?' He glanced around at the geeks in the coffee bar, noisily celebrating their triumph. 'Look at these back-slapping Brainiacs. I do know you, Sally. You liked it best before Step Day, when the Long Earth was just *ours*, right? Long Wyoming was, anyhow. Before I came up with the Stepper box I couldn't step myself, I needed you to take me over, but—'

'You'd read to me. Stories of other worlds, of Tolkien and Niven and E. Nesbit, and I'd pretend that was where we were going . . .' She shut up. Nostalgia always felt like a weakness.

'And now it's all cluttered up by yahoos like these. No offence, Al.'

'None taken.'

'Sally, I know you still spend a lot of time alone. Wouldn't you like to get away to a new world, a raw world, empty except for us – well, us, and a few Martians? Leave humanity behind for a while . . .'

And Lobsang, she thought.

Raup leaned forward, sweaty, intrusive. 'As to how we'd get there, maybe you can already tell that the space programme we're running out of this place is developing a hell of a lot faster than the plod back on Earth. Of course we're able to build on all they learned and reapply it—'

'Get to the point, propeller-head.'

'The point is *we're ready to go*. The first manned spacecraft to Mars. It's waiting at the Brick Moon, just one step away, in the Gap. We wanted to wait until we got confirmation of the planet's atmospheric conditions and so on from these automated landers. But now that we've got that—'

'*We?* Who exactly is going on this mission?'

Raup puffed out his chest and lifted his hefty belly. 'Our crew will be three, just like the Apollo missions. Yourself, your father, and me.'

'You.'

Willis put in, 'I know what you're thinking. But you and I aren't astronauts, Sally—'

'Nor is this puff-ball. Dad, there's no way I'm spending months in a tin can with this guy.'

Willis seemed unperturbed. 'You have an alternative?'

'Does a guy called Frank Wood still hang around here?'

3

Would Frank Wood take a ride to Mars?

In 2045, Francis Paul Wood, USAF (retired), was sixty-one years old. And flying in space had been his dream since boyhood.

As a kid he'd been an odd mix of sports jock, engineering hobbyist and dreamer. He was encouraged by his parents, and an uncle who wrote about the space programme and loaned him a library of old science fiction, from Asimov to Clement and Clarke and Herbert. But by the time his dreams started to take realistic shape, the *Challenger* crash was already history, a disaster that had happened before he was two years old.

Still, he'd progressed. Once he'd been a NASA candidate astronaut, a career development after active service in the Air Force; he'd got that close. Then came

Step Day, when an infinity of worlds had opened up within walking distance of an unequipped human, and spaceships had become instant museum pieces. And so had Frank Wood, it felt like, at thirty-one years old. He had become restless, nostalgic, and without a close family, having sacrificed relationships for a dream of a career. Suddenly he found that *he'd* become the uncle with the connections to the space programme and a trunk full of science fiction novels.

Burdened by a sense of opportunities lost, he'd spent some years hanging around what remained of Cape Canaveral, doing whatever work he could find. But Canaveral, aside from a continuing programme of launches of small unmanned satellites, was little more than a decaying museum of dreams.

And *then* had come the discovery of the Gap, a place where a conjunction of cosmic accidents had left a hole in the chain of worlds that was the Long Earth, and a new kind of access to space. A few years after that Frank, by then in his fifties, had gone out there to find a bunch of kids and young-at-heart types busily building an entirely new kind of space programme, based on an entirely new principle. Frank had thrown himself into the project with enthusiasm, and liked to think he injected a modicum of wisdom and experience into what had felt, in those early days, like some kind of ongoing science fiction convention, and *these* days more like the Gold Rush.

When Yellowstone had blown up back on the Datum, Frank, with many others – including a new friend called Monica Jansson, whom he'd met when Sally Linsay had come here to rescue abused trolls, as she'd seen it – had put aside his own projects and had travelled home to help. Well, Monica was long dead now, and the Datum was kind of settling down to a new equilibrium – or at least people had stopped dying in such numbers as they had been – and Frank felt entitled to go back to his own set-aside dreams. Back to the Gap.

And now here was Sally Linsay in his life again, and her father, with a startling proposition for him.

Would Frank Wood take a ride to Mars? Hell, yes.

They got to work.

4

Outside Madison West 5, at an unprepossessing workshop belonging to a wholly owned subsidiary of the Black Corporation, Lobsang – or rather an ambulant unit, one incarnation of Lobsang – worked on a service of Sister Agnes's Harley. He was convincing at it too as he tinkered, his sleeves rolled up, oil smeared on his hands and forehead and grubby old overalls, even as he lectured Agnes on the state of the worlds in a rather rambling way.

Agnes, bundled up against the biting chill of a Wisconsin winter, was content to tune out his words, content to sit by and watch – and, otherwise, to think. This was January of 2045, over four years after the eruption of Yellowstone, and the worlds of mankind were stabilizing, if not healing, and Agnes, and others, had time to rest. And such moments as this gave her time to get used to herself. To *being* herself again, seven years after her own peculiar reincarnation. She hardly even recalled her given name, these days. She had been 'Sister Agnes' for as long as she could remember, and right now was certain that she still *was* Sister Agnes.

Not that theological doubts often troubled her. Sister Agnes could hardly complain about her new incarnation wrought by Lobsang, to be quick once more in this miraculous artificial body, into which her memories had been downloaded. Of course, to have undergone any kind of reincarnation was somewhat upsetting to a decent Catholic girl, for there was no room for that in the orthodox theology. However, she'd always concentrated on the old maxim that the best course was to do the good that was in front of her, and to put such doubts aside. Maybe God had a new mission for her, in this new form made possible by the advance of technology. Why should He not use such tools? And after all, being alive and apparently healthy was surely much better than being dead.

Meanwhile, what were you to make of Lobsang? In this temporal world he was something like any sensible vision of God, a God of technology, reproducing himself into more and more complex iterations, a being whose consciousness could fly anywhere and everywhere in the electronic world, who could even split himself so that he could be in multiple places at the same time. A being who was *aware*, as no simple human ever could be. Agnes liked the word 'apprehend'. It was a good word that meant, to her, to understand completely. And it seemed to her that Lobsang was trying to apprehend the whole world, the whole universe, and trying to understand the role of the human race in that universe.

Despite all that, Lobsang appeared to be sane, ferociously so in fact – a sanity that burned! As for his character, Lobsang had done some very good work – especially given, of course, that he had the capacity to do a large amount of harm, should he choose. And as far as *she* could see, whatever a theologian might say, he had a soul, or at least a near perfect facsimile. If he was like a god, then he was a benign god.

But Agnes had to admit that Lobsang shared something at least with Jehovah: they were both male and proud. Lobsang loved an audience. He was clever, no doubt about it, extremely clever, but he wanted the cleverness to be *seen*. So he sought sidekicks, people like Joshua Valienté, like Agnes; he needed to let his light shine on their wondering faces.

And yet this new age, after the volcano, was difficult for Lobsang too. Not physically, as it was for the rest of a hungry and displaced mankind, but in some other, more subtle way. Spiritually, perhaps.

Agnes wasn't sure of the cause. Perhaps it was because he had been unable to do anything to avert the Yellowstone disaster. Even Lobsang could only see Yellowstone through the eyes of the geologists, and they had been distracted by the odd phenomenon of disturbances at the stepwise copies of Yellowstone across a swathe of Low Earths – none of which had amounted to much, compared with the eventual Datum eruption. That probably didn't assuage the guilt of one who thought of himself as a kind of shepherd of mankind, however, an agent 'who does the bits God left out', as he once said to her.

Or perhaps it was that the catastrophe that had afflicted Datum Earth, and particularly Datum America, had inevitably knocked a hole in the infrastructure of gel-based stores and optical fibre networks and satellite links that sustained Lobsang himself.

Or, again, perhaps Lobsang himself was actually ageing, in his own way. After all, nobody knew what would happen to an artificial intelligence as it grew older, as its substrate turned into a thing of layers of increasingly elderly technologies, both hardware and software – 'accreting like a coral reef', as Lobsang had once put it – and as its own inner complexity grew ever more tangled. It was an experiment nobody had ever run before.

No wonder then that Lobsang sometimes rambled, almost like a confused and disappointed old man. Well, Agnes was used to confused and disappointed old men; there were plenty of *them* in the hierarchy of the Church.

Maybe this was why she herself was here. Lobsang had brought her back from the grave to be a kind of adversary, a balance to his ambition. Yes, once upon a time she *would* undoubtedly have called herself his adversary, even if her role had always been basically constructive. Now, though, she was – well, what? A friend? Yes, of course, but also his confidante and moral compass – the latter being difficult because her *own* compass had a tendency to spin like a weathercock in a twister.

How was she supposed to have any kind of relationship with such a being? Well, she didn't know, but she seemed to be finding a way. She had a great deal of confidence in herself. She was resilient. She would cope. She always had.

'Consider this,' he was saying now. 'Humanity got to the moon, and you can't say *that* wasn't a remarkable thing. After all, what other creature has got off the planet? And then, what did *Homo sapiens* do? Came home again! Bringing a few boxes of rocks, and a smug feeling of being master of the universe . . .'

'Yes, dear,' she said automatically.

'You could argue that such a species *deserves* to be supplanted by a better breed.'

'If you say so.'

'Nearly done. I've got some tea in the flasks. Earl Grey or Lady Grey? . . . What are you laughing at?'

Agnes tried to look solemn. 'At *you*. For segueing from arguing that humanity deserves extinction to politely asking me whether I would like something so cheerful and normal as a cup of tea! Look – I understand everything you have been saying. Humanity is pretty shallow. It took a trip to the moon for most people even to understand what the *Earth* really was: round, finite, precious and endangered. We can't organize ourselves for toffee. But isn't humanity showing more *common sense*, even at this late hour? Look how well we're coping with the Yellowstone disaster – well, so it seems to me.'

'Hmm. Maybe. Though I've seen some hints that we *may have had some help . . .*'

She dismissed that. 'Oh, don't be enigmatic, Lobsang, it's an irritating habit. And don't assume that we can't change – change and grow. Believe me, I've seen some fine adults grow out of difficult children;

there's potential in everybody. And, frankly, for all the nonsense you spout about how we're doomed to be supplanted, I don't see the new model around anywhere. What happens when they do show up? Should we listen for the sound of jackboots?'

'Dear Agnes, I know that you exaggerate for effect, a ploy which rarely helps matters. No, not jackboots. Something more – helpful. Well, as I hinted so enigmatically. Imagine something subtler – slow and careful and insidious but not necessarily sinister, and yes, better organized than *Homo sapiens* could ever be . . .'

But his voice tailed off, and his expression changed, as if he was responding to some distant call.

You had to get used to that happening. He'd told her all about parallel processing, a concept she hadn't heard of before her reincarnation. This meant running more than one task at once, or breaking down one big job into smaller jobs to be handled simultaneously. Not that she was particularly impressed. After all, *she* had been doing that all her life, thinking about making dinner while also blowing noses and teaching disturbed children how to hold a conversation *and* composing yet another angry letter to the bishop, with the occasional prayer thrown in the mix. Who didn't have to work that way, every day of a busy life?

It did enable her to understand his absences, however. After all, he was steering, as he sometimes said, the narrative of the world.

At length Lobsang snapped back. He didn't refer to whatever had distracted him, and Agnes did not enquire.

He stood up, stretching his back, wiping his hands. 'Done – provisionally. You know, I *could* make this bike the safest in the world. Never skid, never put you in harm's way . . . What do you say?'

Agnes thought that over before she answered. 'I'm sure you could, Lobsang. And I'm very impressed, I really am. And touched. But, you see, a motorbike like my Harley doesn't *want* to be completely safe. A machine like this develops what can only be called a soul, don't you think? And you have to let that soul express itself, not hobble it. Let the metal be hot, the engine hungry . . .'

He stood, and shrugged. 'Well, here's your machine, complete with its hungry engine. Please drive safely – but that, Agnes, in your case, is a wish, not an expectation.'

So she carefully wheeled the Harley out of the little workshop, and guided the bike through the still-sparse rush-hour traffic of this stepwise world, until

THE LONG MARS · 67

she reached open country where she could let the machine play. The wind was strong, but once you got away from the creeping industrialization of this young city – modern-day satanic mills, mostly covered by hoardings and advertisements – you were in a *better* world, the air cleaner, thoughts less melancholy. Over the roaring of the Harley she sang Joni Mitchell numbers, following roads like black stripes through the snow banks all the way around the frozen lakes of Madison West 5.

When she got back, Lobsang told her that Joshua Valienté had come home. 'I need to see him,' Lobsang said urgently.

Agnes sighed. 'But, Lobsang, Joshua might not be so keen to see you . . .'

5

On the day of the launch of the expedition of the *Armstrong* and *Cernan*, Capitol Square, Madison West 5, was like a movie set, thought Captain Maggie Kauffman, not without pride.

Here she was with her crew (make that *crews*) at her side, drawn up in parade order before the steps of the Capitol building, under a clear blue Low-Earth January sky. The air was cold but blessedly free of the Datum's smog and volcano ash. A presidential podium had been set up before the building's wooden façade, a very mid-twenty-first-century image with hovering cameras and a fluttering flag, the holographic Stars and Stripes of America and its stepwise Aegis.

On the stage a few guests waited for the President himself, as he made his latest public appearance at his new capital. There was Admiral Hiram Davidson, commander of USLONGCOM, the Long Earth military command, and Maggie's own overall superior. Beside him was Douglas Black, short, gaunt, bald as a coot and in heavy sunglasses. Black was a 'close friend' of the President as well as a 'trusted adviser', the gossip sites said. Translation: moneybags. He always seemed to show up at events like this. But that was the way of the world, as it had been long before Yellowstone, or Step Day.

Up there too was Roberta Golding, the very young, very slim, evidently very smart and now pretty famous young woman who had rocketed from internship to a place in the President's kitchen cabinet in the space of a few years. Golding, as it happened, had once gone out with the Chinese on their own far-East expedition, as a western student on some kind of scholarship programme. She'd been only fifteen at the time, a rung in the ladder for her spectacular subsequent career. In fact Golding had worked with Maggie's XO, Nathan Boss, advising on the planning of the new expedition to be launched today. Maggie supposed Golding had earned her place on the platform.

Surrounding the party was the usual apparatus of presidential security, including drone aircraft buzzing overhead, and marines stationed around the podium, heavily armed, watchful, some of them sporadically stepping into neighbouring worlds to keep a check on any threat coming from that invisible direction. Further out, a perimeter of police, military and civilian security kept the crowds at a respectable distance from the action. But these crowds were nothing like the numbers you'd once have got in Datum Washington, DC, Maggie thought, on such a day. They were mostly dressed in clothes befitting a still-young colonial city, coveralls and practical overcoats rather than suits, home-made moccasins and boots rather than patent leather shoes. And there were many, many little kids in their number. Since Yellowstone, indeed long before that great dividing line in history, the populations of the stepwise Americas had been booming, and now Cowley's own policies with handouts and tax breaks were encouraging bigger families yet.

And beyond that the scattered sprawl of this new Madison spread away. The wide avenues and open development allowed Maggie a view all the way to the lakes that defined the geography of Madison on all the stepwise worlds, calm, ice white rimmed by blue, glittering in the low January sun. Within the framework of the sparse, elegant, very modern city planning bequeathed by this stepwise community's original founders, smart new establishments that catered for the recent influx of politicos and staffers sat side by side with more practical enterprises, such as stables for your *horse*, not a hundred yards from the Capitol itself. It was nothing like the clutter of the Datum original before the nuke. But it was a beguiling mix of American traditions old and new.

Nobody begrudged Brian Cowley a Constitution-bending FDR-style third term. The consensus seemed to be that whatever the murky processes that had first propelled Brian Cowley to office back in 2036 – at the head of his destructive, divisive, 'Humanity First' anti-stepper movement – he'd stepped up to the plate when the supervolcano had gone up during his innings. Continuity in what was still an ongoing crisis had to be a good strategy, there was no alternative candidate right now who would obviously do a better job – and everybody could see how much the burden was taking out of Cowley himself, who was ageing before everybody's eyes, live on TV. In fact his unofficial election slogan had been 'It's hurting me more than it's hurting you.'

But with his background as a bar-room barnstormer, he did like to put on a performance.

Joe Mackenzie grumbled to Maggie now, as they waited in the gathering crowd, 'What's the man going to do, wait until we all pass out?'

'Don't exaggerate, Mac. The whole thing is a show. This expedition of the *Armstrong* and the *Cernan*, I mean. And damned expensive. We've had to wait for years to do this, while we all worked on the Yellowstone recovery. You can't blame Cowley for milking the moment, that's the whole point of it for him.'

'Hmm,' Mac grunted sceptically. He glanced around at the crews of the two craft in Maggie's small squadron, his expression sour. 'Some expedition.'

Maggie saw her people through his eyes: the Navy crew, the squads of marines adding some muscle. In there was Captain Ed Cutler, whom every man and woman in Maggie's old command had once seen run nutso in Valhalla. There was the small Chinese contingent in their oddly ill-fitting uniforms, a non-negotiable offering of friendship, cooperation and so forth that had been part of the deal that had delivered the advanced Chinese stepper technologies for the US Navy's newest ships.

And there were the trolls, three of them, a small family, wearing the armband stripes that designated them as co-opted members of Maggie's crew. They were visibly unhappy to be stuck in a Low Earth, a world crowded with humanity's stink and suffused with the peculiar mental pressure that generally kept trolls away from dense human populations – yet here they were, and Maggie allowed herself to be pleased by their loyalty.

But Joe Mackenzie appreciated little of this. Approaching sixty, Mac, a veteran of too many years in inner-city emergency departments and battlefield medicine, had become a walking, talking definition of cynicism, Maggie thought – even if there was nobody else she'd sooner have at her side on this first expedition of *Armstrong* and *Cernan*. And now his expression was stony.

'I know what you're thinking,' Maggie said.

'Do you?'

'"What a damn circus."'

'That's the polite version.'

'Mac, this mission is kind of – complicated. We carry a freight of symbolism. The overt purpose of it is to go further stepwise than any ship before us, even those Chinese ships before Yellowstone. But the deeper meaning is that we'll be a visible demonstration of the recovery of America – we'll show that Americans can do more than just shovel ash. Mac, we'll go down in history.'

'Or in flames.'

'And you'll be there to salve the wounds as always.'

'Look, Maggie, I know I'm a crusty old bastard. But as far as I'm concerned all this American-destiny stuff is a lot of hooey. Cowley's only true objective for this trip is just as it was when we went out in the *Franklin*, all those years ago, when Valhalla was boiling up to rebel. To project federal power across the Aegis. To remind those uppity colonials and combers out there who's boss. And as far as *I'm* concerned, our only worthwhile mission objective is to find what became of the crew of the *Armstrong I*.'

'Fair enough. Glad to have you aboard anyhow. Oh, by the way, I'm bringing the cat.'

He flared. 'God dammit, Maggie, why don't you just stick pins in my eyes?'

Suddenly, shadows from the sky striped across the square.

Maggie tipped up her head to see, and shielded her eyes. Precisely at noon, three airships had appeared above their heads.

The two brand new Navy craft, the USS *Neil A. Armstrong II*, and the USS *Eugene A. Cernan*, were whales in the sky. Their predecessors, including Maggie's own old command the *Franklin*, based on Long-Mississippi commercial twain technology, had been a little smaller than the venerable *Hindenburg*. The new *Armstrong*, like its sister, was nearly half as long again, topping out at more than a thousand feet from stem to stern, not counting a protruding comms antenna and massive tail planes mounted with compact jet engines. The crew liked to brag about how that great envelope could swallow the old *Franklin* whole, though that wasn't quite true. But, with *Cernan*, the ship had taken the record for the largest flying machine ever constructed from the old *Hindenburg*. Mac had counselled Maggie not to boast too loudly about that, because after all the *Hindenburg* had been bankrolled by the Nazi party, and ultimately had crashed and burned . . . Maggie had pored over the engineering details as the ships had been designed and constructed, like a kid in a toy store. Now her heart swelled with pride that two such magnificent ships were hers to command.

And between the Navy ships, stepping in at precisely the same moment in a neat bit of synchronization, was a smaller ship but just as sturdy-looking, its hull painted white and blue with a proud presidential seal emblazoned on its flanks and tail fins. Popularly known as Navy One, this twain was the President's own dedicated craft, heavily defended and bristling with armour and, it was rumoured, luxuriously appointed within.

Now, with a hum of powerful engines, a soft downwash of air and some neat navigation, Navy One descended towards the Capitol building, and a hatch in the base of the gondola opened up to allow a staircase to extend smoothly to the stage.

With secret service agents front and back, the unmistakable form of Brian Cowley came down the ramp. The band struck up 'Hail to the Chief', there were good-natured cheers from the gawking crowd out beyond the perimeter, and Cowley worked his way along the line of dignitaries with handshakes. He was an overweight man in a crumpled suit.

Mac grunted. 'Look at him with Douglas Black. Jeez, that's not a handshake, that's a transfer of DNA. Get a room, Mr President.'

'Now, now, Mac. Scuttlebutt is that Black bankrolled the building of these ships, the whole damn expedition. You can't begrudge him his moment in the spotlight.'

'Yeah, but he probably bankrolled the spotlight too . . .'

At last Cowley stepped up to the microphone, and grinned at the gathering before him. 'My fellow Americans, and people of the planet Earth – *all* the planet Earths . . .'

He had always had the easy, graceful command of a natural orator – well, his whole career had been predicated on that one skill – and as his gaze swept over her, Maggie felt herself swell with pride, just a little. Asshole the man might once have been, and might still be, but he was the President, the office was always greater than any one man – and since Yellowstone Cowley had demonstrated that there had been far worse incumbents before him.

Now Cowley looked up at the new vessels, hovering above the Capitol. 'Beautiful new ships, aren't they? The product of American technical ingenuity, and the generosity of our own people and our partners from overseas.' He pointed. '*Neil Armstrong. Eugene Cernan.* I'm sure you all grew up knowing the first of those names. But what of the second? I bet you looked it up before you came out here today.' A ripple of laughter. 'So you see, the names are kind of fitting. And I want you to think of the mission I'm launching today as being a Project Apollo for our generation. This is *our* moon shot – and let me tell you, it's a hell of a lot cheaper!'

After his reward of a little more laughter, he referred back to earlier heroes of exploration: Lewis and Clark, who in the early nineteenth century, under instructions from President Jefferson, had mounted an expedition to survey the peoples and resources of the vast territories acquired by a young America from Napoleon in the Louisiana Purchase, and to establish a route to the Pacific coast. Now, like Lewis and Clark, Captain Maggie Kauffman would lead her ships West, out into the far stepwise reaches of the Long Earth, exploring the footprints of America, mapping, making contact, laying claim.

Mac growled, 'During the re-election campaign he was Roosevelt. Now he's Jefferson. Thinks big, doesn't he?'

'They go to see what's out there,' Cowley said ringingly. 'They will go, not two million steps like Joshua Valienté fifteen years ago, not *twenty* million like the great Chinese mission of discovery five years ago – their target is *two hundred* million Earths, and more. They will map, they will log, they will study, and they will plant the flag. They go to find out *who*'s out there. And they go to extend America as far as the footprint of this great nation can be said to exist. *And*, if it's humanly possible, they will bring home the lost crew of the *Neil Armstrong I*, lost all these years . . .'

Cheers and whoops.

Mac grunted sourly. 'This from the man who used to claim stepping folk were either demons sent by the devil or a species of subhuman.'

'We all make mistakes,' Maggie whispered back with a grin.

Now Cowley was growing more reflective. 'Our nation has suffered a great blow. We all know that; only the very youngest among us cannot remember the time of plenty before Yellowstone, which we compare to the deprivation of the present. Well, recover we will, as the might and resources of the new worlds of the Long Earth come to the aid of the old . . .'

He was battling to be heard now over the predictable cheers.

'This is a time of recovery from disaster. But it is also a time of coming together, of a rebuilding of strength. A time that will be remembered as long as humanity survives. I say to you young people gathered before me: go out in these great Arks of the sky. Go out into the new worlds God has given us. Go out there, and found a new America!'

Even the military crew, supposedly still at attention, broke out into cheers and hat-hurling now. And—

'Why, Mac. I'll swear that's a tear on your grizzled cheek.'

'He's just a soapbox Joe. But, damn, he's good.'

6

In the early days of the cruise into the Long Earth stepwise West from the Datum, Maggie gave her crews time for a final shakedown of the new ships by running at a leisurely one step per second, no faster than commercial twains.

And Maggie got a lot of self-indulgent pleasure in accompanying Harry Ryan, her chief engineer, on his inspection tours.

The crew persisted in calling the *Armstrong*'s habitable compartment the 'gondola', but in fact instead of being suspended below the ship's main body as in older designs, the crew compartment of this craft was entirely contained *inside* the lift envelope, a slab two decks deep built into the forward half of the central plane of the ship, surrounded by the huge lifting sacs.

The intention of this internalized architecture was streamlining, and the *Armstrong* was a sleek bird as a result. But it was also a tough bird; the lower hull, with its loading bays, holds and ground operations bays, was plated by Kevlar armour against attack from below, a tough sheet studded with ports for sensors and weapons.

The crew gondola itself was extensive, reaching back into the body of the ship from the wheelhouse and Maggie's sea cabin in the prow: room for ninety crew and passengers to live and work. Bounded by observation platforms, the upper deck contained the crew quarters and such facilities as the galleys, mess rooms, exercise and training bays, and science and medical labs; the lower deck mostly contained stores and life-support gear.

From the inside, the gondola reminded Maggie of nothing so much as the interior of a submarine. With its metal hull – no iron or steel, of course – and airtight inner partitions, armour-plate hatches over the windows, and sealable, self-regenerating life-support system, it was a world away from the fancy gondolas of the big commercial twain liners that still plied the Long Mississippi route between the Low Earths and Valhalla, with their picture windows and hardwood dining tables for the Captain. If the early expeditions into the extreme Long Earth had taught humanity one thing, it was that you couldn't rely on Datum-like conditions pertaining for ever. Joshua Valienté himself had discovered that when his ship had been wrecked by falling into a Gap, a world where there was no world at all. So the gondolas of *Armstrong* and *Cernan* were built to endure extremes of temperature and pressure, and they could sustain their crews on recycled air and water almost indefinitely, regardless of what horrors were unfolding in the outside world.

Maggie roamed further with Harry, even outside the gondola. She went into the cathedral-like belly of the envelope itself, within the aluminium frame, clambering up ladders and along gantries in the smoky light admitted by the fine translucent hull. The ship carried no ballast; it adjusted its lift by means of huge artificial lungs, into which additional helium could be forced from compressed stores. In all, it was able to lift more than six hundred tons.

The ship's main power came from a compact fusion reactor hung from the structural frame at the stern, a good distance from the habitable sections to reduce radiation risks, its weight balancing the big gondola. The engine room itself was heavily armoured and shielded, designed to survive even a high-velocity crash. At the very crest of the envelope was a bay containing observational gear, antennas, a small atmospheric lab, drone aircraft and even nanosat space launchers – and a bubble observatory, a particularly striking location from which the whole of the *Armstrong* could be seen, stem to stern.

Such tours were a joy. Oh, there were plenty of small technical glitches to fix aboard each boat. But the engineering stuff was almost *fun*, compared with the issues with the flesh and blood passengers . . .

Unlike the *Franklin*, with its relatively small and tight-knit Navy crew, on this trip Maggie had enough civilian academics aboard the two ships to man a small university, covering sciences such as geography, astronomy, ethnology, climatology, mineralogy, botany, ornithology, zoology, cosmology. And smarter people were *always* harder to command.

Take the problem of the trolls, for instance.

For five years now Maggie had kept her little family of trolls on board her vessels, because they were *useful*. Trolls had evolved out in the Long Earth. Through their 'long call' they were in touch with their kind throughout the stepwise worlds. They could even sense some breeds of danger coming well before most humans could respond, such as the imminence of Jokers – anomalous and often hostile worlds in the Long Earth chain. Plus trolls were good, and willing, at heavy-lift jobs of all kinds. Plus their very presence promoted an image of diversity and acceptance which Maggie thought was important to her wider mission of being a kind of ambassador of the central nation and its values to the far-flung Long Earth colonies. And *plus*, dammit, it was Maggie's ship and what she said was the law.

But that didn't stop some crewmen from having problems. The trolls stank, they were noisy, they were dangerous animals loose inside the security cordon of the ship, and blah blah. Maggie had found ways to deal with this. Midshipman Jason Santorini had been with her a long time; he was no high-flyer but was a reservoir of common sense. She'd given him the task of organizing social events involving the trolls – noisy singalongs, for instance. He worked up briefing packages showing how useful the trolls had been aboard the *Franklin*. He'd even had the bright idea of restricting access to the trolls of an evening, when they preferred to huddle up in a corner of an observation lounge and sing, to winners of a prize in a performance-merit competition. Sailors and marines were competitive by nature; anything you had to work at to win had to be worth having, right?

She knew she had a handle on the issue of the trolls when she came upon a mass choir of Navy and marines, joining in with the trolls in the observation lounge in singing a sweet, silly round about feeling good, feeling bad, feeling happy, feeling sad . . .

But then there were the Chinese.

A few days further into the flight, Chief Engineer Harry Ryan asked Maggie to come down to a particularly exotic engineering sub-department: Artificial Intelligence. Contained in vats of Black Corporation gel, enmeshed in fibre-optic cable, here were the dreaming artificial minds who oversaw most of the ship's functions, but whose key role was to step the *Armstrong* across the new worlds – for only sapient minds could step. To Maggie, who had to scrub up to operating-theatre cleanliness standards before even being allowed in here, this was an eerie, somewhat frightening place. What were these manufactured minds thinking, all around her, right now? Were they aware of her presence? Did they resent their enslavement to her purposes?

'Captain?'

'Sorry, Harry.' She tried to focus on her Chief Engineer. 'You were telling me about—'

'Bill Feng.'

'Ah, yes.'

'Look, the guy may have been a big cheese on board the *Zheng He*.'

'More than that, surely. He was the co-designer of all this. The beefed-up stepper technology they've now given us to co-develop.'

'Yeah, maybe. Big shot back home. And his English is good—'

'Mother from Los Angeles. Which is why he's called Bill.'

'That's what I hear. But, Captain, he has his damn nose in everything. He has to be *there*, at every component test, every routine tear-down, every watch briefing, every handover—'

'Always there, in *your* engine room.'

Harry was a big, bluff man, with hands the size of a troll's, it looked like, that belied a delicacy of touch when it came to his precious engines. 'That's about the size of it, Captain. Look, I know what you're thinking. I'm a territorial asshole. It's just—'

'Not at all. It's your domain. I need you to run this place the way you want to. And if Commander Feng is interfering with that we both have a problem. But on the other hand, Harry, he's flown with ships of these new designs across twenty million worlds – that's on the missions we've heard about, maybe more covertly. He ought to be a useful resource. And, look – you know how things are on the Datum, still. You have family there. Everybody knows how much assistance the

Chinese have been providing. Medical supplies, food, even winter clothing.'

'So it's all geopolitics. The Chinese give us handouts and we all have to kowtow?'

'No,' she said sternly, 'and if you use language like that, Commander Ryan, I'll bust you down to grease monkey, so help me. Harry, we have to be gracious. That doesn't make us any less as Americans. This is still your engine room, just as much as it's still my boat. Look, get back to work, sleep on it, and just keep smiling. These things have a way of working out.'

He left, though not with particularly good grace.

Dissatisfied, that night she made a point of hanging around the crew lounges, allowing herself to be bought a couple of beers, watching the dynamics of the Chinese guests with the rest of the crew. Of course they were all different as individuals, one from the other, as people always were. But it was evident that the atmosphere wasn't right.

The next morning she called in the senior Chinese officer on the ship, a Navy commander, and made a quiet suggestion.

By the morning after that she was speaking to Lieutenant Wu Yue-Sai. Wu was a bright thirty-year-old who had aspirations to be an astronaut, had acquitted herself well on the Chinese 'East Twenty Million' expedition – and in particular had done a good job in liaising with English-speaking guests on that mission. By the afternoon Wu had begun new duties in an 'interface' role in Harry Ryan's engine room.

Maggie was gratified that she heard of no more tensions in engineering. And maybe the calm would spread out through the ship from that critical node.

Maggie was the kind of commanding officer who believed in letting issues surface and be resolved as naturally as possible, rather than by her diktat. Mostly it worked out. If any individual didn't get the message, he or she could always catch a slow boat back home for reassignment.

But when Maggie's Executive Officer, Commander Nathan Boss, asked to see her, it wasn't anything to do with trolls, or relations with the Chinese. So Maggie's cat warned her anyhow.

'Then what?'

'The most useful summary is – weaponry.' Sitting on her desk in Maggie's sea cabin, Shi-mi was ghost white. Her voice was liquid human feminine, though reduced in timbre by her small frame.

Weaponry? Maggie wondered what she meant by that. There were plenty of weapons aboard the

Armstrong and *Cernan*; the two airships were military craft. She wanted to ask Shi-mi to expand – but time ran out, and Nathan's soft knock sounded at the door.

Executive Officer Nathan Boss was a competent, solid officer who'd been with her for several years and was overdue for promotion; Maggie suspected he lacked an edge to his ambition. Whatever, she was glad he was on board with her now. Even if he did look disconcerted when he sat down and Shi-mi jumped on to his lap, purring loudly.

'You ham,' Maggie said.

'Sorry, Captain?'

'Not you, Nathan. What's on your mind?'

What was troubling her XO was the presence of Edward Cutler as part of this expedition – not just part of it, he was Captain of the *Cernan* and answerable only to Maggie herself.

'Look, Captain – there's the question of morale. Whatever you might say about Captain Cutler, there are crew on this boat and the *Cernan* who were there that day in Valhalla five years back, when he cut loose of his moorings. Remember he tried to get permission to open fire on that crowd of civilians?'

Of course she remembered. 'It was a rather extreme expression of patriotic duty, I agree.'

He hesitated. 'Then, Captain, you let me go after the guy when he stormed off alone. You didn't see what happened later.'

She'd read the reports, though. Cutler, enraged and frustrated, and completely baffled by the Valhallans' non-violent Gentle Revolution, had finally, and quite without authorization, turned a weapon on unarmed American citizens. Nathan Boss had risked his own life, and indeed his own career, by tackling him with a play straight out of a college football manual. Nathan knew her report on the affair had been thoroughly approving in regard of his own actions; she needed to say nothing more about that aspect now.

'The point is, Captain, plenty of the crew saw me take the guy out too. Fox, Santorini . . .'

'You're thinking of the effect on morale, Nathan. Of seeing a commanding officer behave that way.'

'Well, yes.'

'I think we have to trust our shipmates. And we have to give Captain Cutler a chance to grow into his role. Valhalla *was* five years ago.'

'Yes, Captain.' Now he looked uncomfortable. He even stroked the cat, to calm his nerves. 'But that's not all. Look, I know listening to the scuttlebutt is part of my job. You know I hate it, passing on locker-room bitching.'

She hid a smile. In a way Nathan was too straight-back for his complicated job. But then, she liked him that way. 'Go ahead.'

'There's talk of what became of Captain Cutler after Valhalla. After the investigation he was suspended, he spent some time in a Navy hospital, and then he was transferred to Hawaii, Admiral Davidson's base. The scuttlebutt says he received specialist training there. And that he got his commission for *this* mission because of some kind of special assignment.'

That was new. 'By "special", you mean secret from me.'

'Uh – yes, Captain.'

Maggie said nothing, thinking that over quietly. It wouldn't surprise her, if true. The modern Navy was as full of secrets as any other large, complex, budget-laden and weapons-rich organization. It did surprise her a little if it *was* true and the secret had managed to leak out.

'Whatever the truth about Cutler,' and she supposed she was letting Nathan into her confidence in admit-ting she didn't know any more than he did, 'we're stuck with him, and we can't let this have an adverse effect on morale. That's where the harm will be done.'

He nodded. 'I'll make a joke of it. Sailors are always a gossipy bunch. Soon they'll pass on to something new.'

'Good. Thanks for bringing me this, Nathan.'

'I hope I did right.'

'You have good instincts. But if you do hear anything more concrete let me know. Anything else?'

'No, Captain. Thank you.'

When he'd gone, Shi-mi jumped back on to the desk. The cat asked, 'So what do you think of that?'

'What do *you* think? I assume you know more than either me or Nathan about this.'

'Not a great deal more, I assure you.'

'So there's something in it? Cutler has some kind of secret assignment – something Davidson is keeping even from me?'

'Davidson himself may be acting under orders from above.'

'Why did you say you thought Nathan wanted to talk about weapons? – Oh. You're thinking of *Cutler* as a weapon?'

'Well, isn't he? A man with unshakeable beliefs and a profound loyalty. At Valhalla, suppose Davidson *had* had to order you to open fire on the peaceful crowds that day . . .'

'Umm.' Sometimes, in wakeful nights, Maggie had pondered that, among other unpleasant might-have-beens of her life. 'I guess we would have obeyed his command. But Cutler—'

'Cutler would have been the *first* to fire. Without hesitation and the most enthusiastic. Wouldn't such a man be a useful weapon? Captain, Cutler is here as a means of controlling *you*, in certain circumstances.'

'Hmm . . .'

Maggie had no way to check this out, not without turning the ship around. The only long-range communications system that spanned the inhabited Long Earth was the outernet, a kind of mixture of internet and drop-boxes mediated by the chance passage of travellers and twains – reliable, but slow and in no way secure, and it didn't function too far out anyhow. And there was no ship faster than the *Armstrong* itself to serve as a courier. Maggie was going to have to continue with her mission without access to her command chain, for better or worse.

She took out her frustration on the cat, not for the first time. 'You're damn suspicious, for a bunch of random sparks of electricity in a half-pound of Black Corporation gel.'

'I'll take that as a compliment. But I'm right to be suspicious. *You* should be. There are all sorts of secrets being kept from you on this ship. And if you admitted that to yourself, you might have an evens chance of spotting some of them.'

7

With the stepping rate upped to two a second during operational hours, and with plenty of downtime for testing and system shakedown, the *Armstrong* and *Cernan* were able to cover the best part of a hundred thousand steps a day. So, ten days after Cowley's speech in Madison West 5, the airships were already passing Earth West 1,000,000, and were entering the more exotic band of worlds known to the early explorers as the High Meggers.

Cautiously Maggie allowed herself to relax. Her in-tray of problems both technical and human was dwindling. Despite Mac's gloomy analysis that the true purpose of the mission was power projection by the federal government, she was collecting no issues from the ground either. And after five long years of labour in the Low Earths and the Datum, she was no longer locked into the huge, ongoing and utterly dispiriting relief effort that still spanned much of Yellowstone-blighted Datum America.

She was thinking, in fact, of giving Harry Ryan his head and letting him open up the throttle to full, ahead of the test schedule, and see just what this baby could do.

That was when Douglas Black knocked on the door of her sea cabin.

After an embarrassed introduction by Nathan Boss, Black sat down opposite her, stiffly. The man who stood behind him, no more than thirty years old, close-shaven, glared at her like a recruiting-ground sergeant at a private.

Nathan got out of there as fast as he could.

Maggie hadn't even known Black was aboard, and she resentfully remembered Shi-mi's hints of secrets on this voyage. She had only ever seen this man, Douglas Black, the most powerful, indeed probably the richest industrialist in all the worlds of mankind, from a distance: on stage with the President like back in Madison, or on some media channel, plugging his latest technological initiative, or testifying to yet another senate committee investigating allegations of corporate malpractice. He was smaller than he looked on TV, she thought immediately. Slimmer, older. He wore a plain-looking black business suit and tie. He might have been handsome once, but now his bald pate was liver-spotted, his features, his nose, ears, were old-man prominent, and his eyes were rheumy behind the dark glasses he continued to wear indoors.

Black caught her studying him, and laughed. 'You needn't pull your punches, Captain. I know I'm no oil painting, and a let-down compared with the way the TV people prettify me digitally. Still, check out my youthful smile.' He grinned widely, showing her rows of perfect teeth. 'Decent choppers – one thing money can buy, these days.'

His accent was Bostonian, she thought, old school, like JFK in grainy black-and-white TV clips. Old school, but not particularly old money. Everybody knew Black's story, how he had parlayed a grandfather's oil-money bequest into fortune and power through dazzling technological innovations, *and* had acquired a comet-tail of enemies in the process.

'Mr Black,' she began.

'Call me Douglas.'

'I'd rather not. *You* can call *me* Captain Kauffman. I had no idea you were even on this vessel until you announced your presence to my wretched XO.'

'Ah, yes. I'm afraid we rather caught that young man by surprise, didn't we? Couldn't be helped, I'm afraid. I was smuggled aboard before launch and locked into my private cabin, tucked away in a corner of the gondola – you must come visit. The issue is security, as you can imagine. You must know I am rather, well, *vulnerable*, and I have accreted rather a lot of opponents. So this unhappy subterfuge was cooked up – with the cooperation of your Admiral Davidson and my security people, all mediated by staff from the office of President Cowley. Everybody's been very helpful.' He smiled again, self-satisfied.

Maggie was coldly furious. 'Helpful? Mr Black, from my point of view you're a stowaway.'

He was quite unperturbed. 'How exciting! And at my age. In that case I should say that I do come with some baggage.'

'Baggage?'

'There's Philip here, and a small staff – my personal physician, a few scientific advisers, a planetologist, a climatologist. And some specialized equipment. In addition to the general fragility of age, I have endured a number of transplants, and my regime of anti-rejection drugs compromises my immune system. I need protection, you see. Luckily you have a roomy hold.'

'Good grief. How many tons of deadweight does all that represent? And all smuggled aboard without my knowledge.'

'True. Yet here we are. I don't imagine you're about to throw me overboard?'

'No. But I may do that to this goon of yours, if he doesn't stop staring me down.'

'Philip, be polite.' The man Philip dropped his eyes, but otherwise didn't move a muscle. 'I'm afraid he must stay at my side. Another condition of my security people concerning your kind offer of a berth. Well, not *your* offer, rather the President's . . .' He smiled again after dropping that ultimate name, evidently content to wait while she absorbed all this.

'Well, Mr Black, I can't say I'm not surprised – astonished – to find you here, aboard my ship.'

'That's because you don't know me, yet. I've always been rather more adventurous than my public persona might suggest.'

'I know you pumped a lot of money into these vessels.'

'Yes. Actually I pretty much bankrolled their development – save for the Chinese stepper technology, of course. I've always been glad to support the industries that sustain our armed forces.'

'I know that.' She remembered being shocked at discovering to what extent Black Corporation fingerprints had been all over the fabric of the *Benjamin Franklin*, for instance. She had always suspected that Black must use his infiltration of the military, from the level of his contacts with the senior commanders who approved his enormous contracts, down to the implantation of his devices in every ship of the line, every tank and armoured car and plane – even in the bodies of some of the troops themselves – to garner information at the very least, or more likely to exert subtle control. 'It must have cost you billions, but I guess you bought yourself a berth on this tub.'

'I'm so glad you're taking it this way.'

'Do I have a choice?'

He ignored that. 'You know, I've always followed your career with great interest.'

'I've no doubt you have.' You and others, she thought, remembering the mysterious 'Doctor George Abrahams' who had shown up to offer her troll-call translation technology just when she had needed it, in the course of her mission aboard the *Franklin* – and then had bragged about the way he had manipulated various situations to advance her career. Oh, and he'd then given her a talking robot cat. She believed Black, like Abrahams, represented a node of a wider web of such control and communication. But this was her ship, and she felt the need to regain command of the situation. 'Mr Black, what is it you actually want? Just a ride across the Long Earth?'

'Would that be so surprising? Consider all that I've achieved in my life. As I reach my twilight years, can you not believe that I would want to buy myself such final adventures as this? Think, Captain. We have all become rather blasé about the Long Earth, the tremendous higher-dimensional landscape into which we are so boldly striding. And yet, are there not deeper mysteries of existence? Maybe it's not so strange that a quarter-billion worlds exist for us to explore in this marvellous ship of yours. What's strange is that even *one* world should exist . . . As to what we might find out there: who knows? How could I *not* go on such a mission, if I have the chance? And I must go now, before I depart the universe myself, all too soon.'

'Oh, come on, Mr Black, I don't buy any of that. You're no tourist; you have come aboard with some specific goal.'

'Ha!' He clapped his hands, seeming pleased. 'I always knew you were a bright one. Very well, then. What do *you* think I hope to achieve?'

'How should I know? I didn't even know you were on this ship until an hour ago. Perhaps you're seeking the fountain of youth.'

He raised silver eyebrows. 'You are surprisingly perceptive. I should say no more. There *is* something specific I'm looking for, and if we find it, I'll know immediately. Now.' He began to clamber out of his seat, cautiously; the bodyguard, Philip, lent a hand. 'You mustn't feel you have to make a fuss of me.'

'Believe me, sir, I don't. This is a military ship. You are cargo. And superfluous cargo at that.'

'Well. That's an upgrade from stowaway class, at least. But now that I'm out of the brig, so to speak, I wonder if I could see something of your fine ship. Perhaps I could borrow your charming Executive Officer for an hour or so.'

'I don't see why not. I'll also put Mac, I mean my ship's surgeon, Doctor Mackenzie, in touch with you, to ensure your physical condition is taken care of.'

'That won't be necessary, I assure you. As I said, I have my own physician—'

'That wasn't optional, sir. This is my ship. I'm responsible for your safety, now I know you're aboard. Mac will see you tomorrow.'

'Then I shall look forward to it. Where, if I may ask, is our next stop to be?'

She could answer that precisely. 'Aside from a few test stops, Earth West 1,617,524. Be there in a few days. Where we'll be picking up another crew member.'

And, she thought with dismay, another set of personnel problems for her. But at least it was her choice this
time.

'Perhaps I will have the chance to stretch my legs
there.'

'Mr Black, as far as I'm concerned you won't be setting foot off this ship until she's back in dry dock.'

Black laughed. 'I do admire your straightforward
approach, Captain Kauffman. Farewell for now. Come,
Philip . . .'

8

Sister Agnes was right. Joshua was reluctant to jump when Lobsang called. He'd never really got over Lobsang's failure to save Datum Madison from a terror attack, a nuclear weapon, back in 2030. And, deeper than that, he'd never felt comfortable at how Lobsang, beginning over fifteen years ago already, had ensnared Joshua, a natural loner, in his plans and schemes.

But on the whole, he had to admit, Lobsang had been a force for good, in the Long Earth. Maybe now he was trying to be a force for good again.

Also, according to Agnes, Lobsang was lonely.

And then there was the headache. As he'd become aware of this warning sign inside his own cranium, for sure a sign of some kind of disturbance across the Long Earth, Joshua had been expecting some kind of contact from Lobsang. He was almost relieved when it came.

What the hell. Back to the Datum he went.

Joshua agreed to meet Lobsang in the town of Twin Falls, Idaho, Datum Earth, around a hundred and fifty miles from Yellowstone.

For Joshua, just stepping into the town was problematic now. The ice and the ash on the Datum ground meant that the standing surface was far from the level of the neighbouring stepwise worlds, and unpredictable. So Joshua stepped back to the Datum a respectable distance from Twin Falls, hired an SUV, and drove in.

The roads were open, just, especially the freeways and interstates. There was little traffic save for heavy trucks and a few buses, with bundled-up people sitting behind steamed-up windows: very few private vehicles on the road, few cars like his own SUV, and you could blame the worldwide shortage of gasoline for that.

It went well at first. Then he got caught in a blizzard. He had to follow a heavy snow plough for miles.

When he finally reached Twin Falls, he found it basically frozen. The roads were flanked by ice, old, dirty, layered ice, ice that had already endured for years, ice like you might find on the north pole of Mars, he imagined. And in with the ice was volcano ash, even out here, years after it had stopped falling from the sky, heaps of it swept into corners or consolidated by the ice into hard, gritty banks by the road. Right into the centre of town properties had collapsed from falls of ash or snow, some of them burned out. None of these had been reconstructed, or cleared. This was Idaho, in January. It was like Ice Age worlds he'd visited.

He wondered why people were bothering to stay here at all – and he knew that in fact there were still a few inhabited communities even further north than this. Stubbornness, he supposed, sheer inertia. Or pride: humans, he had observed, had a way of rising to a challenge, refusing to be beaten no matter how overwhelming the odds, returning to their homes on the floodplain when the water receded, to the flanks of the volcano once the eruption was over. Twin Falls was still liveable, just, and so people still lived here, in their homes.

He left his SUV in a motel's parking lot, having agreed upfront a payment for the innkeeper to watch over the vehicle for him until he returned. The innkeeper advised him to siphon out his gasoline before leaving the car, and then tried to dicker over the price they'd fixed. The guy got short shrift from an ill-tempered Joshua, whose weeks-long High Meggers headache had only worsened as he'd come back in to the Datum.

He was a little early for his appointment with Lobsang, so he walked into the centre of town and bought a coffee, paying an astounding price for what tasted like scrapings diluted with sawdust. But at least he got to sit in the muggy warm of the mom-and-pop coffee shop while he waited.

And, after an hour, bang on time, a twain came swimming into the murky sky.

They seemed to have remarkably little to say to each other, face to face, as Lobsang welcomed Joshua on board. Joshua focused on the twain itself.

At two hundred feet long this airship was a small one, compared with Lobsang's own *Mark Twain*, and the mighty commercial ships of the Long Mississippi. Its gondola was no larger than a travel trailer. But, Joshua realized as Lobsang showed him around, the gondola was comfortable enough for two. It had a roomy lounge with expansive windows, and airline-type couches, a galley, a small table, and wall-mounted tablets with animated map displays and readings of altitude, wind-speed, temperature.

As on all Lobsang's airships there were private quarters behind closed doors – machine shops for maintaining Lobsang's artificial infrastructure, tucked neatly out of sight, Joshua had always supposed. But through one half-open door Joshua glimpsed an upright cylinder, maybe three feet tall, intricately etched – a prayer wheel? And behind that a kind of shrine, a golden Buddha in an ornate setting of red and green and gold leaf. A whiff of incense. Another part of Lobsang, Joshua supposed, that was hidden from general view.

There was an earthometer, though Lobsang had warned Joshua that his plan was not to travel stepwise today but to journey across the Datum Earth. They would follow the interstates, the 84, 86 and 15, more or less north and east, and go take a look at the new Yellowstone caldera.

'It's quite a sight, Joshua,' Lobsang said now. 'The caldera. Even for hardened High-Meggers travellers like us. And here it is on the Datum. Horrifying if you think about it.'

He, or rather an ambulant unit, sat with Joshua, in orange robes and with shaven head, and with a rather immobile artificial face, Joshua thought. And his capacity for small talk hadn't improved either. Still, here they were.

Joshua cradled a coffee infinitely stronger and more flavourful than the one he'd been served in Twin Falls, and looked down at the cleared highway below, a band of black cutting across a grey-white landscape. A few trucks moved between the surviving townships, but he also saw horse-drawn buggies, like something out of an open-air museum. Bicycles, too, at least close to the towns. Even what looked like a dog sleigh, cutting across the snow banks. 'Quite a sight,' he said. 'Ten years ago you would never have believed you'd see all this.'

'Indeed. It is as if the climate bands have suddenly shifted a thousand miles closer to the equator, from north and south. So that Los Angeles, say, now has a climate similar to Seattle's before the eruption.'

'I know. I've been there. The Angelinos just hate all that rain and fog.'

'While Seattle itself is more like Alaska. Much of the planet north or south of forty degrees, in fact, has been largely abandoned to the ice. Canada, north Europe, Russia, Siberia – empty, the nations collapsed, the people gone stepwise, ancient cities deserted save for hardy hold-outs. Nelson Azikiwe tells me that little moves in Britain now save for salvage parties from the Low Earths trying to rescue cultural treasures.'

'Nelson Azikiwe?'

'Another of my friends, Joshua. Actually you met him in my reserve in Low Earth Madison on the day of the eruption. I'd like you to link up with him, in fact.'

Joshua didn't respond to that. For 'friends' read 'assets'. Sometimes he felt as much a 'friend' to Lobsang as a chessboard pawn would to a grandmaster. Even so, ultimately he'd probably find himself doing what Lobsang asked.

'The politics of the Datum Earth has been dramatically reconfigured,' Lobsang said now. 'The new powerhouse nations are Southern Europe, North Africa, India, south-east Asia, southern China – even Mexico, and Brazil which is exploiting the final dieback of the rainforest to open up Amazonia to agriculture and mining. There is much jockeying for position in the new order, as you can imagine. China is somewhat disconnected from its stepwise footprints, compared to America and its Aegis, but on the Datum the Chinese are very strong.'

'Good luck to them.'

'But Datum America is prostrate. Not that this concerns you overmuch, I imagine, out in your homestead at Hell-Knows-Where.'

Joshua scowled. 'You know damn well that I don't live there any more, Lobsang. I haven't even been back there in months. You had to send out Bill Chambers to fetch me back from my latest sabbatical, didn't you?'

'I had hoped that you might have been able to come to some reconciliation with Helen.'

'Then you don't know Helen. I guess all the time I spent back here at the Datum after Yellowstone was the final straw – even though she knew it was the right thing to do. I could never get the balance right, not for her, between home, and—'

'And the call of the Long Earth. The two sides of your nature.'

'Something like that.'

'And Dan?'

'Oh, I see him as much as I can. Fine kid – thirteen years old, and already taller than me.'

'And yet your sabbaticals still draw you away . . . How's your hand, by the way?'

Joshua lifted his prosthetic left hand to his throat, pretended to choke himself, and pretended to fight it off. 'It has good days and bad days.'

'I could get you something far better, you know.'

'With *you* inside? No offence, Lobsang – but no.' He held out his mug. 'Have we run out of coffee already?'

The airship travelled at a leisurely pace. It took until evening before they were over Idaho Falls, maybe eighty miles from the caldera. Here Lobsang said they would stop for the night.

At Joshua's request Lobsang lowered the ship so they could climb down to the ground, briefly escaping from the heated air of the gondola, although Lobsang insisted they should return to the airship before dark: 'A lot of bandits out here nowadays, Joshua.'

With Lobsang at his side, Joshua walked around experimentally on a road surface choked with ice and ash drifts, and peppered with boulders of pumice so massive it was hard to believe that any force could propel them eighty yards through the air, let alone eighty miles. The air was bitterly cold, attacking his cheeks and nose and forehead, any part of him that was left exposed by the layers of his cold-weather gear.

He came to a stream, flowing sluggishly. The water was grey with ash, and the tree trunks by the banks were grey-brown. The scene was eerie, the light coppery as the sun went down. And the world was silent. There had been no traffic on the interstate for many miles, but nature was subdued here too; Joshua heard not so much as a bird call, as he inspected the spindly trunks of dead pine trees.

'Kind of quiet,' he said to Lobsang.

The ambulant unit was kitted out in Arctic gear as he was. Its breath, evidently heated and kept moist by some internal mechanism, steamed quite convincingly, a touch of verisimilitude. 'The world is quieter still for me. So many communications nodes and networks have failed or been abandoned. To me, Joshua, it is as if the world is becoming Thulcandra.'

Joshua knew the reference. 'The silent planet. Why did you bring me here, Lobsang?'

'How's your headache?'

'Of course you'd know about that. If you want to know, it's worse than ever. I mean, I usually feel uncomfortable when I'm at the Datum, or close to it, but this is worse . . .' He tailed off, glancing around. He thought he had heard something, breaking the deadened silence. A furtive scuffling. A wolf, starving in this frozen wilderness? A bear? A human, some kind of bandit, as Lobsang had warned him?

Lobsang seemed unaware. 'But this is different, yes? Your headache. You must have a sense that something about the Datum has changed.'

Joshua grunted. 'And so do you, right? You've got evidence, haven't you? Evidence of *something*. Otherwise you wouldn't have called me back.'

'Indeed. Evidence of *something* – well put. Something elusive and difficult to define, yet nevertheless apparent to me, who, despite my post-volcano handicap, still spans the world like a disembodied bardo spirit—'

'Like a what?'

'Never mind. Something real, Joshua. Look – you know me. If nothing else I am a keen student of the folly of mankind, which at times has seemed almost terminal.'

'As we've discussed many times,' Joshua said dryly.

'Well, now something *has* changed. The aftermath of Yellowstone seems to have triggered it. People have responded well or badly. But amid the heroism and cowardice, the generosity and the venality, if you take a global view – and I am scarcely capable of less – it seems to me that humanity's response to Yellowstone has been characterized by a startling outbreak of what Sister Agnes once described as *common sense.*'

And, just as he uttered those words, a figure in an orange jumpsuit, barefoot, with shaven head, materialized out of thin air, already in the middle of a flying leap. 'HAAARRRGGH!'

'Not now, Cho-je!—'

But Lobsang's words were cut off as the newcomer wrapped his legs tight around Lobsang's neck. Lobsang was forced to the frozen ground – but as he fell he stepped away, disappearing, leaving the newcomer rolling alone in the dirty ice, ash staining his orange jumpsuit.

Joshua carried a gun, bronze, steppable. He always carried a gun. Before the guy could stir Joshua had the weapon out in front of him, held two-handed, legs wide. 'I knew I heard something tracking us. Don't move, grasshopper.'

But Lobsang appeared at his side, breathing hard, his robe ripped at the neck. 'It's all right, Joshua. I'm under no real threat. This is just—'

'HYY-AAGH!' The guy on the ground did a kind of back flip, and once more launched himself through the air at Lobsang. But Lobsang dipped into his own forward roll, and the newcomer was sent flying. This time it was the assailant who stepped away, before he hit the ground.

Lobsang straightened up, breathing hard. 'It's one of Agnes's ideas. You see—'

'NYA-HAAH!' Now the assailant, Cho-je, came back into the world *above* Lobsang's head, with his fists clamped together and ready to slam down on Lobsang's crown. But Lobsang ducked, whirled, and caught him with a kick in the stomach – and again Cho-je disappeared.

Joshua gave up. He holstered his weapon, stood back, and watched the fight. It was a blur of kicks, punches, even head-butts that rained in with hard, meat-slapping impacts, and of stepping, as the two figures popped in and out of existence, each trying to get the down on the other. During his travels with Lobsang Joshua had watched plenty of Jackie Chan movies. And out in the

Long Earth he had been involved in his own battles with elves, stepping humanoids honed by the hunt, who could cross between the worlds with such precision that they could materialize alongside you with their hands already in position to close around your throat. This was something like all of that, he thought, hastily mashed together, a high-speed blur of action that was all but impossible to follow.

'HEE-ARR-AARGH!'

'Cho-je, you fool!—'

It ended when Lobsang grabbed Cho-je's left hand, as if to shake it, and, holding on hard, executed a standing somersault. When it was done he was *still holding the hand*, which had been ripped off at the wrist. Cho-je, bemused, breathing hard, looked at the stump of his arm; Joshua saw LEDs spark amid a whitish fluid that dripped to the ground.

Cho-je bowed to Lobsang. 'Nice work! Good to see Sister Agnes's care has not softened you up!'

'On the contrary,' Lobsang said. 'Until we meet again.'

'Until then. If I may have my detached extremity . . .' Lobsang gave him back the severed hand, and Cho-je snapped out of existence.

'So, Lobsang – Cho-je?'

Lobsang was sweating, quite convincingly. 'As I said, Agnes's idea. She has the notion that I'm too powerful.

I need challenges, she says. So I endure an endless routine of toughening up and training. Actually, Joshua, Agnes got the idea for Cho-je from my account of our sparring matches during our voyage on the *Mark Twain*. I do derive enormous benefit in terms of ambulant body control from such exercises, and Cho-je is an increasingly ingenious opponent. By the way, in addition to this training partner, she also recruited another, one of the past inmates from the Home, a rather reclusive young man who has devoted his life to launching ingenious computer-virus attacks on me.'

'Viruses, huh?'

They began to walk back to the twain. 'Viruses are a worse threat to me than any physical violence, no matter how many backups I create. Any synching between my iterations at all leaves me open to a potentially lethal attack. I'm thinking of installing at least one entirely non-electronic backup.'

'Such as?'

'Oh, a few hundred monks in a scriptorium somewhere, endlessly copying my thoughts from one bound paper volume to another. A scriptorium on the moon maybe.'

'One thing has definitely changed about you, Lobsang. Your jokes are no better. But at least now I can tell they *are* jokes.'

'I'll take that as a compliment.'

'And to think that just as this incident with Cho-je occurred you were about to lecture me on "common sense".'

'We can continue that discussion in the morning. The twain is relatively spartan but quite comfortable, I think you'll find.'

'Any good movies?'

'Of course. Your choice. But nothing with singing nuns in, if you don't mind . . .'

9

In the morning they ate breakfast in near silence, and flew on.

Rather than make straight for the caldera Lobsang at first skirted it to the west, following the line of what remained of a south-to-north highway. As they edged closer to the caldera, the increasing thickness of ash began to overwhelm the landscape as it had existed before the eruption. They were entering a true volcanic province, Joshua thought, like a fragment of an alien world brought down to the Earth.

'The civilization of Datum Earth will never recover,' Lobsang murmured, as they peered down at the strange landscape.

Joshua grunted. 'That seems a tough conclusion to come to. It's only been a few years . . .'

'But think about it. We'd already used up all the easily accessible ore, the oil, much of the coal. And the world was already suffering tremendous climate disruption because of all the industrial gases we spewed into the air. When Yellowstone's effects finally fade, the best guess for the future is widespread instability, as the world seeks a new equilibrium after two massive environmental shocks, one human-induced, one volcanic.'

'Hmm. So is this why there's talk of rewilding?'

The idea was, when the winter finally receded from the Datum Earth, why not take the chance to heal the world? All the species that had been driven to extinction on the Datum still prospered in the neighbouring worlds (though once again, Joshua knew, on some of the Low Earths many of those creatures were already in trouble). So, in North America, you could bring back the mammoth and the wild horse and the bison and the musk ox, and the seals in the rivers and the whales in the oceans – just step specimens over, as infants perhaps, to the Datum. Similarly you could let the landscapes and seas recover to their natural state.

'It's a romantic idea,' Lobsang said. 'Of course there's a great deal of work to do before the Datum is even *safe*.'

'Such as, decommissioning nuclear power plants?'

'And waiting for dams to fail, for drained wetlands to flood . . . It will take decades, centuries, for pollutants like heavy metals and radioactive waste to be reduced to safe levels. Even then, where we have driven roads or dug mines into the bedrock, the mark of mankind will linger for millions of years.'

'Makes you proud.'

'If you say so, Joshua. However, an effort to heal this world using the riches of its stepwise siblings seems a noble ambition, whatever the limitations in practice.'

At last, to the north of Yellowstone itself, they paused over what had once been a township. Little remained but a few scattered traces of foundations, the hint of a grid of streets protruding from the ash; much of the rest was buried completely.

Joshua checked a map display; in cheerful white, green and yellow, with finely drawn state and county lines, it displayed the vanished human landscape as it had once been. 'This is Bozeman.'

'Yes. Or was. I thought you'd like to see this, Joshua. I saw from the records that you and Sally went in here on the final day of the eruption itself, when the caldera collapsed. Stepping into danger, seeking to save lives at the risk of your own evanescent existence.'

'We weren't the only ones,' Joshua said without emotion.

The twain dipped in the air, skimming over ground choked by an unknowable thickness of ash and pumice.

'We are still perhaps fifty miles from the caldera,' Lobsang said. 'But this place like many others was caught by the final pyroclastic flow. The eruption ceased when the caldera chamber was empty of magma. The tower of smoke and ash in the air over the volcano abruptly collapsed, and superhot rock fragments came washing out across the landscape at the speed of sound, burying everything for tens of miles around.'

Joshua had been there; he remembered.

'Now Bozeman, Idaho, is at one with Pompeii. It will take years for the ash fall even to cool, let alone for the land to be reclaimed by humans.'

'Yet something's growing down there,' Joshua said. Peering down, he pointed out scraps of green.

Lobsang was silent a moment; Joshua imagined his artificial senses trained on the ground below. 'Yes. Lichen. Moss. Even lodgepole pines. Just saplings, but still – the resilience of life.'

The twain turned its nose and headed south, towards the caldera itself.

'So, Lobsang. Yesterday you told me you were disturbed by a plague of common sense breaking out across the planet? It would be a first, I grant you.'

'I can give you examples . . .'

The screens in the deck flashed up with brief video snips of tales from across the US during the days and years of the Yellowstone disaster:

One little kid in a first-school classroom in Colorado, his teachers having succumbed to an ash infall, quietly organizing his hysterical classmates and walking them out of the building in a line, heads wrapped in wet towels, hands on the shoulders of the person in front.

A young teenager stuck with her grandparents in a care home in Idaho, full of old folks who couldn't or wouldn't step, calmly working out rotas of food sharing and mutual care.

A well-off family in Montana, the mother refusing to leave their home with her surviving children because of one little girl lost, and obviously killed, in the wreckage of an ash-crushed conservatory – her husband going crazy with fear and refusing to stay to dig out the wreck – and an au pair, a girl no more than seventeen years old, organizing the family to dig out the lost one and carry out the body, as that was the only way to persuade the mother to move and save the rest.

Joshua remembered stories he'd heard himself, one from Bozeman in fact, an account of a 'sensible young lady' who had come around with dazzlingly smart advice on how to survive the eruption.

'These anecdotes all involve very young people,' he observed. 'If not children.'

'Indeed. And you'll note that their exploits are not characterized by heroism, or great feats of endurance, or whatever. Instead they are calm, and full of wise leadership – certainly wise for their age. Good judgement, whose value is evident enough even for the adults around them. And a certain cold rationality. They are able to set aside the kind of illusion that comforts but baffles the regular human mind. Consider the woman in Montana with the dead child. She couldn't accept the death. The au pair not only accepted it; she accepted she wasn't going to be able to persuade the mother otherwise, and came up with a strategy to save the family taking that bit of psychology into account.'

'Hmm.' Joshua studied the ambulant's inexpressive face. 'What are you suggesting, Lobsang? You've talked about this before. Are we seeing the emergence of some kind of smarter breed? *True Homo sapiens*, you've always called them – as opposed to regular mankind, a bunch of apes who *call* ourselves wise . . .'

'Well, it looks that way. *If* you are prepared to build a mountain of hypothesis on a raft of a few observations.'

But Lobsang, Joshua suspected, would have more behind his argument than a few scattered fragments of evidence like this. 'So how is this happening? And why now?'

'I suspect those two questions may be linked. There may be some – *incubator*, somewhere out in the Long Earth. Only now, you see, with the advent of widespread stepping, have the products of such an incubator been able to reach the Datum. And perhaps we are seeing the emergence of this new quality under stress. Some gene complex suddenly expressing itself, under the pressure caused by the huge dislocation after Yellowstone. That would explain why we see this *now*, you see. And then there's you, Joshua.'

'Me?'

'Your headaches. This odd psi sense you seem to have for the presence of an unusual kind of mind – and a powerful one. If I screwed a lightbulb in your ear I suspect it would start flashing a red alert.'

'Nice image. Something new in the world, or the worlds, then. And something I'm sensitive to, like I was sensitive to First Person Singular.'

'Not only that, there may be a nascent organization behind it all.'

'An organization? Doing what?'

'My colleague Nelson Azikiwe has an account of an English child – his family are refugees in Italy now – another disturbingly bright child, but this one terrorized by fearful locals. There had even been mutterings of witchcraft. *His* parents, it seems, were approached by another, a teenager. They were offered a scholarship at some kind of residential college, such was the teenager's story, aimed at exceptionally bright children. The parents' account was vague, but they were struck by the eerie calmness of the youngster, the effortless way he seemed to dispose of their objections to his plan.'

'Did they let their son go?'

'With some teenager? Of course not. Although, Nelson says, he *almost* convinced them. Nelson predicts the next approach will be through a front, a more reassuringly elderly adult . . .'

'If this is all so, what do you want to do about it, Lobsang?'

'If this nebulous entity exists, if some *new kind of human being* is emerging in our world, I want to meet it. Talk to it. I see myself as something of a guardian of mankind, Joshua. This new entity may be reaching the end of its own long childhood. As it rises up to adulthood, I want to make sure it means us no harm.'

'And that, I imagine, is where you want my help. Finding these new people.'

'You and a number of others. Ah . . . It is time.'

'For what?'

All the display screens cleared down. 'Look out of the windows.'

For some time the ground had been steadily rising, but it was a fractured ground, ash-blanketed, strewn with immense rocks. It was as if, Joshua thought, they were following debris rays towards a great lunar crater.

Quite abruptly the ground fell away, as if they had sailed over a cliff. Joshua looked down to see a landscape like some gloomy artist's palette: swirls of reddish rock, lava pools that bubbled languidly, sulphur-yellow scum beneath wraiths of steam. His view was obscured by heat shimmer, and he heard switches being thrown in the gondola's air conditioning unit, as suddenly, after hours of fighting off arctic chill, now it strove to exclude the sudden warmth.

And when he looked ahead, beyond the curdled plain below, he saw a kind of cliff face, very far off, blued by the mist of distance, shimmering in heat haze.

Lobsang said, 'This is the caldera, Joshua. The crater. So big you can't really see that it's circular from here. The ground, below, is half a mile down – we're above the collapsed magma chamber. And the caldera's far wall is over forty miles away. We were unlucky actually.'

'Unlucky?'

'The supervolcano erupts every half million years or so. Some eruptions are worse than others – in some, more magma is released, more damage is done. *This* was the worst for two million years. The geologists were able to tell us that much, even though they didn't see it coming. And the result lies around you.'

Joshua had no words.

'Impressive, isn't it? Even to God, it must be quite a sight. Even to *me* . . .' His voice wavered oddly.

Joshua felt a flicker of concern. 'Lobsang? Are you all right?'

Lobsang didn't answer. But he said, more uncertainly, 'I don't ask this of you lightly, Joshua. To travel again, I mean. I have become more aware of the risks I ask you to take when stepping into the Long Earth. Any of us.'

'What do you mean?'

'Have you considered what would happen were you to die out there? I'm referring to the fate of your immortal soul. Can a discarnate soul cross stepwise between the worlds? If you were alone – in a world in which there were no other humans to host your spirit – you might not be able to reincarnate as a human at all.'

Joshua had come across this kind of idea before, mostly from the sort of earnest swivel-eyed zealot who waited to harangue you at twain terminals. It was mildly shocking to hear Lobsang saying this. For all Lobsang's claims about his origin, that he was the soul of a Tibetan motorcycle repairman reincarnated into a gelsubstrate supercomputer, they had never delved too deeply into the mystical side of that proposition. But Joshua thought of the small Buddhist shrine tucked into a corner of the airship. Perhaps Lobsang was changing, reaching for his own deeper roots.

'I take it you've been studying this reincarnation business?'

'Wouldn't you? And I've had a lot of encourage-ment from Agnes in such matters. Buddhism, you know, is essentially a way of working with the mind. By developing the basic potential of the mind you can achieve inner peace, compassion and wisdom. All of us can do this. But *I* am nothing *but* mind, Joshua. How could I fail to be drawn to such ideas, even without my cultural background? As for ideas of reincarnation, I've gone into them deeply. I am familiar with over four thousand texts on the subject, besides my own experience.'

'Oh.'

'Also I have been counselled by Padmasambhava, an old friend in my previous life, now the abbot of a monastery in Ladakh. Which is in India, just beyond

the Tibetan border, and a place where the old wisdom
has been preserved despite the Chinese occupation.
Although Padmasambhava is himself a shareholder in
a Chinese logging consortium . . . I am not losing my
mind, you know,' said Lobsang severely.

'I didn't say you were. But it's odd to hear you
express self-doubt, Lobsang—'

'I think I remember my death.'

That stopped Joshua in his tracks. 'What death? You
mean—'

'In Lhasa. My last human death. And my
reincarnation.'

Joshua thought that over. 'So was it like when Doctor
Who regenerates?'

'No, Joshua,' Lobsang said with strained patience. 'It
was not like when Doctor Who regenerates. I remember
it, Joshua. I *think*. The lamentations of the women, in
the kitchen, when the chikhai bardo came, the moment
of my death. The Tibetans believe that the soul lingers
in the dead body. So for forty-nine days the Book of the
Dead is read over the corpse, to guide the soul through
the bardos, the phases of existence that bridge life and
death.

'I *remember* the reading by my friend
Padmasambhava. Even the Book itself, I looked down
on it from outside my body – the sheets printed from

hand-carved blocks, held between wooden covers. I was dead, I was told. Everybody who came before me had died. That I had to recognize my own true nature, the radiant, pure light of continuing consciousness inside the heavy physical body; and with that recognition, liberation would be instantaneous.

'But after twenty-one days of chanting, if liberation hasn't come, you enter the sidpa bardo, the bardo of rebirth. You become like a body without substance. You can roam the whole world, tirelessly, seeing all, hearing all, knowing no rest. Yet you are haunted by images from your former life.

'Now think about that, and look at me, Joshua: *I* am spread across all the worlds of the Long Earth; I see all, I hear all. What does that sound like but the bardo of rebirth? But to pass on you have to abandon all you have known in this life. How can *I* do that?

'Sometimes I fear I am trapped in the sidpa bardo, Joshua. That I am trapped between death and rebirth – that I have never, in fact, been reincarnated, reborn, at all.' He looked at Joshua with eyes that were dark in the light of a volcano sky. 'Perhaps even you are a mere projection of my own ego.'

'Knowing *your* ego, I wouldn't be at all surprised.'

'And it gets worse. What of the future? *What if I can't die?* If I have to wait for the sun to fade before I am released, who then will be left to read the Book of the Dead over me?'

'Look, Lobsang – this doesn't sound like you. You never did metaphysical doubt. What if this is a false memory? Suppose somebody, some enemy, has uploaded a virus that's whispering into your gel-based head . . . Maybe it's just that kid who Agnes hired to test you. Isn't that more likely?'

But Lobsang wasn't listening. He seemed unable to listen.

The twain shuddered in the turbulent air, a mote above the lunar immensity of the Yellowstone caldera.

10

There was no great space-programme-type fuss before Sally Linsay's journey to Mars: no bone-crunching physical training or survival exercises, no hours in simulators, no photographs on the cover of *Time* magazine. It did take a couple of weeks for Willis, Frank Wood and Sally to get their act together, however. There were briefings, which Sally mostly skipped, almost on principle . . .

And then, at last, astonishingly, Sally found herself in what Raup called a white room: a suiting-up room, for astronauts.

With the assistance of a couple of female attendants in jumpsuits bearing Boeing logos, Sally had to strip off, was given a rub-down with alcohol, and then put on soft white underclothes. Throughout the flight she would have to wear a belt of some kind of medical telemetry equipment around her chest: the corporate rules of GapSpace, Inc. Then came the spacesuit itself, a kind of heavy coverall of some tough orange fabric, with a rubbery, airtight inner layer. You climbed into this backwards through a gap in the stomach, then zipped it all up at the front. Sally groused her way through this, and through a pressure test when she had to screw on her helmet and the suit was pumped so full of air it made her ears pop.

But one of the technicians, a humorous-looking older woman, told her to cherish her suit. 'You're going to be walking on Mars in this, honey,' she said. 'And it's more than likely that it will save your life en route. You're going to come to love her. Based on good Russian technology, by the way – decades of experience have gone into the design of that garment. Look, if you like, we can even sew a little name tag on the chest for you—'

'Don't bother.'

As she was led out of the white room, the techs made her sign her name on the back of a door already covered with hundreds of signatures. 'Just a tradition,' the tech said.

Outside she joined her father, Frank Wood and Al Raup, all suited as she was. Then, with help from the techs, they all bundled into a compact 'stepper shuttle', a cone-shaped spacecraft not unlike an Apollo command module. Raup was to pilot this craft, delivering the Mars crew to the Gap. They were in four seats jammed in side by side, with Raup in the left-hand commander's seat, Willis and Frank in the middle, Sally to the right. The craft had a surprisingly complex-looking instrument panel, most of it in front of Raup, but with basic duplication in front of the others. They wore their spacesuits and helmets but with the visors open. There was a hum of fans, a smell of just-cleaned carpet; it was like being inside a freshly valeted car, Sally thought. Small windows revealed blue English sky.

And a toy spaceman dangled from a chain over Willis's head.

Sally flicked the toy with a gloved finger. 'What's this, Raup? Another dumb astronaut tradition?'

'No. An essential indicator. You'll see. Well, we're good to go. You guys strapped in? Three, two, one—'

There was no more ceremony than that. He didn't even touch any controls.

But Sally felt the subtle lurch of a step.

Suddenly the sky outside the windows was black. That spaceman started to float upwards, his chain slack.

And the shuttle's rocket booster lit up, shoving them hard in the back. They were all strapped tightly into their couches, but even so Sally was startled by the sensation. Maybe she should have paid more attention to the briefings.

The rocket burst lasted twenty seconds, perhaps less. Then it died. Once again the spaceman hung loose on his chain.

And *then* the weightlessness really cut in. To Sally it felt as if she were falling, as if her internal organs were rising inside her. She swallowed hard.

Willis, sitting silently, showed no reaction. Frank Wood whooped.

There were knocks and bangs, and the craft swivelled with tight jerks.

Al Raup produced a flask, squirted out water that hung in the air, a shimmering globe, and then closed his mouth around it. 'OK,' he said. 'The noise you hear is the firing of our attitude rockets, and the manoeuvring system. The shuttle is taking itself in for its docking with the Brick Moon.'

The Brick Moon, an artificial satellite station-keeping in the position of the vanished Earth in its orbit, was the Houston of the Gap, a constant comms presence for space travellers, a place where some basic research was going on, and a link to home. They were to stay there for only a few hours, before boarding their Mars ship, the *Galileo*.

'Everything's automated,' Raup said. 'But because I know some of you paid no attention whatsoever to the briefings, I draw your attention to this big fat red button here.' He pointed.

'You understand we're dealing with the rotation of the Earth here. I mean, the Earth you just stepped off of. When you thought you were standing still on Earth you were already moving through space, being dragged around with the surface of the world – at a speed of hundreds of miles an hour at the latitude of GapSpace. When you step between worlds you keep that momentum, and without compensating you'd be flung away through space. The first time you stepped into the Gap, incidentally, Sally, aboard that airship, it's lucky you stepped back as quickly as you did before getting thrown around too far. Here we have to shed that velocity, so the stepper shuttle burns its rockets, and brings us to a halt relative to the Brick Moon.

'But if we ever want to go *back* we need to accelerate again, to match the Earth's spin. OK? Otherwise you'd be like a leaf in a thousand-miles-per-hour gale. So if all else fails, if I'm incapacitated and you're out of touch with the Brick Moon, press *that* button and the systems will take you home. Comprende?'

'Clear enough,' Willis said.

'The other likely contingencies which we may hit in the shuttle are a drop in air pressure – just close up your suits. There are sick bags in front of you, airline style. Or you may need to use the bathroom. We do have a john in here, which folds out of the wall.' He grinned evilly. 'But your suits do have diapers. My advice is, if you can't hold it in, let it out—'

'Just get on with it,' Sally said coldly.

'Everything's tooty. Just relax and enjoy the ride . . .'

With a speed that was surprising, given Sally's memories of TV images of stately dockings at the International Space Station, the stepper shuttle closed in for a rendezvous with the Brick Moon. The station was a cluster of spheres, the whole about two hundred feet across, each component sphere brightly lettered A to K. The station-keeping satellite had been hastily assembled from prefabricated sections in brick and concrete, doped to withstand the vacuum and filled with airtight pods. Sally had been amazed to learn, during the briefings, that troll labour had been used to manufacture the concrete.

In zero gravity, they scrambled out of the shuttle and through hatches. To Sally the open hatches, surfaces that had been exposed to space, smelled oddly of hot metal.

And on the other side of the entrance hovered a worker, looking strangely like a clone of Al Raup, who handed them bread and a salt dip as they drifted through. 'Old cosmonaut traditions,' Raup said. 'The Russians always got more into this stuff than we ever did.'

Inside the Brick Moon, the big chambers were cluttered with stuff: various kinds of equipment, bundles of bedding and clothing, bags of garbage, bales of what looked like unopened supplies. Every wall surface seemed to be covered in Velcro; more equipment clung there, roughly shoved out of the way.

Sally bounced around, shoving off the walls, getting used to movement in these conditions. Without gravity all these curved-wall compartments felt roomy, despite the clutter. She had a feeling adjusting back to gravity would be a lot tougher.

There was a constant clatter of fans and pumps. Sally saw loose bits of paper drifting in the air currents towards grimy-looking grilles. After five minutes in the dusty air, she started sneezing violently. Dust, hanging in the air, failing to settle out without gravity.

She glimpsed only a few other people in this station during their short visit. Most people just passed through this place, exchanging one specialized craft for another, but there was some dedicated work going on here which Raup showed them perfunctorily. New kinds of materials were being tested, many of them ceramic composites; panels of the stuff were pushed out of airlocks to be tested in the conditions of space. There was a programme of medical testing, of studies of the effects of zero gravity on the human body – repeating studies that dated back to the mid twentieth century and the first spaceflights, but with much more sophisticated gear.

And there were some more intriguing, less obvious projects: on the growth of crystals in the vacuum, on the development of plant and animal life in zero gravity. Sally surprised herself by being utterly charmed by a bank of bonsai trees she found growing in reflected sunlight, vivid colours against the bleak concrete walls.

And from the windows of the Brick Moon, the *Galileo* could be seen to hang in empty space.

Their Mars ship was unprepossessing, just two tin cans separated by a long metallic strut, with a single flaring rocket nozzle at the base of one cylinder, a snub-nosed lander aircraft piggybacking on the side of the other, and sprawling solar-cell wings. The spinal strut was adorned with spherical fuel tanks swathed in thick silvered insulation foam; they looked like huge pearls. There was fuel enough, Sally learned, to push the *Galileo* to Mars and back again. The trip each way would take nine or ten weeks.

The lander was called the MEM, officially the Mars Excursion Module. The upper cylinder to which it clung was the hab module, where the three of them would live for the ride out to Mars, and back. The cladding on the hull would protect them from radiation and meteorites. Light gleamed from windows cut through the cladding, bright and cosy and warm.

They spent twelve hours in the Brick Moon. They stripped out of their pressure suits, which were checked over; they were put through brisk medical tests by an onboard doctor; they had a meal, of paste from tubes and pots, and coffee squirted from bulbs. They all used the bathroom while they were out of their suits.

Then they suited up once more, and crossed into their ship, and Sally Linsay was that bit further away from Earth, and closer to Mars.

11

Earth West 1,617,524: more than a million and a half worlds from the Datum, the original world of mankind, the *Armstrong* and *Cernan* hovered in a washed-out blue sky.

And below, on a green scrape amid arid wilderness on this late January day, smoke rose from the ruins of a city.

Already, just sixteen days into the journey of the *Armstrong* and *Cernan*, Maggie was far from home. She tried to picture, in a kind of human sense, just how far. For example, they had left behind the bulk of the Long Earth's population in just a few *hours*. After Step Day there had been pulses of migration outward into the Long Earth, first the early wanderers, then the purposeful trekkers, and a new wave once twain technology was available and you could ride to your destination rather than walk. Then had come the mass flight from the Datum after Yellowstone, an evacuation of millions, unplanned and unprovisioned, that had overwhelmed all that had gone before.

Even following that, however, the populations of mankind were still relatively concentrated, with a bias towards the 'centre', the Datum and the worlds of the Low Earths. Further out there was a long, long tail, out through the thick bands of more or less similar Earths that humans had given such labels as Ice Belt or Mine Belt or Corn Belt. Valhalla, at around West one point four million, the greatest city in the deep Long Earth, was another useful marker point. That was the limit of the great twain-driven trade routes that had encouraged a certain cultural unity across the developing new worlds. More practically, it was about the furthest point at which you could expect the outernet to work.

But mankind's colonization wavefront had spread further yet, thinning out into the still stranger, still less familiar worlds beyond Valhalla. Such as this one. Now Maggie Kauffman stood with her officers in the science section of her ship's observation galleries, as Gerry Hemingway prepared to brief them on this world, showing imagery taken from the ground and a nanosat in orbit: tentative maps, geological and atmospheric profiles, classifications and analyses.

And all the while that ruined city was spread out beneath the ship's prow, a tangle of dirt tracks and walls and field boundaries. It looked from the air as if it had been smashed flat and then burned out, leaving great blackened scars on the ground – though it was still inhabited, as you could tell from the smoke rising from scattered hearths. Everybody on both craft was a veteran of Yellowstone, of rescue and retrieval operations, and the devastation brought back harsh memories.

There were humans down below. The *Armstrong* hovered over a small huddle of bubble tents, a scraping of tyre tracks, a couple of heavy off-road vehicles. People had come to study this place. But the city itself had been built, not by humans, but by a race of alien sapients. It seemed almost incredible to Maggie to think of that, even as she stood here looking down on a city whose name, translated into human tongues, was something like 'The Eye of the Hunter'. A city that had been built by the race called the beagles.

The three trolls were on the deck, huddled together, peering down at the ruins. They hooted their way through what sounded to Maggie like a softly sung but highly complex version of a funereal hymn, 'Abide With Me'.

For this briefing Maggie had assembled the shore party she was planning to send down to the city. Maggie herself would lead. Wu Yue-Sai was here, as a gesture of cross-cultural friendship with the Chinese. Maggie had never encountered the beagles in person herself, but Joe Mackenzie, her chief medical officer, had relevant expertise; during the post-Yellowstone years he had actually spent time here as part of some kind of biological-stroke-cultural mission – a jaunt he'd told her virtually nothing about.

Wu looked like she was full of nothing but honest eagerness and curiosity. Mac, on the other hand, never the cheeriest of souls, glowered down at the city, almost hostile.

'Hey.' Maggie touched his shoulder. 'You OK?'

'I don't know why you want me in this party.'

'Because you worked here. Even though you never told me about it.'

He avoided her eyes. 'Saw enough of this place back then. Look, why have we stopped? We're going *much* further than this. It's as if Lewis and Clark spent a week hanging out in a Chicago bar before—'

'Well, we aren't Lewis and Clark. We've got different mission objectives. You'll see.'

Hemingway was now displaying global maps, images of this particular Earth. Maggie saw a layout of continents not very much different from those of Datum Earth, but not in quite the right places, landmasses that seemed enlarged, or smeared, even joined together: Australia was connected to south-east Asia by a fat neck of land, the Bering Strait was closed. In the heart of all the continents were the yellow-red stains of deserts. The oceans looked shrunken, and even the polar caps were diminished.

Gerry Hemingway said, 'Some of the climatologists call these worlds Venusian, or Para-Venusian . . . It's all about water. Datum Earth and Venus seem to be at two ends of a band of possible water content levels, for planets like ours. Our Earth has a lot of surface water in its oceans, of course, and in the air, and cycling around in the mantle. Venus may have started out with a similar water lode but lost it all early on. A world like this is somewhere on the spectrum between the two – significantly drier than Earth, not as dry as Venus. There is life here, even complex life, even sapients, but it's sparse, isolated. The early Long Earth explorers, including the first Valienté mission, missed this exception. And its inhabitants. Well, you would, unless you took the time to survey the whole planet.'

Yue-Sai shook her head. 'We always rush, rush across the Long Earth. So we did on the *Zheng He*. So we will on this wonderful craft! One always wonders what one misses, simply through not having time enough to see. So many worlds, so many wonders.'

Hemingway said, 'It was only five years ago that the indigenous sapient culture was discovered. Since then, despite the demands of the Yellowstone crisis, an international consortium of universities has funded stations of observers and contact specialists: linguists, cultural analysts. You see one such camp below. And we contacted the local sapients.' He hit a tab, and the map on his tablet lit up with a scattering of dots, spread around the fringes of the continents, and along the main water courses. 'Here are the main communities we've detected so far. They tend to be small in extent but densely inhabited. That's something to do with the beagles' biology; they like to live in close bands. But they have links of communication and trade that span the continents.'

'And war,' Mac said sourly. 'Their wars span continents too.'

'War, yeah. We understand something of the political landscape. The beagles are grouped into Packs, which roughly correspond to our nations – or maybe what we think of as our races. The North American Pack is ruled by a Mother, as they call her, who's on the west coast, not far from San Francisco Bay. There are local, umm, fiefdoms, each ruled by a Daughter or Granddaughter of the Mother. It's a matriarchy, as you can tell from the language. Males are warriors, workers – breeding partners. Subordinate. Though there's no difference we can detect in levels of intelligence between the sexes.

'And they do have devastating wars. They come in cycles, as far as we can tell from some preliminary archaeology, and their own accounts of their history. A war, and the resulting plagues and famine, causes a population crash, but when the numbers recover, war comes again. Mostly the infighting arises within individual Packs. The basic motivation is Granddaughters trying to displace Daughters, and Daughters trying to displace a Mother. Inter-Pack war seems less common. But in the worst cases you get flare-ups covering a continent – hell, maybe the whole planet for all we know. Afterwards they just build everything up all over again, using the same sites, building slap on top of the smoking ruins. This latest war, however, the first since humans were here on hand to witness it, seems to have been tougher than most.'

Maggie expected Mac to comment on that. Instead he just kept staring out of the window.

'You must have seen something of this,' she murmured. 'Everybody on this boat seems to have secrets to keep from me. You too, Mac?'

Still he would not react. She turned away, obscurely hurt.

'Thank you, Gerry,' she said now. 'OK, folks, we have a mission to fulfil here, as you'll see. Let's get down there and get it done.'

They landed close to the in-situ researchers' huddle of tents.

The senior academic, an Australian called Ben Morton, known to Mac – he couldn't hide *that* from Maggie – was waiting to meet them. A haunted-looking older man, Morton barely acknowledged Mac, before he offered to drive them in the researchers' only vehicle into the beagle town, the Eye of the Hunter.

They bumped along an uneven track, past clumps of forest of low, gnarled trees, like ferns perhaps, and fields roughly delineated with straggling dry stone walls. What looked like grass was cropped by animals: not sheep or cattle or goats, but things like fat deer, and a kind of beefy flightless bird. Some of the fields were tended by workers who went upright, on two legs, swathed in rags and bearing walking staves. Maggie didn't get too close a look. At first glance they looked human – and after all, humans came in a variety of body shapes. But look again at these workers and, elusively, subtly, they didn't appear quite right, the head too large, the waist too low, the eyes set too wide apart.

Her companions took in all this, Hemingway in nervous silence, Mac with a kind of resentful glare. Maggie was growing sure that there was something specific he was keeping from her about his experience here.

Wu Yue-Sai was making notes on a small tablet.

Many of the farms had been looted, burned out, destroyed, Maggie saw from the beginning of the ride. And the evidence of war became more obvious as they approached the heart of the city, and certainly once they'd passed within its low, largely broken-down walls. She suspected the buildings here, of wood and daub, would always have looked irregular, even unfinished to a human eye, and they were oddly set out, clustered along straggling dirt streets – no grid pattern here. But now they were smashed, burned, only a few roughly repaired.

Given the size of the place she saw very few inhabitants, and fewer up close. But one child stood as they passed. Dressed in rags, she held out an empty bowl, her request obvious. It was a scene you might have seen in the aftermath of any human war, Maggie thought. But the child's eyes glittered, her ears were swept back, and a pink tongue lolled from a wide mouth.

At last the truck rolled up beside a more extensive ruin, a fire-blackened crater surrounded by scraps of scorched wall. There was a dog, a big one, bigger than a Saint Bernard, lying in the shade of one fragment of wall. He raised his head to watch them approach. He wore some kind of belt around his waist, Maggie saw.

'Welcome to the Palace of the Granddaughter,' said Ben Morton.

And the dog spoke.

'He-hhr name Pet-hhra. Long dead.' The language was clearly comprehensible English, but spoken with a growl, like a coarse whisper from the back of the throat.

A canine sapient. Maggie had been briefed about this, had even seen recordings. Nothing prepared her for the reality, though. Not even the talking cat in her own sea cabin. *That* was obviously artificial, a smart technological toy. This, though . . .

Her culture shock got worse when the dog stood up. He got up on his hind paws, almost like a trained animal in a balancing act. But then the movement became more fluid, his anatomy seemed to adjust somehow, and he was standing, a biped as fully developed as Maggie was, his waist low but his lower legs supporting him easily. He wore a kind of short kilt, and that belt from which, she saw now, tools dangled. His face did not have the obvious projection of a dog muzzle; it was flat, proportioned something like a human's, but the nose was broad, black nostrils flaring. His ears were sharp and lay back against his scalp, and his eyes were wide apart, unblinking, fixed on her. A predator's gaze. Maggie had a sense of age, from the slightly awkward stance, from grey hairs around a wide mouth.

Age, and injury; one forearm looked almost withered, and he held it against his chest.

He wasn't a dog. He was humanoid, as she was, but moulded from canine clay, as she was from the ape.

She'd asked for this encounter. But not for the first time she wondered whether, in the end, she was going to have the intellectual strength, the imaginative capacity, to face the true strangeness of her long mission, if she felt so overwhelmed by this first encounter with the alien.

'You're a beagle,' she said.

'So we h-have been called, by you. My name to you – B-hrr-ian.' He pulled his lips back, revealing very canine teeth, in what might have been an approximation of a grin. 'I ss-it to meet you like ghh-ood dog. Yes? Now I call.' He tipped his head back and howled, a suddenly very wolf-like sound; Maggie heard the call echo from the remains of the buildings.

Morton raised an eyebrow at the visitors. 'Brian's one of our main contacts here. One of the more, umm, humanized of the local beagles. He has a distinctive sense of humour. Mordant, you might say.'

'Mo-hrr-dant? Not know that wo-hhhrd. Look up later.'

'We've given him English language dictionaries, grade school stuff, and other teaching aids. We're learning a great deal from him.'

'And I too lea-hhrn,' Brian said to the bemused visitors, like the other half of some bizarre trained-animal double act, Maggie thought. 'My job always-ss to learn, when Pet-hhra was alive. G-hranddaughter. Killed in wa-hrr. For he-hrr, my learning useful. Learn of kobolds, learn of humans. Yet she despised me,' he said, and he hung his heavy head and shook it. 'Poo-hhr B-hrrian.'

Mac snorted in disgust. 'Christ. It's like he's begging for a treat.'

'Ignore him,' Morton said. 'Just showing off. He's useful but he can be a real asshole. Can't you, Brian?'

Brian laughed, an oddly human sound. 'Ass-sshole? You come sniff me then, Ben-nn. You know you wan-tt to. Asshole? T-hhrue. All beagles assholes. You see how we kill each other-hrr in war. Over and ove-hrr.'

Now a newcomer arrived, evidently in response to Brian's call, another dog, even bigger. It raced in on all fours but then stood tall, graceful, lithe, even as it slowed before Maggie. This one had clear, ice-blue eyes, was heavily muscled, and stood straight, almost to attention, Maggie thought.

She glanced at Morton. 'Is this the one?'

'We found a volunteer, who seemed to be the type you were looking for.' Morton's shrug said, *Sooner you than me.* 'He's all yours.'

Plucking up her courage, Maggie stepped forward and stood before the beagle. He smelled of musk, of dust, of *meat*; he smelled of animal. And yet his gaze was cool, clear. She said, 'They call you Snowy.'

'Yes-ss,' he said clearly. 'My t-hrrue name—' A guttural growl.

'You understand why I asked for a volunteer? You understand what's to become of you, if you come with us?'

'Ride to scentless wo-hhrlds.' He looked up at the sleek form of the *Armstrong*, and grinned.

Wu said, 'Ah! I understand. A beagle crew member. A fine experiment.'

'The whole journey is an experiment, Lieutenant,' Maggie said. 'Call this one an experiment in cross-sapience understanding.'

Mac stared at Maggie. 'You're kidding.'

'Mac, I didn't tell you before because I knew you'd object—'

'We already got Chinese military personnel on board,' Mac said. 'And trolls. And now this mutt!'

'Ignore him,' Maggie said to the beagle. 'Welcome to the crew of the USS *Neil A. Armstrong II*, Acting Ensign – umm, Snowy.'

'Than-khh you.' And he threw back his head and howled.

As they made to depart, Brian beckoned to Maggie, a very human gesture. 'Wait. Come ss-see my t-hrreasure.' He hurried into the shelter and emerged with what Maggie recognized as a picture – a painting, more likely a print. It was scuffed, dirty; perhaps it had survived a war. But its subject was clearly visible.

Mac grunted. '"Dogs Playing Poker". Old cigarette ads.'

'Gift from Sally Lin-ssay. Good shh-joke, she say. Good joke, good?' And he laughed, in a painful imitation of the human.

'Let's get out of here,' Maggie said.

'You come back-chh. Have mo-hhre pic-sshtures. Play poker-hhr?'

'So, Captain,' Mac said as they began the ride back to the ships, 'does Ed Cutler know about this damn beagle you're bringing aboard?'

'Not yet . . .'

When Snowy walked up the ramp to the airship, Shimi, who usually emerged to greet Maggie when she returned from a surface jaunt, took one look, arched her spine, fled back into the gondola, and wasn't seen for days.

12

Joshua accepted Lobsang's request to seek out and contact his hypothetical new race of superior human beings – his *true Homo sapiens*.

Somehow he never doubted that there was something in Lobsang's theory, his deduction of the existence of a new breed of humanity from what seemed like the slightest of scraps of evidence. Joshua had known Lobsang for fifteen years now; he knew that Lobsang saw the world as a piece, he thought on scales Joshua could barely grasp. He thought holistically, Sally Linsay had once said. If Lobsang had predicted the *true Homo sap* existed, then Joshua was confident they did exist, and if he looked he'd find them.

But where was he to start? Joshua was no scholar, no detective. He wasn't that much of a loner any more – he

was a family man, he had been mayor of Hell-Knows-
Where, and he supposed he would always return to his
deep roots in Madison, where he'd grown up. But he
wasn't entangled in the wider affairs of humanity.

In the event, Joshua's way in to this mystery was
through his friendship with one individual.

In fact, Joshua Valienté had first met Paul Spencer
Wagoner many years before, in Happy Landings, back
in 2031. Paul then was five years old. Joshua, on the
other hand, was twenty-nine.

It had been Joshua's third visit to the place Sally
Linsay had dubbed Happy Landings. He'd come here
the year before in the course of his exploration, with
Lobsang and Sally, aboard the prototype stepper-
airship *Mark Twain*, of the far Westward reaches of
the Long Earth – a jaunt that had subsequently become
known, in some fan circles at least, as 'The Journey'.
Under Sally's guidance they had called into Happy
Landings, more than a million and a half steps from
the Datum, in the course of their outward-bound
trek – and on the way back had called in again, with
the *Twain* now a semi-derelict in the sky, and having
lost Lobsang, after their shattering encounter with the
entity they called First Person Singular. Now, a year
after The Journey, Joshua had been passing through
this particular world, on his way home from a brief,

head-clearing sabbatical – and home for Joshua, just now anyhow, meant a Corn Belt town called Reboot, where he was going to marry Helen Green, daughter of a pioneering family.

He couldn't resist calling in again on Happy Landings.

He wasn't far from the Pacific coast in this version of Washington State. In fact this was the footprint of a Datum township called Humptulips, in Grays Harbor County. Joshua would always remember his surprise on seeing this place for the first time, a township where no township had a right to be, far beyond where the consensus at that time had it that the colonizing wave-front might yet have reached, just fifteen years after Step Day. Yet here it was.

The town hugged the bank of its river, surrounded by tracks that cut off into thick forest. There were no fields, no sign of agriculture. Like the great city of Valhalla a few years later, this was a place where people lived off the natural fruits of the land – and especially in an area as rich as this, as long as you controlled your numbers and spread out a little, that was an easy way to live. And, by the river, in the town itself, visible even from the air during that first visit, Joshua had spotted trolls, everywhere he looked. It was a unique popula-tion, a blend of human and troll – which was maybe what made it so strange in other ways.

Now Joshua strolled alone around the town, roughly centring on the big square by City Hall. The dusk was gathering, but as ever the square was full of smiling townsfolk, and bands of trolls singing scraps of song – people and trolls mixing casually. People nodded politely to Joshua, more or less a stranger making his third brief visit. As always it was all remarkably gentle, civilized, comfortable.

But, paradoxically, that had made Joshua uncomfortable. The community seemed *too* calm. Not entirely human . . . 'It all feels a bit Stepford Wives to me,' was how he'd tried once to express it to Sally.

And she'd said later, 'Sometimes I wonder . . . I wonder if there's something so big going on here that even Lobsang would have to recalibrate his thinking. Just a hunch, for now. I'm just suspicious. But then a stepper who isn't suspicious is soon a dead stepper . . .'

'Hey, mister.'

The kid had stood directly before Joshua, staring up. He was five years old, dark-haired, smut-nosed, wearing clothes that were clean but just a tad too big for him and extensively patched. Typical colony wear, heavily reused. Just a kid, but something in his sharp gaze cut right through Joshua's weary, vaguely muddled thinking.

'Hello,' Joshua said.

'You're Joshua Valienté.'

'I won't deny it. How do you know? I don't remember seeing you before.'

'I never saw *you* before. I deduced who you were.' He stumbled over that word, *deduced*.

'You did?'

'Everybody heard about the airship you flew in before. My parents talked about the people on board. There was a young man, and now he's back, everybody's talking about it. You're a stranger. You're a young man.'

'Good work, Sherlock.'

The kid looked puzzled at that reference.

'So who are *you*?'

'Paul Spencer Wagoner. Wagoner is my father's name, Spencer's my mother's name, and Paul is my name.'

'Good for you. Spencer, like the mayor?'

'He's my mother's second cousin. That's why we came here.'

'So you weren't born here? I thought you had a different accent from most.'

'My mom came from here but my dad's from Minnesota. I was born in Minnesota. The mayor invited us to come because we're family. Well, my mother is. Most people come here by accident.'

'I know.' Although Joshua didn't understand how. That was another mysterious thing about Happy Landings. People somehow came unstuck in the Long Earth, and just drifted here, from all over . . .

Once he'd tried to discuss this with Lobsang. 'Maybe it's something to do with the network of soft places. People drift and gather, like snowflakes collecting in a hollow, maybe.'

'Yes, perhaps it's something like that,' Lobsang had said. 'We know that stability is somehow a key to the Long Earth. Maybe Happy Landings is something like a potential well. And it's clearly been operating long before Step Day, deep into the past . . .'

'How did it fly?'

Again Joshua, exhausted from his journey, had allowed himself to get lost in his own thoughts. 'What?'

'The airship you came in on.'

Joshua smiled. 'You know, it's amazing how few people ask that. How do you think it flies?'

'It might be full of smoke.'

'Smoke?'

'Smoke rises up from a fire.'

'Hmm. That's not a bad try. I think the smoke is actually lifted up by hot air from the fire. And the hot air rises up because it's less dense than cold air. Some airships, balloons anyhow, are lifted by hot air. You have to have burners under the envelope. But the *Mark Twain*'s envelope was full of a gas called helium. It's less dense than ordinary air.'

'What does "dense" mean?'

Joshua had to think. 'It's how much amount of stuff there is in a given space. How many molecules, I guess. Iron is more dense than wood, say. A brick-sized block of iron is heavier than a brick-sized block of wood. And wood is more dense than air.'

Paul screwed up his nose. 'I know what molecules are. Helium is a gas.'

'Yes.'

'Air is a gas. Lots of gases, mixed up, I know that.'

Joshua started to feel nervous, like he was being led down a trail into a thickening forest. 'Yes . . .'

'I can imagine how iron is denser than wood. Do you say "denser"? I don't know that word.'

'Yeah.'

'You could jam in the molecules tighter. But how does that work with gases? If the atoms are all flying around.'

'Well, it's something to do with the molecules moving faster when stuff is hotter . . .' Joshua had never been one to bluff a kid. 'I don't know,' he said honestly. 'Ask your teacher.'

Paul blew a raspberry. 'My teacher is a kind lady and all but she doesn't know squat.'

Joshua had to laugh. 'I'm sure that's not true.'

'If you ask one question and then another she gets unhappy, and the other kids laugh at you, and she says, "Another time, Paul." Sometimes I can't even ask the questions – you know – I can kind of *see* it but I don't have the words.'

'That will come in time, when you grow up a bit more.'

'I can't wait around for *that*.'

'I hope he's not bothering you.' The woman's voice was soft, a little strained.

Joshua turned to see a family approaching, a man and woman about his own age, a toddler in a buggy. The kid seemed distracted; she was singing softly, looking around.

The man stuck out his hand. 'Tom Wagoner. Pleased to meet you, Mr Valienté.'

Joshua shook. 'Everybody knows my name, it seems.'

'Well, you did make quite an entrance last year,' Tom said. 'I do hope Paul hasn't been pestering you.'

'No,' Joshua said thoughtfully. 'Just asking questions I soon realized I had no answer to.'

Tom glanced at his wife. 'Well, that's Paul for you. Come on, kiddo, time for supper and bed, and no more questions for the day.'

Paul submitted gracefully enough. 'Yes, Dad.' He took his mother's hand.

After a couple of minutes of pleasantries, the family said goodbye. Joshua watched them go. He became aware that the little girl, introduced as Judy, had kept up her odd singing all the way through the short encounter, and now they'd stopped speaking he could hear her more clearly. It wasn't so much a song as a string of syllables – jumbled, meaningless maybe, but he kept thinking he heard patterns in there. Complexity. Almost like the trolls' long call, which Lobsang was determined to decode. But how the hell could a toddler be singing out a message that sounded like greetings from a space alien? Unless she was even smarter than her precocious brother.

Smart kids. That was another odd thing he was always going to remember about Happy Landings.

Enough. He had looked around for a bar, and a place to stay the night. He'd left the next day.

But he hadn't forgotten Paul Spencer Wagoner.

And he hadn't forgotten Happy Landings either. And, in the year 2045, he thought of it again, considering Lobsang's suggestion that out there in the Long Earth there could be incubators of a new kind of people. What would such an incubator be like? What would it *feel* like?

Like Happy Landings, maybe?

13

Aboard the *Galileo* the hab module was divided into three levels, and while there were common utilities, such as a galley, toilet and zero-gravity shower, and such universal essentials as closed-loop air and water recycling systems, the designers had assigned a whole level to each of the three crew to serve as his or her personal space. And in the hours and days that followed their booster firing, and their launch into interplanetary space from the Brick Moon, the wisdom of that design was impressed on Frank Wood.

The *Galileo*'s motley crew wasn't going to be a particularly sociable bunch.

Oh, they cooperated over their chores. There were shared maintenance duties: clean the dust filters, check the air balance, scrub down the walls to prevent the mould and algal infestations that tended to grow in untended corners in the absence of gravity. Sally and Willis accepted with good enough grace the work rotas Frank volunteered to draw up. They also quickly got used to the routine of meal preparation, most of it based on Russian space cuisine of decades past: there were tins of fish, meat and potatoes, dried soup and vegetable purée and fruit paste, nuts and black bread, and coffee, tea and fruit juice in bulbs . . . Some crews would have invested a lot of energy in coming up with inventive menus with those limited ingredients, Frank knew. Not the crew of the *Galileo*. Frank also insisted that they all kept up a routine of physical training, to offset the effects of weeks of weightlessness on their performance when they got to Mars. They had a treadmill, and elasticized frames to stress their muscles and bones. This alone occupied hours for each of them every day.

But that left plenty of spare time in each twenty-four-hour cycle – time father and daughter seemed to use, at first anyhow, to get as far from one another as possible.

Willis Linsay immediately disappeared into his own agenda of research and experimentation, using the computer gear and small laboratory he had installed on his personal deck. He seemed entirely unperturbed by being thrown into interplanetary space.

His daughter, meanwhile, a solitary type too, withdrew into herself. She slept a lot, exercised ferociously over and above the required minimum, read for hours using the onboard e-library she'd helped stock. Willis Linsay played a lot of music: Chuck Berry, Simon and Garfunkel. This antique stuff, echoing around the hab module, seemed to disturb Sally. Frank guessed this was the soundtrack of her childhood, and not particularly welcome to have back.

Even though Frank had known Sally from the days of the troll incident at GapSpace years back, he barely got a word out of her, at first. He sensed apprehension in her, however, despite her hard-nut exterior. He had to remind himself that she had actually discovered the Gap in the first place, along with Joshua Valienté and Lobsang. Maybe it was something to do with the fact that she didn't seem to know *why* she was here, why her father had brought her along on this jaunt.

As for Frank himself, he was just thrilled to be out here. For the first few days he gave himself up to a kind of triumphant joy. He'd been to the Brick Moon before, a number of times. Now he was in deep space, at last. Going to Mars! *A* Mars anyhow.

And the scenery, at least at first, was spectacular. Seen from outside, the Brick Moon was a bulbous cluster surrounded by sparking lights and swarming activity – and when the *Galileo*'s fusion rocket opened up he watched that huge, busy complex fall away like it was dropped down a well. A spectacular sight, yes, but it would always be one of Frank's biggest regrets that unlike the astronauts of NASA's heroic age he would never see the Earth itself from space. Of course that was the point. At the Gap you didn't need to escape from the Earth to reach space, because there *was* no Earth. But it did kind of diminish the spectacle.

However, after the first few hours, once the Brick Moon was out of sight, he had the consolation of the stars, any direction you looked away from the sun, an infinity of them. Frank liked to sit in his portion of the hab module peering out into that endless drop, letting his ageing eyes become accustomed to the blackness, his pupils widening to their fullest. And he would make out another peculiarity of this particular stepwise reality: a band of soft dusty light spanning the zodiac, the sky's equator. All this washed past his view, for the whole stack of the ship was rotating on its axis with slow grandeur, a measure taken to equalize the heating of the raw sunlight.

After a couple of weeks, Sally took to emerging from her own space and joining Frank by his windows. Frank was no psychologist, and took a robust view of interpersonal dynamics; in his view it didn't matter if a crew bonded all the way to Mars or not, just so long as they got there in one piece. And he certainly wasn't going to get caught up in what looked to him like a very peculiar father-daughter relationship. So, when Sally showed up, Frank would acknowledge her presence with a nod, but kept his own counsel. Let her talk in her own time, or not.

It was the end of the second day of this tentative companionship before she spoke meaningfully to him.

She pointed at the band of zodiacal light. 'Asteroids, right?'

'Yeah. You can see something similar at home – I mean, in the skies of the Datum. But there's more asteroids here. A whole extra band, actually, between the orbits of Venus and Mars.'

She thought that over. 'Oh. The wreckage of Dead Earth, the planet Bellos smashed.'

'That's it. But it's not wasted. We're out there already, in little dinky rocket ships, mining those fragments of planet for water, hydrocarbons, even iron from what used to be the Earth's core. Easily accessible. And we're manufacturing rocket fuel. Eventually, the plan is, we'll be independent of materials brought over from the stepwise worlds altogether. Some people are planning to *live* out there, on the asteroids themselves. Mind you, others find it kind of morbid that we're feeding off the ruins of a devastated world.'

Sally shrugged. 'I think I lost my capacity for sentimentality a long time ago. Ever since I came across evidence of a few Donner-party disasters out in the reaches of the Long Earth. Butchered human bones. This is just another kind of cannibalism, I guess.'

She said this with such flat finality that Frank had to look away, shuddering.

'Come on, Frank. You're tougher than that. Whatever it takes to survive, right?'

'Sure. So.' He forced a smile. 'How are you finding the trip so far?'

She thought that over. 'Surprising, if I'm honest.'

'Surprising?'

Loosely strapped into her chair, she touched the hull wall. 'For a start, this is kind of a bigger rocketship than I imagined we'd need.'

'Well, the technology's incredible. We're driven by a stream of tiny fusion bombs, pellets of deuterium and hydrogen that are made to detonate by a laser barrage, hundreds of bomblets every second going off behind a big pusher plate. We plan to use it in stacks to assemble more ambitious missions further out, to Venus, even Jupiter maybe—'

'Slow down, Apollo 13, you're hyperventilating.'

'Sorry. This stuff's been my life's work. My boyhood dreams before that.'

'My problem is I don't see why you need a rocket at all. I thought the Gap saved you from all that.'

Frank said, 'Well, to get to Mars from the Datum, you'd have to climb out of Earth's gravity well first. *That's* why you need a Saturn V, even to get to the moon. Using the Gap we don't need a Saturn V to get away from Earth. But we do still need a rocket for the Mars transfer.

'You have Earth and Mars following their circular orbits around the sun, OK? Even when you're in free space at Earth's orbit, you need a boost from some rocket or other to add at least seven thousand miles per hour to your speed to get up into an elliptical transfer orbit, as we call it. You coast all the way to Mars's orbit, and then you need another squirt, six thousand miles an hour this time, to slow down at Mars. And then you land. The whole thing is reversed when you come home. Actually our ICF rocket will provide a lot more push than that minimum.'

'I guess that's all logical enough.'

'Except,' called Willis Linsay, 'that you skipped over the real mysteries behind all this.'

Frank turned to see Willis swimming up the fireman's pole that ran along the axis of the hab module. He asked, 'Which are?'

'How does conservation of momentum work between the stepwise worlds? Or indeed conservation of mass? Sally, if you step from Earth A into Earth B, sixty-some kilograms of mass suddenly disappear from A and appear in B. How come? Mass, like momentum and energy, is supposed to be conserved. These are basic principles of physics – without which, incidentally, this firecracker of a rocketship wouldn't work at all.'

'True enough,' Frank said. 'So what's the answer?'

Sally said, 'Mellanier—'

'That fraud!'

'– would say that the conservation principles work across the worlds, not just in one world. Earths A and B share their mass and momentum, so nothing overall is lost or gained.'

'Whereas *others*,' Willis said heavily, and Frank suspected he was talking about himself, 'argue rather more convincingly that such principles can only work one world at a time. And if you step to world B, you borrow a little momentum from that world – it slows its rotation just a little – and you borrow some mass-energy from its gravity field.'

Frank said, 'Surely you could devise tests to establish which is which.'

Willis shrugged. 'The effects are too small. Some day it will be done. But the latter is the more appealing idea, don't you think? That a destination world somehow welcomes you as you step in, by giving of itself. And of course you *give back* when you step away.'

Sally said sourly, 'If you like your scientific hypotheses to come loaded with emotional freight – yes, I guess that would be an appealing idea . . .'

Frank could sense a lifetime of fencing going on under the surface of this quasi-technical conversation. They didn't even share the same accent. Willis was pretty broad Wyoming, which must have caused him to be underestimated by snobbier academics, while the daughter had a much more neutral accent, as if she'd deliberately distanced herself from her origins, from her father. Frank didn't detect any real animosity between father and daughter. They were too *vivid* for that, the pair of them, much too real personalities in their own right to have that kind of negative relationship. But it certainly wasn't all positive. They were two powerful people, with a shared past, yes, respectful, but wary of each other.

'By the way,' Sally asked now, 'which way's Mars?'

Frank glanced out of the window, thought for a second, then pointed over his shoulder. 'Thataway. It won't show up as more than a spark for, oh, weeks yet. Then we'll see it hanging there like an orange. It has big features, you know, the giant mountains, the canyons, visible from far away – well, you saw the images back in the auditorium. And on *this* Mars there's oceans, and the green of life.'

Sally glanced at her father. 'And is that the point of this mission? To figure out why Mars, this Mars, is warm and wet and alive?'

'Oh, no,' Willis said dismissively. 'That's trivial.'

Frank raised his eyebrows. 'Life on Mars is trivial? Tell that to Percival Lowell. So if life on Mars is just part of the scenery—'

'It's life on the *Long* Mars that I'm after. Life, and mind, and what it might – what it *must* have achieved.'

Sally faced him. 'To what end, Dad? What are you looking for – some kind of technology, like a new Stepper box? And what will you do then? Just turn it loose? Mellanier once compared you to Daedalus, the father of Icarus, the boy who used his father's invention to fly too high and upset the gods. And that's you all over, isn't it? Tinker, tinker for the sake of it, caring not one whit about the consequences. The Daedalus of your age.'

Willis rubbed his chin. 'But Daedalus is supposed to have invented the saw, the axe and the gimlet among other goodies. That's not such a bad charge sheet, is it? And as for—' An alarm sounded softly. 'Ah. That's my latest experiment. Excuse me . . .' Stiff but oddly graceful, he swam through the microgravity to the fireman's pole and pulled himself away to his lab area.

Frank eyed Sally. 'You OK?'

She didn't reply. For a long while she sat silent, withdrawn, quite unreadable to Frank.

Then she said, 'So what could go wrong, Frank? With the *Galileo*. I know they put us through some of the emergency procedures. But that mostly involved us climbing into air bags and floating around helplessly, while *you* saved the day.'

Frank shrugged. 'I think Al and the others figured that was all you would sit still for. And Willis even less. So we fed you the most basic stuff.'

'OK. But I'm here now. And I'm used to relying on myself for my own survival.'

'Sure. Well, there are plenty of contingencies we couldn't survive at all. A massive enough meteor strike. A bad enough failure of the propulsion system during the firing phases – we do have nuclear fusion explosions going on back there.'

'And what is survivable?'

'Plenty. A smaller meteor puncture. A containable fire. An atmosphere leak, or some other failure of the air supply. A drastic power failure. In most of these situations the automatics will save us. In most of the rest, I'll be there to deal with it. And failing that, you can talk to the Brick Moon.'

'And if all those fallbacks fail?'

Frank grinned. 'I'd say the primary key survival skill for you is going to be learning to put your pressure suit on, in the dark, with the air failing around you, and the emergency horns sounding like the opening bars of Doomsday. Once you're in your suit you'll have time to deal with the rest. Takes hours of practice to master that.'

'Well, I guess we have hours.'

And so they started, with Sally learning every inch of the ship and its equipment and various failure modes to the best of her ability, while Willis locked himself away and pursued his own projects.

That was how it was, pretty much all the way to Mars.

14

In her log, Maggie Kauffman noted that it was only once they were past Earth West 1,617,524 – past the world of the beagles, and with that final crewmate on board – that her journey truly began.

Harry Ryan finally declared himself happy with what he described as his 'fusion-cuisine of an engine suite', with robust American engineering wrapped around a core of Chinese gel-based ingenuity, and he permitted Maggie to order full throttle, at last.

Maggie herself was in the wheelhouse when it began, with a few of her officers, ready for any of the multiplicity of breakdowns and disasters that Harry had predicted. Wu Yue-Sai was making notes as ever. Maggie had a fine view of the outside worlds through big panoramic windows – windows with tough ceramic shutters ready to clang shut in an instant in case of emergency.

And she watched those worlds flip by, one after the other, ever faster as the drive cut in.

At first the view was routine, if you could call anything about the Long Earth routine: just one arid world after the next in this belt of 'Para-Venuses', dissolving away at one per second, the rate of her heartbeat. Then the rate increased steadily, up to two Earths a second, faster, and Maggie felt her own heart beat faster in response, her body's rhythms unconsciously tracking the music of the worlds. But as the rate increased further Maggie began to find the strobing of realities uncomfortable. They should be in no danger. It was routine now to test twain crews and passengers for epilepsy, and Doc Mackenzie had ordered everybody aboard to put themselves through a final automated screening before consenting to this engine test.

And still the worlds swept past, faster and faster. Maggie became aware that the Earths flickering below were greener than before, the sky sporadically bluer. They must already be out of the Venus belt, then. But the worlds were now flying past her vision too fast for her to make out any details, nothing save the basics of sky, horizon, land, and the steely shine of the river beneath them – a remote cousin of the Ohio, if the ships' geographers were to be believed.

And then the worlds *blurred*. They reached a certain critical point when the stepping rate was faster than her vision processing system could follow, as if the worlds – each a whole Earth! – were no more than fast refreshes of a digital image. So there was no longer a sense of stepping from Earth to Earth, but more of continuous movement, of flow and evolution. The sun was a constant, hanging in a sky that was a melange of all the weathers, a kind of deep blue blandness. Below, the river spread out across its flood plain like a pale, greater ghost of itself, and forest clumps melded into a greenish mist that lingered over the landscape. It was no longer possible to make out any animals in the individual worlds, any birds; even the mightiest herd in any one world would be there and gone before her eyes had time to see it. Yet there was a sense of continuity, of the connectedness of all these living worlds, these actualized possibilities for Earth. All of this was sporadically illuminated, or darkened, by Jokers, exceptions to the norm, there and gone every few minutes.

And the *Cernan* hung constant in the sky, a reassuring companion – the work of mankind enduring against the flickering of multiple realities.

Now there was a thrum of mighty engines pushing the ship through the air, and the landscape shifted beneath the prow of the *Armstrong*. Continental drift was to some extent an affair of chance, and the positions of the landmasses shifted from world to world, mostly by very little, sometimes by a lot, but cumulatively by significant amounts. So the airships had to navigate geographically, trying to stay roughly over the centre of the North American craton, the antique granite mass at the heart of the continent. Again they were following the precedent of the Chinese expedition five years earlier.

Lieutenant Wu Yue-Sai stood by Maggie, and boldly took her hand. 'It is just as it was for us aboard the *Zheng He*,' she said. 'As if we see these worlds, the whole of the Long Earth all at once, through the eyes of a god.'

Only a few hours later the ships rushed across the Gap, around Earth West 2,000,000, without pausing. Harry Ryan declared himself happy with the resilience of his ships given the test of that dose of vacuum and weightlessness.

The character of the Earths did change somewhat after the Gap, when they paused to sample, image, visit. The worlds became blander, more colourless, with forest clumps dominated by huge ferns. These in turn gave way to more arid landscapes, with the vegetation restricted to the rivers and the fringes of the oceans. The worlds seemed to come in rough bands of similar types, tens or hundreds of thousands of steps wide, analogous to the Belts that had been identified by the first mappers of the Long Earth a couple of decades back.

Hemingway and his scientists tried to label and investigate a representative sample. They stopped to study features of geology, or geomorphology, or climatology – even astronomy, such as unusual features on the moon. They even checked for radio transmissions bouncing around remote ionospheres, and looked for the lights of human-lit fires, for nobody knew how far the colonization wavefront had come in the years since Step Day. The scientists reported that the basic suites of vegetation and animal types were similar either side of the great interruption of the Gap, and that was no great surprise. But they saw no stepping humanoids beyond the Gap: no trolls, no kobolds, none of the species that were common on the lower worlds. Again that was no great surprise, since, Maggie supposed, most steppers would not take the risk of crossing the Gap. But, for a veteran Long Earth traveller, it seemed strange to see worlds where there had never been trolls at all, worlds where the ecology had not been influenced by their massive presence – worlds which had never known the trolls' long call.

On the ships sailed. Data poured in, a torrent.

But it was always life that snagged the attention. And the life they saw got odder and odder.

Most of these worlds seemed to host complex life – that is, animals and plants, more than just bacteria. But the worlds of the Long Earth differed from each other by chance, by outcomes of random events in the past that varied a little or a lot. And the great extinction events that littered Earth's history seemed to Maggie to represent the biggest of all rolls of the cosmic dice. Even worlds closer to the Datum than Valhalla appeared to reflect different outcomes of the big impact that had ended the reign of the dinosaurs on the Datum. There, people had found strange assemblages of beasts that were like dinosaurs or not, like mammals or not, like birds or not.

But where the *Armstrong* travelled now, things got weirder. Maggie learned that there had been another milestone mass extinction on Datum Earth more than two hundred million years before humanity had arisen; a community crowded with the first mammals, early dinosaurs and the ancestors of crocodiles had been smashed. Now, millions of steps from the Datum, they found the consequences of different outcomes of that epochal event, jumbled ecologies where mammalian hunters tracked dinosaur-like herbivores, or insectile predators chased crocodilian prey. There were worlds with crocodiles the size of tyrannosaurs, or raptors the size of mice with teeth like needles . . .

Whatever the details, what struck Maggie cumulatively, as these first days of rapid travel wore by, was the sheer, relentless vigour of an elemental life force which seemed to seek expression anywhere it could, any way it could, on any available world – an expression in living things shaped by relentless competition, creatures breathing, breeding, fighting, dying.

It got overwhelming after a while. Maggie retreated into the familiar routine of work.

15

On the ninth day after the inception of the Chinese drive, Maggie, writing up reports in her sea cabin, barely looked up as she sensed the airship come to a stop, once again. Another science halt; she'd be informed if it was necessary for her to know the details, or if it was thought she'd be interested.

And a day later, with the ship still halted, Gerry Hemingway called. 'Captain, sorry to bother you. You might want to see this one for yourself.'

She checked her earthometer: Earth West 17,297,031. What the hell, she needed some fresh air. 'I'll be there. How's the weather?'

'We're near a sea coast here. Kind of crisp, and it's February. Bring cold-weather gear, and waterproof boots. And Captain—'

'Yes, Gerry?'

'Be careful where you step.'

'See you on the access deck.' She stood, and glanced down at Shi-mi. 'You coming?'

Shi-mi sniffed. 'Will Snowy be there?'

'Probably.'

'Bring me back a T-shirt.'

Maggie Kauffman stood on a sandy beach, by a gently lapping sea. She wondered if this was an inland American sea like in the Valhallan Belt, or if such labels as 'America' made sense any more, as the continents slid around the face of the Earth like jigsaw pieces on a tipped-up tray.

She was here with Gerry, Snowy the beagle and Midshipman Santorini whom she'd assigned as an informal companion for the beagle. Even Snowy, who generally went barefoot, was wearing heavy, improvised boots, she saw. Further away more of Gerry's science team were recording, mapping, monitoring, staring at this unremarkable beach, the ocean, the dunes. There were two armed marines assigned by Mike McKibben, their tough-talking, Scrabble-playing sergeant. Nobody from the Navy side was sure if the marines were attached to parties like this to keep an eye on the local dinosaurs or crocodiles, or on the Navy crew, or on the dog that spoke English.

And two of the party were civilians, wearing odd-looking sensor packs on their shoulders. These were employed by Douglas Black, and sent a continuous feed back to him. Black rarely showed his face outside his cabin, but he was endlessly curious about the worlds they travelled, and liked to explore, if only vicariously.

Well, there were no crocodiles or dinosaurs here, that Maggie could see. Plenty of life in the ocean; she glimpsed fish, seaweed, the remains of some kind of shellfish on the tidal wrack. And crabs, she saw: a hell of a lot of the little bastards running around.

Gerry Hemingway was watching her. 'Captain, we haven't filed a formal report yet. What's your first reaction?'

'That I'm glad you warned me to put my boots on. These damn crabs are everywhere.'

'OK. Fair enough. We've found a whole belt of worlds dominated by crabs and crustaceans. This is the most spectacular so far. Look, if you'll indulge us, we'll show you this step by step. It's a way of checking our conclusions.'

'Show me what?'

'Follow me down to the ocean, please, Captain.'

She glanced at Snowy, who gave a remarkably human shrug, and stepped forward, very carefully.

At the water's edge, Hemingway splashed out a little way. 'What about this, Captain? And this?' He pointed at the seabed, a big patch of pink, a patch of green.

Looking closer she saw the pink was a crowd of shellfish of some kind, like shrimp, and the green was seaweed. 'I don't see . . .' Then she realized that the shrimp things were corralled into a rough square, ringed by walls of stones heaped on the sea-bottom sand, and patrolled by some kind of crab no bigger than the palm of her hand. And the seaweed too was a roughly square patch, maybe six feet on a side. More crabs were working the seaweed, passing over its surface, plucking at the greenery. Working in neat parallel lines, up and down this – *field*?

She stepped back and looked around. The near-shore sea floor of this coastal strip, as far as she could see to left and right, was covered in rectangles and squares like this, green, pink, purplish, other colours. Now she saw it, it was obvious.

'Oh.'

Hemingway was grinning. '"Oh", Captain?'

'Don't get smug, Hemingway.'

'Fa-hrrms,' said the beagle, staring as she was. 'Little fa-hrrms.'

'That's it,' Hemingway said. 'We're evidently seeing careful, conscious, purposeful cultivation by this particular kind of crab. Next step. Follow me, Captain . . .'

They walked along the beach to what looked at first glance like some kind of drainage ditch cut deep into the sand, straight and long and coming out of the dunes. It ran with clear water, down to the sea. Maybe ten feet wide, the surface was cluttered with debris, Maggie saw, maybe litter from the land washed away by some storm . . .

No. She looked again. The 'debris' was flowing in two lanes, one washing down towards the sea, the other back up. And what she'd thought was drifting junk was mostly little squares and rectangles, none bigger than eighteen inches or so on a side, floating on the water. The ones heading downstream carried what looked like waste, empty pink shells and other garbage. The ones coming up from the sea were laden, with 'shrimp', with seaweed.

Snowy bent over, his black nostrils flaring as he sniffed, and briefly Maggie wondered what he saw, what he sensed . . .

What did *she* see?

Those little mats, pale brown in colour, were craft, woven of some kind of reed. Purposefully constructed. They reminded her of big table mats. The seaward ones seemed to be flowing with the current, but those heading upstream were attached by fine thread to more crabs on the bank of the little canal: bigger beasts than those she'd seen on the seaweed farms, hefty, clumsy, labouring to pull their threads. She looked closer, and made out more of the smaller crabs. Each of the big haulage animals had at least one little crab beside him, with a pincer holding – what, a whip? Something like that. And on each of the rafts themselves rode another little crab, or two, and they held handles in their pincers which controlled a kind of rudder—

She stepped back. 'No way.'

'Way, Captain,' said Hemingway, grinning. 'There are many possibilities for life – and, it seems, many possibilities for tool-making, civilization-building. Here, it was the crabs who took the chance. Why not? On the Datum, crabs are as old as the Jurassic, there are thousands of species, and they can be pretty smart, communicating with clacks of their pincers, fighting over females, digging burrows. They don't have hands but you could do some fine work with those pincers.'

'They don't seem to be reacting to us, do they? Half a dozen vast presences looming over them.'

'Too big,' Snowy growled. 'Not ss-see.'

'That may be true,' Hemingway said. 'Maybe they physically can't look upwards. Why would they need to?

Or maybe they just can't process us, visually; we're just too strange, like clouds come down to the ground . . .'

'You mentioned "civilization". I see a lot of rafts and fishers. What civilization?'

He straightened up. 'Just over the dunes, Captain.'

The city of the crabs centred on what Gerry Hemingway believed was a temple complex. Or maybe it was a palace.

A big blocky building with open porticoes faced a long, wide rectangular pool, brimming with murky green water. What appeared to be a sculpture of a crab – like the raft pilots, but *big*, half the size of an adult human – loomed over the 'temple'. Smaller sculptures, of crabs with upraised pincers, stood in a line around the pool, but Maggie thought that these life-size copies looked more like corpses, or maybe cast-off shells.

This complex, of pool and palace, was lined on all sides by more buildings, all more or less rectangular in form, but with softened edges, and all constructed of some hard, brownish substance. The palace, in fact, was the centrepiece of a straight-line grid-pattern of streets, which delineated blocks cluttered with buildings. The canal from the sea led straight into one big area that looked like warehousing, where, Maggie supposed, the incoming food was processed through in one direction, and the sewage bundled up and flushed away in the other. It was a regular city, and laid out in a surprisingly human-like fashion – unlike the irregular beagle city. But all the streets swarmed with crabs, scuttling this way and that. There were no vehicles on the land, but Maggie did see some of the smaller crabs *riding* on the backs of their bigger cousins.

And Maggie could step over the tallest buildings, like Gulliver in Lilliput. Where she planted her feet – with great care – in streets and open areas, the crabs still didn't seem to perceive her properly; they just scuttled sideways around her big boots.

When she looked up she saw the comforting bulks of the twains, like a reminder of reality.

'My God,' she said to Hemingway. 'It's like a model layout. I keep expecting some toy steam train to come rattling around the bend.'

Hemingway seemed to be bursting to explain it all to her. 'Here's as much as we have figured out, Captain. We've been watching for twenty-four hours now. We think *these* ones—' He bent down and pointed to a sample.

'The raft pilots?'

'Yeah. *They* are the smart ones. They're males, who seem to dominate here. These others, the bigger ones, are the females for this species – many crab species have sexual dimorphism. Umm, they also seem to be using other species as draught animals, food stock maybe, construction workers. They don't seem to have discovered the wheel – see, they *ride* the dumber ones?

'The buildings are made of a kind of paste, of chewed-up shell and spit; they have a particular kind of animal that specializes in producing that. You can see there's a big food processing area over there. We can't even guess at the function of the rest of the buildings, the districts, though some are probably residential. On the Datum, crabs like to live in hollows, in caves, even in pits they dig out of the seabed . . .'

Maggie bent to look closer at the stationary crab likenesses around the pool. 'Crabs moult, don't they?'

'They do, Captain. They cast off their outer shells regularly. And maybe that's what this is. Not sculptures, like the big guy over the palace, but moulted shells discarded by – who? The emperor, his ancestors, a line of priests? And it is a *him*, you can see by the size of the shell. And kept for ceremonial purposes here.'

'Lots of guesswork going on here, Gerry.'

'Yes, Captain.'

'Mo-hrre coming,' said Snowy, and he stepped out of the way of the big thoroughfare that led up to the pool.

Here came a regular procession, a whole line of crabs heading for the central complex, most of them raft-pilot size but a few others in there too. Some seemed to have their shells decorated, red, black, purple, maybe with some relative of squid ink, Maggie thought. Others walking alongside clacked their pincers loudly in the air. Conversely there were others, in the middle of the crush, who looked kind of bedraggled, their shells scuffed and scarred. Some even had their pincers missing, nipped off at the joint, perhaps.

The only sounds were the clatter of pincers and the scraping of thousands of shells, a noise like sand on a window.

'Soldier-hhrs with fallen en-hhemies,' Snowy said, sounding almost sad. 'Thei-hrr weapons-ss cut away.'

'Perhaps. The kind of sight we've seen enough of on the Datum, in the past.'

Hemingway said, 'Maybe those guys playing casta-net aren't making noises at random. Some crab species communicate with noises like that. On the Datum the message is usually just "That food is mine", but here it must be more complex.'

Maggie said, 'I wonder what fate awaits these prisoners when they reach that pool . . .'

'Something's happening at the palace,' Hemingway said now. 'Some kind of party coming out.' He snapped at his team, 'Make sure you record every damn moment of this.'

'Yes, sir.'

Maggie bent down to see who was emerging from the spit-and-shell palace. One big crab in the centre of the party was surely the centrepiece of it all. His shell wasn't marked, but he looked heavy, older, even indefinably arrogant to Maggie. He was surrounded by a circle of odd-looking acolytes, pink, vulnerable-looking . . . 'My God,' she said. 'They have no shells.'

Hemingway said, 'Maybe they've just moulted. When it moults the whole crab has to climb out of its old shell . . . Of course these companions look the right size to be females. In some crab species the females are mated just after moulting, when they're softer. Hmm. I wonder if this emperor has some way to keep his harem from forming new shells. Thus keeping them sexually available for whenever he feels the urge.'

'Ouch,' Maggie said.

'Yes, Captain. The procession is reaching the water.'

In the end the fate of the captives was brutal and decisive. One by one they were hurled into the pool, by the adorned soldier types. When the first captive hit the water the pool turned into a frenzy of activity, and was soon a mess of fragments of flesh and shell, and thrashing, struggling victims.

All the captives were thrown in, one by one, with horrible regularity, while the 'emperor' and his consorts looked on.

Hemingway said, 'I wonder what they keep in that pool. Some kind of piranha?'

Snowy said, 'Babies-ss.'

'What?'

'Babies. C-hhrab babies are let out by mother-hrr into water. Swim-mm. Find food. Not like pups, not-tt suckle.'

'Ah,' said Hemingway. 'And in that pool—'

'Babies of rule-hrr of this place. Eat enemy. Make babies-ss st-hrrong. Make them-mm fight each othe-hrr. Happens like this with us-ss. Pups tear-hhr apart fallen enemies-ss of mother-hrr.'

Hemingway and Maggie shared a glance. 'You know,' said Hemingway, 'I bet you're right. I never would have thought of it that way. It makes sense – a cultural logic deriving from the imperative of their biology.'

Snowy had to get that translated into simpler terms. But then he faced Maggie. 'Your thought, my thought-tt, always at mer-hhrcy of blood, of body. Need other blood, other bodies, to p-hhrove thought. My blood not you-hhrs. My thought not you-hhrs.'

Maggie grinned. 'You're right, dammit. That's precisely why I wanted you aboard, Snowy. Different ways of thinking, from a different biological perspective. A way to shed preconceptions we never knew we had. What is the point of the Long Earth if we can't pool our minds?' She studied the beagle. 'I do hope you're forming a more constructive impression of us, crewman, than I hear your people have on your home world.'

Snowy seemed to frown; his expression was always hard to read. 'Con-shh . . . Cons-thrr . . .'

'I mean, *better.* I know you look down on the way we treat our dogs. But we do cherish them, you know.'

Hemingway seemed interested in the conversation. 'Not only that, Captain, some people think that our relationship with our dogs contributed to our own evolution. And maybe, if we follow up this experiment with Snowy, if we continue to work together in future—'

Snowy regarded him gravely. 'Maybe humans-ss be b-hhred better-hrr than before.'

Maggie let her smile broaden. 'Crewman, I'll make a note in my log that you just made your first joke. Now, as for these crab critters—' She crouched down, staring at the bloody scene playing out before them. 'You know, we've got more in common with these little guys than you'd think. We meaning humans and beagles, at the least. Like us they're toolmakers. Like us they build cities. Do we know if they count, Gerry? Do they write?'

'Ah, Captain—'

'You know, if I could find a way to recruit one of these guys on to the crew of the *Armstrong*—'

'*Captain.*' More urgently.

She turned. 'What?'

He gestured, embarrassed. 'The corner of the temple. Your, umm, *butt . . .*'

She turned and looked. 'I demolished the west wing. Oops.'

'They ss-see us now,' Snowy said, looking down.

Maggie saw that the emperor character was waving his big pincers at her in a kind of comical, miniature rage, laying about him, scattering his soft-fleshed concubines. Everywhere pincers were being clattered, a rising tide of soft but persistent noise. She had offended the king of Lilliput, by brushing his palace with her ass. She tried not to laugh.

But then she felt the ground lurch.

Hemingway turned to look. 'Umm, Captain.'

'What now, Gerry?'

'The big crab form on top of this building. The *really* big one.'

'What about it?'

'We thought it was a sculpture.'

'Yes?'

'Well, it isn't.'

'Then what?'

'A moult, Captain. It's another moult.'

'A moult of what? Ah. Of what's emerging from the ground over there. I see. What do you advise, Lieutenant?'

He didn't hesitate. 'Run, Captain!'

They ran, from a crab that burst from its burrow in the sandy ground, a crab the size of a small bear and with the speed of a cheetah, moving sideways or not.

The airships stayed three days, observing, measuring, sampling. They left behind a three-person team of volunteers from Hemingway's department with instructions to study the crab civilization, to make contact if they could – and to survive, at a minimum.

Then they flew on.

16

Frank Wood took a step forward, away from the MEM.

Everything was strange, all the world's familiar elements distorted, here on Mars – on *this* Mars. The sun was shrunken but bright, and the rocks around him cast sharp shadows across the dusty crimson plain. Frank might have been standing in a high desert on Earth, but the air was thinner here than at the top of Everest. Even so this world was relatively clement. It wasn't as bad as the real Mars – Datum Mars. It was cold, the air was thin, but not *that* cold, not *that* thin.

The sky was brownish towards the horizon, but a deep blue if Frank tilted back to see the zenith, though that was tricky in his surface suit with its warm padded layers and enclosing facemask. Somewhere in that sky should have been Earth, a morning star close to the sun. Not here. Not in the universe of the Gap.

He tried another step.

Moving was dreamlike, somewhere between walking and floating. After weeks of weightlessness he was taking time to recover. His body fluid distribution was all off, and his muscles felt feeble despite the hours on the treadmill. His sense of balance was off too, so that this strange new world swam around his head, uncomfortably. But with every step he took, he felt that little bit stronger. This was Frank Wood, aged sixty-one, walking in the Mangala Vallis, an equatorial site with a name given it by NASA mappers from the Sanskrit word for the planet Mars, and if Indo-European was the root of most western languages it might be the oldest surviving name for Mars of all . . . The first human on Mars! *A* Mars, anyway. Who'd have thought it? *This* was a moment that made up for all the years of disappointment when the space programme had shut down after Step Day, and the strain of the flight itself, the weeks of the cruise with no company save a semi-psychotic father-and-daughter tag team, and finally the hair-raising descent to the ground in the Mars Excursion Module, an untried aircraft descending into a virtually unknown atmosphere. None of that mattered, for he'd lived through it all, and he was *here*. Frank whooped, and he did a little jig, and his boots kicked up Martian dirt. And he was *not* going to screw the pooch.

Sally's voice murmured in his earpiece. 'Hey, Tom Swift. Follow the checklist.'

Frank sighed. 'Copy that, Sally.'

He got to work.

First he turned to face the MEM.

The lander was a so-called 'biconic lifting body', a fat-bellied plane sitting on frail-looking skids, its heat-shield tiles and leading edges scorched from the atmospheric entry. Frank walked back to the ship and took a small TV camera from a fold-down platform, and after some fumbling fitted it to a mount on his chest. He took out the flag kit, a fold-out pole and the flag itself in a polythene bag.

Then he set off again, pushing mankind's exploration of this new Mars a few paces further. 'I'm walking away from the lander now. I'm going to work my way over into the sunlight.' Once he was out of the MEM's long shadow he turned around, letting his camera pan across the landscape.

'The picture's a little blurred, Frank. You're going too fast on your sweeps.'

Obediently Frank slowed his rotation. The Martian dust felt a little slippery under his boots. Out here he could see no signs of disturbance from the landing, no dust thrown up by the big wheels. The soil under his feet was virgin: the sands of Mars, by God.

Away to the west Frank saw a line, a soft shadow in the sand. It looked like a shallow ridge, facing away from him. Maybe the lip of a crater. Frank walked that way, further from the MEM.

'Don't get out of sight,' Sally warned.

Frank stopped at the lip of the crater. A few dozen yards across, the crater was a shallow, regular bowl, its rim sharp and fragile. In its base ice glinted, looking as if it was a crust over liquid water. And all around the pool were lumpy forms like footballs, smooth-skinned, tough-looking, and faintly green under a patina of rusty dust.

'They're like cacti,' Frank said excitedly. 'Are you seeing this, Sally? Just as we glimpsed in the lander photos – obviously hardy, desiccation-tolerant – but *no spikes.*' That strange feature struck him immediately. 'I guess there are no Martian critters likely to run up and chomp them for their moisture.'

'You're off the checklist again, Frank.'

'Is that all you can think of, even now?'

'It's your checklist. I'm just following it.'

'All right, dammit.'

It took him only a moment to set up the telescopic flag-pole, and to drive its sharpened tip into the compacted ground. Then he took the Stars and Stripes from its bag, folded it out, and fixed it to the pole. The flag was the enhanced holographic kind, symbolizing the US Aegis. This was a good enough site for the little ceremony, over-looking this Martian garden. Frank set his TV camera on the ground facing him, and made sure he was in the eyeline of the MEM. 'Can you hear me, Sally?'

'Get it over with.'

Frank straightened up and saluted. 'March 15, AD 2045. I, Francis Paul Wood, do hereby claim this land, and all the lands and stepwise footprints of this Mars, as legal territory of the United States of America, to be a dominion of the United States of America, subject to its government and laws—'

Suddenly there was a figure before him.

Frank staggered, shocked. A human, a spacesuited figure, with an outer garment coated in frost, had just appeared out of nowhere. And a stentorian voice sounded in Frank's headset, bawling out a song. Frank didn't recognize the lyrics, but he knew the tune. 'That's the Russian national anthem. What the—'

'Too late to make claim, Yankee! Need bigger flag than that!'

Frank stood straight. 'Who the hell are you?'

'You're late, Viktor,' Willis Linsay called.

The Russian saluted the MEM. 'Nice to see you too, Willis. You going to introduce this fellow here? Hey – what your name, Frank? You want I teach you chorus? Try in English. *Be glorious, our free Fatherland, age-old union of fraternal peoples* . . . Hey, Willis!' He patted a plastic box at his waist. 'Stepper box works on Mars, by the way.'

'I can see that.'

'*Ancestor-given wisdom of the people! Be glorious, our country! We are proud of you!* . . .'

17

The crew of the *Galileo*, with a little help from Viktor Ivanov, their unexpected welcome party – unexpected to Sally and Frank Wood anyhow – spent twenty-four hours closing down the MEM lander, and unpacking its cargo, which included the prefabricated components of two aircraft. Gliders they would be, and light, spindly affairs, as Sally could tell as soon as the parts were unpacked and laid out on fine sheets over the dusty ground. It was in these fragile craft that they would be exploring the Long Mars, she learned from her father. One was to be called *Woden*, the other *Thor*.

It took Sally a few hours to get used to the Martian conditions. In the thin air her pressure suit was doing its best to inflate like a balloon, but there were joints at the elbows and knees and ankles that made moving around relatively easy. It was going to get tougher yet on the stepwise Marses, where the air would be vastly thinner than this. In the lower gravity, one-third of Earth, she could lift massive objects, but once such loads were in motion they tended to keep moving, so she needed to take care. Walking was tricky, and running more so, with a tendency to lift off the ground with every step. Experimenting, she found in fact that running in a gentle jog was easier than walking. But to run properly she needed to keep her body low down so that her feet could push back at the Martian ground, maximizing traction.

Frank gently mocked her efforts. 'We'll have you in astronaut training yet.'

Sally just ignored him, head down, experimenting, concentrating. Being able to run away was a basic survival skill; therefore she intended to master running on Mars.

While Willis and Frank got busy assembling the gliders, Sally got to know their unexpected visitor. 'You liked surprise? You land on empty Mars. God bless America. Whoosh! Big fat Russian here first. Haw! Haw!'

Viktor invited Sally to come and visit his own base, meet his companions there. '*Marsograd*. Willis calls it Marsograd. Not its name, you not pronounce real name. Not far from here, couple hundred miles. On flank of Arsia Mons, one of the big Tharsis volcanoes. We monitor volcanoes, big job, try to understand . . . Come visit.'

Why the hell not? Let Willis and Frank play with their toy aeroplanes.

Viktor's vehicle, which he'd parked in a deep young crater out of sight of the MEM, was a big, tough-looking truck on fat tyres, with a cabin that was a bubble of scarred Perspex. To Sally, it was like some glorified tractor. Inside, the cabin smelled strongly of oil and greasy Russian males, and the air cycling system rattled alarmingly. But it was roomy and warm, and the bucket seats were comfortable enough as the truck rolled away.

Heading roughly north-east they bounced over a rock-strewn landscape, following tracks that the truck had presumably laid down itself. The sky, cloudless today, her second day on Mars, was blue except at the horizon, where it faded to a more Martian dusty red-brown. And there was life here, clearly visible: those things like cacti, round and hard, what looked like trees, gnarled and folded over with small, spiky leaves – even what looked like reeds, or maybe big grass blades, each with one indented side facing the sun. She imagined the blades tracking the sun as it wheeled across the sky during the Martian day.

'Like a story book,' she said.

'Hmm?'

'It's like the way they imagined Mars to be, oh, more than a century ago. Austere but Earth-like, with tough life forms. Like in old science fiction stories. Not the sun-blasted airless desert that we actually found, when the space probes got there.'

Viktor grunted. 'Most Marses like *our* Mars. You see. This the exception. Special circumstance.' He seemed proud of his vehicle. He patted the heavy steering wheel. 'Willis calls this *Marsokhod*. Not its name, you not pronounce. Runs on methane fuel from our wet-chemistry factories. You see.'

'I never even knew the Russians were exploring the Gap.'

He grinned. He was about forty; his face was leathery, crumpled, sweat-crusted after hours behind a facemask, and his black greasy hair was a tangle. 'GapSpace, cowboy outfit in England. Don't know about Russians. Not interested to look. Of course Russians are here. We have base on world on *other* side of Gap, on Baltic coast, high latitude. Called Star City. Like university campus and manufacturing plant and military base, all in one. Also Chinese here, though not so much. Mostly don't know about each other. How would we know? Big empty Earths. No spy satellites. What difference, if one here or all? Gap is door to big universe. Willis know.'

'He would.' Which was presumably how he had known about the true colour of the Martian sky, for instance. 'So the Russians were first here, on this Gap Mars?'

'Of course! Our flags, our anthems. But we help Willis. Why not? Humans together, few of us on big cold world. Now he will explore Long Mars. What he finds, he share.'

Maybe, she thought. 'Listen, Viktor. When we first arrived, you said something about a Stepper working. What Stepper?'

He grinned again. 'Daddy didn't tell you? In back.' He nodded his head at a pile of junk behind the seats.

She twisted and rummaged, bouncing uncomfortably as the truck rode low-gravity high over big boulders, until she found the plastic box that had been strapped to Viktor's side when he'd first shown up. It opened easily after she popped a couple of catches. Inside was a tangle of wiring and electronic components that she recognized as the circuitry of a Stepper, the artificial aid that enabled people to step – most people anyhow, even if they didn't have the natural ability shared by such as herself and Joshua. This was basically her father's invention. The only difference from a thousand such boxes she'd seen before, from tangles lashed up by teenagers to sleek bulletproof models issued to cops and military, was that there was no potato in here, the earthy, almost comical ingredient that powered the box. Instead there was a grey-green puffball. 'What's this?'

'Martian cactus. Native. My colleague Alexei Krilov gives fancy Latin names. Use here instead of potato. Of course we grow potatoes too. Can't make vodka with a cactus. You see.'

It took only a few hours to reach Marsograd.

For the last hour or so the land rose steadily; they were entering Tharsis, province of giant volcanoes, including Olympus Mons. But when Viktor pointed north-west all Sally could see of Arsia Mons, actually one of the lesser volcanoes, was rising land, a kind of bulging horizon. The Tharsis volcanoes, on this Mars as on the Mars of the Datum, were so big that you couldn't even see them from the ground.

The Russian base was centred on a cluster of yellow-ing plastic domes, evidently prefabricated. But huddled around these were structures that looked oddly like tepees, struts of what appeared to be the native 'wood' draped with leather of some kind. *Animal* skins? All these buildings were sealed up with ageing polythene sheets, and connected by piping to creaky-looking air circulation and scrubbing plants. Away from the central habitation, big solar cell arrays sprawled across the rocky ground.

Viktor rolled the tractor up to a plastic tube that turned out to be a crude kind of airlock, good enough on this peculiarly benign Mars. He led her through the tube and into a dome. Unzipping their surface suits as they walked, they came to what was evidently a galley, smelling strongly of coffee and alcohol, overlying an earthy stink of body odour and sewage. On a wall-mounted TV an ice hockey game was playing: Russia against Canada.

Viktor said mournfully, 'TV show. Recorded, stepped across two million worlds and transmitted to us from Gap station. Now no more ice hockey.'

'Because there's no more Russia after Yellowstone?'

'Exactly. We watch same games over and over. Sometimes drunk enough to forget result and bet on scores . . .'

Two more men came bustling in, evidently drawn by the sound of their voices. One was like Viktor, big, dark, maybe fifty; he wore a cosmonaut-type blue jumpsuit with a name tag lettered in Cyrillic and Latin: DJANIBEKOV, S. Viktor introduced him as Sergei. The other, slimmer, blond, maybe under forty – KRILOV, A. – was Alexei, and he wore a grubby white lab coat. These were three men without women, and they stared at her. But Sally met their gazes, Viktor's too, with a certain look of her own. She had been travelling alone in the Long Earth since she had been a teenager, and was a veteran of such encounters. These three seemed harmless enough.

Once that tricky moment was over, they were fine. Indeed, they fussed over her, like kids eager to please. Sergei's English was a lot worse than Viktor's, Alexei's a lot better. Of course even Sergei's English was a hell of a lot better than Sally's Russian, which was non-existent.

They showed her what they called their 'guest room', which was one of the tepee-like shacks. She explored the little space, curious. On the floor was a kind of rug made of thick brown-white wool. The tepee's covering skin felt like ordinary leather, crudely treated, but the Martian wood of the structural frame was so hard and fine-grained it might have been a plastic imitation: this was some adaptation to enhance moisture retention, she imagined.

She returned to the galley. Sergei, gallant but almost wordless, offered her a big baggy sweater evidently knitted of the same wool as the rug. Although it smelled strongly of whoever wore it regularly, she pulled it on;

the sweater was cosy in a base that never quite excluded the Martian chill. They fed her a late lunch, of cabbage and beets and even a couple of tiny, wizened apples, which she imagined were a treasure and a great honour to receive. They offered vodka, which she refused, and coffee, or some imitation of coffee, much-stewed, which she accepted.

Before the light faded Alexei insisted on showing her around the rest of the compound. 'I am the station biologist,' he said with some pride. 'Also the nearest we have to a medic, among other things. We must all play multiple roles, in a team as small as this . . .'

There were clear plastic tunnels connecting the domes, so you could get around the base without exposure to the Martian climate, but there were simple self-sealing airlocks that would close up in the event of a pressure breach. Because the whole base was linked up in this way she never escaped the lingering stink of body odour, but at least it was more diluted the further she got from the central quarters. Alexei insisted that Sally carry her oxygen mask loose around her neck at all times, in case of a wall breach. Sally had survived decades alone in the Long Earth; she needed no persuading about such precautions.

Some of the domes were industrial, where compact, crude-looking machinery cracked the Martian atmosphere and water to produce breathable air and fuels such as methane and hydrogen, or processed the rusty dirt to produce iron. Alexei said they were also working on 'Zubrin kits', which he said were adapted to generate methane and oxygen in the sparser conditions of more typical versions of Mars, like the Mars of Datum Earth. 'You must import hydrogen, to such impoverished Marses. But a ton of hydrogen processed with Martian air will give you sixteen tons of methane and oxygen – a good return, you see.'

They walked through the farm domes, which sheltered laboriously tilled fields of potatoes and yams and green beans. The work these Russians had put in was heartbreakingly clear from the quality of the soil they'd managed to create from Martian dirt. 'Such a challenge, the native dirt is just rusty grit coated with sulphates and perchlorates . . .' They'd even imported earthworms. But a spindly, yellowed crop was their only reward so far.

Beyond the domes, open to the Martian elements, was a small botanical garden Alexei had established, and he proudly showed Sally his collection of native stock. The cacti were shrivelled and tough-looking, and the trees he'd planted, from seeds collected from adult specimens on the slopes of Arsia Mons, were hardly grown.

He took particular pride in showing her a clump of plants a few feet tall, a kind of ice-cream swirl of yellowish leaves on a base of green leaves. 'What do you make of this?'

She shrugged. 'Ugly. But that green looks more Earthlike than Martian.'

'So it is. It's a *Rheum nobile,* a noble rhubarb – or rather a genetically tweaked version. Grows in the Himalayas. Those yellow leaves wrap around a seed-bearing stem within. It's adapted for altitude, you see, for thin air. The yellow column is a kind of natural greenhouse.'

'Wow. And here it is growing on Mars.'

He shrugged. 'One of a suite of plants from Earth that could almost make it on Mars, on this Mars anyhow. And you can eat the stems, yum yum.'

His final surprise, kept in a dome to themselves, was a small herd of alpacas: awkward-looking beasts, imported as embryos from the mountains of South America, scraping at the scrubby grass that grew at their feet. They peered out at the humans, their woolly faces curious and oddly endearing.

'Ah,' Sally said. 'So that's where you get the wool. And the leather for the tepees.'

'Indeed. We hope that the descendants of these creatures may some day become adapted to survival in raw

Martian conditions, on this Mars at least. Of course we may have to genetically engineer Earth-based grasses for them to feed on.

'And if alpacas, why not human beings? Today, this particular Mars is like Earth at an altitude of six miles or so. The highest town on Datum Earth is in Peru, at about three miles. Humans cannot live much higher than that, permanently – or rather *we* cannot. Our children may be different. *This* Mars is almost within reach, for us, for the alpacas—'

'For the rhubarb.'

'Exactly. This was our mission, from the Moscow government. We Russians have always looked to the stars, and the discovery of this near-habitable version of Mars excited our scientists and philosophers greatly. We three were the vanguard; we were sent here to establish how humans might live on this world, as well as to study the life forms already extant here.'

'The vanguard. More should have followed?'

'Marsograd should have been a city by now – such was the plan. But your American supervolcano put a stop to that, as to all Russian ambitions. Still, we are here, and we learn much . . .'

Working pretty much single-handed, Alexei Krilov had been able to establish a great deal about the strange life forms of this relatively clement Mars.

'I have gathered samples from diverse environments, from the deep wet valleys to the flanks of the great volcanoes where life probes at the fringes of space. The cacti have tough, leathery skin which almost perfectly seals in their water stores. The trees have trunks as hard as concrete, and leaves like needles to keep in the moisture. Do not imagine these forms of life are primitive, by the way. They survive in extremely austere environments; they are highly evolved, highly specialized, superbly efficient in their use of mass and energy.

'Both cacti and trees photosynthesize busily – that is, they use the energy of sunlight to grow. And the photosynthesis, by the way, is a form known from Earth; as seems obvious, life on this Mars has been seeded from Earth.'

Sally frowned. 'I don't understand. This is the Gap. There *is* no Earth here.'

'Ah, but there are Earths close by . . .'

When it was young, he said, Mars – every version of Mars – was most likely warm and wet, with a thick blanket of air, and deep oceans. It had been like Earth in many ways – indeed, more generous in those days, and the biologists believed that even complex life, plants, something like animals, might well have got kick-started here on this generous young world within the first billion years or so. It had taken billions more years on Earth.

But Mars was smaller than the Earth and further from the sun, and those facts doomed it. As the geology seized up and the volcanoes died back, and the sunlight got to work breaking up the upper atmosphere, Mars lost a lot of its air. Its water froze out at the poles, or receded to buried permafrost or deep underground aquifers.

'That is how it was on the Mars of Datum Earth, and on most other versions of the planet. But here, you see, *this* Mars has evidently had a regular injection of living things from the neighbouring stepwise Earths.

'Think about it. In our home reality, it was believed that life could be transferred between Earth and Mars, or vice versa, by the great splashes of meteorite impacts. This was called panspermia: the natural propagation of life from one world to the next. But in the Gap, well, there's no originating Earth, but for the last few million years at least there have been stepping sapients. And every time a hapless humanoid falls from a stepwise Earth into the Gap, *it* may be destroyed by the vacuum, but some of the freight of microorganisms it carries will survive, delivered into space with so much less effort than a lethal rock splash. And some of those microbial travellers will survive to seed Mars – not just once, but again and again.'

'I see. I think. Ticks from unlucky trolls, colonizing Mars!'

'More likely stomach bacteria, but yes. If life gets the chance it will proliferate where the water is, in the surface ice, the permafrost, the aquifers. In time great feedback loops would be established – just as on Earth, in fact – living things mediating cycles of mass and energy, and in particular water. This Mars has very similar, if not identical, geology and physics to the Mars of the Datum. It is *life* that has made it as clement as it is, by mobilizing the water and other volatiles. Earth life helped restore the climate – and made it possible for Mars life, the older natives, to flourish. But all this is unusual, you see. Only happened because of the Gap. In the language of the Long Earth, this Mars is a Joker, an exception among Marses.'

'But wonderful nonetheless,' Sally said.

'Oh, yes. But not our discovery, unfortunately. The Chinese discovered a second Gap in the East, five years ago, and observed the same kind of life-spreading mechanism in that solar system. The Chinese! Typical. But even without panspermia, on *all* the Marses, we think, traces of that original native suite of complex life might survive, as spores, seeds, cysts . . . Who knows?

Waiting to be woken up, like Sleeping Beauty, with a kiss of warmth and water.'

'Is that possible?'

He winked. 'Ask your father about life on Mars.'

As the Martian night closed in, the crew of Marsograd, with Sally, withdrew to the galley, the cosiest location. Here they ate another meal, the centrepiece of which was thick steaks of prized alpaca meat, with boiled greenhouse-rhubarb for a sweet, and they drank more coffee, and more vodka, most of which Sally resisted.

Sally felt curiously drawn to these three odd fellows in their shabby hovels. They seemed to have a clear sense of mission. Maybe it was just that she had become so disillusioned with mankind, from the examples she encountered too often. The Long Earth was, in a way, too easy a place to get to; it was only *after* some bunch of idiots had already built their spanking new town slap in the middle of the flood plain of a stepwise Mississippi, and the waters had started to rise, or whatever, that they generally came to Sally's attention. Whereas these Russians had come to a place that was supremely *hard* to survive in, even to get to, and were now showing supreme intelligence, in their slob-like way, in learning about their environment and how to live in it.

But their tragedy was of course that the country that had given them this mission had all but collapsed.

Alexei Krilov's main beef about that seemed to be that the academies to which he would have reported his science results were moribund, if not defunct. 'Nobody to read my papers. No universities to give me tenured posts and science prizes. Poor Alexei.'

Viktor, already drunk, snorted dismissal. 'Academies? On Datum, whole of Russia abandoned now. Gone. Moscow under ice. Polar bears in Red Square. And parties of Chinese working their way in from Vladivostok.'

Sergei had spoken little. 'Chinese bastards,' he growled now.

'Ha! We are last Russian citizens, like cosmonaut in Mir station when Union collapsed, last Soviet citizen.'

'It's not as bad as that,' Sally said. 'Sure, Datum Russia is pretty much uninhabitable now. But most of the population escaped to the Low Earth footprints. The Long Russia survives.'

Viktor grunted. 'Sure. Where struggle to build country begins all over again. Just like after Mongols smashed Kiev. And Napoleon smashed Moscow. And Hitler smashed Stalingrad.' He wagged his half-empty glass at Sally. 'We Russians have saying: "First five hundred years are worst." Cheers.' He drained his glass, refilled it from the flask.

'Chinese bastards!' Sergei shouted now.

Viktor patted Sergei's arm. 'There, there, big fellow. Pah! Let Chinese have frozen ruins of Datum. To us, Long Earth, Long Mars – and the stars!'

They drank a toast to that. Then to the Nobel Prize that Alexei was never going to win. Then to the soul of the alpaca whose life had been sacrificed to provide the steaks they had enjoyed.

And then they tried to teach Sally the words of the Russian national anthem, in English and Russian. She crept out to go to bed at the point they'd got on to the third verse: 'Our strength is derived through our loyalty to the Fatherland. Thus it was, thus it is and thus it always will be! . . .'

18

It was a year after that first meeting in Happy
Landings that Joshua next came across Paul Spencer
Wagoner – this time, in Madison West 5.

'Hello, Mr Valienté!'

Joshua was standing with Sister Georgina, in the
small graveyard outside the Home that his old friend
had run at that point. After the Madison bombing the
Home had been painstakingly reestablished here in
West 5, and the new graveyard held just two stones.
The most recent was for Sister Serendipity, a lover of
cooking whose enthusiasms had always lit up Joshua's
young life – and who, according to Home legend,
had been on the run from the FBI. It had been
Serendipity's funeral that had brought him here, in
fact.

And now Paul's bright voice, older but unmistakable, called to him from across the street.

With Sister Georgina, Joshua crossed the road. It took a while; Georgina was another veteran of Joshua's childhood days, and was almost as old as Serendipity had been.

Paul Spencer Wagoner, now six years old, was standing there with his father. They both looked uncomfortable, Joshua thought, in new-looking Datum-manufacture clothes. But Paul had a black eye and a swollen cheek, and his dark hair looked odd to Joshua, as if roughly cut. Joshua's own little boy, Daniel Rodney, was just a couple of months old, and the Sisters had been cooing over the images Joshua had brought home for them. And there was enough of a father's soul in Joshua now to make him wince at the trouble Paul, still a very young boy, was evidently having.

They quickly introduced each other. Sister Georgina shook hands with Paul and his father, who looked out of place, almost embarrassed.

Paul grinned up at Joshua. 'Good to see you again, Mr Valienté.'

'I suppose you *deduced* I'd be here.'

Paul laughed. 'Of course. Everybody knows your story, about where you grew up. I thought I'd come visit now we live here too, in Madison.'

'Really?' Joshua glanced at the father. 'I thought Happy Landings is a place people generally end up in, rather than leave.'

Tom Wagoner shrugged. 'Well, it got a little uncomfortable for me, Mr Valienté—'

'Joshua.'

'My wife was the Happy Lander. Born there, I mean. Not me. She's one of the Spencers. There are these big sprawling families in Happy Landings, the Spencers, the Montecutes. But she came to college on the Datum, in Minnesota, where I grew up. We fell in love, married, wanted kids, moved back to Happy Landings to be closer to her family . . .'

Sister Georgina prompted, 'So what happened?'

'Well, Happy Landings isn't what it was, Sister. Not as *happy* a landing place, you might say. I think it's been building up since Step Day. Before then it was a kind of refuge, a place where people who had kind of got lost would drift in, and stick. There were the trolls, too, which was always kind of weird to me, but you got used to them hanging around. But these last few years, with everybody stepping all over the place, people kept stumbling upon Happy Landings, and there were just too many strangers. The numbers were getting too high as well, and the trolls don't like too many people. And newcomers – people like me – just didn't fit any more.'

'So you left.'

'It was more me than Carla. She was with her family there, after all. It put us under a lot of pressure, to tell the truth. We came here, got jobs – I'm an accountant, and this is the place for jobs just now, Madison West 5 is growing fast since the nuke – but our marriage is going down a rocky road.' He patted Paul's head. 'Oh, it's OK. He knows all about it. Knows too damn much to be comfortable sometimes.' He forced a laugh.

Now Sister Georgina touched Paul's cheek, his eye. The boy flinched. 'These injuries are recent,' she said. 'So what happened to you?'

'School,' Paul said simply.

Tom said, 'Well, the butchered haircut was given him by a neighbourhood boy. The cheek was the other kids at school. The eye was one of the *teachers*.'

'You're kidding,' Joshua said.

'Afraid not. Guy got sacked. Didn't help Paul. I keep telling him, nobody likes a smartass.'

'It's frustrating at school, Mr Valienté,' Paul said, apparently more puzzled than distressed. 'The teachers always make me wait for the other kids.'

Tom smiled wistfully. 'His headmaster says he's like a young Einstein, ready to take on relativity. But his teachers can't teach him beyond long division. Not their fault.'

'Mostly I sit and read. But I can't keep quiet when I see people making mistakes. The other kids in class, or the teacher. I know I should keep quiet.'

'Hmm,' Sister Georgina said. 'And these bruises are your reward.'

'It's like people care more about their pride than about what's correct, about the truth. What kind of sense does that make?'

'We've had worse than bruises actually,' Tom said now. 'Some of the parents have asked for Paul to be removed from the school. Not just because he's disruptive, though he is, if I'm honest. Because they're – well, they're scared of him.'

Sister Georgina cast a concerned look at Paul.

Tom said, 'Look, don't worry, we can speak frankly. He understands all this better than I do.'

'I have been reading about people,' Paul said in a matter-of-fact way. 'Psychology.' He pronounced it *puh-sike-ology*. 'I don't know a lot of the words, and that slows me down. But I get some of it. People are scared of strange stuff. They think I'm not like them. Well, I'm not. But I'm not *that* different. One woman said I was like a cuckoo in the nest. And there was the man who said I was like a changeling, left by the elves. Not a human at all.' He laughed. 'One kid said I was E.T. Not from this world.'

Sister Georgina frowned. 'Well, look – this is a time when people are scared anyhow. The coming of stepping was a big change for all of us. And now we've had the nuclear attack and everybody's been affected by that. At times like this people want scapegoats, somebody they can comfortably hate. Anybody different will do. That was why people blew up Madison.'

Joshua nodded. 'When I was a kid I always tried to keep my own step ability hidden. I felt the same, I knew how people would react if they knew, if they thought I was *different*. Sister Georgina here can tell you about that; she was there. And that was on the Datum. Out in the Long Earth, I've seen it for myself, you have a lot of small, isolated communities. People are growing up superstitious, more than in the big Datum cities—'

To Joshua's surprise, Paul's response was angry, almost a snarl. 'At least in Happy Landings there were other kids like me. Smart, I mean. Not here. Here they're all dumb. Well, I'd rather take a few punches from the kids at school than be like *them*.'

Tom took his son's hand. 'Come on, we did what we came for, you said hello to Mr Valienté, now we need to let these good people get on with their day . . .'

Joshua said Paul could come and see him any time he could find him, wherever he 'deduced' where Joshua was. And Sister Georgina offered Tom any support the Home could give him, and his unhappy family.

When they'd gone, Joshua and Sister Georgina exchanged a look. The Sister said, 'This place Happy Landings has always sounded odd to me, from your descriptions. Whatever's going on there, I hope our modern generation of witch-hunters don't find it any time soon . . .'

19

The two gliders, *Woden* and *Thor*, sat side by side on the red dust of Mars.

The gliders were spindly constructions, supremely lightweight. Their wings were long – fifty or sixty feet, each wing longer than the entire fuselage – wings surprisingly narrow and sharply curved, which was something to do, Sally learned, with managing the flow of the very sparse Martian air. But the slender hulls of the gliders had been intelligently designed, Sally discovered as they got the ships loaded up, with a lot of room for food and water, surface exploration gear, inflatable domes for temporary shelter, spares and tools to maintain the gliders themselves – and some items that surprised her, such as emergency pressure bubbles, each big enough for one human, and little drone aircraft to act as eyes in the sky.

And, poking around the hulls, Sally discovered that each ship carried a whole stack of Stepper boxes, ready to be fitted out with Martian cacti.

Willis was proud of the design, and bragged about it at length. 'You can guess the design principle. These gliders will be our equivalent of twains back on the Long Earth. We'll ride in the sky as we step, safely above any discontinuities on the ground – ice, flood, quakes, lava flows, whatever. Airships would be no use in this thin air – they'd have to be too big to be practical, and we don't have the lift gas anyhow. But the gliders are based on designs that have successfully flown at ninety thousand feet on the Datum, which is about the air pressure on the local Mars – higher on *this* Mars, of course . . . The gliders will only step the way twains step – a controlling sapient does the stepping, that is the pilot, metaphorically carrying each ship stepwise. We probably won't travel too far laterally. We'll do a lot of circling. That way, if we crash, there's at least a chance that we could step on foot back to the MEM. Another failsafe option. Right, Frank?'

Before they launched, Sally said she had two questions. 'Two ships, right?'

'Well,' Frank said, 'we could carry three persons in one ship at a pinch. We're taking two ships for backup.'

Sally thought almost fondly of Lobsang. 'You can never have too much backup.'

'Right,' said Frank.

'Two gliders, then. We need two pilots, from the three of us.' She looked at them. 'So, question one: who's driving?'

Frank and Willis both put their hands up.

Sally shook her head. 'I won't waste my time arguing with two old-guy control freaks like you.'

'You'll get your turn,' Willis said. 'We'll need to rotate.'

'Sure. I'm happy to ride shotgun. Do I get to choose who I ride with?' And before they could answer she snapped, 'You got the short straw, Frank.'

'That's all I need. A back-seat driver.'

'Don't push your luck, Chuck Yeager . . . And, Dad, here's my other question – why all the Stepper boxes?'

'Trade goods,' he said simply. He wouldn't expand further.

She glowered at him, but said no more. This kind of secretiveness was typical – the way he'd known all about the Long Mars before they'd even come here, the way he'd been working with the Russians on Mars who he hadn't mentioned until they landed, the secrets of Mars itself – 'Ask your father about life on Mars' – and now these Steppers, carried for a contingency he clearly foresaw but wouldn't discuss. He'd been this way since she was a teenager; it was a way of keeping control, and it had always made her coldly furious.

But she'd known all about his personality when she signed up for this jaunt. The time to challenge him would come, but not yet, not yet.

Frank was focusing on the flight. He said sternly, 'We're going to take this in stages. We're going to suit up fully, in case of cabin leaks, and we're going to make our very first step *on the ground*. Then, if all goes well, we'll launch and step further in the air.'

Willis scowled. 'OK, Frank, if you insist. Safety first.'

'That's the way to stay alive. Let's get on with it.'

On their last night, the Russians insisted on taking them all over to Marsograd, served them coffee and vodka and black bread with some kind of algal paste, and made them watch a movie, called *White Sun in the Desert*. Viktor explained, 'Old cosmonaut tradition. Movie watched by Yuri Gagarin before historic first flight in space. All Russians remember Gagarin.'

Frank fell asleep during the movie. Sally just sat through it, trying to avoid conversation with her father.

In the small hours, in the dark, they were driven back to the gliders in the Russian rover. They arrived a little before dawn. The MEM was a silent hulk in the dark, sending reassuring status messages to Frank's tablet, waiting to take them home.

They clambered out of the rover, and the Russians rolled away.

In their already familiar pressure suits the three of them crossed to their aircraft, and boarded. Soon Sally found herself sitting in a cramped bucket seat, looking at the back of the helmeted head of Frank Wood, in the pilot's bucket seat in front of her.

Even before this first limited trial Frank insisted on running a few more 'integrity checks' before going any further.

Then he called back, 'OK, let's do this. The ground test first. *Thor*, this is *Woden*. You hear me over there, Willis?'

'Loud and clear.'

'Sally, I have my Stepper box; I'll do the stepping. For now I'll carry you and the ship. OK?'

'Copacetic, Captain Lightyear,' Sally said.

'Yeah, yeah. Just take this seriously; it might keep you alive a little longer. Willis, on my zero. Three—'

Before he'd got to 'two' Willis's ship had winked out of existence.

Frank sighed. 'I knew he'd do that. Here we go—'

Stepping on Mars, Sally discovered, felt just like stepping on Earth. But the landscape beyond the hull of the glider changed dramatically, a more significant difference than most single steps on the Long Earth, unless you fell into a Joker.

Around the two gliders, still sitting side by side on the ground, the basic shape of the landscape endured, the eroded remains of the Mangala valley, the rise to the north-east that was the beginning of the great bulge of Arsia Mons. But aside from that there was only a plain of dust littered with wind-sculpted chunks of rock, under a sky the colour of butterscotch. No life here.

The MEM, of course, and the tyre tracks left by the *Marsokhod*, had disappeared.

Frank theatrically tapped one of the display screens before him. 'Air's all gone. Pressure down to one per cent of Earth's, and – yep, it's mostly carbon dioxide. Just like our Mars.'

They clambered out cautiously. In the thin air Sally found her pressure suit inflated, subtly, making it stiffer to move around in. Frank and Sally checked each other's suit, checked the glider cab. They took care over this, at Frank's insistence; a failure of their gear over in the Gap Mars would have been survivable – here, probably not. The average Mars was lethal. Unprotected, Sally would be killed by the lack of air, the cold, the ultraviolet. Even the cosmic rays sleeting through the thin atmosphere inflicted a radiation dose equivalent to standing five miles from a nuclear blast, *every six months.*

Frank looked east, to the rising sun, holding up his hand to shield his faceplate from the glare, until he found a morning star. Earth, Sally realized, a feature missing from the sky of the Mars of the Gap. Frank opened a hull hatch and pulled out a small optical telescope and a fold-out radio antenna.

Willis came walking over from his own glider. 'At last, *this* is an authentic Mars. Just like our own. The way Mars is supposed to be.'

Sally said, 'I thought the Gap Mars was barren. I didn't realize how much life there was, visible even in a casual glance. Not until now, when it's all been taken away.'

'You'd better get used to it.'

Frank was peering through his telescope, listening in to his radio gear. 'You were right, Willis.'

'I usually am. What about specifically?'

Frank pointed at the sky. 'That's Earth. We came East, right? The GapSpace facility is one step East of the Gap. But there's no radio signals coming from *that* Earth up there. No lights on the dark side. If *that* was the GapSpace Earth we'd see evidence of it, hear it.'

Sally tried to get her head around that. 'So we took a step into Long Mars. But it doesn't – umm, run parallel to the Long Earth.'

'It seems not,' Willis said, peering up into the sky. 'The Long Earth chain of stepwise alternates, and the Long Mars chain, are independent of each other. Intersecting only at the Gap. That's no surprise. They're both loops in some higher-dimensional continuum.'

Sally felt neither wonder nor fear. She'd grown up with the strangeness of the Long Earth; a little more exotica now hardly made any difference.

Frank, as ever, stuck to the practical. 'What that does mean is that our only way home is back this way – I mean, back to the Gap universe, and the MEM, and *Galileo*, and a ride across space.'

'Noted,' said Willis. 'OK. Anybody need the bathroom again? Then let's get these birds in the air.'

To launch, each glider was fitted with small methane-burning rockets. The craft would scoot along the ground and fling itself into the air, gliding when the rockets were shut down. The gliders carried plenty of methane and oxygen propellant, and were equipped with versions of the Russians' Zubrin factories, small processing plants, to manufacture more if they needed it.

They took their time to pace out a launch runway across the dusty plain, kicking aside any rocks big enough to cause a problem. Then they lined up the ships. From the air they would look like Lilliputians, Sally thought, toiling to move these fragile toy aeroplanes.

At last they were ready.

Willis went up first, in *Thor* this time. That was yet another precaution by Frank; he kept two warm bodies on the ground ready to help in case the first flight attempt ended in a crash. Willis put his glider through banks and turns and rolls, testing out responses in a way that would have been impossible in the thicker air of Gap Mars.

When they'd got through that programme and Willis reported he was happy, Frank and Sally climbed aboard *Woden* and took off in their turn. The methane rockets were noisy and gave a firm shove in the back.

But soon they were gliding, high over Mars.

They flew in silence broken only for Sally by her own breathing, and the whirr of the miniature pumps in the pressure suit pack she'd stowed behind her couch. There wasn't a whisper from the Martian air that must be flowing over the glider's long narrow wings. The cabin was a glass blister that gave a good all-round view, and Sally found herself sandwiched between a cloudless yellow-brown sky and a landscape below of much the same hue. Lacking any contrasting colour to the universal buttery brown, from above the landscape looked like a model, a topographic representation of itself chiselled out of soft clay.

From up here she could make out the distinctive form of Mangala Vallis, as she'd studied it in maps en route to Mars, a complex network of valleys and gullies flowing out of the higher, more heavily cratered ground to the south. It very obviously looked as if a great river had once run here, leaving behind bars and levees and islands, carved out and streamlined by the flow. But the water was just as obviously long gone, and the landscape was clearly very old. The valley features cut across the most ancient craters, huge worn ramparts that would have graced the moon – but the islands and levees were themselves stippled with younger craters, small and round and perfect. Unlike Earth, Mars was geologically static, all but unchanging, and had no mechanisms to rid itself of such scars.

The horizon of Mars, blurred a little by the dust suspended in the air, seemed close and curved sharply. And to the north-east she saw the land rising up, and imagined she saw the mighty flank of Arsia Mons looming into her view. Mars was a small world but with outsized features: volcanoes that stuck up out of the air, a valley system that sprawled around half the equator.

Nowhere in this landscape did she see a glimpse of life, not a speck of green, and not a drop of water.

'When do we start stepping?'

'We already have,' Frank said. 'Look down.'

Although the gross features of the landscape below the banking gliders endured – the horizon, the mighty carcass of Arsia, the outflow channels – now she saw that details were changing with every heartbeat: a different pattern of newer craters on the older landscape to the south, subtleties in the finer twists and turns of Mangala's complex of channels to the north. Then there was a blink, she was in a crimson-tinged darkness, and the glider was buffeted as if it had driven into turbulent air. Just as suddenly the darkness cleared, and the gliders flew on.

'Dust storm,' called Willis.

'Yeah. Not very comfortable,' Frank replied. 'But we've got no vents to clog, no engines to choke. These storms can last months.'

'But we don't need to stick around to see it,' Willis said.

They snapped into the buttery sunlight of the next world, and the next. The Marses slid past below, one every second.

As they flew on, things became relaxed enough that Sally was able to loosen her faceplate and open her suit.

The stepping was no faster than the old *Mark Twain*, the prototype stepper airship she rode across the Long Earth with Lobsang and Joshua Valienté fifteen years ago, no faster than a modern commercial cargo-carrier, and a lot slower than the fastest experimental craft, or even the best military ships. But it was fast enough, she thought, for this journey into the utterly unknown.

Except that it seemed like a journey into the utterly identical. There were simple step counters in the cabin, and she watched the digits pile up as time passed: sixty worlds a minute, over three thousand an hour. At that rate, on the Long Earth, they would have crossed over sheaves of Ice Age worlds, fully glaciated planets, within the first hour or more; after ten hours or so they would be crossing into the so-called Mine Belt, a band of worlds with quite different climates, arid, austere . . . Even on smaller scales the Long Earth was full of detail, of divergence. Here there was nothing, nothing but Mars and more Mars, with only the most minor tinkering with detail at the margins. And not a sign of life anywhere: dead world after dead world.

She did, however, notice an odd sensation at times, a sense of *twisting*, of being drawn away . . . She knew that feeling from her jaunts on the Long Earth: it was a sense that a soft place was near by, a short cut across the great span of this chain of worlds. She supposed that to someone like Frank that would seem unimaginably exotic. To Sally, these subtle detections gave a glow of familiarity.

The gliders flew on, banking like great birds in the empty skies. They had set off not long after dawn. As the Martian afternoon wore on, Sally decided to try to sleep, asking Frank to wake her when they got to Barsoom.

20

As it happened, Sally slept only a couple of hours before she was woken, not by Frank, but by another sudden lurch of the glider. She sat up with a start, reaching for her faceplate.

The cabin seemed dark, and she wondered if they had fallen into another storm. Then she realized that it was merely that the sun was low, setting in the west, and the colour was draining from the sky – but that colour, in this particular world, was a kind of bruised-purple, not the usual dusty brown.

Frank and Willis were talking quietly over the comms. Frank said, 'Flying into this world with its thicker air was like slamming into a wall. Worse than the dust storm. We didn't anticipate that.'

'Yeah, but the gliders are coping.'

'Possibly we could rig some kind of cut-out, so we don't step further. Or maybe go up to higher altitude, where the air will never get catastrophically thick . . .'

As they talked Sally surveyed her surroundings. They were banking over a plain of dust and broken rock, not far north of the mouth of the enduring Mangala feature. In nearly twelve hours of travelling they had crossed more than forty thousand worlds, Sally saw, glancing over Frank's shoulders at the instruments. And now this, something new and different. The air here was thicker, and oxygenated, and contained water vapour. It wasn't as generous an atmosphere as Gap Mars, but more so than any other they'd passed through since, it seemed.

And on the ground below there was movement.

At first Sally, peering down, saw what looked like ripples in the dust, but ripples that slid and evolved as she watched. The low sun cast long shadows which made this diorama easy to follow.

Then a kind of body emerged from the dust.

She saw a gaping mouth, then a tubular carcass, coated with chitinous plates that glistened in the low sunlight. It was almost like watching a whale surface from the sea. Then that great mouth opened wide, scooping in the sand. Now Sally saw more such shapes emerge from the ground, none of them as large as the first: young, perhaps, immature versions. They glided through the dust, propelled by flippers; Sally counted a dozen pairs of limbs on the big leader.

'Life on Mars,' she breathed. 'Animal life.'

'Yeah,' Willis called. 'Like whales in a sea of dust, filter-feeding. And there's no Gap *here*. This may have some common root with the life of the local Earth. But it's a very remote relation indeed.'

'It's hard to get a sense of scale.'

Frank said, 'That big mother is the size of a nuclear submarine. And maybe it, she, *is* a mother . . . What a vision!'

Willis grunted. 'It's logic. An ecology shaped by its environment. Here, the dust must be fine enough to act as a fluid, to support something like a marine biota—'

'Oh, keep the lectures. *Look* down there! It's like a homage to old science fiction dreams. There was a book I grew up with, published twenty years before I was even born – I learned more about ecology from that novel than I ever did in class – and if you could ever argue that science fiction has no predictive value—'

Sally said gently, 'Turn it down, fan boy.'

'Sorry.'

Willis said now, 'Shall we go back to something resembling rationality? Why are we seeing these – whales – in this particular world? Because it's warmer and wetter here – not by much, but some. The local air contains a lot of volcanic products. Sulphur dioxide—'

Frank asked, 'Volcano summer?'

'I guess so.'

'Just as you predicted, then, Willis.'

'We need to confirm it. I'd like to deploy a probe here. A slow drone will do; we have some designed to be carried by balloons. If it was a supervolcano, a Yellowstone, the most likely location is Arabia, a very ancient terrain on the far side of the planet. Maybe that's where we'll find the caldera.'

Sally frowned. 'I'm not following you. What have volcanoes got to do with anything?'

Her father said, 'I think this world is a Joker. Look, Sally, life – extant, complex, active life anyhow – is going to be rare in the Long Mars. In the Long Earth, the worlds are mostly living, but the Jokers, the exceptions that have suffered from some calamity, are often free of life. Right? Here it's the other way around. The Long Mars is mostly dead. It's *only* the Jokers, rare islands of warmth, that can host life . . . When it was young, Mars was warm and wet, with a thick blanket of air, and deep oceans. Like Earth, in many ways. And life got started.'

'But Mars froze out. Alexei told me about this.'

'But life persists, Sally, life huddles underground, clinging on as spores, or as bacteria munching hydrogen or sulphides or dissolved organics in long-buried salty aquifers – even as encysted hibernators. Resistant to heat and cold, to radiation, to aridity, to a lack of oxygen, to extreme ultraviolet . . .

'And sometimes life has the chance to do more. Imagine for instance an icy asteroid captured in Martian orbit, gradually breaking up, raining its mass on to the planet, seeding it with water and other volatiles . . .'

He sketched other ways for a Mars to come alive, if briefly. A massive asteroid or comet impact could leave behind a crater so hot that it might stay warm enough for centuries, even millennia, warm enough to host a liquid-water crater lake. Or there might be 'axial excursions', as Willis put it, times when the planet's rotation axis tipped or bobbed, bringing sunlight to the polar regions, and shaking up the world with earthquakes and volcanism. Again, there was more of that on Mars than on the Earth, because Mars had no massive, spin-stabilizing moon. Indeed, it seemed from their observations so far that most Marses had no moons at all; the twin moons of the Mars of Datum Earth, Phobos and Deimos, evidently captured asteroids, were unusual – the Datum Earth Mars, it turned out, was itself a Joker.

'And on *this* world,' he said, 'this Joker, we're coming to the end of a volcano summer. Mars is still warm inside. Every so often the big Tharsis volcanoes blow their tops. On Earth, volcanoes are disasters. Here they belch out a whole replacement atmosphere, of carbon dioxide and methane and other products, and a blanket of dust and ash that warms the world up enough for the water to come gushing back out of the permafrost.

'On this Mars a recent eruption has warmed the air, for a hundred or a thousand or ten thousand years. Seeds, dormant perhaps for megayears, sprout hungrily, and the Martian equivalent of blue-green algae get to work enriching the volcanic soup with oxygen. Those little bugs have evolved to survive, and to be *efficient* when they get their chance. It must be an incredible sight, Mars turning green in just a few thousand years, like a natural terraforming. And life forms like the whales down there have their moment in the sun. But then, sooner or later, quickly or slowly, the heat leaks away, and the air starts to thin. The end, when it comes, is probably rapid.'

Sally nodded. 'And then it's back to the dustbowl.'

'Yes. The Datum scientists believed they had mapped five such episodes, five summers lost in deep time, on *our* copy of Mars. The first was about a billion years after the planet formed, the last one a hundred million years back . . .'

'And similarly,' she said, 'if we travel across the Long Mars, we're going to find rare islands of life – as rare in stepwise space as those episodes on a single Mars are rare in time.'

'Something like that. That's my theory, anyhow. And it seems to be borne out so far.'

'Look at that,' murmured Frank, looking down. 'One of those babies got separated from the pack.'

Sally looked down to see. The infant whale, if it was an infant, had indeed become detached from the pack that surrounded the big mother.

And a new type of creature emerged, as if out of nowhere, to attack the lost little one. Sally glimpsed huge forms, with flexible armour plates but much more compact than the whales, like big hungry crustaceans with eyeballs on stalks. They all scooted across the surface of the dust, or just under it.

When they caught the infant whale, they fell on it. The whale thrashed and struggled, throwing up great sprays of dirt.

Willis called, 'Are we recording this, Frank?'

'You got it,' Frank said. 'Each of those crustacean predators is the size of a truck. And notice how they move: low down on the surface, or even under it. I bet that's a low-gravity adaptation; they're clinging to the ground for traction, for speed. You want we should go down, take some samples? My vote is no, by the way; it looks kind of hazardous down there and our gliders are somewhat fragile.'

'We go on,' Willis said. 'After all, it's not life I'm after but sapience, and I don't see much sign of that down below. Another hour? Then we'll pick some safely dead world to camp for the night. On my zero: three, two—'

Sally caught one last glimpse of the scene on the torn-up ground below. What looked like blood seeped from a dozen wounds in the baby whale's hide, as the crustaceans ripped and tore: blood that was purple in the low light.

And then the scene was whisked away, to be replaced by lifelessness, a plain of scattered rocks that might not have moved for a million years, casting long meaningless shadows as the sun set on another eventless day, on another dormant Mars.

21

Professor Wotan Ulm, now of the University of Oxford East 5, author of the bestselling if controversial book *An Untuned Golden String: The Higher-Dimensional Topology of the Long Earth*, appeared on a news channel run by the Britain West 7 Broadcasting Corporation, responding to questions on the nature of 'soft places', as those mysterious short cuts, widely rumoured to be more than mere stepper legends, were increasingly becoming known.

'I do see that going through a soft place would be like wearing seven-league boots, Wotan – may I call you Wotan?'

'No, you may not.'

'But it would help if I understood *how* you can make these seven-league-boot jumps.'

'Actually a better metaphor for a soft place is a wormhole. A fixed passageway between two points. As in the movie *Contact*. You remember that?'

'Is that the porno where—'

'No. *Stargate*, then. What about that? Oh, for some modern cultural references. Never mind! There is in fact some relevant theory. Young man, have you ever heard of a Mellanier Sequence diagram?'

'No.'

'It'll never be properly drawn until they invent n-dimensional printing, but basically it portrays the Long Earth as a tangled ball of string. Or, if you can stomach it, as a vast intestine. Datum Earth is a dot somewhere in the region of the appendix. Mathematically this tangle may – and I emphasize the "may" – be represented by a solenoid, a particular mathematical structure like a self-crossing string, a mixture of linear order and chaos . . . You look as blank as a chimp faced with a banana fitted with a zip. Well, never mind.

'The point is that simple Stepper technology allows us to move "up" or "down" the gut, you see, along the string of worlds. But Mellanier, even before the existence of the soft places started to become widely known, argued on theoretical grounds that it might be possible to break through into an adjoining strand.

Rather than walk all the way around the string, you see. An effective short cut.'

'Mellanier. I do remember him. Face all over the media a few years after Step Day. Princeton, isn't he?'

'That's him. He got a lot right, but only dipped his toe in the theoretical waters.'

'You don't seem to like him very much, Wotan. Why should some rival academic from Princeton get your goat?'

'Because Claude Mellanier is a fraud who fed off the analyses of Willis Linsay, *and mine*, repackaged them, dumbed them down, and passed them off as his own.'

'The man won a Nobel Prize, didn't he, Wotan?'

'That's because the Nobel committee are idiots nearly as blithering as you.'

'Also he published a bestselling book—'

'And don't call me Wotan. Oh, must you plant me before these pithecine buffoons, Jocasta?'

22

By the end of February, the *Armstrong* and *Cernan* had passed Earth West 30,000,000. There was no particular celebration – and nor had there been a few days back, when the ships had passed 20,000,000, and so beaten the five-year-old Chinese record. Not in the public spaces anyhow, at Maggie's quiet order.

With the sheaf of worlds dominated by crabs and other crustaceans far behind, now they passed through a band of worlds where – as the biologists discovered on scooping up samples of pond scum – not only was there no multicellular life, no animals, no vegetation, there was often no evidence of complex *cellular* life: that is, no cells with internal nuclei, like those of Maggie Kauffman's own body. Only the most simple of bacteria dwelled here, in mats and banks.

The crew called these 'purple scum worlds'.

Still, in such worlds there could be complexity, of a different sort. They found structures like stromatolites, mounds of bacteria built up layer by layer in the sunlight, mindlessly cooperating in what might on Datum Earth have been called primitive ecosystems. But after billions of years of a different evolution, there was nothing primitive about *these* structures. Especially not the ones that crept up on an unwary crewman, taking samples with her back turned . . .

Two days' flight later, at around Earth West 35,000,000, after millions of scum worlds all more or less identical, they encountered another band of worlds with their own peculiarity. Here oxygen levels in the air were very low, carbon dioxide high. The airships stopped at random on one such world – Earth West 35,693,562. Biologists in oxygen masks cautiously explored the shore of an arid continent. Even by the standards of the 'purple scum' worlds, this was an Earth poor in life.

It took some detective work on a larger scale to figure out the cause. Under Gerry Hemingway's prompting, Maggie authorized the launch of balloons, sounding-rockets, and one of their small stock of precious nano-sat launchers, and a global map was assembled. Here, North America had united with most of the world's other continents, rafts of granite floating on mantle currents, to form a single supercontinent – like the Datum's Pangaea, Maggie was told, which had broken up a quarter of a billion years back. One huge continent, and nothing else but ocean.

And supercontinent worlds, it turned out – just as the Chinese had found, Maggie discovered, consulting with Wu Yue-Sai – weren't particular hospitable to life. The continent's vast interior was worn down and arid; it was like one gigantic Australia, with only the coastal regions showing any kind of fecundity. The expedition pushed on, across one supercontinent world after another – the 'Pangaean Belt', the geographers called it. They saw no sign of life more complex than stromatolites at the coastal fringes, and if some kind of exotic critter roamed the tremendous plains of some footprints of these world continents, well, Maggie was content to leave the discovery to future travellers.

The Pangaean Belt turned out to be about fifteen million worlds thick. *Fifteen million*: sometimes Maggie struggled to grasp the significance of such numbers. The width of the Pangaeas alone was ten times the stepwise distance between the Datum and Valhalla, for instance, a reasonable measure of the width of the Long Earth as colonized by human beings in the generation since Step Day. Yet, travelling at the airships' nominal cruise speed, they crossed it in a week.

After the Pangaeas, fifty million worlds from home, they entered yet another purple scum belt, where at least the scattered continents provided varied scenery. The atmospheric and climate conditions were often close enough to the Datum that Maggie could authorize shore leave without significant protective clothing, and her crews of very healthy, mostly very young people could escape from the roomy but confined interiors of the gondolas. But there was nothing to do down there, nothing to see – pond scum didn't count – and people kind of clowned around aimlessly. There was only so much fun you could get out of lobbing rocks at stromatolites.

Snowy, the beagle, was different, however. Maggie watched him stride alone across the most featureless of landscapes, his extraordinary animal-human body held erect in the Navy uniform Maggie had had specially tailored for him, his wolf eyes glittering, his head tipped back so his nostrils could drink in the local scents. He seemed to find something of interest in every world they called at. And he kept his own log, a vocal record rigged up for him by Harry Ryan since his people mostly lacked conventional literacy. Maggie promised herself to get that log transcribed and studied. She had the feeling it would describe a voyage perceived quite differently from the human crew's experience. Which, of course, was why Snowy was here.

She tried to talk to Mac about Snowy, and whatever problem the two of them had. All she got was stony silence, a Mac speciality when he was in the mood.

When Snowy was off the ship Shi-mi would come out of Maggie's rooms and run around the gondola of the *Armstrong*, presumably letting off steam in her own way, and submitting to being spoiled a little by the crew. Save for Mac, of course.

They pushed on, thousands upon thousands of steps. Even Jokers seemed sparse out here. Maggie fretted that the journey was turning into a kind of experiment into mass sensory deprivation. An unexpected hazard for a pioneer, she thought.

At first they kept the nominal cruise speed at a little over two million steps a day, achieved by stepping at fifty steps per second for around twelve hours' run-time per day. Maggie was mindful that she was running two essentially experimental ships here, and Harry Ryan – backed up by his Chinese counterpart Bill Feng with whom, after initial suspicion, he had formed an unlikely buddy-buddy partnership – was resistant to any change to his preplanned test routines. But Maggie pushed Harry to up the running time to eighteen hours a day, enabling a transit rate closer to *three* million steps daily, rather than two. That still allowed for two hours' downtime for the engine in the average watch, and she permitted Harry to have one full day per week without any stepping, for tests and overhauls on both boats.

Meanwhile she tried to keep the crews occupied. Luckily the gondolas were big enough to allow room for physical exercise and training, even in flight. She got together with Sergeant Mike McKibben, the commander of the two chalks of marines she had on board the airships, and fixed up joint exercises to keep both contingents happy. She also allowed, with caution, some competitive sports between the two services, Navy versus marines, from squash to Scrabble, McKibben's surprising pet love.

She did quietly order Nathan to ensure that her crews' salaries were firewalled so they couldn't be gambled away on the turn of a high-scoring tile.

'Yes, Captain. Should I warn Mike McKibben to do the same for his guys?'

She grinned. 'Let's see if he thinks of that for himself.'

'Yes, Captain.'

Even at the increased rate, it took nineteen more days before they left behind the purple scum.

Joe Mackenzie, one night towards the end of that interval, revealed to Maggie that he too was keeping a kind of log of the trip.

'My God, Mac, is everybody on these damn ships keeping a diary? We're like a dysfunctional White House.'

'It's a solitary habit, but there are worse. And, according to my personal log – you know, it's hard to grasp the scale of what we're doing here, because epic stepwise journeys are *new*, whereas we've been making long geographical journeys on Earth since, what? The Vikings, the Polynesians? But even so it seems to me we're coming up on a milestone, of sorts. Look – when Armstrong flew to the moon, he was undertaking a journey on a scale that dwarfed anything in human history, or indeed prehistory. The distance to the moon, two hundred and forty thousand miles out, is about sixty times the radius of the Earth. OK? Now, Datum to Valhalla is the civilized Long Earth, as much as it's civilized at all. That's around one point four million steps. And sixty times that distance, stepwise, is—'

She figured it quickly. 'About eighty-four million.'

'Which milestone we're due to pass tomorrow.' He raised the glass of single malt she'd poured for him. 'Whatever comes next for us, in comparison with other human achievements we've achieved our personal moon shot, Maggie.'

'I'll buy that. And a good excuse for a celebration,' she said, always thinking of crew morale. 'Let's round it up to a hundred million. Sounds neater.' She glanced at a calendar. 'Looks like we'll get there on April Fool's Day.'

'Seems appropriate,' Mac said.

'We'll have a day's R&R, make a couple of speeches, take photographs, plant a flag.'

'I was thinking it would be a good place to throw out the cat. But fine, do it your way.'

23

Not far past the hundred-million-step milestone, the purple-scum band gave way to yet another sort of world: another band in which multicellular life had emerged. It was a welcome island of scenery after long stretches of purple scum worlds – or sometimes, for the sake of variety, green scum. Yet the creatures they encountered in these worlds were not like anything anybody had seen before.

Earth West 102,453,654: on this world the land had been colonized by things that looked like trees, but were actually, said the biologists, a kind of much-evolved seaweed. Things like sea anemones crawled over the ground, browsing. And the canopies of these kelp-like forests, and much of the world below, were dominated by a kind of jellyfish.

Jellyfish, living in trees.

These were tremendous leathery creatures, typically as massive as a troll. Their permanent habitat seemed to be the shallow sea, and while some crawled out on to the land, others *flew*, rocketing out of the ocean on water pumped from their mantles, and then gliding using fins protruding from their carapaces as 'wings' to reach the tree tops.

The canopy was laced with natural cables, like lianas but probably not. The jellyfish would descend on these cables for smash-and-grab raids on their cousins on the ground, and on other life forms like the anemones. Once the watching scientists even observed a kind of war, as one band of jellyfish from one forest clump hurled cables and nets over at another clump, and attacked in force.

All this was recorded from the air, by the human visitors. Off-duty crew spent all their spare time at windows or in the observation galleries, gazing down. Captain Kauffman vetoed any shore leave, however; the oxygen level was so low the party would have had to wear facemasks and carry tanks, and thus encumbered would have been terribly vulnerable to the predatory flying cnidarians of the branches above.

Bill Feng surprised Maggie by showing a peculiar fascination with the spectacle below – a peculiar interest in living things for a man she'd taken as a standard-issue engineer, anyhow. The Chinese said in his oddly accented English, 'I have a military background myself, but I have never been one to cherish war for its own sake. Now we have travelled a hundred million steps from the Datum, we are finding life systems entirely unlike our own – and yet we still find war. Must it always be so?'

Maggie had no satisfactory answer.

Having logged, recorded and sampled these worlds, the ships pressed on.

Now that there was something to see out of the windows Maggie reduced the cruise rate to the nominal two million steps a day, but when this sheaf of worlds, which the biologists called the Cnidarian Belt, gave way after only a few more days' travel to the purple scum, Maggie quietly ordered an increase in the stepping rate once again.

At Earth West 130,000,000, approximately, reached seven days after they had left the Cnidarian Belt – seven more days of purple scum – the expedition reached a new kind of world. Here a typical Earth's air seemed depleted of oxygen altogether – there was merely a trace in an atmosphere dominated by nitrogen, carbon dioxide and volcanic gases, and that trace,

Gerry Hemingway told Maggie, was probably put there by geological processes, not by anything alive. These were worlds, then, where oxygenating life had never formed in the first place, where there had been no discovery of the complex trick of photosynthesis, the use by green plants of the energy of sunlight to crack carbon dioxide to acquire its carbon for life-building, and incidentally to release excess oxygen into the air.

The airships had been designed in anticipation of such conditions. In the absence of atmospheric oxygen the great jet turbines which pushed the craft around the sky had to be fed oxygen from an internal store. Faced with a new engineering challenge to test his craft, Harry Ryan was in his element, and Maggie was fascinated; in this mode the technology was like a scramjet. But inside the gondola the air, now fully recycled by necessity, soon smelled stale.

Beneath the prow, meanwhile, the landscapes were more dismal than ever. Only a biologist could love the strange purple-crimson slicks and mounds of anaerobic bacteria that were the emperors of these worlds. Maggie quietly ordered that the accelerated stepping rate, three million steps a day, be maintained for now, but she warned Harry Ryan to be sure to watch the crafts' onboard reserves. She didn't want to have to try to walk back home through this.

It was the issue of oxygen, in fact, that caused her to have her first long conversation with Douglas Black since her most distinguished passenger had come on board the *Armstrong*.

Maggie made her way to Black's suite of rooms. She had Mac at her side; she was here to back up the doctor's complaints.

She'd asked for this meeting, but even on her own ship Douglas Black wasn't a man who would come calling. And it didn't surprise her that Black kept them waiting on his doorstep. His man Philip told them he had just woken up from a nap.

Mac muttered, 'Damn arrogance.'

'Let's just play it low key for now, Mac, and see what he has to say for himself . . .' And then the door opened.

Black had a team of aides, but only one servant on hand today, Philip the overbearing bodyguard, who gave the two officers a quick guided tour of Black's suite, glaring at them throughout.

The suite, a grand name for a set of cabins which Black had fitted out at his own expense, was less luxuriously appointed than Maggie had expected. There was a small galley, for Black insisted on having his food prepared for him exclusively, from fresh ingredients where possible – evidently Philip was also the chef. The lounge area was equipped with deep, adjustable chairs and couches, and a bank of information-processing gear, screens, tablets, storage units.

At first glance Black's bedroom looked to Maggie like a compact intensive care unit, with one big gadget-laden bed draped in a transparent curtain – it was effectively an oxygen tent, Mac murmured – and surrounded by monitors and drip-feeds, even what looked like a telesurgery robot arm. One small cot in the corner, behind a light partition, must be where Philip slept, on guard twenty-four seven.

It was the oxygen tent, Maggie knew, that Mac had an issue with.

Black, at ease in his lounge, sitting in a massively engineered wheelchair, wore a loose, comfortable-looking kimono jacket, silk trousers, slippers. Even in the enclosed submarine-hull artificiality of the gondola he wore his sunglasses. He smiled, his wizened face creasing, as he himself poured them rather good coffee. 'So – welcome to my lair, Captain Kauffman. That's the sort of thing people expect me to say, isn't it? Shall we get down to business? I'm aware that your doctor here has been taking an interest in my welfare, but I have brought my own medical establishment, as you can see.'

'But,' Mac growled, 'on this ship, where I'm chief surgeon, you do fall under my purview nonetheless.'

'Of course. I bow to your authority; it can be no other way.'

Maggie said, 'I'm afraid that's where the friction is coming from, sir. Specifically your use of oxygen.'

'Captain, I have assured Doctor Mackenzie that I have brought my own supply, my own replenishment and recycling equipment – it's like a regular little spaceship in here.'

'You nevertheless are plugged into the ship's supply,' Mac said. 'It's inevitable, an engineering constraint. And you, sir, are using up a hell of a lot. Captain, I wouldn't have raised it, but since right now there's no spare oh-two outside the hull, we need to discuss this.'

'I don't understand, Mr Black,' Maggie said. '*Why* are you using all this oxygen?'

Mac broke in, 'To fill his hyperbaric chamber all day and all night. You saw the tent over his bed, Captain. He lives in the damn thing, breathing air with an oxygen content whole percentage points above the Datum Earth level.'

'OK.' This sounded nothing but kooky to Maggie. She'd had a long day before this meeting, but she wished now she'd got herself better briefed. 'I'm no medic. Why would you want that, Mr Black?'

'For the most profound of reasons. To regain the one thing that all my money can't buy me – not yet, anyhow. You joked about my searching for the fountain of youth, Captain. Well, in a sense – *so I am.*'

For the next few minutes he ran her through a discourse, complete with a picture show on one of his big tablets, of the treatments he was taking, not just to slow down the ageing of his body but actually to reverse it. Hormones that declined with age were replenished, including growth hormones, testosterone, insulin, melatonin, others, to let them repair and restore body functions, as they would in a youthful body. There had been attempts at genetic repair using retroviruses to make and break DNA strings, removing damaged or undesired sequences. Back in the Low Earths Black was promoting experimental methods involving stem cells to regenerate tissues, even whole organs.

He spread liver-spotted hands. 'Look at me, Captain. I have always exercised, eaten well, avoided most vices. I have been fortunate in being spared many common illnesses. And of course my decades-long precautions against the ambitions of assassins have borne fruit, so far.' He tapped his skull. 'Mentally I seem as sharp as ever, my memory is good . . . But I am eighty years old; my time is running out. There is so much more to see, so much to do. Consider the mission we are undertaking right now! Can you see that I would do all I can not to leave just yet? Can you blame me?'

'All right. But what's that got to do with oxygen?'

'It's one of the therapies,' Mac said. 'And one of the flakier ones.'

Black inclined his head. 'I won't argue with a medical man. But you won't condemn me for exploring all the options, will you? Yes, the use of excess oxygen is controversial. But – look where we are. Look out the window! There is no oxygen here, and these worlds are all but dead. It is oxygen that promotes the life force. Why, you yourself use it in extremis for a patient, do you not, Doctor? The word is "oxyology", Captain. The use of a high oxygen partial pressure to promote healing, the rejuvenation of the body. It is cheap, it is easy, and some claim to have proof that it works, on ants and mice and so forth. Why not try it?'

Mac would have argued some more, but Maggie raised a hand. 'I think I get the picture. But I don't yet see what kind of "fountain of youth" you're seeking aboard this Navy ship, Mr Black.'

He would only smile. 'All I can say is that I will know it when I find it – if it exists.'

Maggie stood. 'I think we're done here. Look, Mac, we're watching our oxygen usage closely, but we've a complement of ninety, and Mr Black's consumption, given his private supply and even with his tent, is going to be only a fraction of that. We can cope, for now. But,' she said to Black, 'I'll put my chief engineer on alert. And if we need to impose any kind of emergency measures I'll have to restrict you to a regular crew allocation, sir.'

'Of course.' He looked faintly offended. 'I would never let my own interests put at risk a single one of your young charges.' He looked from one to the other. 'Is our business done? Am I allowed down from the naughty step?'

Maggie laughed gracefully, and nudged Mac until he forced a smile.

'Then, if you've time, let's have fun. Please, do sit again. Perhaps you'd like to look over the latest package of science updates prepared for me by your kind Lieutenant Hemingway. I'm sure you know it all already, but the images can be startling.' He nodded to Philip, who got up to make preparations; soon the room's screens filled up with curtains of purple and crimson. 'Who would ever have imagined that life even without the power of oxygen was capable of such beauty, such inventiveness of design? Can I offer you more coffee? Or perhaps something stronger . . .'

24

And so, over the years, Joshua had kept in sporadic touch with Paul Spencer Wagoner, as the strange little boy grew up into a somewhat stranger young man. He'd felt it was a kind of duty. Joshua was probably the boy's only contact, save for his immediate family, from his childhood in Happy Landings. Joshua Valienté was always big on duty.

But he was also curious. And in Paul Spencer Wagoner there seemed to be a lot to be curious about.

As far as Joshua could tell, Tom and Carla Wagoner had always tried their best with Paul, and his little sister Judy; certainly they had never hurt the kids. But when their marriage broke up, cracking under the stress caused by the kids, Joshua guessed, Tom was left to deal with Paul alone. And what Tom couldn't cope with was when his son, growing in knowledge if not in wisdom, and acquiring a certain power mentally if not physically, turned on his father.

Paul was just ten when he was taken away from his father.

'Paul knows me too well,' Tom said to Joshua, when they met at the Madison Home in the spring of 2036. Joshua was back to see how the Sisters were coping in the aftermath of the death of Sister Agnes, the previous year. 'How I broke up with his mother,' Tom said, 'and she took little Judy away. By the way, Carla's coping no better than me, I can tell you – she has just the same issues with Judy as we had when Paul grew up. And he knows how I screwed up at work. Paul *saw* all that, he understood far more about it than any damn kid ought to. About what's going on inside my skull, I mean.' He shook his greying head regretfully. 'When he takes me apart over some flaw or foul-up, it's – crushing. I don't feel like a father with an uppity kid. I feel like a pet dog being punished. Totally subordinate.

'But it's worse when he's deliberately cruel. Oh, I don't mean physically, I guess I could handle that. He can slice you to pieces with words. Damn kid. And you know what the worst of it is? He does it just because he can. For fun – no, not even that. For curiosity. To see what happens when he opens you up, like cutting open a frog. He doesn't know what he's doing, he is just a kid, but . . .'

A little digging revealed that Paul's sister Judy had by now also been taken away from her mother. And, such was the whim of the care system, the siblings were kept apart.

Paul, meanwhile, it was clear, was not happy, not settling anywhere, and in danger of spiralling out of control. After a couple more disastrous attempts at foster care, Joshua pulled a few strings. Paul was taken into the Home in Madison, and placed under the stern but perceptive care of the Sisters.

After that, Joshua saw him more regularly. The boy remained a mystery, though, to Joshua and the Sisters, as he grew into a strange maturity.

25

Willis Linsay appeared to be right about the stepwise geography of the Long Mars, Frank Wood observed.

Most of the stepwise Marses, at a first glance, as seen from the gliders riding in the high, thin air, were all but exactly the same. The pilots kept their dust-streaked birds hovering over their landing-site area of the Mangala Vallis, a huge arid landscape, and generally little changed from world to world, as it had been from the beginning. As Willis had predicted the only relief for Mars came from the occasional Jokers, worlds where, for some reason, there was warmth, moisture, a brief chance for any surviving life to express itself.

But all of these beneficent accidents seemed limited in *time*. It might take years, centuries, millennia, maybe even tens of millennia, but at last the eruptions would cease, the volcanic gases would clear, or the crater-lakes freeze over, as Mars returned to its regular state of lethal stasis. In fact, more often than they found functioning biospheres – like the world of the sand whales they'd encountered fortuitously early in their voyage – the travellers came upon traces of recently extinguished life. Aside from dust storms, not much happened on Mars; erosion was slow, and such traces could linger.

For example, about two hundred thousand steps East of the Gap, the gliders had swept over what looked like the remains of a mighty ocean that must have covered, if briefly, the plains of the northern hemisphere. Sites like Mangala showed signs of having become sea coasts, and Willis pointed out stranded beaches, what looked like a petrified forest a short distance inland, and salt plains on the dried-out ocean floor.

When they swept down for a closer look, they saw conical casts on the seabed, casts as tall as pyramids created by some immense snake – maybe a relative, in a common-origin sense, of the sand whales they'd seen before – and scattered plates like abandoned armour that might have come from something like the crustacean predators. Even bones, resembling a huge ribcage as if of a whale, sitting on a dry ocean floor.

At last, on the twelfth day, some half a million steps East of their starting point, they came upon traces of sapience. They found a city.

Set upon the high land to the south of Mangala, straight-line avenues still showed under the dust, and towers loomed, tall and bone-white. But there was no sign of extant life.

They had got in the habit of swapping over crew and rotating piloting responsibilities, to keep everybody fresh and experienced, and so that the pilots got used to the quirks of both machines. The day they found the city, Frank was riding shotgun as Sally piloted *Thor*, while Willis flew *Woden* solo. And so Frank was able to take in the scenery as Sally took the bird down close to the ground, and swept towards the city.

One peculiarity of their flight was that, such was the thinness of the air, the gliders needed high speed to keep aloft; that wasn't so noticeable at high altitude, but close to ground level you whipped along like a swallow chasing a fly. So the city loomed out of nowhere, and suddenly Frank found himself racing over avenues of broken flags between towers of ivory, impossibly tall, cracked and shattered. Frank couldn't resist it; he let out a rebel yell.

Sally grunted. 'I'm trying to concentrate here.'

'Sorry.'

'How's the data capture?'

Frank glanced at a tablet beside his seat, which showed megabytes of data from imaging systems, sonar, radar, an atmospheric sample suite, pouring into the glider's compact memory. They even had radio receivers listening out for any evidence of transmitters; Mars's ionosphere was feeble and would be a poor reflector of radio waves, but you never knew, and it seemed remiss not to listen. 'All in hand,' he said. 'Quite a place, isn't it? From the air the city looked like – I don't know – a chess set. From here, down and dirty, those towers look like cracked teeth. But taller than anything you could build on Earth.'

Willis called over, 'That's the low gravity for you.'

Sally said, 'But the towers didn't save them when the final wars came. Look down.'

Now, in the rubble-littered roadways and even inside some of the smashed buildings, Frank saw wreckage: segments of casing, articulated limbs, as if torn from some immense spider. They were made of some kind of metal, perhaps, or ceramic. These fragments were broken, crushed, blown open, and the road surfaces and walls were pitted with bomb craters. All of this was covered with a fine sheen of rust-red dust, wind-blown.

Frank asked, 'Why do you say "final wars"?'

Sally said, 'Because evidently there was nobody left to clean up when it was done. Many of these Joker islands-in-time must have ended in wars, mustn't they? When the climate collapsed, the survivors would have fought over the last of the water – the last trees to burn – maybe they made sacrifices to appease their gods. All patterns familiar from Datum Earth's history; that's what *we'd* do. Stupidity is a universal, it seems.'

In this city like a vast cemetery, that cold remark made Frank wince.

Willis said, 'I doubt if there's anything more for us here. I'll go down to take a few samples. Follow me if you like.'

Frank saw *Woden* dip towards a broad flat area outside the city. He asked Sally, 'How about it? Need to stretch your legs?'

'I'll be fine. You?'

'Skip it. I'm doing my couch yoga as we speak.' To conserve the methane fuel they needed to launch from the ground, they were trying to minimize landings.

Sally tugged on her joystick. *Thor's* nose lifted, and the glider spiralled into the high air. Once again the city was reduced to a toy-like diorama, with no visible trace of bomb blasts or insectile war machines.

Frank switched to the internal intercom, so Willis couldn't listen in. 'So, Sally.'

'What?'

'"Stupidity is a universal." I've heard you say that kind of thing before. Are you serious?'

'What's it to you?'

'I'm only asking.'

'Look – I didn't *grow up* despising mankind. I had to learn it. You know my background . . .'

He knew the basics. Most of it he'd learned from Monica Jansson, who, late in her life, Sally had grown close to – close at least in Sally's terms – when they had pulled that stunt of liberating a couple of trolls from GapSpace. And then Jansson had become close to Frank, all too briefly, before he'd lost her.

Sally Linsay had grown up a natural stepper, but from a mixed background; her father, Willis, was not a natural. Before Step Day, her mother's family – like, it seemed, many dynasties of naturals – had, understandably, kept their peculiar superpower to themselves, but they'd used it when it suited them.

'I was stepping when I was a little kid,' Sally said now. 'My uncles would go hunting in the Low Earths with crossbows and such, and they knew to watch for grizzlies. Dad was always more a tinkerer than a hunter, and he built a stepwise workshop for himself, and dug a garden. I'd take him over there and I'd help him out, and he'd make up stories and such, and play games. The Long Earth was my Narnia. You know Narnia?'

'That's the one with the hobbits, right?'

She blew a raspberry. 'To me, stepping was a joy. And it was a useful experience, because I was surrounded by smart people who understood what they were doing, and used the gift wisely, and took precautions.

'Then came Step Day, and suddenly every idiot with a Stepper box could go out, and guess what? Next thing you know they're all drowning or freezing to death or starving, or getting chomped by some mountain lion because the little kitteny cubs were so *cute*. And worst of all is that all those idiots took not just their idiocies with them into the Long Earth, but their petty flaws too. Their cruelty. Especially their cruelty.'

'And especially cruelty to trolls, right? I know that much about you, from when you showed up at the Gap.'

She was sitting ahead of Frank in the glider's pilot seat; he saw her back stiffen. Predictably she had become hostile. 'If you know all about me already, why are you asking?'

'I don't know it all. Just what I heard, from Monica for instance. You became a kind of rogue. An angel of mercy, helping save these "idiots" from themselves. But also—' He sought for a non-antagonistic term. 'You became the conscience of the Long Earth. That's how you see yourself.'

She laughed. 'I've been called many things, but not that before. Look, most of the colonized Long Earth is far from any semblance of civilization. If I see a wrong being committed—'

'A wrong in your opinion.'

'I make sure the wrongdoers know about it.'

'You act as a self-appointed judge, jury – and executioner?'

'I try not to kill,' she said, somewhat enigmatically. 'Oh, I punish. Sometimes I deliver the perps to justice, if it's available. Dead folk don't learn lessons. But it depends on the situation.'

'OK. But not everybody would agree with the value judgements you make. Or the way you assume the right to act on those judgements. There are some who'd call you a vigilante.'

'What's in a word?'

'You see, Sally, what I'm struggling with is this. It was your father who did this, who *caused* Step Day. And now all these "idiots" are polluting *your* Long Earth, as you grew up seeing it. Killing the lions in your Narnia. Right? Is that the real problem? The fact that it was your own father opened it all up—'

'What are you now, some kind of analyst?' She was practically snarling.

'No. But after my military service I saw a number of analysts myself, and I know the questions they ask. Look, I'll shut up. Your business is your business. But,

Sally – do good, OK? But watch that anger of yours. Think about where it comes from. We're all a long way from home, and we rely on each other, and we need to be in control. That's all I'm saying.'

She wouldn't reply. She just kept flying the glider in wide, over-precise loops, until Willis had done his work and came flying up to join them.

Then, after a quick synchronization of their data stores, they stepped away, the chessboard city vanishing from beneath their prows.

26

More lifeless Marses, sheaf after sheaf of them, day after flying day, broken up by landings each night on yet another copy of the Mangala landscape, and occasional pauses for exploration.

On the thirtieth day they landed for the night on a world not far short of Mars East Million – a million steps East of the Gap – and Frank Wood went for a brief walk in the dark, bundled up in his pressure suit. This night the twin stars of Earth and moon were particularly prominent, riding high in the east. This was a typical Mars, like the Mars of the Datum sky, a world about as lethal as it could get and still have any kind of similarity with Earth. But it was a pleasure for Frank to land anyhow and stretch his legs.

These walks had become Frank's habit, uncomfortable and faintly risky as they were, a way of putting some distance between him and the Linsays. Just a few minutes each day, so Frank's own personality had room to breathe, and recover something like its proper shape. Walks on worlds that might be forty or fifty thousand worlds apart, so far were they travelling each day, and yet all so alike – so similarly dead. On this night, as on many nights on these desolate Marses, he wondered what the point of it all was: all these empty worlds, an emptiness made worse by the brief and rare windows of habitability they found, almost all slammed shut with the finality of extinction. Was it crueller to have lived and died, or never to have lived at all?

And what was the meaning of it all – was *every* world inhabited by intelligence going to be Long like this Mars, like Earth? He imagined a sky full of threads of Long worlds, like broken necklaces drifting in some dark ocean. Maybe you could have a Long Venus – a Long Jupiter, even, if mind ever took hold there. But *why*? Why should it be that way? What was it all for? He suspected he would never find a satisfactory answer to such questions.

Just do your job, airman.

As it happened they came across traces of another near-miss civilization the very next day, only fifty thousand worlds plus change past the meaningless million-step milestone.

The crater was a few tens of miles south of Mangala itself, the glitter of metal easily visible from the air, and spotted by their image-processing software as they stepped through.

This time Frank was piloting Willis as the gliders flew over. The crater was a great bowl in the ground, deep and clear-cut, maybe a half-mile across. But its inner surface gleamed with some kind of metallic coating. From a height, Frank could see that the bowl itself was littered with inert objects, crumpled and fallen: machinery of some kind, perhaps. And some parts of the crater, and the land near by, were blotted black, as if bombed from the air by immense bags of soot. The crater appeared to be joined to a wider landscape by straight-line trails of some kind, but they were old, faint, dust-choked.

Willis growled, 'Another close call, dammit. Another still-warm corpse. I see no movement, am picking up no signals. You want to take us down, Frank? Sally, station-keep.'

'Yes, Dad,' came a dry reply. Sally tolerated being ordered around by her father in situations like this, but just barely.

Frank dipped the glider's nose. As they skated in towards the bowl of the crater, Frank noticed that swathes of the surrounding terrain were glassy, glinting in the weak sunlight as the land flowed by under the glider's prow. He remarked on this to Willis.

'Yeah,' Willis replied. 'And look in the crater.'

As they skimmed over the bowl one more time, Frank saw that the crater's inner surface appeared to have been coated with sheets of some kind of metal, but the lining was extensively damaged, torn away by explosions – and melted, in part. 'Radiation weapons? Lasers?'

'Something like that. I think this may have been some kind of telescope – like Arecibo, rigged up in the natural bowl of the crater. If the surface was mirror-like, maybe it was optical. You'd get a great view of Earth with a thing like that, given its location.'

They flew deeper into the bowl itself now. Frank was wary of any surviving superstructure, but he saw nothing: the destruction had been comprehensive. Piled up in the bowl's depths was a tangle of smashed equipment, much of it of elaborately sculpted metal. At first he could discern no signs of life, no biology down there. But then he made out shards of chitin that looked vaguely familiar.

'Put us down,' Willis said. 'We may as well take a few samples. Sally, stay aloft . . .'

They came down a short distance from the mirrored pit, and walked over.

When they clambered down into the pit itself, clumsy in their pressure suits, the deep cold seemed to intensify. At the bottom, there was no sign of recent activity; a layer of windblown dust seemed undisturbed. Willis snipped a few samples of metal components, the reflective surface, the chitin-like remains.

Frank said, 'This shell stuff looks familiar. Like traces of the crustaceans we've been seeing from the beginning.'

'So it does. There is a certain consistency, isn't there? I'm thinking of what we've seen: the crustaceans, the whales. A kind of common palette; maybe we're going to find distorted versions of those families wherever we go, differently evolved.

'I think I see how it would work . . . You have a rapid evolution of life forms, species, families, genera, while Mars is young. Pretty much identical on every world of the Long Mars. But then a given Mars shrivels, and whatever survives has to hibernate, aestivate. Mostly Mars stays dead, but on Jokers like this the root stock takes its chances when they come, adapting in different ways depending on the details of the environment. An endless reshaping of the same primordial stock – variations on the theme of whales and crustaceans, and maybe other sorts we've yet to identify.' As he spoke Willis kept working, patiently studying the melancholy debris. 'I'll run this through the assay gear on the glider.'

'I take it the tech artefacts you're looking for aren't here.'

'No. Disappointingly. Though this is the highest culture technologically we've encountered.'

'You'll know it when you see it, will you, whatever it is?'

'You can bet on it.'

'How do you even *know* this thing exists?'

Willis didn't look up from his work. 'This is Mars. On such a world it's a logical necessity.'

Frank knew that they were all getting on each other's nerves anyhow, but this deliberate obscurity of Willis's increasingly niggled him. What was he, a chauffeur who couldn't be trusted with the truth? 'Secrecy and certainty, huh? Those traits have helped your career, have they?'

Willis just ignored him, which annoyed him even more.

'Sally compared you to Daedalus. I looked him up. In some versions of the story he invented the labyrinth on Crete, where they kept the Minotaur. Problem was, he didn't think through the consequences. Made the labyrinth so intricate it was hard to pin down the beast if you needed to slay it. Not only that, it had a design flaw. With a simple ball of thread you could make a trail to find your way out – Daedalus never thought of *that*.'

'Is this storytelling going anywhere, Wood?'

'Maybe you are more like Daedalus than you think. What will you do with this bit of Martian tech, if you find it? Just unleash it on the world, like the Stepper box? You know, you and Sally, father and daughter, you both treat mankind like it's some unruly kid. Sally slaps us around the back of the head when she thinks we're misbehaving. And you, your way of teaching us responsibility is to hand us a loaded gun and let us learn by trial and error.'

Willis thought that over. 'You're just sore because you're an old space cadet. Right? Step Day stopped you from getting to fly around in the space station measuring the thickness of your piss in zero gravity, or whatever those guys did up there for all those years. Well, bad luck for you. And whatever *we* do, at least we have mankind's best interests at heart. Me and Sally, I mean. Now. Does this conversation have any point, Frank?'

Frank sighed. 'Just trying to figure you two out.' He looked down at the silent war zone. 'God knows there isn't much else to do on this trip . . .'

'Ground party, *Thor*.'

Frank tapped the control panel on his chest to switch over his comms circuit. 'Go ahead, Sally.'

'I'm picking up some residual background radiation.'

Now there was movement, out of the corner of Frank's eye. A vent of some greenish smoke, puffing into the air from a pile of dust-coated debris.

Sally said, 'The builders and warriors are long dead, but maybe the junk they left behind isn't. Suggest you get out of there.'

'Copy that. Come on, Willis.'

Willis followed without arguing as Frank clambered out of the pit. Frank glanced up at Sally, flying high in the air, a Martian Icarus. Then he looked away, concentrating on where he put his booted feet on the uneven slope.

27

Everybody on Maggie's airship thought they'd have to get out of the 'Anaerobic Belt' before they came across complex life once more. As it turned out, everybody was wrong, and not for the first time.

Earth West 161,753,428: ten days after they'd entered this thick band of oxygen-free worlds, the twains drifted over a landscape teeming with life, big, complicated, active life. Evidently this was a new complexity band – but, this deep into the stepwise worlds, the life forms they saw below were very different from anything they'd encountered before.

Maggie was standing in the observation gallery with some of her senior crew. These included Mac and Snowy the beagle, at her insistence, in the vague hope that forcing the two of them into the same space might bring to a head whatever issue was bubbling between them. Not yet it hadn't. And, as it happened, Captain Ed Cutler was here too; he'd come over for his weekly face-to-face with Maggie.

The ships, side by side, were drifting through a yellowish sky laced with very odd-looking clouds, over a greenish sea, that lapped against a shore of pale brown streaked with scarlet, purple. The very colour scheme was distracting, as though it had come out of some doped-up college student's imagination. On the land were banks of what had to be vegetation, including what looked to Maggie like 'trees', tall structures with trunks and some kind of leaf-like arrangement on the top, evidently a universal formation wherever you needed light from the sky but had to be rooted to the ground for nutrients. But those 'leaves' were crimson, not green. Gerry Hemingway had told her they were busily photosynthesizing, leveraging the sun's energy – but unlike Datum trees, what they seemed to be absorbing from the air was not carbon dioxide but carbon monoxide, and what they were producing was not sweet oxygen but hydrogen sulphide and other unpleasant compounds. Around the clumps of 'forest', meanwhile, stretched swathes of some kind of 'prairie' of more diverse vegetation, but nobody knew what the hell grew there yet.

And, among the vegetation, animals moved. Nothing like Datum animals. Maggie made out a disc, translucent, huge, like a cross between a jellyfish and a Hollywood UFO, that slithered and slurped and morphed its way over the land. No, not just one disc: a whole family, a herd maybe, big adults with little ones skittering alongside. Gerry Hemingway wondered if they moved by some kind of ground effect, like an airship.

It didn't aid comprehension that all this was played out at a manic speed, as if the world outside was stuck on fast-forward. Hemingway's biologists suggested that was something to do with the higher temperatures of this world, an increase in available energy. Still, whatever the justification, Maggie wished all this shit would just *slow down*. And—

'Mao's eyebrows!' That, astonishingly, was Lieutenant Wu Yue-Sai. She turned to Maggie and blushed. 'I must apologize, Captain.'

'The hell you must. What do you see?'

Wu pointed. 'There. No, there! In the trees – it is long, muscular, like a snake. A huge one. But—'

But this 'snake' hurled itself through the air, from tree to tree. No, it did more than that, Maggie saw; it was streamlined, kind of like a flexible helicopter blade, and it was wriggling as it moved through the air.

It was purposefully gliding – even flying, if you wanted to stretch a point.

Gerry Hemingway whistled. 'A twelve-foot-long flying snake. Now I've seen everything. No, wait – not yet I haven't.'

For the 'snake' had hurled itself on one of the disc creatures, a little one, an outlier. There was a hiss of steam, the disc wriggled and thrashed, but Maggie saw the snake sink *inside* the disc, and once within, it began to twist and tear its way back out again.

'Eating its victim from the inside out,' Mac said. 'Having burned its way in with some kind of acidic secretion. Charming. Everywhere you go, herbivores and carnivores, the dance of predator and prey.'

Maggie forced a laugh, to try to lighten the mood. 'Maybe, but I bet you never thought you'd see it quite like this, did you?'

Cutler was standing rather stiffly beside Maggie. He never was one for social occasions. He said now, 'I suppose we need to find somewhere rather more isolated for a safe landing for our shore parties, Captain? The crews could use some R&R; we've been cooped up a long time . . .'

The group fell silent at this. Maggie felt embarrassed for the man.

Mac had no such compunctions, however. 'Captain, are you suggesting we actually send crew down there?'

'I don't see why not. We've landed on exotic Earths before.'

'Sir, do you *ever* pay attention to the science briefings from your officers?'

Maggie murmured warningly, 'Mac . . .'

'Not if I can help it,' Cutler said defiantly.

Mac looked around. 'Gerry, do you have what's left of that first drone we sent out, so we can show it to the Captain here? The damage to its hull – no? . . . Never mind, I've a better idea.' He made his way to the wall of the observation gallery, where a series of lock-boxes had been fixed to allow the collection of atmospheric samples. He donned a protective glove, reached inside and pulled out a flask of gas, yellowish in the deck's fluorescent lights. 'The air,' he said, 'of Earth West 160,000,000 plus change. And do you know what we found in here, Captain?'

'No free oxygen, I know that much. Water vapour?'

'Good guess. But not just water. Highly acidic water. Captain Cutler, that's the story of this world. The oceans are more like dilute sulphuric acid. So are the rivers. So's the rain. And so is the blood of these creatures down below, the couple we managed to snag with drones. Why, you just saw it in action, as that snake thing must have concentrated its bodily fluids to burn its way into that protoplasmic beast—'

'Ed,' Maggie said quickly, hoping to defuse the situation, 'the science boys think that on this world, in this band of worlds, water, I mean neutrally acidic water, isn't what life uses as – what's the term, Gerry?'

'A solvent. Which means, in this context, something to provide a liquid environment within which the chemistry of life can happen. On Datum Earth, we use water. Here—'

Cutler asked, 'Acid?'

'That's the idea,' Mac said. 'There's a whole biosphere based on that simple fact, that difference. But we've barely started to scratch the surface.'

Hemingway said, 'We have here a suite of life that's made up of the same basic molecules as us, Captain Cutler, but with an entirely different chemical basis. Perhaps the plants absorb carbon monoxide and secrete hydrogen sulphide. In any event it would be extremely hazardous, to say the least, for a human to venture down there without very heavy protection.'

Maggie said, 'But the ships are sound. The hull, the envelopes can withstand the dilute acidity of the rain. Obviously we're keeping our internal air supply sealed off. I'm sure you'd have been briefed by your XO if she'd perceived any problems, Ed.'

Cutler was quite unperturbed, Maggie saw. He was a man whose mind was thoroughly compartmentalized, and he liked it that way. The nature of these exotic worlds, unless his ship was directly endangered, was something he didn't need to hear about, and he'd no doubt instructed his crew in that regard. Still, he seemed to show a flicker of curiosity as he asked now, 'So what went wrong?'

Hemingway stared at him. 'Pardon me, sir?'

'I mean, how did these worlds get this way, instead of producing regular oxygen-breather types like us?'

Hemingway said cautiously, 'Well, we can only guess, sir. We've only spent a couple of days with a whole new kind of biosphere.'

Maggie smiled. 'Guess away, Gerry, you're all we've got.'

'We think that these worlds, for whatever cause, must have gone through a phase of extreme heat when they were younger. Maybe they were like Venus, for a time, with thick atmospheres, ferocious heat at the surface. The thing about Venus, though, is that we've always suspected life was possible up in the clouds, where it's cool enough for life, if you pick the right altitude. There could be some kind of bug tapping solar ultraviolet, and using whatever chemical resources it can find to live on up there. Notably droplets of sulphuric acid – because the acid, you see, has a higher boiling point than water, and is available as a solvent where liquid water isn't . . . The point is, maybe *this* Earth was like Venus, *our* Venus, when it was young.'

'OK. But this world isn't like Venus now.'

'No, sir. But maybe it – recovered. Cooled down again, rather than suffer the full catastrophic heating of our Venus. It became more – well, Earthlike. But that acid-based life, once it got a foothold, stayed in control. And the result is the acid biosphere you see below.'

'Hmm. Sounds kind of pat to me. And I— What the— *Back!*' To Maggie's blank astonishment, Cutler pulled his handgun, crouched down, and pointed it two-handed at the hull wall.

Then she turned and saw the snake.

It came twisting and turning, riding the yellowish air – yes, it was undoubtedly flying, purposefully. And it was heading straight for the ship, for this observation gallery, and what must look like fresh meat to a flying, acid-blooded, snake-like predator . . .

'Keep calm,' snapped Nathan Boss. 'It can't do us any harm. The hull, the windows, are resistant to—'

The beast slammed into the hull, its whole body sprawled across the window. Maggie got a nightmarish glimpse of the animal's underside, an array of suckers and ribbed flesh and things like tiny lips that mouthed the window surface. She even saw some kind of liquid come squirting out, fizzing. She remembered the fate of the jellyfish down on the ground, and her skin crawled at the imagined touch of acid.

And Ed Cutler ran for the wall, towards the snake, gun in hand. 'I got this,' he said.

Maggie grabbed for him, missed. 'Ed! No! Let that thing off in here and you'll either crack the hull and kill us all, or the ricochets—'

'I'm not a fool, Captain.' He jammed the weapon into one of the air-sample lock-boxes. 'These things will self-seal, right? Same design on the *Cernan*. Eat this, acid boy.'

And he fired the gun. The noise was enormous in the enclosed space. Maggie saw the projectile pass through the snake's body and splash away into the air, leaving a ragged hole. The animal thrashed and squalled, and lost its grip and began to fall away.

'Let me finish him off,' Cutler said, changing his stance, repositioning the gun.

'For Christ's sake stop him!' Maggie yelled.

Mac was the closest, Snowy the fastest. Between them they hauled Cutler away from the window, and Mac forced the weapon out of his hands.

Cutler stopped struggling, and they released him. 'All right, show's over.' He was breathing hard, his face flushed; he glowered a look of pure hatred at the beagle, then turned to Maggie. 'Decisiveness, Captain

Kauffman. That's a quality usually attributed to me, in the face of danger—'

'The only danger here came from you and your weapon. Get off my ship, you idiot.' She deliberately turned her back. Then she approached Snowy and Mac, who were standing awkwardly side by side. 'Good teamwork, you two.'

The beagle nodded gravely. 'Thank you, Captain.'

Mac just shrugged.

Maggie said, 'Good work, in spite of the fact that you avoid each other like the plague. So, you going to tell me what's going on between you two?'

Snowy said reluctantly, 'Matter of – honou-hhr . . .'

'Honour? What about?'

'Murde-hrr my people.'

'Who? Mac? Are you serious? . . . Ah, look, we need to sort this out. In the meantime – Mac, with me.'

'Yes, Captain.'

She led him to the window and looked down. She could see the snake where it had landed, twisting, struggling. 'We're supposed to be explorers. We only just show up here, we don't even get out of the ship, and we start shooting. Killing. Except we didn't kill that thing.'

'No, we didn't.'

'Badly wounded, though. And it's in a lot of pain, in my non-medical opinion.'

'Can't disagree with that, Captain.'

'So what are you going to do about it?'

'What do you mean?'

'I mean, get down there and fix it, that's what.'

'How the hell am I supposed to do that? You heard Gerry describe its life system. What do I use for anaesthetic, battery acid?'

'Figure it out. You're the doctor. Think what you might learn about the anatomy of these creatures.' More softly she said, 'And think what an impression you'd make on the crew, after Cutler's performance.'

He opened his mouth, closed it, and, very visibly, began to think. 'Hmm. Well, if Hemingway is right about the ecosystem here, an animal like *that* must live off some combination of the plants' products, regardless of what they are. I'd need Harry Ryan to knock me up canisters of hydrogen sulphide, sulphur dioxide.'

'Ask him.'

'And I'll need thick gloves. Thick, thick gloves . . .' He walked away. 'Hemingway, you'd better come give me a hand down there.'

Maggie looked down once more at the writhing acid snake, then turned away and returned to work.

There were more acid worlds, many more, in a belt that turned out to be millions of steps wide, a good fraction of the width of the great belt of complex water-solvent biology worlds that encompassed the Datum itself, and containing just as much diversity of form. A belt dominated by a form of life whose existence had been entirely unsuspected, before this mission.

And still they sailed on.

28

So, with Lobsang's urging to find out more about the anomalous outbreak of intelligence among mankind ringing in his ears, and with memories of previous encounters stirring in his memory, in the spring of 2045 Joshua went to see Paul Spencer Wagoner.

Nine years after Paul had first been admitted to the Home, he was still in Madison, in fact still based at the Home. Now aged nineteen, Paul had been allowed to stay on in an informal capacity of 'care assistant'. It had been similar for Joshua. Even as he'd grown to a young adult Joshua had needed the shelter of the Home, or so he'd felt, to keep his own stepping ability private. Did Paul, with his abnormal intellect, feel that way too?

'But there was no harm in *you*, Joshua,' said Sister Georgina, now an old lady, all but immobile, with a smile like a sunbeam. 'There's no harm in *him*. Inasmuch as there's no harm in the hurricane, or the lightning strike. Nothing *intentional*. Not really . . .'

Joshua had seen Paul a few times in the years since the boy had been brought here, whenever he called in to the Home. They found they shared a morbid sense of humour, and would play jokes on the long-suffering Sisters, often involving the detaching of Joshua's artificial hand. But you had to be careful. Not all Paul's jokes were a lot of fun for other people.

And now, as soon as Joshua got to the Home, somehow it wasn't a surprise to see a young girl come running out of the front door crying, and Paul Spencer Wagoner half-heartedly following her, very obviously trying not to laugh.

Paul let Joshua take him for a coffee in downtown Madison West 5, on a pale imitation of the old Datum city's State Street. Paul insisted on paying, however; he had a wallet full of credit cards.

Across the table, he eyed Joshua. 'So, good old Uncle Joshua. Honorary uncle, anyhow. Back to check up on me, are you?'

The challenge wasn't serious, Joshua saw. Nor was it playful, quite. It was more of a probe, a test. This wasn't the Paul Spencer Wagoner Joshua had known before. He had hardened. Joshua saw a young man who was growing up to look like his father – ordinary-looking, really, not too handsome, not too plain. His thick dark hair was his best feature. His clothing was a jumble, with no evident sense of style or colour coordination, not that Joshua was any kind of fashion guru. It looked like he had raided the spare clothing locker at the Home and come out wearing whatever suited, whatever was practical for the day.

He had beefed up, filled out, and Joshua wasn't surprised; no matter how smart he was, or rather *because* he was so smart, a kid like Paul needed to be able to defend himself physically. Once Joshua had even taken him to some sparring sessions. Joshua himself had sparred with Bill Chambers and other buddies as a boy – scenes later replayed with Lobsang, in much stranger circumstances. But Paul had scars he was always going to bear: one misshapen eyebrow, a broken nose, the remains of a nasty laceration on his neck.

Joshua just ignored Paul's opening sally. He asked instead, 'So, who was she? The girl at the door. What's the story?'

'The girl?' To Joshua's surprise, Paul had to think for a moment before he dug up her name. 'Miriam Kahn. Local family, met her at a barn dance. Always liked barn dances, you know.'

'You? Really?'

'Is it so surprising? They were always big on barn dances out at Happy Landings. Well, there wasn't much else to do. And with the fiddle players working away, and the trolls singing their rounds . . . I mean, the events are trivial, the repetitive music, the baby steps, but it is such a joy to throw yourself into the *physical* from time to time, isn't it? We are not after all disembodied intelligences. Dancing and sex. Great sport, both of them. A kind of animal madness comes over you.'

'So. Is that all that Miriam Kahn meant to you? "Sport." Is that what you said to her?'

'Oh, of course not. Well, not in so many words. Joshua, we *love* sex. My kind, I mean. And sex between *us* is the best of all, a union both physical and mental, of equals.'

And Joshua wondered: *My kind?*

'But the trouble is there still aren't many of *us* around. And so we turn to other partners. Look, Joshua, I know you're less easily shocked than most. But that's what I think poor Miriam picked up on. Sex with her, with one of *you* – well, can you imagine having sex with a dumb animal, a beast? I don't mean some bizarre High Meggers thing, a lonely comber with his mule . . . Like mating with *Homo erectus.*

Have you heard of that species? Fully human from the forehead down, anatomically. But from the eyebrows up, the brain of a chimp, more or less, scaled up for the bigger body. Can you imagine coupling with one of those? The animal thrill of the moment – the beautiful, empty eyes – the crashing shame you'd feel when it's over?'

'You're telling me that's how it was for you and this Miriam?'

'More or less. But I can't help myself, Joshua. It hurts me as much as it hurts them.'

'I doubt that very much. Paul, what did you mean by *your kind*?'

Paul smiled. 'I've been meaning to tell you, when you showed up again. I know you can keep a secret, because you kept enough of your own, didn't you? Look – I'll show you. I have my Stepper box. I know you don't need one. I've paid, let's get out of here—'

He stepped away with the slightest pop of displaced air, leaving his coffee half-finished.

When Joshua had first built a Stepper box of his own, on Step Day, aged thirteen, he had stepped out of the Home in the city of Datum Madison, and into forest, primeval, untouched, unexplored, as far as he could tell. Since those days, thirty years on, the Low Earths had soaked up most of the stepwise migration away from the Datum, including the big flow since Yellowstone had popped.

But – and even Joshua sometimes forgot this – a stepwise Earth was a *whole world*, as big and roomy as the original, all but empty of humans before Step Day, and it could absorb a large stepping population while keeping much that was wild and primitive.

Thus it was that, only a few steps away from West 5, in the footprint of Madison itself, Joshua found himself in a forest glade as untouched as any unexamined world in the High Meggers, in this little corner at least. It was the old trees that gave it away, Joshua always thought. If you saw a *really* old tree, centuries or even millennia old, bent out of shape by the vicissitudes of time and coated with exotic lichen and fungi, you knew you were in some-place no farmer had ever cleared, no logger had ever plundered.

And in this glade a dozen young people, from middle teenagers to twenty-somethings, were at play.

Most of them sat around a heap of food, canned and film-wrapped, a hasty picnic. Two of them, both girls, swam naked in the small pool that was the centrepiece of the glade. And three others, two boys and a girl, were having noisy, giggling sex off in the shade of the trees. It might have been any bunch of kids at play, Joshua thought. Save for the inventive open-air sex. And save for the way they spoke to each other continually, a kind of high-speed jabber that sometimes sounded like compressed English, sometimes like the baby-talk produced by Paul's sister Judy all those years ago, which Joshua still vividly remembered. Joshua could understand barely a word.

And they weren't like ordinary kids in the way that the nearest of them immediately rounded on Joshua when he stepped in with Paul, all armed with bronze knives, and a couple further out with raised crossbows.

'It's OK,' Paul said, hands held high. He squirted out some of the high-speed babble.

Joshua was still subject to suspicious stares, but the knives were lowered.

'Come have a sandwich,' Paul said to Joshua.

'No thanks . . . What did you say to them?'

'That you're a dim-bulb. No offence, Joshua, but that was obvious to them already. Just from the way you looked around, with your jaw slack. Like you showed up dragging your knuckles, you know?'

'A *dim-bulb*?'

'But I also said you're the famous Joshua Valienté, that I've known you since I was a little kid, that I trusted you to keep our secret. So you're in. Not that there's much of a secret to keep. We move the whole time, never visit the same place twice.'

'Why do you need to do that?'

'Well, we've all got scars, Joshua. If you want to know why, ask the people who gave them to us.'

'All right. You say these are *your kind*.'

He grinned. 'Actually we have a name. We call ourselves *the Next*. Not presumptuous at all, right? We thought about other names. The "Wide-awake", compared with you sleepwalkers, you see. "The Next" is catchier.'

'How did you find each other?'

He shrugged. 'It's not so hard in the Low Earths. You people keep good records. A lot of our kind have problems at school and the like. And a lot of us have been institutionalized, one way or another, Joshua. Spent time in places like the Home, foster care agencies – in lunatic asylums, juvenile penal institutes. Also there are family names that can provide a link. Spencer, my mother's maiden name. Montecute.'

'Happy Landings names.'

'Yeah. That was the breeding ground, or one of them. We don't fit in your world, Joshua, but at least we leave a trace as we pass through it. Having said that, there must be some who *do* fit in, who keep their heads down, who find a place in your society somehow. We haven't found any of them yet. They may be aware of us . . . I guess we'll meet up some day.'

'Hmm. I'll be honest, Paul. The way you keep saying *us* and *you* is disturbing me.'

'Well, that's bad luck for you, Joshua. Get used to it. Because it's been obvious to me ever since I hooked up with others of my kind – for the first time since they took my little sister away, and I had no one to talk to – that we *are* a different kind, fundamentally. That's not to say we haven't had a few disputes. We're arrogant sons of bitches; we're all used to being the brightest in our own little circle of dim-bulbs. But when we're together, we just race away.

'Joshua, you needn't think we're cooking up the next atom bomb here. We're super-smart, but right now we don't *know* anything. Nothing much more than *you* know, I mean, and half of that's wrong and the rest is mostly illusion . . . We're like the young Einstein in that patent office in Switzerland, staring at an empty notebook, dreaming of flying on a beam of light. He had the *vision*, but lacked the mathematical tools, yet, to realize his theory.'

'Modest, aren't you?'

'No. Nor immodest. Just honest. For now we're more potential than achievement. But that will come.

Already is coming, in a way.' He glanced at Joshua. 'I saw you watching me in the coffee bar. Wondering where the hell I got my money from, yes? It's all legal, Joshua. We're particularly good at mathematics, an area where you don't necessarily need a lot of life experience to excel. Some of us came up with investment-analysis algorithms – it wasn't hard to find loopholes in the rules, ways to beat the system. We don't play the markets ourselves; we just found middle men to sell the software. That kind of thing – that's how we make our money.'

'Sounds like you're playing with fire. You need to be careful.'

'Oh, we're careful. It's not as if we need to spend much anyhow. Not for now, not until we figure out what we're going to do, where we're going to go . . . Look, Joshua, one reason I brought you here is because I thought you would *understand*. For us to gather like this – it's not about mathematics or philosophy, or making money or whatever, not even about the future. It's just about being with others like ourselves. Can you imagine how it was for a kid like me, alone? To be surrounded by a bunch of upright apes with minds like guttering candles, and yet who had built this vast civilization full of rules and a crushing weight of tradition, none of which makes any sense if you just *look* at it . . . And having to act like you're the same as everybody else. Then, can you imagine what it's like, for the first time in your life, to find people who can keep up with you? For whom you don't have to slow down, or explain – or, worse yet, pretend? Where you can just *be* the way you need to be?'

Joshua met Paul's intense stare, trying not to flinch. Paul was just a not particularly well-turned-out nineteen-year-old boy. His face was smooth, young, his brow clear. But his eyes were like a predator's eyes – like the eyes of a cave lion, and Joshua had encountered plenty of those out in the Long Earth in his time. He had met at least one super-intelligent entity before, he reminded himself, in Lobsang. But even Lobsang's artificial visages showed more empathy than he detected in Paul's gaze.

Joshua was afraid, and he was determined not to show it.

To break the moment Joshua glanced over his shoulder, where the three-way coupling, uncomfortably noisy for him, was still going on. 'I can see you also get a lot of hot sex.'

'Well, that's one thing. When I'm with Greta or Janet or Indra, it's not like it is with a dim-bulb girl, like poor Miriam Kahn. It's real, it's the whole of me engaged with the other, not just my hormones expressing themselves. We don't even have to obey your rules, your taboos.'

'I can see that.'

'People fear us because we're smarter than them. I guess that's natural. But what they don't see is that we're fundamentally *not interested* in them, you know? Not unless they're standing before us, getting in our way. It's each other that fascinates us. Enriches us. And I thought *you* would understand because you were special too, weren't you, Joshua? When you were my age, or younger. You thought you were the only natural stepper in the world.'

'Yeah.' And it wasn't until he was twenty-eight years old, in fact, when he'd met Sally Linsay, that Joshua had first fully understood that he wasn't alone, that there were whole *families* of secret steppers out there, if you knew where to look.

'Maybe you remember how it felt to have to hide, to pretend. And what you feared they might do to you, if they found you out. Well, you've told me as much.'

'OK, Paul. Look, I appreciate you trusting me this far. Showing me all this – showing me yourselves. I know it cost you to do this, that you're taking a risk. Maybe going forward I can help you some more.'

Paul grunted, sceptical. 'How? By being the latest in a long line to tell us how we have to "fit in"?'

'Well, maybe. But I'm Joshua Valienté, king of the steppers, remember. Maybe I can find you a better place to hide. The Long Earth's got a lot of room. And I can show you a better way to live out there. Ways to set traps and snares, to hunt.'

'Hmm. Let me think it over—'

But there was no more time for talk. Because that was when the cops arrived.

There were twenty of them, maybe more, an overwhelming number, and they just stepped right on into the forest glade. They seemed to have everything spied out. They jumped on the kids, and took away or smashed their Stepper boxes. Joshua saw just one girl, evidently a natural stepper, get away, but a couple of cops headed off after her too.

Joshua had heard of this kind of tactic, evolved by the Low Earths' police and military after three decades of dealing with steppers, and their ease of escape and evasion. You did your surveillance. You went in hard, without hesitation, without warning, with overwhelming force. You immediately took away the Stepper boxes from those who used them before they had a chance to react. And you made natural steppers helpless, usually by rendering them unconscious immediately. The theory was brutal, and the reality, if you were on the end of it, even more so.

And, cuffed himself, pushed to the ground, Joshua was able to see who had betrayed them, those Paul had called *my kind, the Next.* It was Miriam Kahn, who Joshua had last seen broken-hearted and running from the Home.

She pointed coldly at Paul. 'That's him, Officer.'

29

Long Mars, one point five million steps East, as near as dammit. More than forty days into this stepwise trek.

And suddenly the crimson plain below the gliders was full of action.

Frank was at the controls of *Thor*, with Sally sitting behind him. Frank's first glimpse was of dust rising from charging vehicles, a herd of some tremendous beasts racing, a glint of metal – and *fire*, fire shooting out like flame-throwers in the Vietnam jungle.

Frank's first reaction was to pull on his joystick, lifting the nose of the glider up and away. He yelled to Willis in *Woden*, 'Climb! Climb! We don't want that flame weapon to reach us!'

'Roger that,' Willis replied more calmly. 'But I don't think that's a weapon, Frank. Take a closer look.'

When he had the glider climbing smoothly, Frank did take another look, through a panel on his console with an image he could zoom in with a touch. He saw again those big animals (*how* big? – his mind recoiled from making an estimate) fleeing over the plain, some kind of herd of them – maybe a dozen, big and small, adults and children. From above they looked like storybook dinosaurs, massive bodies with long necks, long tails balanced front and back, and galloping legs. 'They're like sauropods, maybe,' he suggested.

'Maybe. But those "sauropods" are bigger than anything we ever had on Earth,' Willis said. 'I'm recording a total length of two hundred and fifty feet, from nose to tail. Like eight blue whales laid end to end. Total height about fifty feet. A lot bigger than even *Amphicoelias*, which, I'm reading now, was the largest sauropod on Earth. That's Martian gravity for you. *And* they've got a dozen pairs of legs each. No wonder they're so fast. Also armoured, with bands of shell on their backs.'

Sally said, 'Those sand whales had a dozen pairs of flippers. Same anatomy.'

'I think they're this world's versions of the sand whales. Descendants from some common root. Look at the necks, like tubes, and those wide mouths. And – oh, my word—'

One of the big beasts stopped and turned, skidding in the dust of what looked like another dried-up lake. It rose up, uncurling its body so two, three, four sets of limbs were off the ground, and lifted its mighty neck to grow *tall*, and it loomed over the vehicles following it – Frank hadn't got a good look at them yet – and it opened that big sand-whale mouth and belched a gout of flame. The fire licked down at the hunters, whose vehicles turned and scattered.

'There's your napalm thrower, Frank,' Willis said.

'A fire breather,' Sally said. 'What a sight.'

'Just as well it can't fly,' Frank said practically.

Willis, in *Woden*, snorted. 'Probably just igniting methane from its digestive system.'

Frank forced a laugh. 'In the service, I knew a guy who lit his farts with a cigarette lighter.'

'Don't spoil the magic,' Sally said. 'That's the nearest thing to a dragon I'm ever likely to see.'

'And think about it,' Willis said. 'For some reason *this* Mars is evidently full of life, and vigorous life. Why would a beast that size need armour plating, and a flame-thrower? Imagine its true predators.'

'*True* predators?'

'As opposed to those hunters down below, Frank. And by the way – too late about avoiding being seen.'

Frank, with an effort, looked away from the big beast at bay.

The little flotilla of vehicles behind the flame-breathing dragon scattered and slowed, and as the dust settled around them Frank made out details. The vehicles weren't carts, they had no wheels; they were more like sand-yachts, sail-driven, riding on some kind of skid system. The dust-coated structures looked so primitive technologically he guessed they were made of wood, or some local equivalent. Their occupants, two or three to a yacht, were nothing remotely like humans. They were crustaceans, a form familiar from other encounters, but in this particular evolutionary arena they had developed supple armoured bodies, long manipulating limbs that held weapons: spears, bows perhaps.

And, yes, the gliders had been seen. Frank saw what looked like raised chitinous fists waving, even a spear thrown in futile threat into the air.

He said, 'I'm guessing we don't go down there.'

'I wouldn't,' said Sally. 'And look over there.' She pointed over Frank's shoulder.

There were more hunters chasing more land-dragons, further away across the plain, oblivious, it seemed, to the presence of the gliders in the sky. As one party caught up with a fleeing beast, Frank saw spears protrude from its hide, and ropes fixed to the spears hauled a handful of yachts along in its wake. It must take some skill to plant a thing like a harpoon between those armour plates. One boat turned over, scattering its occupants, and Frank got a glimpse of the skids, which were white as ivory.

He said to Sally, 'Those skids look like bone. Maybe these guys are like the old nineteenth-century whalers who used to build bits of the beasts they brought down into their boats . . . Sally, what's that you're singing?'

'It's called "Harpoon of Love". Just a stray memory – never mind.'

Willis growled, 'And look ahead, to the north.'

Frank levelled the glider and looked that way, away from the bloody commotion below him. And he saw, standing up from the smooth flatness of the seabed, a series of dark bands, slender, vertical, black against the purplish sky of this world.

Monoliths. Five of them.

All this was too much for Frank to take in. 'I don't believe it. Land-dragons? Crustacean whalers in sand-yachts? And now this?'

Sally said, 'What, would you prefer another dead Mars?'

'I'm at the limit of my scope's resolution,' Willis called back. 'And this damn air is full of dust, and moisture. But I think those slabs bear some kind of inscription.'

Frank said wildly, 'What inscription? Prime number sequences? A build-your-own-wormhole instruction manual?'

'Something like that, possibly,' Willis said, reasonably patiently in the circumstances. 'The legacy of the Ancients.'

Sally snapped. 'What are you talking about? What Ancients?'

'Oh, come on,' Frank said with a smile. 'This is Mars. This is the story of Mars, which is always an old world, old and worn down. There are always monuments left behind by the Ancients, the vanished ones, enigmatic inscriptions . . .'

Willis growled, 'Let's stick to reality. We're not going to know any more until we take a copy of those inscriptions back home for a proper analysis.' His glider tipped towards the monoliths. 'We have to get in there and record it all, maybe take a sample of the monolith material itself. Then we'll go on—'

'After finding *this* you want to go on?'

'Sure. This is wonderful. But it's not what I came looking for. And—'

Behind him, Sally cried out. 'Ow, Jeez, my *head* . . .'

An instant later, Frank felt it too.

For the rest of that day, they tried every way they could think of to get close enough to the monoliths to record their surface images. But something was blocking their approach.

If they flew in, or even if they landed and tried to walk in, they all suffered blinding, agonizing headaches. Sally was reminded of the pressure Joshua Valienté claimed he had felt in the presence of the huge entity they knew as First Person Singular. Or the way the trolls were repelled by the density of human consciousness on Datum Earth. Evidently humanoids shared some kind of faculty, a sensitivity to mind – a faculty that these hypothetical 'Ancients' were able to manipulate.

Willis tried to trick the mechanism by moving to a stepwise world, moving in closer to the monolith site, and stepping in – but the pain nearly disabled him, even stepwise where there was no direct trace of the monoliths.

They tried sending in their drone aircraft, but another defence strategy came into play. The little planes were just pushed away, physically, as if by an invisible hand in the air, until they reached some limit beyond which their automatic guidance cut back in, and they would turn and try again. Willis wanted to try sending in one of the gliders under remote control, but the others vetoed that.

'Whatever is written on there,' Frank sadly concluded, 'it's not meant for us. Those Ancients of yours are keeping us out, Willis.'

'Oh, we're not beaten yet. We'll find a way.'

They landed a safe distance away from the sand-whalers.

Later, as the light was fading, as they were setting up a bubble tent for the night, Sally pointed to the north. 'Look. At the feet of the monoliths. My eye was caught by something . . . I see a dust trail. And are those sand-yachts?'

They were, Frank confirmed, by looking through binoculars held up to his pressure-suit faceplate. Three, four, five of the whalers were rushing past the base of the monoliths as if they didn't exist. 'They aren't even slowing down.'

Willis said, 'Infuriating. Those sand-whalers have absolutely no idea what they're dealing with here. The monoliths are just a feature of the landscape to them.'

'Which,' Sally said, 'might be why they can get so close.'

Frank said, 'Maybe the monoliths are meant for them, some day – not us. Listen, I'm satisfied we're far enough from those whalers that they won't bother us tonight. But you don't take chances. I think we should keep some kind of watch in case those guys come visiting.'

'Agreed,' Sally said.

Willis stood there, still in his pressure suit, thinking. 'We ought to send up one of the gliders. Just to make sure they don't sneak up on us.'

Frank considered. 'That seems excessive, Willis. A drone will do just as well.'

'No, no.' He strode off. 'I'll take *Woden*. Better to be sure . . .'

Of course there was no stopping him. And of course he'd lied. He'd had no intention of serving as some aerial sentry.

Once he had *Woden* in the air, there was absolutely nothing Frank and Sally could do to stop him turning the glider's nose south, towards the main party of whalers.

'He hasn't even got the comms system on, damn him,' Frank growled, frustrated, twisted up with anxiety. 'What the hell's he doing?'

Sally seemed calm. 'Gone to find a way to get those images he wants,' she said. 'What else? That's what my father does. He goes and gets what he wants.'

'He'll get himself killed, that's what he'll go and get. He's your father. You seem cool about it.'

She shrugged. 'What can I do?'

Frank shook his head. 'If you fix up the tent, I'll go check over *Thor*. Make sure we're ready to go get him out of there fast if we need to.'

'Fair enough.'

In the end Willis didn't make his approach to the whalers until first light.

Frank, who had spent a fretful, sleepless night swathed in his half-closed pressure suit, was wakened by a soft beep from the comms system. 'Sally. He's online.'

She sat up immediately; she always slept very lightly. 'Go ahead, Willis—'

Frank found himself staring at a screen image of the upraised carcass of a giant insect-like creature, taller than a man when it stood upright. Over a tough-looking exoskeleton it wore belts and bandoliers containing tools, loops of rope, and it held a spear in three, four of its multiple limbs, a spear with a rope attached: a harpoon. All this was seen through a greyish mist. And the creature was pointing the spear straight into the camera.

'Convergent evolution,' Willis's voice murmured.

'Willis?'

'You're seeing what I'm seeing, through my helmet cam. Convergent evolution. That harpoon might have come from a Nantucket whaling ship. Similar problems demand similar solutions.'

Sally asked, 'What's that grey mist? The vision's blurred—'

'I'm in a survival bag.' A gloved hand appeared, pushing at a translucent wall. 'In my pressure suit, in a bag.'

The bags were simple zip-up plastic sacks with small compressed-air units. They were meant for decompression emergencies when you couldn't reach a pressure suit; you just jumped in a bag, zipped it up, and the released air would keep you alive for a while. You had very limited mobility, with tube-like sleeves for arms and legs to allow some capability; essentially you were supposed to wait for rescue from somebody better equipped.

'I rigged out a few bags to provide the local air, so these whaler guys can use them.'

Sally frowned. 'Air bags? Why do these guys need air bags? They *live* here.'

'I'm recording this encounter in case it doesn't work out. You might learn from my mistakes next time.'

Frank snapped, 'Next time what?'

'Next time you approach these guys to go in and record the monolith inscriptions for you.' He held up his other gloved hand; it held, awkwardly, a small handheld cam, and a stack of Stepper boxes.

Sally said, 'I understand the cam. You need to photograph the monoliths – or get the whalers to do that for you. But why the Steppers?'

'I told you, right at the beginning of all this. Trade goods. *Steppers* – something that was going to be valuable to whatever kind of sapient we encountered. Even though you need a spacesuit to survive a single step, on these Joker Marses. Hence I'm giving them survival bubbles too . . .'

It took some pantomiming for Willis, surrounded by spear-wielding, expert-hunter, six-foot-tall crustaceans, to get over what he wanted. First he showed the whalers what a Stepper could do for them. He finished its assembly, a question of pushing a few plugs into sockets, and then turned the switch, stepped away to the hunters' bafflement – and popped back into the world behind the lead guy, to their obvious consternation. 'That's it, fella. You get the idea. Imagine creeping up on Puff the Magic Dragon using one of these. Now you try. But you need to finish it for yourself, if it's to work for you. And you're going to need to use the survival bubbles, otherwise the Mars to either side will kill you in a breath . . .'

Only an hour later he had the crustaceans' apparent leader in a comically incongruous plastic bubble, stepping back and forth at will, and jumping out of nowhere to alarm his buddies. Or possibly *her* buddies, Frank corrected himself. He couldn't help noticing that one of those companions came in for particular humiliation with the new tool: some kind of rival to the leader? A father, brother, son, mother, sister? Whatever, he was jumped on, tripped, shoved, pushed over.

Sally said, 'If these beasts bear any kind of similarity to human personalities, that guy is going to be seriously pissed at Dad for this.'

'Yeah,' Frank murmured. 'That's one angry young prince. Or whatever.'

As the morning wore on, Frank watched with increasing impatience. And at one point he thought he heard a sound like distant thunder. The sky was cloudless. Were storms even possible on this version of Mars?

The crustaceans were fast learners. They quickly grasped the potential of the technology, and soon picked up the idea that in exchange for the magic Stepper box, all Willis wanted was for them to take his handheld cam as close to the monoliths as they could get.

'If this doesn't work, nothing will. I also gave them seeds for the Martian cactus that powers the box. That comes from the Gap Mars, and there's a good chance it will grow here too . . .'

'My God,' Frank said. 'You just encountered these creatures. And yet within a few hours you've given them their own Step Day.'

'It's not like that,' Willis said sternly. 'Remember, the Stepper is only an aid to releasing an ability to step that's innate in the first place. There *had* to be some sapient Martians who could step, or, surely, there'd be no Long Mars at all. But stepping is a lot less useful here, because the worlds neighbouring a habitable island like this are almost always going to be lethal. I'm only giving them what they have already, Frank. And besides, it's going to take a Renaissance *and* an Industrial Revolution for these guys to be able to figure out the meaning of the Long Mars, let alone how to make decent pressure suits.'

'But they are clearly inventive, technologically,' Sally said.

'And brave,' Frank said. 'They learn fast too—'

'Oh well, Pandora's box is open now. Or would you and that ass Mellanier say that's the wrong myth, Frank? Look, we need to stay in this world long enough to get the monolith data. Then we can move on. But I suggest we get the gliders in the air soon.'

'Why?'

'I think I'm learning to read these guys' body language. They seem a little anxious. Remember how I speculated about what kind of predator could make a two-hundred-and-fifty-foot-long animal grow armour plate? That thunder you thought you heard a while ago – I heard it too – that ain't thunder . . .'

30

Earth West 170,000,000, and more. It was May now; the expedition was in its fourth month.

Around the patient, solid forms of the *Armstrong* and *Cernan*, strangeness shivered, in worlds gathered in great sheaves. Worlds where the only oceans were shrivelled, briny lakes in wildernesses of rock. Worlds where the continents had never formed, and the only dry land was a scattered handful of volcanic islands, subsiding into tempestuous seas. Worlds where different forms of life itself had prevailed.

Gerry Hemingway and Wu Yue-Sai were concocting a probabilistic theory about the prevalence of complex life in the Long Earth based on the statistics they were gathering. Almost all Earths had life of some kind. But only around half of all Earths had atmospheres enriched by oxygen from photosynthesis, and only one in ten hosted multicellular life, plants and animals. Perhaps the stepwise geography they were mapping represented something like the history of life on Earth in time, projected across the higher-dimensional spaces of the Long Earth. On Earth it had taken billions of years for full photosynthesis to be evolved, and multicellular life was, relatively speaking, a late arrival. The more complex the life, the harder it was to evolve. Maggie didn't pretend to follow this argument, and thought it was probably premature to jump to conclusions anyhow.

Around Earth West 175,000,000 they again found a divergence from the simple-cell purple scum worlds. There was complexity in this island of worlds, but not at the level of a cell, or groups of cells, but at a more global scale. There would be a whole lake, even a sea, swarming with microbial life, yet all linked in hierarchies of communities, all contributing to a single, compound, protean life form. Fifteen years back the Valienté expedition had discovered one such entity, in retrospect freakishly close to the Datum: the beast Joshua Valienté had called First Person Singular, of a type that had since been named 'Traversers'. Maybe this band of worlds was the ultimate origin of such creatures.

Given Valienté's experience, the airship crews knew to be cautious here.

And still the ships plunged on into the unknown. Maggie was fascinated by the evolving panoramas of land, sea and sky she glimpsed through the windows of the observation galleries, and intrigued by the closer-up glimpses of the worlds they stopped at to sample in more detail. Yet, as they flew on, day after day, something in her recoiled from the bombardment of strangeness. And longed to come to some terminus.

On Earth West 182,498,761, Maggie watched an expedition of spacesuited crewmen explore yet another distant relation of North America, rich with intricately complicated and entirely unfamiliar life forms.

Gerry Hemingway arranged for one specimen to be brought up to the *Armstrong*. This was set up in a lab deep in the bowels of the gondola, with lamps that simulated the local daylight, under a plastic dome in which the methane-rich, oxygen-depleted local atmosphere could be reproduced. When he was ready, Hemingway invited Yue-Sai, Mac and Maggie to come and inspect his latest display.

They gathered around and peered down, frowning. Under the air dome, in a tray of local soil, stood what looked like a small tree, with a woody trunk and purple leaves. A yellowish thread was wrapped around the trunk, and yellow-white flowers poked out among the purple.

'It's like bonsai,' Mac said.

Yue-Sai laughed. 'Yes, as developed by some fellow on hallucinogenic drugs. That's the Japanese for you!'

'Just tell me what you see,' Hemingway said, reasonably patiently.

'A tree,' Maggie said briskly.

'Exactly. Though not remotely related to any tree species on the Datum, now or in the past.'

Mac said, 'But like all trees it's competing for the light. So it's photosynthetic. I suppose you could tell that from the purple and yellow leaves, the little flowers.'

Hemingway said, 'Yes. So, on this world there are clearly multi-celled forms, and some of them are photosynthesizers. But look closer at this specimen. They are *both* photosynthetic.'

Maggie scratched her head. 'They? Both?'

'Both the life forms you see here.'

Yue-Sai leaned closer to the dome. 'Actually it looks like a tree being attacked by something like a strangler fig.'

'Not *attacked* . . . I'm not being fair. I've had the benefit of a full biochemical analysis of these specimens.

Lieutenant Wu, on our Earth all life is based on DNA. Yes? We share DNA and its coding system and so on with the humblest bacterium. So we can say that all life on the Datum derives from a single origin. Even to get to that point, the DNA-life origin, there had to be earlier selections, by various evolutionary processes: the selection of a set of amino acids to work with, twenty out of the many possible alternatives, the choice of what kind of DNA coding to use . . . But other choices were possible. There may have been other origins of life, based on different choices. If so, those other domains were wiped out by our kind, the triumphant survivors.'

Mac grunted. 'Genocide, even at the root of the tree of life. So it goes. Hemingway, I'm guessing from your big build-up that things are different here.'

'They are. There are two life forms, under this dome. The tree is based on DNA like our own, and amino acids like our own set. But the other, the "fig", has a *different* suite of aminos. It uses a different genetic coding, with some of the information carried in a DNA variant, the rest in proteins—'

'Wow.' Mac straightened up. 'Life from *two origins* survived here?'

'So it seems. Who knows how or why? Perhaps there was a refuge, an island . . . For one thing the fig's chirality is different. Organic molecules aren't symmetrical; we describe them as left-handed or right-handed. All *our* aminos are left-handed. The aminos in the "tree" are left-handed. The aminos of the "fig" are right-handed.'

Maggie shook her head. 'So what? What does that mean?'

Mac said, 'I guess a left-hander couldn't eat a right-hander.'

'Well, it couldn't digest it,' Hemingway said. 'They could destroy each other. But look what they're actually doing.' They bent to see again. 'The fig is using the tree for support. You can't see another detail – in their tangled-up root systems the fig pays the favour back by bringing nutrients to the tree.'

'It is cooperation,' Yue-Sai breathed. 'No genocide here, Doctor. They work together to live. Cooperation, across two domains of life! What a wonderful discovery. My faith in the universe is restored.' She playfully patted Hemingway on the shoulder. 'There, you see! If two alien beings such as this can cooperate for their mutual benefit, why not us Chinese and you Americans?'

'I was born Canadian, not American,' Hemingway said, uninterested. He bent closer to the intertwined plants.

Maggie came to an impulsive decision. 'Let's leave this busy guy to his work. Mac, come with me.'

Mac raised an eyebrow. 'Problem, Captain?'

'Yeah,' she said privately. 'This issue with you and Snowy – enough with the frosty glares and moody silences. It's festered long enough, and I need to know what the hell the problem is.'

'What's brought this on now? Was it that tree and the strangler fig, living in harmony? You'll start singing "Ebony and Ivory" next.'

Glowering at him, she said nothing.

He sighed. 'Your sea cabin?'

'You bring the single malt.'

Shi-mi insisted on sitting in. Maggie insisted she stay out of sight, under the desk.

And, making it clear he resented being ordered to do so, Mac told Maggie the full story.

'Here's the main thing you got to remember, Captain,' Mac began, as he sipped his malt: his favourite, Auld Lang Syne. 'We meant well.'

'"We meant well." My God, I wonder how many sins have been justified by that line?'

'Look – this all happened in 2042, '43. A couple of years after Yellowstone. At that time the *Franklin* was still running Low-Earth relocation missions . . .'

As Maggie remembered too well. Military twains with their holds full of wide-eyed refugees, men, women, children, being taken away from their volcano-smashed homes and deposited in entirely unfamiliar worlds . . .

'If I recall you had about a year away from the *Franklin*.'

'Yeah,' Mac said, 'before I was called back to advise on the fitting-out of the new *Armstrong* and *Cernan*. You were somewhat busy, Maggie. And you didn't ask any close questions about what I'd done with my year away.'

'Hmm. Nor did I check the crew files. No need in your case. So I thought.'

'You wouldn't have found much, not without digging. The outcomes were kind of covered up . . . Maggie, I was sent to West 1,617,524.'

She knew that number, and wasn't surprised. 'The beagles' Earth. Snowy's world.'

'Yeah. I was conscripted – under Admiral Davidson's command, but it was a commission from higher up. I was part of a multi-service, multi-disciplinary party sent to establish some kind of formal liaison with the beagles, after the first contact in 2040. President Cowley and his advisers thought it was important to mount the mission even at a time of national emergency, to make sure we had a foot in the door. We were basically military, but there was genuine scientific interest, of course. We had anatomists, linguists, psychologists, ethnologists. Even a dog trainer. Look, it was a successful project. You saw the extension that's still running, under Ben Morton.

'We studied every aspect of the beagles' society, every aspect we were allowed to see anyhow, and we snooped on much of the rest. Maggie, beagles can't step, even with a Stepper box. Hell, you know that. Aside from that, they seem to be richly intelligent, individually just as smart as we are.

'But here's the headline. Despite their smarts, their culture is impoverished. I don't mean just technologically, materially, though they are stuck at the level of Stone Age herdsmen – or were, before the kobolds sold them iron-making and a few advanced weapons.'

Kobolds were something of an embarrassment: cunning humanoids, parasitical on human culture, and evidently using scraps of it to disrupt the destiny of others.

Mac said, 'The beagles' art is primitive, they don't have complex writing, their religions and civilization forms are crude. Their science is non-existent, although they have a decent tradition of trial-and-error medicine – based mostly on battlefield experience.'

Maggie frowned. 'So what? Maybe beagles don't need writing, for instance. I know that the beagles communicate by scent, by hearing – those howls Snowy likes to run off into the night to make . . . And didn't modern humans hang around for an age after *they* evolved, before they started painting caves and flying to the moon?'

'It's true. But in the end we did take off, there was a kind of spiral of invention. And, Maggie, though we've had calamities since then – the collapse of empires and shattering plagues and such – our progress has pretty much been, well, I won't say "upward", that's a value judgement. At least in the direction of more complexity. Yes?'

'OK.'

'And we tend not to lose what we invent. Oh, individual civilizations lose it all, but—'

'I get the picture. Once iron-making is invented, it stays invented. And the same isn't true of the beagles, I'm guessing.'

'That's what we found. You see, the beagles go through booms and crashes, catastrophic crashes. Because their societies aren't stable.

'It all comes from their breeding cycle. The problem is that beagles breed like dogs – that is, they breed copiously, with huge litters. A beagle Pack is a martial matriarchy, basically, with the authority of the Mother being expressed down through Daughters and Granddaughters, even Great-granddaughters. So if you have a period of peace you end up with a population boom – and, more significantly, far too many Daughters and Granddaughters.'

'Hmm. All of whom have an eye on the throne. I learned that from talking to Snowy. To kill you honourably is seen as a gift.'

'All very Klingon. Anyhow, any period of peace—'

'Inevitably ends in over-population and a devastating war.'

'That's the idea, skipper. In the end the conflict generally goes continental if not global, as Packs invade warring neighbours, and the rival Daughters rip each other to pieces over the spoils. Each period of recovery lasts no more than a century, maybe two, and then everybody's busted back down to hunting and gathering, and it all starts again.

'We learned this from the archaeology, but also from the accounts of the beagles themselves. They *know* what happens to them; they have oral traditions, histories shading into legend. But all they seek to retain from each cycle is weapon-making. They don't tend to save farming technology, for instance. Each Pack hopes that its descendants will be the ones to win the big global war next time. Which is why their weapons tech is relatively advanced, and little else is. Although their doctors are an exception, I have to say. They at least try not to forget all they learned.

'Anyhow, you see that the cycle of their history is quite unlike ours. And though they seem to have been around a lot longer than we have – maybe a half-million years according to some first guesses – they've been limited in their development. And all because of a flaw in their biology.'

Suddenly Maggie saw where this was going. 'A *flaw*. What's that but a value judgement?'

Mac growled, 'They have too many babies, too many litters. Their medical science doesn't go much beyond the treatment of traumatic wounds. They haven't even come up with the *idea* of contraceptive treatments . . .'

'And then in walk a bunch of idealistic humans, with simplistic theories and advanced biological science, and an impulse to meddle.'

'Maggie, it wasn't as crude as that. Imagine what we found when we got there. Snowy's people had just all but wiped themselves out. The ruling elite gone. This time the damage had been worse than ever because of high-energy weapons they'd been trading from the kobolds. We felt we had to do something. I mean, the fix was so *easy* to research, from what we know of dog anatomy, and easy to administer.'

'How did you do it?'

'In the water supply. Dropped by drone aircraft, across the continent. We didn't make the females unable to bear pups; we just reduced the litter sizes. We thought that was the best way; later, when they perceived the benefits, we could explain what we'd done, give them a choice.'

'My God. I guess we do have a track record of this kind of meddling with populations back on the Datum . . . So what happened, Mac?'

'The beagles we treated, when they stopped having big litters, thought they were cursed by their gods, or maybe infected with some plague by their enemies – a plague that made them nearly infertile. We tried to explain what we'd done, but they wouldn't listen.'

'They didn't blame you?'

'It was more that they don't take humans seriously. Their internal politics blinds them to everything else. The Daughters and Granddaughters turned on each other, each suspecting the other of poisoning or infection. And the neighbouring Packs, seeing their continuing weakness, started invading, from all corners. As things heated up, some of them *did* start to point the finger at us. We got out of there.'

'I bet you did. And the war got even worse, right?'

'We let it burn out. Then Ben Morton led the first party back in . . .'

'God knows what the long-term consequences are going to be. "Murder my people." That's what Snowy said. Got it about right, didn't he?'

Mac poured another slug of whisky. 'You know me. I'm a doctor, Maggie. I meant to help.'

'I thought the first principle of medicine was to do no harm. Well, you should have told me all this before. Oh, get out of my sight, Mac. Go back to work – no, hell, go find Snowy. Try to talk to him. Don't expect forgiveness; you don't deserve any. That's an order, by the way. And send him to see me.'

Snowy eventually showed up the following day. Shi-mi got out of the sea cabin a quarter-hour before he arrived.

Knowing the background now, Maggie tried to judge Snowy's mood, towards Mac, towards human-ity in general. 'Mac says they were trying to help you. Mistakenly, maybe, but—'

'Not hell-p. Cont-hhrol.'

'I don't think that was the intention.'

'Cont-hhrol.'

Well, maybe he was right. Even if the party of med-dlers hadn't understood their own deeper motives. 'Yet you flew with us. You're here now, talking to me.'

'Lea-hrrn about you.' He gazed at her, huge in the small human-scale cabin, his wolf eyes wintry. 'Some good, some bad, in stink-chhrotch kind.'

'Thanks.'

'Good in Mac, even. Docto-hhr. We have docto-hhrs.'

'Yes. He's a good man, if misguided sometimes—'

'But not cont-hrol beagles. Never-hhr again.'

'I understand . . .' Her comms light sparked.

He stood, saluted smartly enough, and left.

The comms call was an urgent one, from Ed Cutler on the *Cernan*. The sister ship had gone on alone, probing deeper into this band of worlds, which Gerry Hemingway had informally named the Bonsai Belt. Now it had come hurrying back. 'Captain Kauffman, you'd better come see this.'

'Tell me what you found, Ed.'

'The wreck of the *Neil Armstrong I*.'

31

Earth West 182,674,101. Another world of the Bonsai Belt, with roughly the same suite of dual-origin life.

And a crashed airship.

The *Cernan* had detected it through a radio beacon, picked up as it had sailed through this world in the course of its explorations. Maggie had ordered the comms teams to check for radio signals, routinely, at each step, even under fifty-steps-per-second cruise; a fraction of a second was enough to detect if such a signal was present. As far as the geographers could tell, the *Armstrong* had come down in a scrap of continental terrain that, on other worlds, would underpin much of Washington State. The *Cernan*, and now the *Armstrong II*, had had to travel a thousand miles laterally to reach the site.

The profile of the *Armstrong I*, an airship of the same class as the *Benjamin Franklin*, was unmistakable from the air.

'It looks like a whale carcass, dropped from the sky,' Mac said.

The crew were fascinated by the huge wreck, as they hadn't been by any of the natural wonders they'd seen so far. That was the Navy for you.

'And there are survivors,' Maggie pointed out.

You could tell that immediately. Near the fallen ship, rectangular fields had been scraped in the loamy ground, though the crops looked sparse. There were structures like tepees, evidently assembled from scavenged components of the *Armstrong*. And Maggie could see people, down there on the ground, looking up and waving. Among them were recently landed crew from the *Cernan* in their distinctive uniforms.

'Come on down, Captain,' Cutler called up. 'The air's fine in this world, the water's clean, the hospitality's great, and the potato fritters are cooking already.'

That made Maggie grin, but at her side Mac frowned. 'Is he for real? That doesn't sound like Ed Cutler.'

'Isn't he allowed to be pleased with himself? Finding the *Armstrong* was one of our mission goals, remember. And if there are survivors—'

'Maggie, my eyes are kind of rheumy these days. But those guys don't look to be wearing anything like Navy uniforms, or marine gear.'

'Well, they evidently turned into farmers, Mac.'

'Maybe. But *I* would dig out the old rig when Navy ships came calling. Wouldn't you? If only to avoid being shot at. And besides, Cutler hasn't sent up any identification of those characters with him. You'd think he would have; we have the *Armstrong*'s crew roster.'

'Hmm.'

'Look, we don't know anything about how the *Armstrong* got here, who these guys are.'

'OK, you old spoilsport. We'll take precautions. But I think you're being over-cautious. Hey, Nathan.'

'Captain?'

'Do we have any Fourth-of-July fireworks on this tub?'

The XO grinned. 'We have multicolour flares.'

'Break them out.'

'My name is David.'

Maggie led her party in from the set-down site, past the wreck of the *Armstrong* and towards the little habitation. The man who greeted them was young, no more than twenty-five, twenty-six. Good-looking, confident, with an accent she couldn't quite place, he walked boldly up to her and shook her hand. With him were four others, three women, one man, all about the same age. All very impressive, was Maggie's first take, even if the clothes they wore were pretty ragged.

And none of them had been crew of the *Armstrong*.

Maggie introduced her own team, drawn from both *Armstrong II* and *Cernan*: Mac, Snowy, Nathan, Wu Yue-Sai, others. The strangers stared at the beagle, but did not seem alarmed.

Cutler was beaming from ear to ear, like he'd found Santa Claus. He introduced David's companions. 'Let me see if I remember.' He pointed. 'Rosalind, Michael, Anne, Rachel. All with the same surname – Spencer – not siblings, but from one extended family, Captain.'

David patted him on the back. 'Well remembered, sir!' They broke away into a huddle of friendly chatter.

Maggie murmured to Mac, 'You're right. That's *not* like Ed Cutler. Is he *blushing* to be praised by that boy?'

Mac said, 'These characters are somewhat – what's the word? *Charismatic.* That's my first impression. My mother once took me to Houston, when they were still flying astronauts on the shuttle. Place full of function-aries, office workers. But when an astronaut walked through the room, every head turned . . .'

Maggie was aware of a soft friction at her leg. It was Shi-mi, rubbing her face on Maggie's trouser, hiding behind her legs.

Maggie knelt down and whispered, 'I thought you didn't come out when Snowy's around. Or Mac, in fact.'

'The dog smells me. I know he *smells* me . . . But this is important. Danger, Maggie Kauffman. Danger!'

'What, from these shipwrecked characters? What kind of danger?'

'I'm not sure. Not yet. Listen, Captain. Post a guard. Set up your men around a perimeter so they can't all be taken out at once. Have the airships monitor your movements. If I were you I'd send one ship over the horizon, or step it away . . . Take precautions. Whatever you think best.'

Maggie frowned. But she remembered Mac's cautious appraisal. 'OK. Against my better judgement.' She summoned Nathan and gave orders to pass on to the crew, and McKibben's marines.

'**Please, be** our guests. We are *so* pleased you found us at last . . .'

David and his companions led the party of officers past the wreck, through the fields, towards the tepees. Maggie could see that the tepees were indeed built of materials scavenged from the *Armstrong*, aluminium struts, fabric from the broken envelope. As they walked, two of the women were talking quietly. Their speech was fast, fluid, as if speeded up, and Maggie couldn't make out a word.

Gerry Hemingway slowed, his attention evidently snagged by what he saw in the fields. They didn't look too impressive to Maggie, just scratches in the dirt, but there were potatoes and beets growing. However, what caught Gerry's eye was a field in which some of the native life was growing, like a display of bonsais. Their colours were strange, their scent unfamiliar, exotic. And the tiny trees seemed to be wired up in a kind of net of fine cables, no doubt more salvage from the airship, that were fixed to their roots. The cables led to a bank of batteries, and glass jars of water that bubbled languidly. 'You go on, Skip,' he said. 'Let me take a look at what they're doing here.'

She nodded. 'OK. But don't be alone. Santorini, stay with him.'

'Yes, Captain.'

The largest tepee was spacious enough for a dozen people to sit on blankets in the dirt. The day was warm, mild, still, and a heavy sheet that covered the door was thrown back. In a hearth in the middle of the floor a small fire burned. Maggie, Mac, Cutler, Nathan Boss, Wu Yue-Sai crowded in. Rachel had gone off with the rest of the crew, while Michael prepared some kind of hot drink on a frame over the fire.

David sat on a box, overlooking his guests, with Rosalind and Anne at his side.

Mac grunted at the layout. 'Guy's like a Saxon king with his thanes.'

'Yes,' Maggie said. 'But he has the character for it, you have to admit.'

'Hmm. And look how Wu is staring at him. Like she'd have his babies here and now . . .'

David said now, 'As I said – we are so glad you came. You can see we are stranded here, just the five of us, the only survivors of the *Armstrong*. Of course we could all step away. But we aren't even sure how far we are from home.'

Nathan Boss rattled off the number of the world for him. David thanked him, and to Maggie's chagrin Nathan looked pleased to be favoured, just like Cutler.

David said, 'But the number scarcely matters. Even if we could step so far we could not walk through the lethal worlds you have crossed already – worlds without oxygen, worlds whose whole biospheres are soaked in sulphuric acid. And we could not contact you. We had to wait for rescue.' He grinned. 'Now you can bring us home.'

And what an honour that would be for her, Maggie thought helplessly. Like she'd found Elvis. The guy really did have an air of command.

She tried to snap out of it. 'So tell us what happened.'

Mac grunted. 'In fact, you can start by telling us how the hell you came to be aboard the *Armstrong* in the first place.'

David appraised the two of them. 'You are skilful, Captain. You ask the soft questions, while allowing the Doctor to wield the baton.'

'If only we were that smart,' Maggie said ruefully. 'And anyhow this isn't an interrogation, David. Please just answer the questions.'

'We are from a community you know as Happy Landings. You would be able to determine that much from the *Armstrong*'s log.'

Mac nodded. 'I know of it. Somewhere around a million and a half steps from Datum, right? Kind of a peculiar place, Captain. Explains the accent, I suppose.'

David said smoothly, 'The first *Armstrong* called there, on its own journey to the far stepwise West. We five were selected as passengers, guests, for the next leg of the journey. We were thrilled. Off to the far Long Earth, aboard a military twain! But things went badly wrong. The engines – the crew lost control . . .'

Maggie left it to Mac to question them closely about the details of the incident. David and the others were vague about places and times – what precisely the engineering problem was, where exactly in the greater Long Earth they were when the crew lost control, what their stepping rate was, how the crew tried to handle the situation.

After a time, while Mac continued the question-and-answer, Nathan Boss tugged Maggie's sleeve. 'Captain – does Mac have to interrogate them so hard? They survived a wreck. They've been stranded here, cut off from the rest of mankind, for years. In the middle of an alien ecosystem too. They're damned impressive to have survived at all, let alone to be so – composed.'

'They are, aren't they?'

'Of *course* they aren't going to know the engineering details of the crash. The crew will have kept them isolated, as safe as possible, protected from the crisis . . .'

Yue-Sai was on Maggie's other side. She seemed to have got over her first star-struck reaction. 'But even so they seem very vague about it all, for individuals evidently so intelligent.'

Maggie noticed that Rosalind and Anne were observing this sidebar discussion. Again they whispered to each other, and again Maggie strained to catch that peculiar high-speed talk of theirs.

Yue-Sai said, 'Captain, if I may, I would like to go inspect more of this little colony for myself.'

'You do that.'

As Yue-Sai stood up, David smiled and held out a hand to her. 'Please, don't leave us.'

It was a request, not a command. Yet it seemed to have a peculiar effect on Yue-Sai. She stood frozen, as if unwilling to disobey him. But then she shook her head, turned away, and left the tepee.

'And you say there were no survivors,' Mac pressed now. 'From the crew, I mean. None but the five of you.'

David spread his hands. 'What can I say? They kept us safe – in an inner cabin, far from the gondola walls – while they struggled to save the ship. We broke out later, after the crash. I can show you the cabin if you like.'

'I'm sure you can.'

David described how over the following days, weeks, they had taken the bodies, bagged up, to a burial site some distance away. 'We needed to stay here, by the wreck. We needed its raw materials for our survival, and we knew any rescue attempt would be drawn here. We buried the bodies decently.'

Mac pressed him on exactly where. David was vague, as if distressed to be pushed to recall such a difficult time.

'All the questions you ask, Doctor Mackenzie – look, the *Armstrong* crew saved us. They gave their lives to do so. This is the noblest sacrifice imaginable. Really, is there anything else to be said?'

Even Maggie felt there wasn't. 'Let's take a break.'

Quietly, however, she detailed Nathan to keep David and the others as busy as possible. 'The rest of you, spread out. There are only five of them, they can't tag us all.' Then she turned to Mac, who remained expressionless. 'I don't know if anything's wrong here. But—'

Mac said, 'These kids are just too damn likeable. Right?'

'Something like that. I'd prefer to take a look around myself . . .'

32

Maggie found that the reactions of the crew to these Happy Landers was extreme – mixed, but extreme. 'Like they all love them or hate them,' Mac growled. 'Mostly they love 'em,' he admitted.

In those terms, Gerry Hemingway was a lover.

'You should see what they've done with the native ecosystem, Captain. Those experimental fields out front? You understand we have a mix of life origins here on this world, with Datum types – our DNA type – mixed in with at least one other kind. Well, they've been experimenting, through domestication, even a little genetic tinkering using equipment scavenged from the *Armstrong*'s lab. They're developing useful crops, for food, fabrics, drugs, from the DNA stock. And they're using the partner life forms to support that – as nitrogen fixers, for instance, pest control, even using them as natural, self-repairing supports for the crops.'

'And that affair with the wires and the batteries and the jars?'

'Power production. Milking the photosynthesiz-ing plants for energy to be stored in the batteries, or to crack water for hydrogen. They've made incredible progress, though it's hard to judge the details – hard to judge exactly what it is they've done, they don't seem to write stuff down. And when they try to explain it – Rachel spent fifteen minutes with me, she was open enough, but—' He shook his head. 'I was a slow starter at grade school, you know, Captain. Made up for it later. Speaking to her, to this kid from the boonies, from some place where they don't even have proper schools – this kid who must have been self-taught in every discipline we discussed – Captain, she made my head spin. I felt like I was back at grade school again, and she got kind of impatient when I couldn't keep up, like she wasn't used to being asked to clarify her statements.'

Mac grinned. 'Well, that's how you make the rest of us feel, Gerry.'

Maggie said, 'Shut up, Mac. So they're – well, they're smarter than us. More inventive, faster learning.'

'I'd say by a significant degree,' Hemingway said seriously.

'I'd agree with that,' Mac said. 'And not just smarter academically. Smarter with people too. You can see it by the way they're *dazzling* everybody. It's all subtle signals, subtexts, body language. All working just under the radar of the conscious mind.'

'But they ain't foolin' you, huh, Mac?'

'Maybe I'm better at recognizing this stuff than most. I did some psychology options before they let me out into the wild, you know. Once did a term paper on Hitler. How he got so many people to do what he wanted. You can analyse it quite specifically.'

Hemingway scoffed. 'You're not seriously comparing David, say, to Hitler.'

'These guys are *worse*, potentially. Hitler had the charisma but he wasn't all that smart – probably wouldn't have lost his war otherwise. These characters are smarter than us – Maggie, I'd like to try IQ tests and such on them, I predict they'd break the scale. Definitively smarter. And smart people can fascinate, baffle, like a magician bamboozling a five-year-old kid.'

If Hemingway was a fan and Mac an immediate sceptic, Wu Yue-Sai, despite seeming briefly dazzled herself, was definitely growing suspicious. She showed Maggie around the rest of the settlement. Most of the fields were scratches, the structures half-finished. And, in a roughly dug pit, there were heaps of ration packs from the downed *Armstrong*, all scraped clean, even MREs, military-class meals ready to eat, usually a last resort when it came to cuisine choices.

'Captain, one must have sympathy for their plight. Whatever happened to bring them here, we have five Crusoes, pitched into an alien wilderness with a challenge to survive. Yet they are five young people, strong, healthy and *very* smart, who have spent *years* here. And, aside from their remarkable experimental set-up which Lieutenant Hemingway has shown you, they have made remarkably little progress. It's as if what they have achieved, save for the basic provision for shelter and so on, has been – well, for show. Half-finished, abandoned.'

Mac grunted. 'Eating off ship's rations while meddling with the plants' genetic make-up. Five Doctor Frankensteins.'

'But no Igor,' Maggie said with a grin.

Wu Yue-Sai said slyly, 'Actually I understand that reference. It is odd you should say that, Captain. I think they *do* have an Igor.'

'What do you mean?'

'Look here.'

She showed them one of the secondary structures, a rough tepee that contained nothing but a heap of fire-damaged clothing, presumably hauled from the crash. Yue-Sai had examined the structure closely, even pulling the supporting struts out of the ground. And she had found, roughly scratched into one strut – far enough down that it would have been buried, out of sight – a pair of initials.

'SA,' Mac read. 'There's no "S" among the group we met.'

Yue-Sai said, 'Indeed not. Then who is SA? Was it SA, in fact, who built this structure?'

At that moment Snowy came running. When he really wanted to move fast he went down on all fours, big, strong, wolf-like, and very animal, despite the adapted uniform he wore, the gloves on his paw-hands. He was a bizarre and terrifying sight.

When he reached Maggie he stopped, straightened up, as if morphing back to human form, and saluted her. 'Captain. I have ff-found . . . You ss-see.'

Making his own investigation, he'd followed scents. That was very wolf-like, Maggie thought. Covering a lot of ground quickly, he'd followed one trail to a clump of forest, of comparatively tall trees in this bonsai world. In the heart of the wood he'd found a cage, swathed in silver survival blankets under a covering of leaves – those blankets would have rendered the set-up invisible to infrared sensors, Maggie realized.

And in the cage, Snowy had found a man, bound and gagged, in the remains of a marine uniform.

Maggie immediately snapped out orders. 'Nathan, go round up those superstars and tie 'em down. Use lethal force if you need to.'

Nathan Boss hesitated for one second – that was the glamour fighting against Navy discipline in his head, Maggie thought. Then he said, 'Yes, Captain.'

'Mac, Yue-Sai, Snowy, come with me. Let's go rescue that marine.'

It wasn't hard to bust open the cage.

When they'd got through, Maggie went in herself to release the man. She pulled the gag away from his mouth tenderly. He was filthy, rough-shaven. He whispered hoarsely, 'Thank you.' Yue-Sai had a water flask. She passed it over and he drank greedily, his gaze flickering nervously from one face to the next. 'Hey, Wolverine,' he said at length. 'Don't eat me.'

'He's a member of my crew,' Maggie said reassuringly. 'His name's Snowy. Acting Ensign Snowy.' She turned to Mac. 'Now do you see why I brought him along?'

'Thank you, Snowy,' the marine said seriously. 'Without you finding me – well, I reckon those damn Happy Landers would have left me for dead, after you took them off this place. Probably only kept me alive after you showed up as an insurance policy. Or hostage, maybe. They think things through, all ways up.'

'I know you,' Maggie said. She smiled. 'Though I've seen you looking better. You served under me on the *Franklin*.'

He grinned. 'Until you booted me off for screwing up a ground patrol at a place called Reboot, Earth West 101,754, Captain.'

'I remember. Sorry about that.'

'No, you were right.'

'Lieutenant Sam Allen, right?'

'Yes. US Marines. But I'm a Captain now.'

'OK, Sam. This is Joe Mackenzie, my ship's surgeon.'

'I remember you too, sir.'

'Sure you do, son.'

'I'll have Mac look you over, and get you out of here and up to my ship. And then we'll have a serious talk with David and the rest.'

'Captain—'

'Yes, Sam?'

'My wife and kid. I guess they'll think I'm dead.'

He was on the verge of tears, and Maggie imagined a five-year flood, pent up. 'I know they're fine. I met them at the—'

'The funerals?'

'They're waiting for you in your family home. Benson, Arizona, right? Where you grew up. We'll take you back, son. We'll take you back.'

'Are we under arrest?'

David and the others sat on the ground, out in the open, hands visible. Armed marines circled them, well out of range, and the scene was being watched over by two airships.

'Well?' David snapped. 'If so, under what authority? Military, civilian? Do you claim to be acting under the US Aegis? Can such a concept be any more than a fiction in a world so remote that the very genetic basis of life is different – where nothing like North America, even, is recognizable?'

Maggie studied him. He was handsome, forceful, quite unafraid, very impressive. He seemed to have a sense of entitlement about him, a right to power over others, that she had seen in scions of old-money families, for instance. And yet there was more than that, something outside human norms. Something compelling, hypnotic.

She murmured to Mac, 'If I start falling under his spell, pinch me.'

'I'll do that, Captain.'

Sam Allen, showered, fed, tended to by Mac, in a fresh uniform that didn't quite fit him, stood by

Maggie. 'Don't let him take the lead, Captain. He's smart with words. Even when he doesn't know what the hell you're talking about, he can work it out awful fast. Filling in the gaps, figuring stuff out. Before you know it, he has your head spinning like a top.'

David sneered at him. 'I wonder how you survived at all, among us.'

'By not listening to a word you said, pretty boy.'

'OK, David. Let's just hear it. The unvarnished truth, please. You come from Happy Landings. You grew up there, right?'

From a fragmentary account drawn from David and the rest, interspersed with more of that high-speed private language between the others – and interrupted by Sam Allen, who during his years here had picked up more of the truth than David and the others seemed to have realized – Maggie pieced together the full story. Almost everything they'd been told so far was a lie. But the five had come from Happy Landings.

Happy Landings was a strange place, that was clear enough. Even in the annals of USLONGCOM, the Long Earth military command, it was a legend, a piece of exotica, an odd little community off in the wilds that seemed to have been around long before Step Day. Some kind of natural accretion point for steppers, where trolls lived alongside humans, in apparent harmony. And where, to any visiting outsider, a lot of the kids seemed alarmingly bright . . .

Maggie had insisted that Shi-mi join her in these sessions for background briefings. Now the cat murmured privately to Maggie, 'Did you know that Roberta Golding was from Happy Landings, originally? And now *she* is in the White House.'

Even before Yellowstone, before the great flood of refugees out of Datum America and the rest of the planet, there had been trouble in Happy Landings. Since Step Day many more people had been moving around the Long Earth than the earlier handful of natural steppers, and more had been arriving in Happy Landings than the community could absorb. Everybody was upset by this sudden flux of outsiders. These were people who didn't fit in with the local ways and didn't *want* to – and, worse for such a private community, started to feed back accounts of peculiar features to the Datum authorities, and attracted still more unwelcome attention.

'They were in turmoil,' David said, with some contempt. 'The mayor. Our so-called leaders, elders all of them.'

'Let me guess. You stepped up to help.'

'Our insights were deeper, those of us of the younger generation. Our minds qualitatively stronger.

Qualitatively. Do you understand what that means, Captain? We *think* better than those who went before us. This is a demonstrable fact. And this despite our lack of years.'

Mac growled, 'You offered to take over, did you? A benevolent dictatorship.'

'We offered leadership, if that's what you mean. We would not have excluded the elders. We knew we needed their knowledge, experience. But the wisdom was ours.'

'Ah. The wisdom, and the decision-making. I'm guessing your offer was politely refused. And I'm guessing you were prepared for that refusal.'

It had been a kind of coup d'état.

'We had acolytes in all the townships,' David said, sounding almost dreamy, like a kid recounting some feat at school sports. 'We had weapons. Our planning was meticulous, our preparations entirely unsuspected. One morning, Happy Landings woke up in our control.'

'It didn't last long,' Sam Allen said with contempt. 'Their glorious reign. Getting them out was bloody, however. Captain Stringer – of the *Armstrong I* – knew more of the detail than I ever did. What's for sure is that by the time this bunch were put down, there were a lot of dead, among their own followers, I mean, as well as those who supported the "elders", as they put it.

These five were the ringleaders. Five twenty-year-old Napoleons. According to the mayor, they showed no remorse.'

'Remorse?' David said, as if surprised by the word. 'To feel remorse would imply that one accepts some mistake, would it not? We made no mistake. Our rule would have been the optimal way forward, for Happy Landings. This can be demonstrated logically, even mathematically—'

'I don't want to know,' Maggie snapped.

'The elders seemed unsure what to do with them,' Sam said. 'They don't practise capital punishment in Happy Landings. They didn't want to lock them up for ever, for as sure as eggs is eggs they'd bust out some day. And they didn't want to turn five young psychotic geniuses loose on the rest of humanity.'

'Well, that was benevolent,' Mac said wryly.

'And then, in the middle of all this, our twain showed up in the sky . . .'

After making the crew of the *Armstrong* welcome, the elders of Happy Landings made a request of the Captain. They knew the ship was going on, further West, into the deep Long Earth; its mission was a kind of pre-Yellowstone precursor of Maggie's own. They wanted Stringer to take David and the rest to – well, some place like this. A world so far out in the reaches of the Long Earth that they could never physically walk back. A permanent exile. Some day, perhaps, they could be brought back home, if they repented, reformed, or if some way could be found to contain them safely. In the meantime, the rest of humanity would be safe.

Maggie frowned. 'How would the elders even know such a place as this existed? The *Armstrong I* was the first to go out there.'

Sam Allen smiled. 'They deduced it. They proved to themselves it had to exist, that the kind of waves of deadly worlds and such that *you* found must be out there. They aren't as smart as these kids, but smart enough. And they were right, weren't they? Well, Captain Stringer agreed. I think he figured that if he couldn't make the exile idea work, he could always ship 'em back to the Low Earths, and deal with them there.'

'But it all went wrong,' Mac said gloomily.

The five of them had seduced half the crew and bamboozled the rest. They soon broke out of their secure quarters, and found ways to bypass the ship's controls.

'And the damnedest thing is that some of us, the crew, were *helping them*,' Sam Allen said. 'You wouldn't believe it if you saw it, Captain. They can read you like a book – hell, before they rose up I once tried playing poker with 'em and they cleaned me out.

Their men preyed on our women, and the women on our men. It was like they could read your mind. And they set everything up so smart, when they rose up they had got hold of almost everything before we even knew what they were doing. Well, Captain Stringer, and me, and some of the others, we organized to fight back. That was when the killing started.'

Mac grunted. 'That's what you get when you breed little Napoleons. So they started two wars before they were twenty-one years old.'

Allen went on, 'This time they won. David and his gang, and his followers among the crew – they *won*. We'd gone further out than this world – I'll give you the reference, Captain. There are more folks awaiting pick-up out there, more survivors of the *Armstrong* . . .'

David, in control of the vessel, had ordered a sweep of the ship, rounded up any survivors among the crew. Then he'd had them put off the ship. Even those who had supported the Happy Landers were dumped; they could not be trusted.

All but Sam Allen, who, when he saw how things were going, had hidden away, in the interior of the *Armstrong*'s vast envelope.

The rest of it was simply told. The *Armstrong* had been turned back. David and the others, living it up in the Captain's quarters, began to lay plans on how to make a second, successful takeover attempt at Happy Landings. How they would then march on the Lower Earths, even the Datum itself. Allen just hid out.

As soon as the *Armstrong* was isolated from the stranded surviving crew on the one hand, and from the worlds of humanity on the other, Allen had emerged from hiding and caused a wrecking crash – here.

'I had no plan beyond that point, Captain Kauffman. Figured I didn't need one – I probably wouldn't survive the crash, or for long afterwards even if I did. After we were down and stranded they debated killing me.' Now he shuddered, showing emotion for the first time. 'Not out of revenge, you understand. They did it coldly, Captain. Logically. Like I was a broken-down horse to be disposed of, or a dog gone wild. Like my whole self, my life up to that point – my wife and kid, dammit – didn't matter at all. They really do think they're different from us, Captain. Above us. Well, maybe they are, for all I know. But they kept me alive, in the end. Put me to work. Thought I might yet have knowledge they could use. And maybe they had some plan to use me as a hostage, if the worst came to the worst. Like I told you, they think things through every which way. I had to build that cage in the woods myself, the cage I was to be kept in.'

'With your initials on it,' Yue-Sai said.

'Oh, yes. And I marked other stuff they made me build for them. They may be smart, but they ain't all-seeing. I knew somebody would come by some day, seeking the *Armstrong*. And so did they. That's why they didn't attempt to repair the ship, or rig up environment suits so they could walk out, or take their farming seriously, or anything like that. They knew there would be a follow-up mission. You were to be their ride home, I guess. All they had to do was wait for you – and take you over, like they took the *Armstrong I*.'

Mac turned on David. 'So that's the story. How do you plead?'

David frowned. 'Is this suddenly a trial? Do you believe this man's drivel?'

'Every word of it.'

'I plead duty, then. Duty to my kind, and yours.'

My kind. That phraseology chilled Maggie. She murmured to Mac, 'They seem – passive.'

He grunted. 'Not passive. Just calm. Some of the accused at Nuremberg were like this. He's confident. He believes he's in control, still – or will be soon.'

David said now, 'You need not take us back to Happy Landings. Take us back to your worlds – the Low Earths. We have learned of Yellowstone, from your crew. Let us help rebuild the Datum Earth. Our leadership, our wisdom, would be invaluable at such a time. Indeed, from what we have heard from your crew it sounds as if some of us have been at work there already, quietly.' He smiled. 'It is our duty to help you. It is *your* duty to allow us to do so, Captain.'

Maggie shook her head. 'You'll have to show me your study on Hitler some time, Mac. David, you really are good. There's about twenty per cent of me longs to agree with you.'

'Then let yourself agree. We offer you order. Security.'

'Hmm. The security of the sheep in the fold? The order of the serf under the lord of the manor, like poor Sam Allen here? No, thanks.

'I think this is the safest place for you, for now; if you'd been able to break out of here you'd have done it by now. So we're going to complete our mission. We'll collect the *Armstrong* crew en route. We'll call back here on the return leg. Maybe we'll take you home, if I think we can do it securely . . . Well, that's my plan. Whereas you're confident you can bring me down, aren't you, if you get the chance? Like poor Stringer. Well, you won't get the chance, not from me. If I'm not absolutely certain I can have you contained I'll just leave you here, and kick this particular ticking bomb upstairs when I get back to USLONGCOM. I'll leave a team to keep you under guard. Mac, work with Nathan and McKibben to pick a bunch of ornery souls who won't fall for their blarney. Sam, you can advise them on that.'

'Yes, Captain.'

'For sure you're going to face charges in federal courts – sabotage, murder. Whether or not this place is under the US Aegis, Happy Landings certainly is, and so was the *Armstrong*.' She stood up.

David said smoothly, 'But I have not yet finished speaking, Captain.'

Even now, the tone of casual command. 'But I'm done listening to you. OK, Sam, you come with me. You've done a hell of a job here. Dinner at the Captain's table for you . . . Mac, we ought to fix up some kind of counselling for the crew affected by this. I'm thinking of Gerry, for example. And Wu.'

'Good idea, Captain.'

'Hmm. Why not book us all in? All who've had contact with these characters. Yes, me too. I feel like I need a detox of the soul. Now let's get out of here.'

33

After Joshua Valienté was released from custody by the cops who had apprehended Paul Spencer Wagoner and his companions, he told Lobsang what had happened.

And Lobsang asked another of his friends to help.

Nelson Azikiwe, who was once more assisting David Blessed at a Low Earth footprint of his old parish in England, quickly ascertained that Paul Spencer Wagoner, and his companions from Madison, had been part of a wider group of Next youngsters swept up without notice in a snap action coordinated by police, military and Homelands Security: an action that spanned the American Aegis of the Long Earth. By May 2045 Paul and some of the rest had been transferred to a facility at Pearl Harbor, the old naval base on the Datum Hawaiian island of Oahu.

Oddly, Nelson wasn't very surprised to learn about the existence of the Next. After all, Lobsang had been anticipating the rise of something like these Next for many years, and he and Nelson had discussed such possibilities at length. Once, for example, five years ago, on a twain hovering over a living island, seven hundred thousand steps West of the Datum:

'Humanity *must* progress,' Lobsang had said. 'This is the logic of our finite cosmos; ultimately we must rise up to meet its challenges if we are not to expire with it. You can see that. But, despite the Long Earth, we *aren't* progressing; in this comfortable cradle we're just becoming more numerous. Mainly because we have no real idea what to do with all this room. Maybe others will come who *will* know what to do.'

'"Others"? . . . So you believe that the logic of the universe is that we *must* evolve beyond our present state, in order to be capable of such great programmes. Seriously? Do you really believe a brave new species can be expected sometime soon?'

'Well, isn't it at least possible? At least logical?'

Nelson remembered those conversations with Lobsang very well, on that living island. Where there had been a woman who wore a red flower in her hair, a woman called Cassie with whom Nelson had made sensational love – only once, but that had been enough.

It had been one of the most vivid moments of his life – and one of the most incautious, given that neither of them had used any kind of protection. He wondered often how Cassie was, and berated himself as a coward for not going back again, and resolving that he would, just as soon as the latest crisis was over. But there was always another crisis, and another, and never a good time . . .

Even then, Lobsang had known they were coming, this race of superhumans. Of course he had – Lobsang was tuned in to the deeper currents of the whole world, of all the worlds of the Long Earth. And so, it appeared, it had come to pass. But in the end *Homo superior* turned out to be a bunch of scattered children who needed Nelson's help, said Lobsang.

So be it.

The island state of Hawaii, Nelson discovered, had been spared the effects of Yellowstone as much as had anywhere in the world.

The Navy facility itself had been built into an old bombproof shelter near the base. Though now shared with the Air Force, the facility was still the headquarters of the US Pacific Fleet, as well as serving as the base of USLONGCOM, the Long Earth military command under Admiral Hiram Davidson. To Nelson

Azikiwe, when he flew in, the facility, flattened under heavy Pacific sunlight – a naval base swarming with military, an underground bunker proof against steppers (and even if you could step away into a Low Earth footprint you'd still be on Hawaii, you'd still find yourself on an island surrounded by thousands of miles of ocean) – could hardly have been more secure.

That is, a more secure prison.

It had taken a good deal of ingenuity for Nelson to concoct a story to get him inside this facility. His cover was that he had volunteered to serve as a kind of chaplain to the inmates. His background as a Church of England vicar helped make that a lot more plausible, of course.

And his network of online buddies known as the Quizmasters had been extremely helpful in setting up his cover – well, this kind of operation was their cup of tea, as his parishioners back in St John on the Water might once have said. Of course they were generally so bright that some of them might well be Next themselves. On the other hand, there was always a downside to the Quizmasters. Nelson found he had to work hard to distract them from their ongoing obsession of the last five years that Yellowstone had either been an act of war, directed against the Datum US government by its enemies, or set up *by* President Cowley's administration for purposes of its own.

The military transport plane had begun its final approach. Nelson focused on the issues of the present.

Once off the plane, Nelson was led through a short blast of open-air heat that made him feel all of his fifty-three years, and into a surface building. He found himself in an anteroom with air conditioning, potted plants and a receptionist behind a desk: a room full of Pacific light. Save for the insignia of various command units on the wall, it was like the waiting room for an upmarket dentist.

An officer came out to meet him, a woman, fortyish, in a crisp Navy uniform. 'Reverend Azikiwe?'

'Call me Nelson. I'm freelance these days.'

She smiled, pushed back a lock of greying blonde hair, and shook his hand. 'I'm Louise Irwin. Lieutenant. I'm in operational control of the treatment of the patients here. We've corresponded, of course, but it's good to meet you in person.' She led him out of the room, nodding to the receptionist, and used a swipe card to guide him through a doorway. They walked down a narrow corridor with low polystyrene ceiling tiles, very mid-twentieth century. 'How was your flight? Those military transports can be a little rough. The room we've assigned you is in a neighbouring block. If you need some time to freshen up—'

'I'm fine.'

'You'd rather go straight to see our charges, wouldn't you? It's a very understandable reaction. There really isn't any substitute for encountering them in person. That's true of most psychiatric patients, of course. You're going to need full security clearance but I can swipe you through for now.'

They came to an elevator that opened for Irwin's card. It descended smoothly, if slowly.

Nelson asked, 'Is that how you think of them? As patients? Not as prisoners?'

'Well, that is my background. I trained as a psychiatrist, and found I needed a little more excitement in my life, and I joined the Navy. Now I'm a psychiatrist who travels.' She smiled again.

'I guess we're all chameleons. We chop and change during our lives.'

'As you have,' she said, studying him with an evident insight that felt faintly disturbing to Nelson. 'I read your file, of course. Anybody allowed in a facility like this has to have a biography as long as my arm – and *you* came with top personal recommendations, to serve as our inmates' personal chaplain. A kid from the South African townships who got his chance through a Black Corporation scholarship; a respected archaeologist; a Church of England vicar . . . You've adopted many roles.'

Nelson knew all about the 'personal recommendations'. His credentials for being allowed in had essentially been engineered by the Quizmasters, along with Lobsang, through a web of behind-the-scenes contacts – including a little help from Roberta Golding, he'd been surprised to discover, the rather glamorous, in-the-news White House staffer who'd taken some kind of personal interest in the inmates of this place since they'd been brought here, though for now Nelson had no idea what her connection was to all this. On the other hand the substance of his record as seen by the US Navy had mostly been genuine. When lying, it was always best to tell as much truth as possible. And he really did intend to serve as a chaplain for these imprisoned children, to the best of his ability, until the time came for his deeper purpose to be revealed.

The elevator slid to a halt. The doors opened smoothly to reveal a metal-grille walkway, suspended over a kind of compartmented pit.

Irwin led him along this pathway, and Nelson found himself looking down into a series of rooms: *into*, for these rooms all had transparent ceilings, even the bathrooms, though Nelson imagined that some visual trickery ensured the ceilings looked opaque from underneath. The rooms individually didn't seem all that impressive, or unusual. They were like small hotel suites, each a bedroom-cum-study equipped with TV and computer terminal and other gear, a small bathroom. The rooms had been personalized, with posters and souvenirs, clothing in the cupboards (all of which lacked doors) or heaped on the floor. Nelson felt as if he was looking down into something like an upmarket campus dorm. But heavily armed and body-armoured marines patrolled this high walkway, pointing their weapons down into the rooms below.

In most of the rooms there was a single person, alone – all young, aged maybe five years old to early twenties, both sexes, varying ethnicity – some fat, some thin, some tall, some short. Ordinary-looking, at first glance. Some had company, an adult or two, generally talking quietly. There was a lounge where a few of these inmates gathered, and a small crèche where infants played amid a litter of toys. Both crèche and lounge were supervised by adults, men and women in civilian clothes. One room was more like a small clinic, where a girl was having samples taken, blood, a cheek swab for DNA.

And Nelson soon spotted Paul Spencer Wagoner, the friend of Joshua Valienté, alone in a room, reading on a tablet.

Through Lobsang and Sister Agnes, Nelson had at last got to meet Valienté properly, and to know him.

Joshua was a man whose Long Earth exploits Nelson had studied for many years – and, Nelson suspected, another ally of Lobsang's in whatever long-term game that mysterious entity was playing. Joshua had asked Nelson to look out especially for this Wagoner kid, who had wound up in the same kids' home, Sister Agnes's Home, as Joshua himself a few decades earlier . . . And now here was Wagoner in this military cage.

Lieutenant Irwin was saying, 'A few hundred of these individuals are known in the American Aegis, though the sweeps continue. This is the largest single group we're holding. Of course there must be others of foreign nationalities. So. What's your first impression?'

'It's a prison. An impressive facility. But it is a prison.'

She nodded. 'We're wary of them. We don't know what they're capable of—'

'They're in glass boxes, like lab rats. With armed guards twenty-four seven. You have young teenagers in there. Can you really give them no privacy?'

'These were the security protocols mandated. We try to normalize their environment as much as possible. You may baulk at this confinement, Nelson. They look like ordinary kids, don't they? Ordinary young Americans. But they're not. Any contact with them and you'll find that out for yourself. In fact they distinguish themselves from us, you know. They do call themselves *the Next*. Of course they're only youngsters. But they have quite a lot of money behind them, actually, or some do. Also some of their parents have the resources to fight this. The Navy is having to dig deep fending off petitions from some fancy lawyers.'

'Hmm. Fancy lawyers who are arguing about such irrelevancies as these kids' constitutional rights, I imagine. US citizens swept up and imprisoned without any semblance of due process. A few foreign nationals too?'

She raised an eyebrow. 'I'm going to enjoy debating such issues with you, Nelson. But I suspect you are rushing to judgement. We had to do *something*. And remember, I am a naval officer. The purpose of this place is to maintain national security.'

'They don't seem such a terrible threat to national security to me.'

She nodded. 'Well, that's one of the things we are here to ascertain. Generally they are no trouble, from a disciplinary and control point of view. Most of them quickly adapted to confinement, actually, which is because so many of them have been through processes of care, fostering, even prison at the juvenile or adult levels. They are institutionalized, *used* to confinement. Says something about how well our society has been able to handle these individuals, right? And if they do play up they are removed from this part of the facility.'

'To where? A punishment block?'

'A special therapy facility.' She studied him. 'You do use judgemental language. You need to keep an open mind, Nelson. Until you get to know them. They are extraordinarily acute – perceptive, controlling, manipulative. In person they can be very difficult to deal with, one to one. But it's when they get together that – well, they take off. Their talk is incredible, rooted in English but super-fast and dense. We have linguists analysing their talk, as best they can. Whatever they are discussing, we can at least measure the sheer *complexity* of the talk. And that itself is far beyond the norm. I was shown a transcript, of a kind of argument being developed by a girl called Indra; there was a single sentence that went on for four pages. *That* is one of the simpler examples. Often we don't even know *what* they are talking about—'

'Concepts beyond the human, perhaps,' Nelson said. 'As unimaginable to us as the mystery of the Holy Trinity would be to a chimp. If these kids really have arrived in the world equipped with these super-powerful minds, they must come up against the limits of our mere human culture very quickly.' He smiled. 'How wonderful it must be, when they are free to talk together. How much they must be discovering, beyond the imagination of any human who ever lived.'

She was watching him. 'You know, I think you're going to make a fine chaplain. But let me tell you something even more remarkable. Even more *different*. We have a few infants here – and we're monitoring even younger subjects, even babies, who are still with their families. Before the age of about two, the young ones will try to talk – well, as human infants do. They gabble out stuff that's entirely incomprehensible to us, and mostly incomprehensible to the older ones – but not totally. Again the linguists have analysed this stuff; they tell me it's like investigating the structure of dolphin song. These infant gabblings are languages, Nelson. Meaning they have actual linguistic content. We arrive in the world with the capacity for language, but we have to learn it from those around us. Next babies, trying to express themselves, *invent their own language*, independently of the culture, word by word, one grammatical rule after another. Only later do they start to pick up the language of the rest. And, still more remarkable, the others incorporate some of the infants' inventions into their own shared post-English tongue. It's like an entirely new language is emerging, mutating at a ferocious rate, right in front of our eyes.'

'When you let it happen. When you let them speak to each other at all.'

She didn't react to that. 'It's important you understand what we're dealing with, Nelson. These children represent a different order, a step change. Something new.'

'Umm. And yet they *are* children, in our care.'

'So they are.'

'I think I should get settled in. I imagine there are superior officers I need to be presented to.'

'I'm afraid so. Also you need to get through your security processing.'

'Then I'd like to talk to some of the inmates. One at a time, to begin with.'

'Sure. Any preference who first?'

As if at random, Nelson pointed down at Paul Spencer Wagoner. 'That one.'

Nelson was allowed, in fact encouraged, to speak to Paul in the nineteen-year-old's own room.

Nelson could see that made the security set-up easier to manage, but he wasn't sure about the psychology of it. When *he* was nineteen, twenty, he hadn't had a room of his own, but he was pretty sure that if he had, he would have seen it as an imposition to have some stranger walk in and start talking about God. This was the condition of the meeting, though, and Nelson made the best of it.

Paul's room was only sparsely customized, by the standards of others Nelson had seen – or rather, had looked into from above. Posters on the walls: a galaxy image, exotic Long Earth beasts, a singing star Nelson didn't recognize. On the desk, a phone, tablet, TV, though Nelson had learned that the connections you could make on these devices were sparse and tightly controlled, here in this facility.

Paul himself, slim, dark, was dressed in a black coverall. All the inmates here had to wear coveralls, Nelson had learned, but at least you got a choice of colours, and only the most defiant chose Gitmo orange. Paul evidently wasn't the most defiant. He just sat on the edge of the bed, arms wrapped around his torso, legs crossed, a blank expression on his face. A classic sulky-teenager pose.

Nelson sat opposite, on a chair. 'I bet you didn't choose any of this stuff,' he said as an opener. 'The posters and such. This is some elderly Navy officer's idea of what people your age like, right?'

Paul returned his stare, but gave nothing back.

Nelson nodded. 'Lieutenant Irwin, who showed me around earlier, said a lot of things about you and your colleagues in here.'

Paul snorted, and spoke for the first time. '"Colleagues"?'

'But the most perceptive single word she used, in my view as far as I've formulated it, was this: *institutionalized.* And that's what you're falling back on now, right? The blank stare, the silence. The old tricks you learned to survive, in one institution or another. That's OK. But you were lucky, you know. I can tell you there are worse institutions to fall into than the one that caught you, in the end. I mean the Home in Madison West 5.'

Paul shrugged. 'All those nuns.'

'Right. And Joshua Valienté. He's a friend of mine. He sends his regards.' Nelson stared at Paul, trying to send a subliminal signal. *You aren't alone. Joshua hasn't forgotten you. That's why I'm here, in fact . . .*

Paul just smiled. 'Good old Uncle Joshua. The magic stepper boy. Maybe *he* should be in some cage like this. What is *he* but the vanguard of a new human species?'

'Well, in fact there are similarities. The whole Humanity First movement, that brought President Cowley to power, grew out of fear of steppers.'

'I know. That bunch of nuts blew up Madison because of it. The nest of the stepping mutants.' He mimed an explosion with his hands. 'Ka-boom!'

'Can you understand people feeling that way? About you, I mean?'

'I understand it in the abstract. The way I understand much of how you dim-bulbs think. Just another aspect of the madness that grips most of you, for most of your waking lives. It goes back to witch hunts, and even deeper. If something goes wrong – it's somebody's fault! Find somebody *different* to blame! Burn the demon! Fire the ovens!

'Oh, of course they've come for us. They were always going to. At least this prison they put us in is secure. I suppose we should be grateful for the organized madness of the US government, which is protecting us from the *disorganized* madness of the mob. But after all, we haven't actually *done* anything to anybody, have we? We aren't like steppers, who could in theory walk into your child's locked bedroom and so forth. That's something worth fearing. All *we've* actually done so far is make a little money. But that was enough to condemn the Jews under Hitler, wasn't it?'

Nelson studied him. He was coming across now like a defiant youngster, a member of some punk-revival band, maybe, out to shock. Nelson realized he had no real idea what was going on in Paul's head. 'But you have the potential for much more than that in the future. Do you believe it's rational that we should fear you?'

Paul studied him back, as if briefly interested in what he'd said. 'Insofar as you're capable of being rational at all – yes. Because we are a different species, you know.'

These words, delivered matter-of-factly, were chilling. 'You mean, unlike the steppers—'

'Who are genetically identical to the rest of you. Stepping is just a faculty, like a gift for languages, that people have more or less of. We are all potential steppers. *You* are not a potential Next. The bumbling dim-bulb scientists at this facility have confirmed what we have long known. We have an extra gene complex. This is expressed physically in new structures in the brain, specifically the cerebral cortex, the centre of higher processing. They're studying that here too, though thankfully without cutting our heads open, at least not yet. *My* brain contains a hundred billion neurons, each with a thousand synapses, just as yours does. But the connectivity seems to have been radically upgraded. In your head, the cortex is like a single sheet of crinkled layers, folded up inside the skull – spread out it would be around a yard square – with about ten billion internal connections. The topology of the cortex in my head is much more complex, with many more interconnections . . . It cannot be modelled in less than four dimensions, actually.'

'Hence you're a brighter bulb.'

Paul shrugged. 'The biological definition of a species is the ability to interbreed. Our claim of species differentiation is blurred, but it is real enough.' He smiled. 'Do you have a daughter, Nelson?'

The question took Nelson by surprise. He remembered that living island, a woman with a red flower in her hair . . . 'Probably not.'

Paul raised his eyebrows. 'Odd answer. Well, if you did, she could serve as an incubator for my child. Who would be one of us, not one of you. Does that offend you? Does that frighten you? Does it make you want to kill me? Perhaps it should.'

'Tell me how this has happened. If you understand it yourself.'

Paul laughed in his face. 'Oh, you seek to manipulate me through challenging me. I will tell you only what the dim-bulbs in this place must already have figured out. It's not hard, after all. I was born in Happy Landings, as you probably know. And I am a Spencer, on my mother's side. You've heard of the place.'

It had loomed large in the talk of Lobsang and Joshua.

'If you know about Happy Landings, you know about the trolls. Nelson, the secret is the trolls. Happy Landings is infested by them, and their presence has shaped that particular society. Not every human being gets along with the trolls, and vice versa. With time, there has been a selection pressure. Only a certain *kind* of human is welcomed to Happy Landings. Even some of those who are born there know, somehow, it is not for them. There is nothing mysterious about it, nothing psychic, merely a question of complex group dynamics spanning two humanoid species, humans and trolls, working over centuries – many generations, long before Step Day, as the place was accidentally populated by natural steppers. But the outcome, unplanned, unintended, is that there has been a selection for a greater human intelligence. Of course there must have been some competitive advantage. Maybe only smarter humans can accept the blessing of the company of trolls . . .'

'And the result is what I see before me?'

He shrugged. 'Right now Next are emerging all over. Many colony worlds are in turmoil because of the great population flow from the Datum, after Yellowstone. Maybe it's something to do with the stress of all that. Dormant genes suddenly expressing. But, and I'm sure your dim-bulb scientists have worked this out, many of the emerging Next can trace their ancestry back to Happy Landings, especially to the old dynasties, the Montecutes, the Spencers. *That's* the source of the new genetic legacy.'

And a random memory came back to Nelson: Roberta Golding, who had done so much to set up his own assignment here, was originally from Happy Landings . . .

'But on the other hand,' Paul said now, 'we could only have arisen in the Long Earth. Happy Landings, the forcing ground, is a uniquely Long Earth phenomenon, is it not? The unconscious mixing of two separate humanoid species could never have happened on the Datum. The trolls could never have survived at all on Datum Earth, not alongside *you*, you clever apes, smart enough to destroy everything around you, never smart enough to understand what it is you are losing in the process . . . The trolls needed to be protected by the Long Earth, protected from *you*, in order that they could participate in the production of *us*, in such crucibles as Happy Landings.'

'"Such crucibles." Are there others?'

'Oh, yes. Logically it must be so . . . Anyhow, you're a chaplain. I thought you were here to talk about God, not Darwin.'

Nelson shrugged. 'I'm being paid by the hour, not by the topic. We can talk about whatever you want to talk about. *Do* you have any views on God?'

Paul snorted. '*Your* gods are trivial constructs. Easy to dismiss. Animistic fantasies or mammalian wish complexes. You are lost children longing for papa, and casting his image into the sky.'

'Very well. And what do you believe?'

He laughed. 'Give me a chance! I'm nineteen years old, and in jail. We've had no time to address such questions, not yet. I can tell you what I *feel*. That God is not *out there* somewhere. God is in us, in our everyday lives. In the act of understanding. God is the sacredness of comprehension – no, of the *act* of comprehension.'

'You should read Spinoza. Maybe some of the yogis.'

'If we have the time we may come closer to the truth. And if we have a *lot* more time, we may be able to render it into a form even you dim-bulbs can comprehend.'

'Thanks,' Nelson said dryly. 'But you say *if*. You're implying you won't be granted that time.'

'Look around you.' He waved up at the blank ceiling. 'Look at the uniformed ape with an assault rifle up there. Or so I deduce his presence. How much time do *you* think the dim-bulbs will allow us?'

'And do you fear that, Paul? Do you fear death?'

'Hmm. Good question. Not individual death. But there are so few of us still, Nelson, that death for us means extinction of our kind. And I fear *that*. For all that is left unsaid, all that is left undiscovered, unexpressed. Are we done? I'd kind of like to watch some TV now.'

Nelson paused for one second, considering. Then he rapped on the door to summon the guard.

34

The crew of the *Armstrong I* were not difficult to find, a few worlds further out from the Napoleons, and unreasonably grateful for their rescue. Maggie allowed a day's partying to celebrate.

Then the mission continued. The airships *Armstrong* and *Cernan* pressed on into the unknown.

The airships had left West 5 in January. It was now May, and life on board wasn't getting any easier, especially when they crossed through uninhabitable worlds, and the ships had to be locked down. Harry Ryan was growing quietly concerned about the state of his engines. The quartermaster, Jenny Reilly, sent Maggie depressing reports about the ships' ability to withstand a continued push across worlds that could not provide them with even basic necessities – edible foodstuffs, oxygen, sometimes there wasn't even potable water. The crew were exhausted, stir-crazy and increasingly fractious. Joe Mackenzie fretted about their health, the illnesses and injuries they were slowly accumulating, and the steady depletion of his medical supplies. But then, he always did.

But despite all the niggling problems Maggie still had her eyes on the nominal target she'd been given for this mission: to reach Earth West 250,000,000. The best estimates showed that the goal was still well within the ships' consumables budget and system lifetimes. And it was after all a prize worth achieving; once it was done everybody on board would go to their graves still cradling the memory of it. This jaunt would dwarf the famous Chinese expedition to East 20,000,000 five years ago – and it would by quite some way surpass even the one-way journey of the *Armstrong I*, which had ultimately reached the world of the young Napoleons, more than a hundred and eighty million steps out. *That* was a fantastic journey that had for too long gone unreported and needed its story told, even if it would take some of the gloss off what she'd achieved in *Armstrong II*.

The trouble was that the final leg from Planet Napoleon to Good Old Quarter Billion, as she had taken to calling it, represented over a quarter of the total mission still to be completed – at least three weeks' running time, probably more like over four. And of course they would have to come back the same way.

And as the journey wore on, and the Earths became ever more exotic and challenging, Maggie sometimes felt as if it was only her own willpower that held the mission together.

The latest narrow band of worlds hosting complex life, the Bonsai Belt, had terminated at around Earth West 190,000,000, and they found themselves drifting once more over endless purple scum worlds.

Earth West 200,000,000 was another numerical milestone that Maggie used as a chance for a couple of days' rest, recuperation, systems check. But the world itself was one of another band blighted by supercontinents, one hemisphere a vast bowl of Mars-red desert, the other a featureless mask of lifeless ocean. The oxygen levels were low here, and she couldn't in all conscience sanction any shore parties, which did nothing to help morale. Then, beyond Earth West 210,000,000, oxygen levels once more collapsed entirely. This persisted even though, after around West 220,000,000, the supercontinent features abruptly fractured.

And beyond that point, the crews of the airships *Armstrong* and *Cernan* encountered increasingly unfamiliar and difficult Earths.

There were a lot more Gaps, for one thing, holes in the Long Earth that had to be cautiously, but hastily, traversed. Worlds with very exotic biota. Such as a thin band of worlds dominated by tremendous trees, trees whose slim trunks towered *above* the twains, and Gerry Hemingway's best guess was that they might be three miles tall, their canopies – wonderfully, impossibly – higher than most mountains . . .

There were worlds where the atmosphere was much thicker than on the Datum, or much thinner. The crews had to battle with the buoyancy of the ships in such unfamiliar airs, and the engineers fretted about corrosion by acidic gases, and the battering of ultraviolet from the unscreened sun.

There were worlds with one moon, bigger or smaller than the Datum's, or many moons, or no moons at all.

There were even worlds where the gravity was different. On the low-weight worlds the ships floated over landscapes that generally looked more or less like the Mars of the Datum sky, with thin air and huge mountains and canyons that could span continents. In the partial gravity the airships were difficult to handle, the crew played jumping games, and the trolls hooted in dismay, tumbling. On other worlds, though, the gravity was stronger than on the Datum. Under thick blankets of atmosphere, winds scoured landscapes bare of any life but stunted-looking trees. The ships, their buoy-ancy inadequate, were pulled towards the ground, and if they lingered any length of time the crew complained that it felt as if packs of rocks had been loaded on their backs, like a punishment-detail training exercise.

Hemingway had some ideas about what was going on. At the root of Earth's formation was violence, as a cloud of dust spinning around a young sun had col-lapsed into rocks that smashed each other to pieces – or, sometimes, collided to form bigger rocks, which in turn formed bigger rocks yet . . . Emerging from this chaos, Datum Earth with its moon had in the end been born as a result of a final titanic head-on collision between two young worlds, one Earth-sized, the other the size of Mars. It was all a series of accidents; it could have turned out lots of other ways. And now Maggie was finding sheaves of worlds so remote from her own that even that primordial sculpting had turned out differently.

Gerry wondered what this was telling them about the nature of the Long Earth, the relation of these par-allel worlds to each other, and stepping.

'How far away from the Datum model in terms of Earth's formation can you go, before it's no longer Earth at all? We know that even if an Earth is miss-ing altogether you can step into the Gap remaining, but at least an Earth *once* existed there. But what if, for instance, an Earth hadn't congealed at all – what if we found a cloud of asteroids kept from aggregating by some nearby gas giant, say? Is that where the Long Earth would terminate at last, and no more stepping would be possible?'

Well, they hit no such terminal condition on this jaunt. But to Maggie's mind the most remarkable Earth of all was West 247,830,855.

This Earth was not a planet at all, but a *moon*: a mere moon, of a greater body. The moon-Earth was smaller than the Datum, hotter, the air denser – more geologically active, Gerry speculated, because of tidal squeezing by its big primary world. 'It's a mutant cross between Earth and Io, moon of Jupiter,' he said gleefully. Yet even here they found life, and complex life at that. One drone returned a striking image of what looked like pterodactyls to Maggie, huge bony flyers swooping around an active volcano.

And the sky was dominated by the primary, a nameless world that had no counterpart in the solar system of Datum Earth. This too was a rocky world, more like Earth than a gas giant like Jupiter, say, but many times more massive than Earth itself. It was a big angry ball that hung unmoving in the sky, though the sun wheeled beyond it; the Earth-moon was so close to the primary that it was tidally locked, with one face turned forever to the giant world. And as the primary itself turned it revealed sprawling continents, tremendous oceans, dense, smoggy air, and flaring volcanoes to match the activity on its Earth-moon.

They stayed a full twenty-four hours to study this object. Maggie thought the crew took more amateur photographs of this world than of any other sight they'd come across, save only the wreck of the *Armstrong I*.

And, most tantalizing of all, on the primary's darkened hemisphere, they saw lights. Maybe only campfires, but still . . .

'It's maddening,' Maggie said to Mac. 'We'd need a spaceship to get over there. We stepped a quarter of a billion worlds to get here. And now we can't cross a few thousand miles to go see all that.'

Mac only smiled. 'We have to leave something for the future to achieve. Damn, this bottle of Auld is empty. This ship is running out of single malt, just like most other essential supplies. I think I have an emergency ration in my cabin . . .'

Bowing to a petition by the scientists, and some of the more adventurous crew, Maggie left a small party behind to explore this Earth-moon further. Then they moved on.

35

On May 24, 2045, four months after leaving the Low Earths, the US Navy airships *Armstrong* and *Cernan* reached their nominal target of Earth West 250,000,000.

The world itself turned out to be unprepossessing, barren, ordinary, but at least you could land on it with a facemask, walk around a little. The crew built a stone cairn, affixed a bronze plaque, set up a Stars and Stripes, took a few photographs. When Wu Yue-Sai showed images of a similar ceremony performed by the crews of the *Zheng He* and *Liu Yang*, who had reached Earth East Twenty Million, they built the cairn up a bit to make sure it was bigger than the Chinese one. The trolls looked out from the observation galleries – they weren't about to wear facemasks to go outside – and sang a sweet barbershop-quartet kind of song, over and over as a round, that sounded as if it had been selected to celebrate the journey, about how it was mighty nice, a trip to paradise, with my baby on board . . .

Even Douglas Black came down to the surface, with his aide Philip at his side. At Maggie's quiet order, while he was off the ship Mac was never more than a few yards from Black, with full medical kit to hand. Black looked around, smiled, chatted, and allowed himself to be photographed alongside the crew, but refused to do any more than that. This achievement was the crew's, he said; he was only a passenger, cargo. He did collect a handful of the local dirt, and slipped it into a plastic bag: a mundane souvenir of an unprecedented journey. Maggie rather liked his lack of ostentation.

There wasn't much else to do here. Some of the crew played an improvised game of golf as a tribute to Alan Shepherd, an American hero who was one of their own, a Navy man who had once played a golf shot on the moon.

Then they turned the ships around, metaphorically speaking, to head Eastwards, and home.

At this point Douglas Black made another rare emergence from his suite, and asked a special request of Maggie.

They had logged Earth West 239,741,211 on the way through, but had not lingered long. Now they returned, for a longer stay.

This was one of the smaller worlds, with a mere eighty per cent of Datum Earth's gravity. On the local version of the North American craton, tremendous glacier-striped mountains strained for a sky laden with fluffy water-vapour clouds, and in the valleys impossibly spindly trees clustered. The animals too were tall, slender, graceful, even though a peculiar six-legged body plan had prevailed. This world was, according to Douglas Black, just like a Chesley Bonestell painting, and all of them save Mac had to look up that reference to see what he meant.

When Maggie authorized shore leave, the crew loved it. Delightfully, thanks to an atmosphere that happened to be especially rich in oxygen, you could walk around with no special protection whatsoever. Harry Ryan and his engineers wandered around planning how they would span mighty gorges with graceful viaducts. Snowy was at last able to indulge his appetite for the hunt, and went bounding away. Even the trolls seemed happy here, despite the low gravity, and they sang a new song, playfully taught them by Jason Santorini: 'Lucy in the Sky With Diamonds'.

When the moon came up, Maggie could see the grey and the white, the lunar seas and the highlands, were all wrong. Proof, if she needed it, that this was far from home.

But – as Douglas Black announced to Maggie as they walked in convincing-looking grass, with Philip shadowing them, and Mac silently looking on – Black intended to stay here. 'I found my real estate, at last,' he said.

'Hmm. On this world of all the worlds, of all the possibilities for life on Earth that we saw?'

'I always knew what I was looking for, Captain. I had a quite detailed specification, and my staff have scrutinized the records of every single world we stepped through. And this place fits the bill, most nearly, of all those we have witnessed. Now, I have prepared for this possibility. In my sealed cargo I have everything required to establish a home here, safe, secure, provisioned. For now I need only Philip at my side, my staff, my equipment. I would ask only of you, Captain, that you take the news of this place back to the Low Earths, announce this location, stepwise in the Long Earth and geographically – I will give you the name of an appropriate agent to handle this, although of course the regular news channels will disseminate it – and in due course others will follow me here.'

Maggie was puzzled. But when she asked Mac's advice, the doctor shrugged, evidently having no particular objection.

Maggie said, 'I'll tell you the truth, Mr Black. You might not be alone. Some of my younger crew are thinking of jumping ship and staying here. It's an open secret. Thanks to my XO I can tap into the scuttlebutt.'

Black seemed delighted. 'I would be glad of the company of young people. Of course we could assist each other . . . And are you thinking of permitting this?'

'Why not? I can't let the manning numbers run down so far that the ships themselves are compromised, of course. But we have some slack. My mission is more about planting flags than planting colonies, but my orders don't expressly forbid it. It would extend the US Aegis in a concrete form, a pretty long way out. And it will be an international colony, if Lieutenant Wu is serious about staying.'

'Ah! That delightful young officer. She would be very welcome. Her children will be tall and slender and have big chests for the thin air. Just like the Martians of Ray Bradbury! What do you think, Captain? How about yourself? You are healthy, still young. You too could stay, build bridges, raise babies.'

'Oh, I think my own duty is clear, Mr Black. It's home for me, with my ship.'

'Of course, Captain. But will you allow me one privilege? Earth West 239,741,211: an efficient but cold label. Let me name this world, as if I were its discoverer. I will name it Karakal. Please record it in your log.'

That baffled Maggie, who had been expecting some name like *Blackville*.

But Mac recognized the reference. '*Lost Horizon*. The Tibetan mountain where they found Shangri-La, in Hilton's novel.' He looked around. 'Ah, I see now. That's the clue. You picked a world of gravity so low that even a lard-bucket like me can leap like a basketball star, and oxygen levels so high the air is like wine. Of course, I should have guessed. This Earth, you hope, is going to turn out to be a machine to keep you alive. Even reverse your ageing. Like this whole world is an extension of that oxygen tent you have in your cabin! Your very own Shangri-La.'

'That indeed is the idea, Doctor.'

Maggie asked, 'Can partial gravity really reverse ageing?'

Mac grinned. 'It's one of the oldest space-buff dreams, Captain.'

'Yeah, but I thought low gravity was bad for you – leaching away the calcium from your bones, wasting your muscles, messing with your body's fluid balance . . .'

Black said, 'That's true for *zero* gravity, Captain. Partial gravity is different. Surely *this* world's pull will be sufficient to keep the muscles strong, the juices flowing as they should, with appropriate diets, exercise regimes and so forth. But by allowing the body to spend less energy just fighting gravity – the cells will oxidize more slowly, the joints, the ligaments, the dubious architecture of the spine will all be stressed significantly less – there *is* a strong argument that life spans could be significantly extended.'

Maggie turned to her chief surgeon. 'Mac?'

He spread his hands. 'There's an argument, maybe. But not a shred of hard evidence. Very little research has been done on the effects of partial gravity, and won't be until the day we have data from long-duration stays on Mars or the moon. However, it's Mr Black's choice, his money.'

'Oh, come, Doctor; at my age, my position in my life, don't you think it's a gamble worth taking? And it's not just my money by the way. I'm representing a consortium of backers – none of them adventurous enough to take this trip with me, but all willing to follow, in the next year or two. They will come with their staff, their own doctors . . .' He smiled. 'Now do you see the vision, Captain? Among my backers are Americans, Europeans, Chinese, politicians and industrialists and investors, some, frankly, closer to the dark edge of the law than others. Old money and new – some indeed who made a fortune out of the Yellowstone aftermath, for every disaster is an opportunity for somebody. Some people, you know, got rich even out of the fall of the Roman Empire. The Long Earth is still young, and we are very wealthy indeed; with time we'll find ways to wield our influence even from this remote world. Now if you'll excuse me – come, Philip, we need to find a location for our first settlement and get established before the airships leave . . .'

Maggie stared after him. 'A community of the fabulously rich, Mac. Rich and ageless, if this all works out as he dreams.'

'Well, it might. Oxygen and low gravity – that's quackery, probably. But they'll be bringing in teams of researchers who'll have nothing else to do but find something that *does* work.'

'And if so it really will be a Shangri-La. Without the monks.'

Mac grunted sceptically. 'Or a community of struldbrugs, like *Gulliver's Travels* – undying but ageing, and growing more and more bitter. A gang for whom even death will no longer bring an end to their clinging to wealth and power. Think of all the monsters of history who you wouldn't want to see still around today, from Alexander through Genghis Khan to Napoleon . . .'

'It might not be like that. Maybe they will give us a longer perspective.'

'Hell of a gamble if you ask me. So are you going to allow this, Captain?'

'I don't see I'm in a position to stop him. He's not crew, Mac.'

'I guess. Well, I'm glad *I* won't live long enough to see what grows from the seed you planted today.'

'You old cynic. Come on, let's get back to the ship and go home.'

36

The *Galileo* crew had left behind the world of the sand-whalers and the monoliths with, as far as Frank Wood was concerned, a sigh of relief.

And it was only when they were safely in the air, passing over yet more clones of dead Mars, one every second, that Frank began to relax, that the military man inside him began, grudgingly, to release his hold on events. How they had got away from ferocious fire-spitting land-dragons and harpoon-hurling sand-whalers – not to mention some kind of monstrous unseen Martian tyrannosaur – without harm to themselves or their equipment, he had no idea. And he kept remembering that crustacean prince, as Frank had labelled him (or her) in his head, humiliated by his leader with one of Willis's Stepper boxes. What kind of consequence was that going to have? But, he supposed, that was a problem for the future, not for right here, right now.

In the days that followed, while Willis paged through the screeds of images the whalers had retrieved for him from the monoliths, and Sally sank back into her own default mode of wary silence, Frank spent a lot of time asleep, nerves slowly recovering. He wasn't as young as he used to be.

And he was only peripherally aware of the new Jokers the expedition came upon, and paused to study.

A flooded Mars, where, it looked like, the whole of the northern hemisphere was drowned by an ocean. Here beasts not unlike the sand whales roamed the land, while what looked like cities floated on tremendous rafts on the sea. 'Fishermen', crustacean types, came ashore in land-yachts to hunt the whales, just as on Earth land-dwellers harvested the fruit of the sea . . .

A drier Mars, whose copy of Mangala Vallis was nevertheless covered by forests, of tough, low, needle-leaved trees. Willis was tempted to linger here because he thought he saw two forest clumps in slow-motion conflict with each other: a war waged at the speed a flower grew. 'Birnam Wood besieging Dunsinane!' he said. But they could not afford a long enough stay to study this slow encounter properly . . .

A plain covered in rocky coils, like heaps of rope. Willis's first guess was that these were some kind of volcanic extrusion. But when he took *Thor* down for a closer look the coils unwound into pillars of basalt, gaping mouths opened, and gouts of flame shot out at the hastily retreating glider: another variation on the theme of sand whale . . .

Once, Sally swore, on a moist but chill Mars, a glacial Mars, she saw a herd of *reindeer*, off in the northern mist, coats shaggy, antlers held high, animals much larger than their terrestrial equivalent. But the others could not see it, and the cameras could not penetrate the mist for a clear image. None of them understood what this vision, like a race memory of the Ice Age, might mean . . .

And, every so often, Frank thought he saw flickering forms in the valleys of Mangala, far below. Translucent sacs, like survival bubbles; gaunt forms like landed sand-yachts. As if they were being followed. Probably the product of paranoid dreams, he thought.

Finally, eleven weeks since the landing and nearly three million steps from the Gap, Willis Linsay said he thought he had found what he was looking for.

37

To Sally, piloting Frank in *Woden*, it was just another dead Mars. As seen from a high altitude the basic shape of the landscape, the tangle of Mangala Vallis below, the great rise of the Tharsis uplands to the north-east, looked much as she remembered it from spacecraft images of the Datum-Earth Mars, taken decades ago in a reality all of three million steps away.

Behind her, Frank, sleepy, grumpy since they had run out of caffeinated coffee a week back, was also unimpressed. 'What the hell can he have found, if even a new set of Commandments from God on those damn monoliths wasn't good enough?'

'It's not visible to the naked eye,' said Willis from *Thor*, his voice crackling over the comms. 'I've had optical and other scanners searching for it, from both gliders.'

Sally said, 'Tell us where to look, Dad.'

'More or less east. You won't see it, not from here. Use your screens . . .'

Sally fooled with her screen, looking in the direction he'd told her, exploring the bulging Tharsis province landscape under the usual featureless toffee-coloured sky. She saw a lot of horizontals, the uneven horizon itself, craters reduced to shallow ellipses by perspectives, gullies on the uplifted flanks of the volcanoes, all painted a monotonous brown by the ever-present dust. No odd shapes, no unusual colours. Then she allowed the software to scan the image for anomalies.

'Oh, my,' said Frank. Evidently he had done the same thing, about the same time. 'I was looking at the ground, the landscape. The horizontals.'

'Yeah. When all the time . . .'

There was a *vertical* line, a scratch of very un-Martian powder blue, so fine and straight and true it looked like an artefact of the imaging system, a glitch. It rose up out of the landscape from some hidden root. Sally let the image pan, following the line upwards. What was this, some kind of mast, an antenna? But it rose on up into the sky – up until the imaging system reached the limit of its resolution, and the line broke up into a scatter of pixels, still dead straight, fading out like an unfinished Morse code message.

Frank said reverently, 'Arthur C. Clarke, you should be seeing this. And, Willis Linsay – respect to you, sir. You found what you were looking for, all this time. I get it now.'

Willis said, only a little impatiently, 'OK, let's get the fan-boy stuff out of the way. I take it you understand what you're looking at.'

'A beanstalk,' Frank said immediately. 'Jacob's ladder. The world tree. A stairway to heaven—'

'What about you, Sally?'

Sally closed her eyes, trying to remember. 'A space elevator. Straight out of those wonders-of-the-future books you used to give me as a kid.'

'Yeah. Future wonders of my *own* childhood, actually. Well, here it is. A cheap way of getting to orbit, basically. You put a satellite in orbit to be the upper terminus of your elevator string. You need it to hover permanently over the lower terminus, which is on the ground. So you put it over the equator, or close to, at an orbit high enough that its period matches the rotation of the planet.'

'Where they station the communications satellites.'

'Right. Mars has about the same day as Earth, so a twenty-four-hour orbit does the trick here too. Then you just drop a cable down through the atmosphere—'

'The engineering details of *that*,' Frank said dryly, 'are left as an exercise for the reader.'

'Then you fix it to the ground station, and you're in business,' Willis said. 'Once it's in place, no more expensive, messy rockets to get off the planet. You get a cable-car ride to the sky, fast, cheap, clean. In principle this technology will work on any world. Any Mars. *This* Mars is better than our own, in fact, because it doesn't have any pesky low-orbit moons to get in the way.'

Sally was plodding through the logic of this situation. 'Let me get this straight, Dad. You *predicted* you were going to find a space elevator on Mars – I mean, somewhere in the Long Mars. How did you know? Who built it? How *old* is it? And why do you want it?'

'How did I know? It was a logical necessity, Sally. Any advanced society on a Joker Mars is going to strive to reach space, before the window of habitability closes, as close it must. And if a spacegoing culture does arise, then a space elevator is going to be something they're going to reach for, because it's so much easier to build here on Mars, than on Earth. *Who* built it? Irrelevant. Somebody was bound to, given enough time – enough chances, in the worlds of this Long Mars.

'As to why I want it – look, we need this back on Earth.

'The big challenge for a space elevator is getting hold of a cable material strong enough. On Earth, you'd need a cable twenty-two thousand miles long, and said cable has to hold up its own weight, against the pull of gravity. If you used fine-grade drawn steel wire, say, you'd only be able to raise your cable through thirty miles or so before it would pull itself apart like taffy. That's a long way short of twenty *thousand* miles. In the old days there was much fancy talk of special materials with a much higher tensile strength – graphite whiskers and monomolecular filaments and nanotubes.'

'You understand this was all before Step Day,' Frank said. 'When because of *you*, Willis, everybody got distracted by travelling stepwise instead of up and out, and the dreams of opening up space were abandoned.'

'OK, my bad. But, Sally, the point is that building an elevator on Mars is much easier than on Earth. The lower gravity, a third of Earth's, is the key. Satellites orbit a lot slower than around Earth, at a given altitude. So the twenty-four-hour synchronous orbit is only eleven thousand miles up, not twenty-two. And you can use materials of much less tensile strength to make your cable. You see? That's why space elevators are a much more accessible technology on Mars than on

Earth. But if we can take this cable stuff home – learn its lessons, retro-engineer it to find out how it works, enhance its performance for Earth's conditions – we'll skip decades of development and investment.

'Think about it. What a gift for humanity, just when we need it. Once you have an elevator, access to space is so easy and cheap that everything takes off. Exploration. Huge developments like orbital power plants. Resource extraction, asteroid mining, on a vast scale. Some of the Low Earths have populations of tens of millions now, since the Yellowstone evacuations. And as they industrialize, if they *start* with easy access to space, they'll be able to keep it clean and safe and green from the beginning. We could have a million-fold industrial revolution across the Long Earth, on worlds as clean as my garden in Wyoming West 1, Sally, where you used to walk me as a kid. And as for the Datum itself, given the depletion of oil and coal and mineral ores there, this is the *only* way the old world can ever recover.'

'You *are* playing Daedalus again, aren't you?' Frank said. 'I guess the historians will call it Beanstalk Day this time.'

'Things have a way of working out. Stepping did, didn't it?'

'Sure. After a slew of social disruption, economic chaos—'

'And a billion lives saved during Yellowstone. Whatever. Anyhow this conversation is irrelevant because—'

Sally said, 'Because you're going to do this anyhow.'

'Yep. Come on, let's head over; I want to find the root station before it's dark. Then we'll need to figure out how to acquire some kind of samples to take back. The cable is the thing; if we get pieces of that material the rest is detail.'

Sally pushed at her joystick; the glider climbed higher, banking to the east. 'One more question, Dad. So you figured that somebody would have come up with the space elevator idea, somewhere on the Long Mars. All you had to do was keep stepping until you found it. But how did you know it would be *here*? I mean, geographically. If I understand it right you could grow a beanstalk anywhere along the Martian equator.'

Frank said, 'Let me try to answer that one. We've been tracking the big Tharsis volcanoes. Right, Willis? Stick a beanstalk on top of Olympus Mons and you're already thirteen miles up towards your goal, *and* above eighty per cent of the atmosphere, thus avoiding such hazards as dust storms.'

'Actually Pavonis Mons would be a better choice,' Willis said. 'Not as big but slap on the equator. Yes,

Frank, that was how I figured it; Tharsis had to be a site, if not the only one . . . Hmm.'

'What?'

'I'm getting better visuals now. Up here, out of the dusty air. As it happens the cable line doesn't quite line up with the summit of Pavonis. Engineering details. Soon we'll know for sure. Come on.'

They flew on, Sally tracking Willis, heading steadily east, away from the setting sun, over slowly uplifting land. The shadows speared out from the rocks and pooled deep in the craters, where Sally imagined she saw mist gather.

At last she thought she could see the cable itself with her naked eye, a baby blue scrape down a sky turning a bruised purple. She tilted her head, watching it spear up, up out of her vision, impossibly tall.

'Like a crack in the sky,' Frank said. 'What's that old song?'

'It makes me feel kind of giddy,' Sally said. 'In an inverted way. I'm glad I can't see the anchor satellite, poised up there. What if this thing broke and fell?'

'Well, the cable would wrap around the planet as it rotated, and cause a hell of a lot of damage. There was a novel called *Red Mars*—'

'It's not going to fall,' Willis said.

'How do you know?' Sally snapped.

'Because it's very ancient. If it was going to break and fall, it would have done so by now. Ancient, and lacking maintenance for a long time.'

'And how do you know *that*?'

'Look at the ground below.'

The featureless plain was scattered with meaningless shadows. No structure, Sally realized. No sign even of a relic.

Willis said, 'Think where we are. At the foot of a space elevator, this should be the hinterland of a port that serves a major chunk of the planet. Where are the warehouses, the rail lines, the air-ports? Where's the city to house the travellers and the workers? Where's the farmland to feed them all? Oh, I know whatever race built this probably had totally different ways from the human of solving those problems. But you don't build a space elevator unless you want to bring materials down from space, or ship goods back up into space, and you don't do that without some kind of facility to handle stuff on the ground.'

'And there's nothing down there,' Sally said. 'How much time, Dad? How much time to erode everything to invisibility?'

'I can only guess. Millions of years? But the elevator survived all that time, the dust storms and the meteor impacts – and its own exotic hazards, such as solar storms and cable-snipping meteors further up. Whoever built that built it well . . .'

Suddenly the wonder of it hit her, the strangeness of the situation. Here was the product of a long-vanished indigenous civilization, about which Willis could have known *nothing*. Nothing about their nature, the detail of their lives – their rise, their fall, their evident extinction. And yet, from the sheer planetary geometry of Mars, he had deduced they must exist, or must have existed, and they must have built a space elevator. And he was right, here was that final monument, their last legacy, with everything else about them worn to dust. As if they had only ever existed for this one purpose, to fulfil Willis's ambition. And he, in turn, had crossed two million Earths, the Gap, and three million copies of Mars, in the utter certainty of what he would eventually find. Not for the first time in her life she wondered what it must be like to live inside her father's head.

'OK,' Willis said, 'we're coming up on the base of the cable. We're still a ways short of Pavonis Mons. I guess the base could have been relocated . . .'

The gliders dipped towards the ground. They lit up the darkling landscape ahead with their searchlight beams, and Willis fired off a couple of flares. The artificial light made the cable gleam, a mathematical abstraction above the chaotic jumble of the plain.

At last Sally saw where the cable touched the ground – but it did not stop there. The blue line dived down into a circle of darkness, foreshortened from this distance. At first Sally thought it was a crater. Then, as the gliders flew overhead and looped past the cable itself, she realized she was looking down into a *hole*, a shaft that might have been a half-mile wide – smooth, symmetrical, a well of darkness.

Willis growled, 'I pinged it with my radar. That's where the cable goes, all right; that's where the root station is. Down there. Damn thing is over twenty miles deep.'

That shocked Sally. '*How* deep?'

'Deep enough to contain a decent thickness of air.'

Frank the trained astronaut took over. 'Deep enough that we wait until the morning before taking a look inside.'

Willis hesitated. Sally knew his instinct would be to uncoil a rope and just plunge down there with a flashlight, Martian night or no Martian night. But at length he said, 'Agreed.'

Frank said, 'You hotshot pilots just make sure you don't run into that cable on the way in to landing. I'm guessing that if this thing has lasted as long as you say,

Willis, then if we pick a fight with it our gliders are going to come off worst . . .'

And as they came down, Sally thought she saw a light in the landscape, off in the distance, far away from this beanstalk root. A single light in the dark that was extinguished when she looked again. If it had ever existed at all.

38

In the morning the three of them resolved to hike to the pit, leaving the gliders behind. That was basically Frank and Willis's plan. A plan that entailed leaving the gliders unguarded . . .

Sally didn't contribute much to the discussion. She was doubtful about the plan, however. This was Mars, a typical Mars – a dead Mars, aside from whatever they were likely to encounter in the pit. There were no real hazards here. Even a dust storm, pushed by Mars's feeble air, would barely leave a mark of its passing. The only real danger was an unlucky meteor strike, and no sentry could ward off that. To post a guard, thus splitting their tiny team, would have been absurd.

Wouldn't it?

Sally was cautious by nature; living alone in the wild worlds of the Long Earth had made her so, long ago. But her caution was of a different degree to Frank's. He thought in terms of physical effects, equipment failures – a meteor strike, a solar flare, a leaky pressure hull. While Sally had learned to think in terms of malevolent life – creatures out to kill her, one way or another. Maybe she was importing an over-caution bred on a too-alive Earth to a too-dead Mars where it wasn't appropriate. Maybe this was just a distraction.

Wasn't it?

She went along with the guys' plan. But in her head a small alarm sounded softly, continually.

And she remembered that light she'd thought she'd seen, glowing in the Martian night.

So the three of them walked to the pit. In the bright daylight the thread of the cable was even more striking than in the twilight, a brilliant eggshell blue like no natural colour Sally had seen on any of the millions of Marses they had visited.

As they walked, Willis held up a small sensor pod to study their target. 'That cable is about a half-inch thick,' he said. 'A finger's width. You know, I'm betting it doesn't *need* to be that thick.'

'A safety factor,' Frank suggested. 'Maybe the apparent thickness is mostly dummy, a lightweight safety coating. You don't want to be slicing off the wing of your flying machine—'

'Or your limbs—'

'On a super-strong thread that's too fine to even see.'

As they talked Sally was studying the ground, the lip of the approaching pit. 'No raying.'

'What?' Frank asked.

'No splash debris, like from any other crater on Mars, or the moon.'

'Umm,' Frank said. 'But there is a crater wall, of sorts . . .'

The ground rose up as they neared the lip, hard-packed under the dust, to become a circular barrier maybe fifty feet tall, Sally saw as she crested it, a wall that ran right around the rim of the hole in the ground. This was a *big* feature, it was obvious now they were standing on top of it, a hole a full half-mile across encircled by this smooth wall. Away from this highest point, which was a broad ridge so Sally had no fear of falling, the lip fell away smoothly, funnelling into the ground. From here she could only see the upper sections of the interior walls of the pit itself, which looked like compacted Martian rock.

Willis cautiously knelt down, tied a fine rope to a handheld sensor pod, and lowered it into the pit, paying out the rope, clumsy with his gloved hands. 'Yeah, this pit is indeed just about twenty miles deep; the radar confirms it. And pretty much the same radius all the way to the bottom. It's a cylinder.'

Frank said, 'Surely no meteor could create a pit as deep and orderly as this. A bigger impactor doesn't drill a deeper hole, it just melts more rock, and you get a wider, shallower crater.'

'Hmm,' Willis said. 'I can imagine how it could be done. A string of small impactors coming down one after the other. Deepening the hole before it had a chance to infill.'

Frank pulled a face, looking dubious. 'Maybe. If this *is* artificial I can think of easier ways to build it. Like with a massive heat weapon. Like we saw used in war, back on world – what was it?'

'About a million,' Willis said. 'The Martian Arecibo.'

'But,' Sally said, 'that's a long way from here, step-wise. We've seen no evidence of cross-stepwise transfer of technologies, or even life forms, here on Mars.'

'True. But convergence of technology types isn't impossible,' Willis said. 'We have directed-energy weapons, and we're not even from Mars.'

Sally shook her head. 'We've got nothing but guesses. *Why* would anybody build this, though?'

Willis was monitoring the results coming back from his sensor pod. 'I can make a guess at that. This pit is *deep*. The Martian atmosphere's scale height is only around five miles. At twenty miles deep, you'd expect the air pressure to be around fifty times its value on the surface. Up here you have a typical Martian-surface atmosphere, a scrape of carbon dioxide at about one per cent Earth's sea-level pressure. At the bottom of this pit, and my instruments are confirming it, that's up to about fifty per cent.'

Frank whistled. 'That's better than on the Gap Mars.'

'Right. Which is about as hospitable as we've found it, anywhere across three million stepwise copies. That's why they built this pit, Sally. As a refuge.'

'From what?'

Willis said, 'From the collapse of the air. Maybe there was something like a volcano summer here – a deep one, a long one—'

Frank said, 'Long enough for some breed of Martians to come up with a space programme.'

'Right. But, like all summers, eventually it came to an end. The heat leaked out, the snow started falling at the poles, the oceans froze over and receded. The usual story.'

Sally thought she saw it now. 'This pit is a refuge.'

'Yeah. And it couldn't be simpler. The pit would keep its air, water, even if civilization fell.'

Frank said, 'And the elevator?'

'Maybe they moved the root station here, before the end, from Pavonis or wherever else. Kind of romantic, but *very* long-term thinking. They lived in a hole in the ground to make sure they saved their air and water, but they kept their ladder to the planets.'

Sally peered into the pit. 'So what's down there now?'

'Life,' said Willis. 'I can tell that much. There's oxygen, methane – the atmosphere is unstable, chemically. So something must be photosynthesizing away, pumping all that oxygen into the air.' He glanced around, at the way the slanting morning sunlight caught only the upper surface of the pit walls. 'No, not photosynthesis. Not primarily anyhow – not enough direct light, in the depths. Maybe it's like the deep-sea organisms on Earth, out of sight of sunlight, feeding on seeps of minerals and energy from underground. We're close enough to the Tharsis volcanoes for that to work; the big magma pockets under those babies must leak a lot of heat.'

Sally asked, 'So this is the last refuge of their civilization. Where's the city lights, car exhausts, radio chatter?'

'None of that, I'm afraid. There is one splash of metal.'

Frank looked startled. 'Metal?'

'An irregular form. Down on the floor of the pit.'

Sally said wistfully, 'All this makes me think of Rectangles.'

Willis wasn't interested, but Frank glanced at her. 'Where?'

'A Long Earth world I discovered with Lobsang and Joshua. We called it Rectangles, for the traces of foundation ruins we found on the ground. Another site with relics of a vanished civilization.'

'Right. And a cache of high-tech weapons.'

She looked at Frank in surprise. 'How did you know that? Oh. Jansson told you.'

'We spoke a lot. Especially when she was in her last days, during Yellowstone. Told me a lot about her life. Her time with you—'

'We'll have to go down,' Willis said, cutting across their talk. 'Into the hole.'

Sally took a breath. 'I was afraid you'd say that.'

'In the spirit of noble exploration, I suppose,' Frank said.

'No. So that I can get up close and personal with that cable. And get a look at the root station.'

'OK,' Sally said dubiously. 'Suppose, hypothetically, we agree we're going to do this. How? We don't have twenty miles of rope – do we, Frank?'

'No. Anyhow we'd need a lot more, for doubling up, fail-safes.'

'We don't have winches, or jet packs—'

'We fly down,' Willis said. 'We take one of the gliders, and fly down.' He looked at them both. 'You're going to say no, aren't you? Look. You can see how wide this pit is. A half-mile across – plenty of room for a spiral flight, down and back up.'

'The air at the base is a hell of a lot thicker than the design optimum, Willis,' Frank protested.

'You know as well as I do that fifty per cent bar is still within the performance envelope. And besides, there's a lot of heat seeping out of this hole in the ground. We can ride back up using the thermals; that will help.

'Here's the plan. Two of us will ride one glider down, leaving the other glider on the surface as backup, together with one pilot. We can offload stores before the flight. There are obvious fallback strategies, if anything goes wrong. Maybe we could even climb back up, out of this pit. The gravity is a baby.'

Frank said, 'Why not send down a drone plane?'

'Not equipped to take samples.'

'But—'

'End of discussion,' Willis said. 'We came here for that damn space elevator. We ain't going home without a piece of it. Got that? OK. Let's get down to specifics.'

They argued about how to split the crew. They agreed that one should stay on the surface, two descend. Which one, which two?

In fact the logic was clear. Willis was always going to go into the pit. Sally was the least good pilot, but as the youngest and fittest she had the best chance of climbing out of that hole in the ground if things got bad enough. Frank, meanwhile, the best pilot, was the obvious choice for the reserve on the surface.

Willis and Sally it would be, then.

Willis fretted through the day that Frank insisted they took in offloading *Thor*, the glider to be used for the descent, testing through its systems one more time, checking over their pressure suits and other gear, working out communications protocols and the like. And if Willis was restless, Frank was visibly unhappy, whether because the stunt was so obviously dangerous or because he was the guy left behind to mind the store, Sally wasn't sure.

Come the evening they had a hot meal in one of the bubble tents, washed up, and took to their sleeping bags early. The plan was to rise at dawn and use the full day to descend, do whatever had to be done at the base of the pit, and climb back out again before the sun fell.

That night Sally slept no better and no worse than she had during the whole trip. Another legacy of her solitary, nomadic life: she had adapted to getting by on whatever sleep she could snatch, as and when she got the chance. She was always aware, though, oddly, of the thread to the sky just a couple of miles away, silent, ancient, with space at its tip and some kind of fallen culture at its feet. Her life had always been odd, even before Step Day. Just when she'd thought it couldn't get any odder . . .

Thor lifted, propelled by the methane rockets, as obedient and responsive as ever. Willis was piloting.

Once they were into their glide Willis made one circle over the landing site. Sally looked down at the ground, at *Woden* gleaming bone white in the morning sun, and their bubble tents like blisters on the scuffed Martian dust. Frank Wood stood alone, staring up. He waved, and Willis waggled the wings in response.

Sally still had that faint alarm bell ringing in the back of her head. There was something about this situation that wasn't right, that they hadn't thought through or prepared for. Well, Frank Wood was more experienced than Sally in this kind of situation, less intelligent than Willis maybe but calmer, more capable in many ways. If something did blow up, she'd have to rely on Frank's instincts to save the day.

Thor turned away from the landing site and towards the pit, and Sally turned her attention to the challenge facing her.

They were over the pit in only a couple of minutes. Willis, getting the feel of the craft, took *Thor* banking in tight circles over the opening, keeping one eye on the elevator cable. 'I can see the cable easily,' he said with some relief. 'Also I rigged up a proximity sensor that will ping if we get too close. Short of flying straight at the damn thread, we should be OK.'

'Don't tempt fate, Dad.'

'Now you sound like your maternal grandfather, Patrick. Remember him? The gloomy Irishman. OK, let's take her down.'

He began a lazy spiral around the axial cable, cutting the speed, Sally guessed, as low as he dared without risking a stall. Soon they were descending towards the mouth of the pit, the low sunlight wheeling through the glider cabin – and then, with a smooth wash of rising shadow, they fell beneath the lip of the hole, with its artfully consolidated ridge. The sun caught only the uppermost stretch of the wall of crimson rock, and soon they were falling into the darkness.

Sally felt an odd sense of claustrophobia. But that was logical, for her, with the instincts of a natural stepper. Sally had grown up knowing in her bones that as a last resort, whatever difficulty she got into, she could always just step away, even without a Stepper box. Even on the Long Mars that was true, though she would generally just be swapping one lethal landscape for another. But you couldn't step out of a pit, a hole dug into the ground, because there would be earth and bedrock in the worlds to either side stepwise. A pit, a basement, a cellar, even a mine, was therefore a simple defence against stepping aggressors, as had been figured out very early after Step Day, even by neighbourhood cops like Monica Jansson.

On the Long Mars as on the Long Earth.

She was trapped in a cage one world thin.

As she descended twenty miles.

Into the dark.

Towards the unknown.

It came as a relief when Willis switched on lights, shining front and back of the glider and to either side, picking out the wall on the one hand and the cable on the other. The floor was still too far below to be visible. The wall of the pit was layered, with a spray of sun-blasted dust on the surface, then a mass of rubble and gravel and ice – and then the bedrock, itself deeply cracked, a record of the huge primordial impacts that had shaped this world. She wondered if these walls had needed some kind of consolidation, to keep this tremendous shaft from collapsing. Maybe Mars's lower gravity, and its cooler interior, helped with that.

'Piece of cake,' Willis said as he piloted the glider. 'Just got to hold her steady. And get used to the thickening air. Worst danger is I'll fall asleep at the wheel.'

'Don't even joke about it, Dad.'

'You keep watching, the walls, the ground. I have cameras working and other sensors, but anything else you spot—'

'I can see something.' The wall, in the plane's spotlight, was no longer featureless, she saw. The rock face, as rough as ever, was etched with a kind of zigzag spiral. 'Stairs,' she said. 'I see stairs. Big ones, four or six feet deep, it's hard to tell from this vantage. But they're stairs, all right.'

'Ha! And we're not a mile deep yet. Should have anticipated stairs. A culture careful enough to build this hole in the ground in anticipation of its entire civilization collapsing was always going to install something as simple as stairs.'

'Why don't they reach all the way to the surface?'

'Maybe they just eroded away. I have the feeling this pit has been here a long time, Sally.'

After that, for a time they descended in silence. The circle of Martian sky above them receded, a coppery disc, like a coin. From above, the ship must look like a firefly spiralling down the barrel of a cannon. Still the base of the pit was invisible.

At about twelve miles deep Sally thought she saw more detail on the wall, and she had her father level out for a closer look.

'Vegetation,' she said, watching carefully as the glider slid past the walls. 'Stumpy trees. Things like cacti. Dad, this is like what we saw on Gap Mars.'

He checked the air pressure. 'Yeah, we're up to about ten per cent of a bar already. I guess this is the lower limit of tolerance for that vegetation suite. And there must be just enough sunlight down here to support their kind of photosynthesis. Remarkable, isn't it, Sally? We keep seeing the same biospheric suite, essentially, taking its chance wherever it can, wherever the environment lets up its stranglehold, even just a little. I can feel the air thickening, getting kind of bumpy . . .'

So it was. Sally guessed that the pool of air trapped in the pit was turbulent, stirred up by the heat from below and falling back when it cooled. She tried to watch for more evidence of life on the walls, but mostly she monitored the glider's increasingly ragged descent.

'OK,' Willis said at last. 'Less than a mile to go. Pitch black down there. Radar's showing ground. I'm going to put her down on as smooth a patch as I can find – and not far from that anomalous metal heap I detected from the surface.'

She stayed silent; she could only distract him. She checked the seals of her own pressure suit, and telltale sensors monitoring Willis's suit.

Only in the last few seconds did she see details of the pit bottom, which looked as if it was encrusted with life, a multitude of shapes and colours gaudy in their panning lights, quickly glimpsed. It was like a seabed, like looking down into a fish tank.

'Here we go . . .'

The landing was bumpy. Through the fabric of the craft Sally heard scrapes, crackles, liquid noises, before they came to rest.

Willis glanced back over his shoulder at her, and grinned. 'Once again, a piece of cake. Come on, let's see what's out there.'

Sally clambered cautiously out of the glider.

The only light came from splashes from the glider's floods. The disc of sky, far above at the top of this rock chimney, was too remote even to see – although, glancing up, following the blue thread of the beanstalk cable, Sally thought she saw something moving, falling, occluding what light there was.

The ground, as she'd glimpsed just before the landing, was coated with life, most of it static: purple-green
bacterial slime, and things like sponges, things like
sprawled trees, things like banks of coral. The glider, on
landing, had cut parallel tracks through all this, tracks
that glistened, moist. The air was comparatively thick,
the place was comparatively warm – this was indeed as
welcoming an environment as she'd found on any Mars
so far. And it surely had to be fed by energy supplied
by mineral seeps from the deeper ground, moisture
perhaps leaking from some aquifer; there could be no
meaningful input of sunlight down here – and no rain,
on a typically arid Mars. Unless the pit had some kind
of microclimate of its own, she thought, with captive
clouds and rainstorms all contained within its walls.

Walking away from the glider towards the elevator
cable, she turned her head from side to side, sweeping
her helmet flashlight. Aside from the cable itself, and
the basic architecture of the pit, there was no sign of
structure, of sentience—

Something moved, cutting across her beam from
one pool of shadow to another. She whirled, alarmed.

It was a crustacean, she saw, flat to the ground like
those she'd seen at some of their early stops, its chitinous armour gleaming with colours that must be, normally, entirely invisible. Indeed it had no eyes, she saw,

none of the eye stalks she'd noticed on those surface creatures.

'You poor thing,' she said. 'You really have been down here a long time, haven't you? Long enough not just for your culture to have fallen apart, but for you to have evolved out your sight . . .'

The creature seemed to listen. Then it scuttled back into the dark.

Keeping a wider lookout Sally walked on, heading for the cable. Even from here she could see that there was no obvious root station, no structure; the cable just seemed to sink into the deep rock, which was covered by a tide of dark-adapted life . . . But, she saw, the cable itself was scuffed, frayed, only a few yards above the ground level.

'Hey, Dad.'

'Hmm?' As ever, Willis sounded distracted, not quite paying attention to her.

'Bad news is the root node is buried somehow. I suppose if the builders had the power to melt out this pit, they could have just sunk the node in molten rock . . . Good news is the cable is frayed here. Like something clipped it. We might be able to get your samples after all.'

'Uh huh. And I think I've found what did the clipping. Come see.'

She turned, sweeping the glow of her helmet light. She saw Willis in his suit, standing straight, his back to her. He was holding something, in the shadows. And beyond him, nearer the pit wall, she saw a gleam of metal.

It was a spacecraft. A stubby nose and part of a wing poked out of the heavy clay, badly damaged. And she saw scrapings, where Willis had cleared dirt from around a hatchway.

'What the hell?'

'Recent,' he said. 'Comparatively. Given that the ship hasn't yet eroded to dust. Maybe they came from some other world – the Earth of this universe, even. Whatever, they must have tried to land down here—'

'They were even worse pilots than you.'

'They actually *clipped the cable*. What if they'd cut it entirely? We could have lost everything.'

She walked forward for a closer look. The ship had obviously come down hard, and was ripped open, but it must have looked weird enough beforehand. There were padded things with grooves in them that could have been seats. She glimpsed what looked like bones, gleaming beneath rotted fabric.

And Willis was holding a skull; it was crested, arrow-shaped and two or three times bigger than a human head.

Again something moving overhead caught Sally's eye. She tipped her head, angling her flashlight, trying to find it again. Something pale, flapping.

'The ship doesn't concern us,' Willis said. 'Leave it for the expeditions from the universities. We'll take images, a few samples. Bits of bone. Maybe this skull. Then we'll get our chunk of cable material and get out of here . . .'

The thing that was falling from above came closer now, drifting slowly in the thickening air, the low gravity, flapping gently, like a damaged bird. As it settled to the life-crowded ground, not far from Sally, she saw that it was a ceramic panel fixed to aluminium struts, painted with the corner of a Stars and Stripes, clearly visible.

It was a piece of *Woden*.

39

*T*hor burst out of the hole in the Martian ground and into the light of midday.

Mars, more than half as far again as Earth was from the sun, had always struck Sally as a murky kind of world, swathed in twilight colours. After emerging from the pit, though, it seemed dazzlingly bright, the opened-out landscape huge, and it took her a few seconds to get her bearings.

Then she saw chunks of wrecked glider scattered all around the rim of the pit, bone-white fragments chopped and chewed as if by some huge jaw.

As soon as he had gained some altitude from the thermal uplift that he got from the pit, Willis immediately turned the glider's nose westward, towards their overnight camp. He dipped low for speed; the glider whipped across the rock-strewn ground. There were tracks, Sally saw, like ski marks, cutting across the thin lines of Neil Armstrong spacesuit-boot footprints the crew had made yesterday between their camp and the pit rim.

Then she was distracted by something moving, out in the distance. It raced over the rocky ground, drawn by a mud-brown sail, riding on some kind of ivory-white runners, raising a big rooster-tail of dust. Just as she'd seen a million worlds back: it was a sand-whaler.

Back at what was left of the camp, they circled over the wreckage. The glider was so comprehensively trashed that Sally could barely make out its narrow-winged cruciform layout. Their bubble-dome shelters were still standing, amid scattered bundles of gear, food, water, blankets, clothing, bits of comms and science gear.

And, in the camp, there was Frank Wood, she saw to her relief, standing and waving at them, apparently uninjured, his pressure suit intact.

Sally called down, 'Frank? You OK?'

'See for yourself.'

Willis called, 'I'm putting her down.'

Frank turned, scanning the horizon. The racing form, the dust cloud, was a good distance away. 'Yes. Do it. He's far enough away for now. We need to salvage as much of our stuff as we can. But, Willis, keep the launch booster primed for takeoff. We can't afford to lose our last glider.'

'Noted.' Willis dipped the nose and brought the glider down in a hasty, bumpy landing.

Sally immediately unbuckled and opened the canopy. 'In fact, Dad, why don't you stay on board? Stay ready to take her up and out of the way of danger.'

Again Willis hesitated, thinking it over. 'That makes sense.'

Sally strode over towards Frank, who called back, 'Now do you see why I insisted on fall-backs?'

'Not the right moment for a lecture, Frank,' Sally snapped.

'So how was the pit?'

'Nor for a travelogue. Frank, I get the feeling we haven't got a lot of time here.'

'You're right.' He glanced over at the dust plume again. 'I was looking east – the way you two had gone. He came in out of nowhere, from the west. He just drove his sand-yacht straight into the glider, severed a wing in the first pass. I was near the bubble domes. I grabbed a strut from the wreck – nearest I had to a weapon – I stood by the bubbles and the rest of the gear while he tore into the glider again. Well, he smashed up the bird, and then he took chunks of it off to the pit. I saw him throwing the gear in. He's smart, you know; he's modified the survival bags to give himself a lot of flexibility.'

'He?' Willis called. 'Who the hell is this?'

Frank looked across at the glider, bleakly. 'You should know, Willis. Remember the whalers, a million worlds back? You traded them Steppers, for access to those monoliths. Do you remember how it went? One of those ten-armed characters got hold of your boxes and survival bubbles, and started lording it over another of them—'

'You called him the prince,' Sally said.

'Yeah. That was one pissed-off crustacean. Well, my guess is he got hold of one of those Steppers and all the survival bubbles he could steal, and he took off step-wise, chasing us.'

Willis grunted. 'Why would he do that?'

'Dishonour,' Sally said. 'Revenge. Just as Frank has been saying. Maybe you destroyed his social standing in front of his peers, Dad. Shit. I *thought* I saw something following us. A light in the dark. I didn't figure it out, never put it together.'

'And you, Willis,' Frank said, 'this is all your fault. You inflicted a Step Day on those guys, just like you did to humanity. It was just a means to an end to you, a way of getting to the next stage in your grand plan. You never thought of the impact it might have on *them*, did you? And it's already been a pretty savage one judging by this guy's obsessive, murderous rage.'

Sally watched the dust plume. Was it coming closer? 'I think Frank's right, Dad. And now he's coming back for more.'

Frank punched a fist into a gloved palm. 'And we've been standing here yakking and haven't loaded a damn thing. We can't let him get at the second glider, Willis—'

Willis hesitated no longer. He fired up the launch rocket and the glider leapt into the air, wheeling over the two of them on the ground. 'Listen,' he called down. 'I'll draw him off with the glider. You get the stuff packed up. When he's out of range I'll come back – the glider is a hell of a lot faster than that damn sand-yacht – and we'll load up and step away.'

'Come on.' Frank led the way, collapsing the bubble-dome shelters, bundling up pallets of food and water. Sally followed his lead, making for the wreck of the *Woden* to see what she could salvage.

Willis dipped the glider over the sand-yacht, and Sally saw that, yes, the yacht was turning, following the bird in the sky. Willis called, 'He'll follow us when we step. But he's not going to be able to get any closer to us while we keep moving stepwise.'

'Dad,' Sally said urgently. 'Why not just kill him?'

'I got nothing to kill him with.'

'Come on. I can't believe you didn't pack any weapons. Some kind of handgun adapted for Martian air.'

'Believe me. I didn't.'

She hesitated. 'OK. Well, I did. In the back of the food lockers, on both the gliders. I stowed away crossbows. To work them, you just have to—'

'Found them. Took them out. Dumped them. Sorry, kid.'

She felt unreasonably enraged. 'Why the hell? Listen to me, Dad. Weapons like that have helped keep me alive a long time in the Long Earth—'

'Don't hold with weapons. Wouldn't expect that from a guy from Wyoming, would you, Frank? Weapons kill people, in the hands of idiots. And since most of the human race are idiots—'

Sally yelled, 'Including me, you pompous old tyrant? Including Frank, for God's sake?'

'Anyhow we don't need weapons to get rid of this guy. He'll destroy himself soon enough. He can't do me any harm up here. And then, the ride home. It won't be comfortable but we'll make it. Look, he's a long way out, and heading away now. I'll come back in and—'

Sally saw a blinding light coming from the plain, from the sand-yacht dust plume, directly under the glider's elegant form. And a spark, bright as the sun of Earth, lifted up into the sky, trailing black smoke.

A spark arcing straight up at *Thor.*

Though Willis banked with impressive reflexes he only had a second or two to react. Sally saw the spark rip through the fabric of the glider.

When Willis came back on line, Sally heard alarms sounding in the background, patient artificial voices explaining the nature of the damage. 'Shit, shit . . .'

'Dad, what the hell was that? Some kind of rocket?'

'I think it was natural. Like the dragon-beasts, like those fire-breathing columns we saw. It's like a methane-burning worm, flying through the air, using that burning breath as a rocket exhaust. A living missile. Maybe the whalers cultivate them, as weapons. Saved that up for a surprise when he needed it, didn't he? These guys are pretty smart.'

Frank said, 'Yes, they are. And you thought the prince couldn't touch you.' Despite the peril of the situation for them all, angry as he was, Frank sounded like he was almost gloating. 'You were wrong again, Linsay.'

'We'll discuss my personal flaws later. Listen, the wings are intact, but my controls are mostly shot, and I'm losing pressure . . . I'm coming down. Let's stick to the plan. We'll load up what we have, launch again, get out of here. There should be time before he reaches us. When we've outrun him stepwise we can land, make proper repairs—'

'Just get that bird down here,' Frank snapped.

And Sally was watching the dust plume. 'He's closing. I think you keep underestimating this guy, Dad. He is a hunter, from a culture of hunters.'

'Yeah, yeah. Later. Coming in.'

The landing was heavy, but, as Frank remarked, in these circumstances any landing that left the fuselage intact was acceptable.

To Frank's curt orders, Willis stayed in the cockpit, at the controls, ready to get the bird back in the air at short notice. Frank and Sally, meanwhile, began to bundle their goods into the glider's slim fuselage. They had to work around the scorched, gaping hole in the rear where the rocket-worm had passed straight through.

Frank muttered and growled. 'Hell, I hate the idea of launching again without taking care of that damage.'

'We have to. And we can't leave the gear behind.'

'I tried stepping, you know,' Frank said. 'When he came in for his first passes. Sally, he stepped straight after me. Even with the anti-nausea drugs, stepping slows me down, just a little. Not him, not the prince—'

'Don't talk,' Sally said. 'Just load.'

'And we're below capacity too. We're going to have to leave stuff behind if—'

'Shut up.' At the foot of that racing dust plume, Sally saw another spark of light, this time racing over the ground. Racing towards her, she realized. 'He's firing at us, this time. Dad, incoming. Get her up again, now.'

'Roger that—'

The glider scraped into the air with a flare of booster rockets.

And Frank Wood was standing there, staring at the approaching rocket-worm.

Sally leapt forward. She endured an age of low-gravity slow-motion falling towards Frank. At last she slammed into him, her arms around his waist, pushing him to the ground.

Not a heartbeat later the rocket-worm hammered into the ground. Sally felt the pressure wave, feeble in the thin air, a stronger blast of heat.

When it was over she was on top of Frank, who was on the ground, on his back, gasping. She rolled off him, clumsy in her pressure suit.

Frank said, sitting up, 'What the hell – would he have hit?'

'He was damn close.'

'If it is some kind of living being, this weapon – internal methane and air sacs – I wonder how close you can aim it?'

Willis called down from the spiralling glider, 'If it's alive, maybe it aims itself. Meanwhile he's coming back for more, on that damn sand sled of his.'

Sally saw the looming dust plume. There was a figure on the deck, beneath the big sail: that body like a huge upright centipede, incongruously wrapped in the plastic sac of a survival bag, wielding some kind of spear.

Frank stood, breathing hard. 'By Christ, I'm getting old. *Look* at that bastard. He's relentless.'

Sally glanced up. 'Keep on climbing, Dad. Just stay out of the range of the rocket-worms.'

'Roger. But what about you two?'

Frank faced the plume of dust. 'We split up.' Without hesitating he turned and began to run, clumsy in his suit, across the dirt. He looked back once, still running. 'Move out, Sally. Thataway.'

She stood frozen for a heartbeat.

Then she began to run in the opposite direction. She ran with her head down, her body tilted forward, her boots thrusting back at the crusty ground. She had practised running on Mars. This moment was why.

'He can only come for one of us at a time,' Frank called. 'He can strike at us from a distance, but this way at least one of us has a better chance. And if we keep on moving, maybe we'll wear him down.'

'Maybe. We could have just stood and fought.'

'With what? This is the better way, Sally. Weaken him, finish him later.'

'Dad? What can you see from up there? What's he doing?'

'Hesitating. He's by the campsite, what's left of it. Making another couple of passes through the wreck of the *Woden*, just for fun, I guess. Listen, I've a better idea. I'll come down, pick one of you up.'

Frank seized on that immediately. 'Do it.'

Sally said, 'Leaving one at his mercy?'

'We'll deal with that when we get to it,' Frank said. 'Come on, Willis, do it.'

Sally stopped running, breathing hard, and looked up at the circling glider. Willis hadn't yet made his move to land, she saw. Looking back she could see the sand-yacht, the trail its runners made in the dirt, the bulky form of the whaler swathed in the survival bag. And beyond that, the smaller figure of Frank, still running awkwardly. From the point of view of her father, up there, the situation must look perfectly symmetrical, she thought. The hunter at the centre, his two prey to either side, more or less equidistant. Whoever of them Willis chose to pick up first was going to have a markedly better chance of survival than the other; she knew that, and so would Willis. So who would he choose?

She was Willis's daughter. She imagined that for most people that would swing it. But Willis was no ordinary father.

Still Willis hesitated. He was actually thinking it over. Choosing between her and Frank Wood, who to save, as she waited.

At last, with a dip of its wings, the glider came out of its banking circle, like sliding off an invisible summit in the air, and swept down towards the ground.

Heading straight at Sally.

In the glider, Sally and Willis watched from the air as the whaler's yacht closed on Frank Wood, trailing plumes of red Mars dust. Frank made his last stand, lashing out with his gloved fists as the yacht made pass after pass. There was nothing they could do to help.

Finally the crustacean jumped off his yacht, hitting the ground running, though he was obviously impeded by the layers of survival bags he wore. He leapt straight at Frank, driving his spear forward even as he completed the low-gravity stride. Frank tried stepping even now, but the crustacean went straight after him, so that the two of them strobed between the worlds, fighting in the dirt.

Then the spear slammed into Frank's faceplate, shattering it.

The noise of Frank's ragged breathing cut out of the comms link immediately, and he shuddered and toppled back.

And Willis shifted them stepwise, over another crimson Martian plain, under an identical buttery sky. The scene of devastation and death below was gone, whisked away as if it had never happened.

40

There was nothing to say. So, at first, they said nothing.

They were stepping West now – West, back the way they had come, back to the Mars of the Gap, and, ultimately, home.

Sally made her way to the rear of the pressurized compartment, where a small bathroom was partitioned off. Here she opened her suit, for the first time since leaving the campsite to explore the pit – it seemed days ago, it was only hours, it was still early afternoon on Mars. She breathed in cabin air that felt suspiciously thin, with a faint tang of burning. No doubt there were leaks in the pressurized inner hull after the battering the glider had taken, on top of the hole ripped into the fuselage by the rocket-worm. They could be dealt with later. For now she just took some time to herself, to loosen her suit, wash herself down with wipes, empty her suit's piss collection tank.

Time away from her father.

When she joined him again, he was still at the controls. The glider was facing geographic west, appropriately enough, and the shrunken Martian sun was starting to descend across stepwise landscapes all but identical save for the usual flickering changes of detail, the scattered rocks and craters, the patterns of shadows. His faceplate open, Willis glanced over at her, and held up a small glass vial with some kind of whisker within. 'Some day we'll come back out here and give Frank Wood a proper burial. Later yet, they'll build a statue to him. A three-hundred-foot tall statue of Mars rock. And it was all for this.'

'Beanstalk cable.'

'Yep. We got what we came for, whatever it cost us. And with this we're going to change the world. All the human worlds.'

'Again.'

'You better believe it. Listen, Sally. I've checked over the systems. With just the two of us the supplies we managed to salvage ought to be sufficient to get us home. But we have other problems. *Thor*'s not going to make it back, not all the way. We took too much damage. Lost too many fluids for one thing, coolants, hydraulics. Even our methane-fuel factory is failing.'

She sat down in her couch, behind him, and shrugged. 'She did well to keep flying at all, after a rocket attack.'

'Yeah. Well, we're going to need to ditch.' He paused. 'And I'll need you to tell me where.'

She understood what he meant. She closed her eyes and *felt* the stepping, the slow rhythm of it, again, again, again, one a second, like a deep pulse inside her head. And, under that, she had a vague, misty sense of the wider topology of this Long Mars, just as she always had of the Long Earth. A sense of connections.

Her father wanted her to bring him to a soft place, a short cut in the Long Mars. There they would ditch . . .

'And I'll take you home,' she said, completing the thought aloud. 'Through the soft places, as Granddad Patrick used to call them. Holding you by the hand, like when I was a little kid taking you to your tool shed in Wyoming, West 1.'

'That's the best plan I got. It was only ever a fall-back concept, Sally. I mean, it was a logical anticipation, but I didn't know for sure if there would be soft places here, if you would be able to detect them, use them . . .'

'Use them to save you. You and your precious cable whisker.'

'Well, it is precious, Sally. More precious than anything.'

'More than the life of a man like Frank Wood?'

'The rights of an individual, the life of one man, are as nothing compared with the value of a technology like this. We're talking about the destiny of the species.'

She felt cold, sluggish, passive. As if she had to work through this one step at a time.

'When you were up in the glider, and Frank and I were on the ground – we were waiting for you to choose which one of us to save. You hesitated.'

He said nothing.

'I mean, most fathers would save their daughters instinctively. Right? I think Frank would have understood. But *you* – you hesitated. You were calculating, weren't you?'

'I—'

'Here's what I think. You weighed us up, Frank and me. Frank's the better pilot. Given an operational glider, Frank would have been more useful to you than me. And also Frank was obviously better equipped to handle the *Galileo* and take us home. But you assessed the damage, and you figured, no, the glider wasn't going to make it, you were going to need the short cuts. As for the *Galileo*,

well, you watched me train on the emergency procedures, and I guess we'll have support from the Russians
at Marsograd when we need to fly home. We'll cope with
Galileo. But the soft places were the key item.

'All of which meant you needed me more than you
needed Frank. It wasn't about family, or loyalty. Your
only consideration was which of us had the greater –
utility – to you at this point in the mission, given the
probabilities going forward. And it happened to be me,
because of the soft places. Which is why you saved me,
not Frank.'

'What do you want me to say—'

She cut across him. 'And – of course – this was why
you contacted me in the first place. Summoned me to
the Gap, to Mars. Your first contact with me in years,
out of the blue, out of nowhere, the father who turned
the whole world upside down and went missing when
I was still in my teens. It wasn't me you needed alongside you. It was my ability you wanted. I was a backup
option, in case the gliders failed. A human dowsing
rod. Nothing more than that.'

He seemed to think that over. 'So, what's your point?
You seem to think I've acted unreasonably. Is that it?
But, Sally, I'm not a reasonable man. Reasonable men
are like Frank Wood. He just accepted it when his
career choices shut down. He drove a damn tour bus

at the Cape, until he heard about the Gap, somehow. Then he just drifted again, until you happened to show up with that policewoman . . . In the end he accepted his death, down there in the dirt. I'm not like Frank Wood, just accepting what the universe throws at me. I'm unreasonable. I change the universe.'

She wasn't angry, to her own surprise. Maybe she'd seen too much crap out in the reaches of the Long Earth to be angry at the failings of mere human beings any more. Even her father. What did she feel, then? Disappointment? Perhaps. But this was the way Willis had always behaved. Pity, then? But who for? Willis, or herself?

'Yes,' she said. 'You are a man who changes the universe. But you're also my father—'

'Grow up,' he snarled.

And so Sally took her father back through chill tunnels, the soft places of the Long Mars.

At the Gap Mars, Viktor and Sergei and Alexei made them welcome once more, though they were saddened by the loss of Frank.

Then Sally and Willis crossed space, back to the Brick Moon and GapSpace. Aside from dealing with necessary business, they had no significant conversation, in the weeks it took them to reach home.

Immediately on her return, Sally sought out Frank Wood's family. She hated such obligations. But she knew there was nobody else who would tell how he died.

And she visited the grave of Monica Jansson, in Madison West 5, to tell her too.

That was when she got a message from Joshua Valienté.

41

I t was the end of August, and the return of the Navy airships USS *Neil A. Armstrong II* and USS *Eugene A. Cernan* from their expedition into the remote Western reaches of the Long Earth, that precipitated the crisis for the Next children in their prison-hospital at Hawaii. Because Captain Maggie Kauffman and her crew brought home the 'Napoleons' who had destroyed the *Armstrong I.* Monsters who were immediately identified as Next.

Nelson suspected it was simply the image of the rogues' leader, who called himself only David, that did the most damage to the cause of the Next. This was not some institutionalized, broken child, like Paul Spencer Wagoner and the rest. David was an adult, tall, arrogant, commanding, defiant as he stared out of the cage into which his captors put him, gazed into the lenses of the news cameras. A Napoleon indeed, a daunting superman.

Around David and his kind, inchoate fears crystallized. Something had to be done about the Next. The question was, what?

A conference call was hastily set up, involving senior staff at the Pearl Harbor base as well as administration officials in such secure locations as had survived across the post-Yellowstone continental US. On Hawaii, the meeting was projected in a complicated hologrammatic conference room, an expensive piece of kit.

It seemed inevitable to Nelson that even in the mid twenty-first century, even after the huge dislocation of the last few decades, most of the delegates were white, middle-aged men.

Nelson himself wasn't allowed to contribute unless specifically invited in the course of the discussion, but he was allowed to watch from a glass-walled booth. To his surprise he found himself sharing the booth with Roberta Golding, who he knew had come to Hawaii supposedly on her own fact-finding mission. He had met her in person once before, at a party thrown by Lobsang just before the Yellowstone eruption. But they had not spoken then; she had been very young. Now she had played a part in arranging his own cover here.

He supposed it was coincidental that Roberta was here in person when the *Armstrong* crisis blew up. But then he reminded himself that Golding herself was from Happy Landings . . . Maybe it was no coincidence at all. Secrets colliding with secrets. What was her true role? How much did she believe *he* knew of all this?

As they took their seats Nelson introduced himself; Roberta responded coolly, but pleasantly enough.

'Quite a set-up,' Roberta said, as they watched the conference delegates file in, or coalesce from clouds of pixels.

'Yes. I imagined you'd be in there with them.'

'Oh, this is far above my pay grade. And it's mostly military, you'll notice. The President's Science Adviser is chairing the session, and she's one of the few not in uniform.'

'Indeed. Reminds me of nothing so much as a Cold War military bunker. Oh, sorry.' Golding was only around twenty years old herself – only a little older than Paul Spencer Wagoner, he reflected. 'Maybe that's too dated a reference for you.'

'No, no. I have studied the period. Perhaps the most perilous of all manifestations of dim-bulb madness.'

Her obviously deliberate use of the Next term 'dim-bulb' startled him, and he looked at her with his perceptions of her shifting rapidly.

The Science Adviser called the meeting to order. She announced that the group had been convened by President Cowley as a 'Special Contingency Task Group', in response to the evidence returned by the crews of the *Armstrong* and *Cernan*, and other data relating to the Next, including the study of the internees here at Hawaii. The objective of the session was to make recommendations to the administration concerning next steps.

Admiral Hiram Davidson, chief of USLONGCOM, was head of the chain of command that had controlled the mission of those Navy ships, and he spoke first, giving a brief rehash of what Captain Kauffman and her crew had found out there in the reaches of the Long Earth, and what they'd done about the 'ragged-trousered Hitlers', as he put it, that they'd shipped home. 'As to what's going on in this base right here, for a summary of that I want to bring in Lieutenant Louise Irwin . . .'

Irwin spoke well, concisely, intelligently, even with a degree of compassion. She briefed the delegates on what had been learned of the Next in the time they'd been under surveillance in this controlled facility, and – as she reported more cautiously, under pressure of follow-up questioning – what had been surmised of their potential. Apparently unawed by the stuffed shirts around her, she neither condemned nor supported the

Next; rather she gave a cool assessment of their intellect, their psychology, their capabilities. Even so, Nelson thought – or perhaps because of her analytical tone – she made the Next children sound pretty scary.

Roberta murmured, 'I've spoken with Irwin a few times. The inmates here have been lucky to have her around.'

'I'd second that,' Nelson said.

'Anyhow, so much for the background briefings. Now the debate begins . . .'

Somewhat to Nelson's surprise, the next speaker, the head of DARPA, an advanced research agency responsible to the Department of Defense, spoke quite passionately in favour of protecting the Next. He was a stout, red-faced man, a classic desk-jockey type; his rather visionary words didn't fit his image, Nelson thought, as he began to speak.

'Before we convened I consulted some colleagues here, including representatives of the National Science Foundation, NASA, and also some members of the President's Science Advisory Committee.' DARPA nodded to other wise heads present. 'And we all agree there are potentially great scientific benefits to be derived from this situation. If there *is* some kind of speciation event going on here – and that *very* much remains to be demonstrated – well, consider how much we might learn of humanity, our common genetic heritage, the nature of natural selection.

'And if these "Next" individuals do indeed have intellectual capacities considerably above the norm, then who knows what we might learn from them directly? I don't just mean new technologies and so forth, advanced mathematical techniques maybe . . . I mean *ideas*. Remember, even human history shows that what may seem an "obvious" discovery to one culture may bypass another altogether, such as the discovery of writing, or the use of the wheel. As an example, think about this. With open mind and simple but systematic observations of the natural world, one of the ancient Greeks or Romans, Pliny for example, could easily have come upon the theory of natural selection – a simple but brilliant idea. Instead we had to wait two millennia for Darwin and Wallace. Who knows what progress we might have made if Pliny had got there first? And who knows what *other* obvious-in-hindsight notions we have missed?'

A representative of the Department of Defense grunted at that. 'Pliny? Who the hell was he? I always said you guys in DARPA are a waste of money. Listen, I'll tell you the only thing we'll learn from these screwed-up wiseacres, if we give them a chance. And that's how to *serve* them.'

A CIA chief responded, 'Well, that's not necessarily true, General. Not if we can control them. Imagine the defence applications of super-brains.'

'*If* we can control them.'

'Granted,' said CIA. 'And there are options to achieve that. They've already been chipped. I mean, implanted with trackers.'

Nelson stiffened; he hadn't known that, and he was sure the inmates hadn't known either.

DoD grinned. 'Ought to implant them with weaponized chips. That's the way to control them.'

CIA looked faintly disgusted. Then he went on, 'But we need to think of the wider picture. This is an issue for humanity, not just America. The Chinese are going to have their own "Next" too. The Russians. The rising nations of the equatorial belt on the Datum. We need *our* Next to counter *theirs.*'

The DoD laughed out loud. 'So what are we getting into, an arms race of the Brainiacs?'

The Science Adviser intervened. 'We seem to persist in describing these young people as a danger, a threat. Is that necessarily so?'

That generated a buzz of conversation. On the anti-Next side, delegates pointed to their private, non-decipherable languages. The fact that they had already been making money by producing investment-analysis algorithms that defied existing market safeguards. The fact that *they looked like us*, that they were an insidious, insider threat, cuckoos in the nest, like an alien invasion from within our own DNA . . .

And then there was the inarguable fact that a handful of young, unarmed, untrained Next had been able to bamboozle experienced Navy officers, capture a twain, and slaughter many of its crew and abandon the survivors. That incident proved that these Next could be a real and present danger, the military officers argued. There had even been some incidents on Hawaii, attempts at manipulation by the imprisoned children here. Some of the marine guards had had to be rotated; others were in counselling. 'Real Hannibal Lecter stuff,' said DoD.

Protests to counter that perception, such as the assertion from the Homelands Security representative that individuals later proven to have Next characteristics had quietly, unannounced, done heroic work in helping the post-Yellowstone rescue and recovery efforts, sounded feeble in comparison.

Nelson felt increasingly uncomfortable as he listened. 'I don't like the subtext to all this. What's been said beneath the words: *they aren't like us, and that's why we need to destroy them.* That's what they're really saying. My own background—'

'South African,' Roberta murmured. 'I know. You are sensitive to such undertones. And you are right to be. America, indeed mankind, has undergone revolutions of the spirit in the last generation, from the discovery of the Long Earth to Yellowstone – and now this. People retreat to default positions in such circumstances. Protect what they have.'

'"People." Dim-bulbs, you mean?'

She didn't respond to that. 'Within the administration itself there has been a kind of emotional coup. Everybody knows that it was the undercurrent of resentment against steppers cresting in the Humanity First movement that gave President Cowley his power base in the first place.'

'It seems to me Cowley himself has grown beyond that. He reaches for the centre ground. He wouldn't have got re-elected otherwise.'

'True. But behind the scenes, some of the President's closest aides and advisers from those days are still around. Perhaps the stain lingers even in the President's own soul. And that darkness has come to the fore, in this different context, under the pressure of events. There is a gathering mood to *do something*. To strike. It is nothing to do, really, with questions of national security, and still less the survival of the species. Such a policy is believed to accord with the perceived public mood. And perhaps it does. People need scapegoats. Ah, the conference may be coming to its conclusion . . .'

The President's Science Adviser summed up the position, the options, and the mood in the room. 'This place "Happy Landings". This is the source, you say?'

'The nest,' growled the CIA. 'The genetics confirms it.'

'One source,' said the FBI. 'No doubt there are others. But many genetic linkages trace back to Happy Landings. Right now it is a primary hub.'

'OK.' The Adviser turned to Davidson. 'And our relevant assets, Hiram? USLONGCOM is your domain.'

'The *Armstrong II* and *Cernan* are the best ships we got. They can be out there in days.'

The DoD grunted. 'Those ships carry some serious weaponry; we made sure of that before they went off into the dark. Admiral, just make sure your troll-lover Captain Kauffman is forced to ship out Ed Cutler too. Then we might have a serious card to play . . .'

Nelson said, 'What kind of weaponry? . . . Good Lord. They're actually considering a military response, aren't they?'

Roberta said evenly, 'The conclusion is as I anticipated. The game is nearly played out.'

'And what of the inmates here? What will be done with them? Nothing good, I imagine. Certainly they will never be freed.'

She turned to him, her face serious, intent. 'They are young, you know. For all their arrogance, their difficulty. *I am like them* – I know you see it.'

He did see it now. He thought that she must need iron self-control to keep up camouflaging behaviour in the high-intensity hothouse of Madison West 5, the new DC.

'I was once enough like them to understand. How it is to be *different*, how it is to be surrounded by blank faces and empty heads, to *know* there is nobody you can talk to, no parent, no teacher, no way you can empty your head of the insights rattling inside it. And to be frightened, almost all the time.'

'Frightened?'

'The Next can read people, remember, with an acuity you dim-bulbs lack. They look at an adult and it is as if they are reading that person's mind. They can clearly see the indifference, the malevolence, the lust, the calculation, behind the smile. All this is very visible even to the smallest, most helpless child. We see the world clearly. We have no illusions,' said Roberta bleakly. 'We are too intelligent to be comforted by any of your stories, your gods and heavens.'

Nelson considered. 'Once I saw Paul crying in the night. This was from the viewing walkway. I did not disturb him.'

'I used to cry at night too.'

He considered that. 'Do you call yourself Next, then?'

She smiled. 'Labels like that are for youngsters. As if we're comic superheroes. I don't fret about labels. And I am – different. I am less developed than some others here, but, having been raised in human society for most of my life – and with good teachers – I have decided my best place is here, out in the human world, serving as a sort of – interface.'

He smiled. 'One hell of an interface if you're in the White House itself.'

'I try. But my maternal grandmother was a Spencer too. I have deeper loyalties; it's my family being discussed here. I can find ways to get the inmates out of here.' She faced him. 'Will you help?'

'Of course I will help. It's why I came.'

'What must we do?'

Nelson thought of Lobsang, and Joshua Valienté – and what he knew of Joshua's friend Sally Linsay, and her facility with soft places . . . 'There are ways.'

The meeting had come to its conclusion. The delegates stood up, mingled, those in the same geographical locations shaking hands. Then, one by one, their hologram representations winked out of existence.

42

Nelson Azikiwe contacted Joshua, and Joshua contacted Sally, fresh back from the Long Mars via the Gap. And together they worked out a soft-place escape route from the Hawaii facility.

Joshua and Sally were smuggled into the base, and they started stepping out the Next inmates, one batch after another.

They tumbled through the soft places, hand in hand, Joshua and Sally and the final group of the Next.

Even to Joshua, king of the natural steppers, whenever he followed Sally Linsay through this strange network of linkages it always *felt* as if he was falling out of control down some kind of invisible shaft, and a cold one too, a deep chill that sucked the innermost heat out of his body: the toll exacted by the universe for this miraculous fast transit.

But it was fast, that was the point. Happy Landings was more than a million and a half steps from Datum Earth. From the breakout from Hawaii, following Sally and Joshua, passing from soft place to soft place, the party of refugee Next made it all the way to their destination in the equivalent of a dozen steps, no more.

And they emerged in the open air, in scrub country, no more than a mile from the centre of Happy Landings itself. Sally gave her charges a moment to get their breath, sit in the dirt, sip water from their flasks.

Joshua walked among them, checking their condition. They might be young geniuses but they were comparative stepping novices. As soon as they started recovering the youngsters began to gabble at each other in their own complex post-English rapid-fire speech. The most remarkable thing was how they would all talk at once, all of them speaking and listening at the same time. Joshua imagined megabytes of information and speculation passing between them through this crowded network of language.

Joshua was relieved this was the last party they'd had to liberate from the Pearl Harbor facility. It included Paul Spencer Wagoner himself, and his kid sister Judy, and others Joshua didn't know so well. It was done, at last.

Joshua walked a short distance away to get his own bearings, and, climbing a bluff, he looked down on Happy Landings. He saw the squat bulk of City Hall at the centre of the community, with a few smoke threads rising from overnight hearths into the morning air, and heard the gentle rush of the river. The air was unspoiled Washington-State fresh, heavy with the scent of forest.

Sally joined him. 'How's the headache?'

'Worse. I *can* sense them somehow, Sally. These young eggheads. A new kind of mind in the world. Or worlds.'

'Like First Person Singular.'

'Yeah. Not a faculty I welcome. Maybe it's useful sometimes.'

'I had a dose of it on Mars. Long story. So here we are, back in this creepy place.'

'Creepy? Sally, you brought me and Lobsang here in the first place.'

'Yes. But I always did feel there was something odd about Happy Landings. Even when I came here as a kid . . .'

She had once told Joshua how her natural-stepper family used to bring her here, and how she never felt she fitted in, and he'd read between the lines about how she had felt about that.

He nodded at the Next, engaged in their eerie super-speech. 'Well, if all this is the product of Happy Landings, your intuition was right. But even so – you've crossed three million Marses, and you think *this* is odd?'

She shrugged. 'The more you travel, the more you see commonalities. The whole time I was on the Long Mars we were hopping around on the flanks of big shield volcanoes—'

'Just like Hawaii, on Earth.'

'Right. Made me feel at home. By comparison with the company of the Next, anyhow. So what are they talking about now?'

Joshua glanced over. 'Hey, Paul. What's the hot topic?'

'The soft places,' Paul called back. 'What their existence tells us about the higher-order topology of the Long Earth . . .' Even as he spoke Paul was distracted by the ongoing chatter of the others, their eyes shining with enthusiasm. Reunited with his peers, he was unrecognizable from the sullen boy-man Nelson Azikiwe had described encountering in isolation in Pearl Harbor. 'Why, just the observations we've been able to make during that brief journey have enabled us to extrapolate swathes of the pan-dimensional structure. We don't have the language to describe it – we don't even have an agreed mathematical notation to record it . . .'

Sally said with a trace of unease, 'My father's been the world expert on Long Earth structure up to now, before *you* lot came along.'

'All things must pass, Sally,' Joshua said.

'Yeah.' She pointed to a trail. 'We'd best get them moving . . .'

The Next youngsters got to their feet.

Paul, with some reluctance, broke away from the rest and faced Sally. 'Umm, before we move on – we want to thank you, Ms Linsay. You saved us from that prison. Maybe you saved our lives, the way things were going in there.'

'Don't thank me,' Sally said in her usual cold fashion. Compared with these kids she showed her age, Joshua thought; in her late forties now. But, her body taut, her face lined and weathered, her hair greying, she was fitter than any of them, Joshua included. 'Thank whatever benevolent deity enabled me to find a soft place just stepwise of the military facility where they were holding you. Thank Joshua, if anybody. And thank Nelson, who saw a crime being committed, as I did when I was told about it. I put a stop to it, is all.'

Paul seemed interested. 'A crime in your judgement. Though not in the judgement of the US administration, obviously. Of the government, of the nation that defines the laws you live by.'

'Not that *I* live by necessarily.'

'So you have your own moral code? Do you believe there are universal moral values, or is it up to the individual to discover her own inner truths? Do you follow Kantian imperatives or—'

'Paul,' Joshua said earnestly, 'shut up. Sally meant to say, "You're welcome." There are times and places for a philosophical debate.'

Sally looked over to Happy Landings. 'Well, we've got bigger troubles than that.'

'What do you mean?'

'We brought these kids home. But things aren't right over *there*. Listen.'

Joshua stood with her. 'To what?'

'The trolls.'

'What trolls?'

'Exactly.'

And Joshua realized it now. Of all the human communities he'd ever encountered, Happy Landings was the most suffused with trolls, a place where trolls and humans lived side by side. As Paul had once told him, that was the true point of the community; that was the secret of how it worked. And wherever trolls were, they sang, all the time. This close in Joshua ought to be able to hear them in the town itself, and away from the centre, in the woods and clearings.

But the trolls had gone. It was an eerie echo of 2040, when in response to wider disturbances the trolls had withdrawn from all the human worlds . . .

'Trouble's coming,' he said. 'But what kind of trouble?'

Sally looked up at the sky. 'Maybe that kind.'

Two huge airships had materialized right over their heads, their heavy envelopes emblazoned with the Stars and Stripes, their plated undersides bristling with observation ports and weapons. Having arrived step-wise, the ships turned their vast prows towards Happy Landings. Joshua felt a warm downdraught of air from their turbines.

The Next youngsters gaped. Then they picked up their scant belongings and began to hurry towards the town, Paul and his sister Judy leading the way, hand in hand.

43

Twenty-four hours after the *Armstrong* and *Cernan* took up station over Happy Landings, Captain Maggie Kauffman summoned Ed Cutler, Captain of the *Cernan*, over to her sea cabin aboard the *Armstrong*. 'We need to discuss your note,' had been her only order.

Then, on second thoughts, she asked Joe Mackenzie to join them.

Before the officers arrived, Shi-mi rubbed up against her leg. 'Why Mac?'

'Because I feel I need a voice of sanity.'

'*I'm* a voice of sanity.'

'Yeah, right. Just keep out of the way.'

'Oh, I always keep out of *Mac's* way . . .'

Mac arrived first, in his green medical scrubs, straight from work, crumpled, informal. 'What a circus this all is,' he said as he threw himself into a seat. 'That idiot Cutler.'

'I agree, a circus. But it's what we have to deal with. Want a drink?'

Before he could reply, in walked Captain Edward Cutler, carrying a small briefcase. He was in full uniform, and insisted on standing to attention and saluting.

Mac grinned sourly. 'About that drink, Captain. You got any grain alcohol and rainwater? That's your poison, isn't it, Ed? Got to think about the purity of your bodily fluids.'

Cutler frowned. 'I have literally no idea what you're talking about, Doctor.'

Maggie glared at Mac. 'I do. Not the time for old movie jokes, Mac. At ease, for Christ's sake, Ed. Sit down. Just tell me again what you put in your note.' A handwritten memo delivered to Maggie personally by Cutler's XO, Adkins, evidently a trusted officer.

'Well, you read it, Captain—'

'You really have a tactical nuke aboard the *Cernan*?'

Mac gaped. 'What the hell are we talking about here?'

'We're talking about a nuclear weapon, Doctor. Which I didn't even know we carried until we got here. Which, it seems, we also carried all the way to Douglas Black's new Shangri-La and back again, entirely without my knowledge. Which Ed Cutler knew we had all along . . .'

'It has about the firepower of a Hiroshima.' Cutler pushed the briefcase across the desk to her; she didn't open it. 'The enabling mechanism is in the case, along with a copy of my orders. It's self-explanatory. You'll need one other officer to authorize its use, but that's your choice, doesn't have to be me.'

'Oh, it's nice to know I have some leeway.'

'I'm just the delivery system, if you will.' He was clearly glowing with self-righteousness, and the sheer pleasure of fulfilling his covert orders.

Mac said, 'Let me make sure I got this clear. We carried this damn bomb—'

'And a maintenance facility for it.'

'It gets better. All the way to Earth Quarter Billion and back?'

'Yes. It wasn't specifically loaded for this mission, to be brought to this place. To *Happy Landings*.' He said the silly name as if it were heretical. 'It was meant to provide you with an option, Captain. In case of a certain kind of threat.'

'What the hell kind of threat demands a nuke?' Mac growled.

'An existential threat. A threat to the whole human species. The mission planners had no clear idea what that might prove to be, Captain. They had no idea what was out there in the Long Earth in the first place – what threats we might encounter, what trouble we might stir up.'

Maggie said, 'I can imagine a lot of threats against which a nuke would be no use at all.'

'True. As I said, Captain, the intention of the orders was only to give you an option, and my task was to ensure that option was in place when you needed it.'

'In your judgement.'

'In my judgement, yes. The choice was always yours, however. To use it or not. Admiral Davidson was always clear that a twain Captain has a great deal of autonomy, being so far out of contact with the chain of command, was he not? So it is with this.'

He was right about that, of course. Before Step Day the armed forces, like everybody else, had got used to a wired-up world where you could speak to anybody, anywhere, with a delay of only fractions of a second. But when the great dispersal across the Long Earth had come, all that had broken down. Maggie in the remote High Meggers had been as out of touch with USLONGCOM as Captain Cook had been with the Admiralty in London, when he stopped at Hawaii. And old models of distributed command dating from the eighteenth or nineteenth centuries had had to be dusted off. Yes, Maggie had a vast amount of autonomy out in the field; she'd been trained to face decisions like these.

She said, 'But I never anticipated facing *this* situation, Ed, you and your damn nuke.'

Mac growled, 'And what's the overwhelming threat that requires us to consider this option? A bunch of smart-ass kids?'

'Who broke out of the high-grade military facility they were confined in, Doctor.' Cutler shook his head. 'Who took down a USN ship. Who are a new kind of being walking among us, of unknown capability. They are clearly a "potentially existential threat" within the meaning of my orders. And this place, Happy Landings, is some kind of locus, a source. A nest, if you like. We were sent here—'

Mac snapped, 'To study the place! To speak to the people! We've gondolas stuffed with ethnologists, anthropologists, geneticists, linguists, to achieve this. Those were our orders.'

'All that was just cover,' Cutler said dismissively.

'Hmm,' Maggie replied. 'And in your note you say that you've already implanted the nuke. Even before telling me about its existence.'

'Again, orders, Captain Kauffman.' He tapped the briefcase. 'Now all you have to do is make your decision. From this unit you can disable the weapon, we can retrieve it, take it away. Or—'

'OK, Ed, you've said your piece. Get out of here.'

He stood up, smug, smooth, neatly groomed. 'I've fulfilled my own orders. But if you need any more input from me—'

'I won't.'

When he'd gone at last, she reached under the desk. '*Now* I need that drink. Fetch the glasses, Mac. Christ. As if I didn't have enough to deal with concerning the fall-out from the mission.'

Mac just nodded sympathetically. Their long journey had left a loose end. On the way back they'd been able to retrieve the party Maggie had left to study the crab civilization of Earth West 17,297,031. But earlier, at the moon-Earth, West 247,830,855, there'd been no trace of the equivalent science party. Given the state of the ships' supplies it hadn't been possible to stay long to investigate, and Maggie was reluctant to strand anybody else, any search party, given the uncertainty about when if ever a new mission might be sent out here. So they'd come home, leaving behind supplies, beacons, messages – Stepper boxes – in case the missing crew found their way back to the rendezvous point. Maggie hated to lose people. On her return she'd thrown herself into the work of contacting the families, before

Davidson had called her in for a fresh assignment, and sent her out once more – to *this*.

And now, here she was sitting on a nuclear weapon like an unhappy hen.

'That guy Cutler,' she grumbled as she poured Mac his whisky. 'Never known a guy who fit his role in life so well.'

Mac grunted. 'And wouldn't fit anywhere else. Whereas you are a bit more amorphous. Which is why he reports to you, Maggie, and not the other way around. Our senior commanders aren't entirely idiots, not all of them.'

'A ringing endorsement. But, you know, there was scuttlebutt about Cutler and his role in the mission even before we left the Datum in the first place. I remember Nathan Boss coming to me with below-decks rumours about Cutler having some kind of special assignment from Davidson.'

But Mac was dismissive. 'So what? Look, Ed Cutler doesn't matter any more. He's done his job. All that matters is how you use that switch on the desk before you.'

'I feel like smashing the thing, Mac. That's the truth. I'm being asked to consider, not just the fate of these few "Next", whatever the hell they are, but everybody else in this community too. This is a nuclear weapon we're talking about. There'll be collateral damage—'

'But you can't just push this choice away.'

'No, I can't. I need to take this seriously.'

'A career-defining moment?'

'More than that, Mac. Life-defining. Whatever I decide I'm going to have to live with it for the rest of my days.' She massaged her temples. 'One thing's for sure. Sitting in here staring into my own conscience won't be enough. I need to open this out. Take some advice.'

'Hold a hearing,' Mac said.

'Hmm?'

'Get a couple of advocates. One to argue each position, to nuke or not to nuke. They don't have to be proponents of the position they defend. Just logical about it.'

'That's not a bad idea.' She looked him in the eye. 'Guess what? You just volunteered.'

He sipped the single malt. 'I thought that might happen. It'll be a pleasure.'

'I'm afraid it won't be.'

'Come again?'

'I can't call on some swivel-eyed bigot to argue the case *for* a nuke. Ed Cutler, for instance? I need somebody sane. You, Mac.'

'Hold on a minute. You need me to argue *for* the nuking?'

'You just said the advocates don't have to be proponents of their cases, personally—'

'I'm a doctor, for Christ's sake. How can I possibly argue for mass slaughter?'

'By setting your conscience aside, and appealing to logic. Just as you said. You're a doctor but you're also a military man. Look at it this way, Mac. If the logic *you* come up with is compelling, then the argument will have been won.'

'You spoke about needing to live with this action for the rest of your life, one way or another. If I was to win the argument – I couldn't forgive myself. Not even a priest could pardon that.'

'I appreciate what this will cost you, Mac. Will you help me?'

'Is it an order?'

'Of course not.'

'The hell with it. The hell with you.' He drained his glass, and stood up. 'When?'

She considered. 'The nuke is concealed, but it won't stay that way. Twenty-four hours, Mac. Back here.'

'Christ, Christ.' He made for the door. 'Who will you get to argue the case against?'

'I don't know. I need to think about it.'

'Christ.' He slammed the door on the way out.

Maggie sat back, sighed, considered another whisky, decided against it.

Shi-mi slid out of wherever she'd been hiding and leapt on to the desk. She sniffed the briefcase, electronic eyes gleaming with suspicion. 'I did tell you that Cutler was aboard as a weapon, Captain,' she said.

'Yes, yes.'

'My intuition was good. But even I didn't imagine it would be quite so literally true as this.'

'OK, smartass. The question is, how we go forward from here.'

'You have a choice to make,' Shi-mi said. 'This idea of a hearing is a good one. But as Mac asked, who should argue to save the Next?'

'One of *them*, I guess.'

'No. It can't be one of the Next.'

'Why not?'

'Consider the logic,' Shi-mi said. 'The whole point of the case against them is that these Next are not human. They're a new species. That's precisely why they're a threat to humanity. As a consequence this is a *human* decision to make. It can't be made, even in part, by the Next themselves. You need a human to argue their case for survival, a case *based on the interests of mankind*, not the interests of the Next. Of course that advocate can gather evidence from whoever he wants.'

'Why do you say "he"? Who are you thinking of?'

'Joshua Valienté.'

'The super-stepper guy? You know him?'

'He's an old friend.'

'Why aren't I surprised? And he's here? How would you know that? . . . Ah, the hell with it. Of course you'd know. Can you find him, ask him to come in?'

'Leave it to me.' The cat jumped down from the desk.

44

As she prepared for the 'hearing' with Mac and Valienté, Maggie had time to wonder why it was her who happened to be in this particular hot seat in the first place.

Admiral Davidson must have been under intense pressure, from the White House on down, to have authorized the loading of covert weapons of mass destruction on to ships that were supposed to be Lewis-and-Clark explorer vessels in the first place, and then more so to mandate the deployment of a nuke against Happy Landings, a civilian settlement within the US Aegis. But Maggie had known Davidson a long time. And he'd proved in the Valhalla rebellion back in '40, for example, that his instincts were not to fire first. Maybe handing this poisoned chalice to

Maggie was Davidson's way of ensuring that it never got spilled.

But all that was irrelevant, Maggie thought now. However she had ended up with this responsibility, she was on the spot. And as had been pressed on her since the moment she got the command of the *Benjamin Franklin*, let alone the *Armstrong*, as a Navy twain Captain she had the autonomy to act as she saw fit, whatever the circumstances. Cutler was right. Hers was the choice to make, not Davidson's or anybody else's, no matter how she had got here.

Before she knew it, it was time.

Almost exactly twenty-four hours after that meeting with Mac and Ed Cutler, Joshua Valienté was shown into Maggie's sea cabin by Ensign Snowy, Maggie's beagle crewman. Mac was already here, in full uniform for once, with a tablet full of notes on the desk before him, looking as grumpy as hell. He stood when Joshua entered, and he acknowledged Snowy curtly.

Before he left, the beagle leaned forward and sniffed Joshua's face. Maggie knew by now that this was close to a beagle's way of shaking hands, toned down in some physical details for human society.

'Joss-shua. How is-ss you-hrr back?'

'Not even a scar.'

'And the hh-and?'

Joshua flexed his artificial fingers. 'Better than the original. No hard feelings.'

'Good to hav-vve ss-seen you again, Joss-shua.'

'You too, Krypto.'

After Snowy left, Joshua sat down, and Maggie ran through a quick round of introductions. An orderly pushed in a trolley laden with water, coffee, soft drinks. Maggie herself got up to pour the drinks, water for Mac and herself, but Joshua asked for coffee – that was an authentic detail, she'd never known a pioneer type turn down the chance of good coffee.

Joshua Valienté wore patched jeans, a practical-looking jacket over a denim shirt, and an Indiana Jones hat he hung on the back of his chair. He looked the part, a Long Earth pioneer, and Maggie wondered if he'd dressed down for the occasion to make the point. Probably not, she tentatively decided. This was the authentic Valienté. But he looked as uncomfortable as did Mac, in his own way.

Once they were set with their drinks, Maggie locked the door.

'OK, gentlemen, this is it. Bathroom is through the other door, over there. Otherwise nobody comes in or out until we've – sorry, *I've* – made a decision here. It's entirely up to us. We are being recorded, however, for the court-martial that's probably coming my way later.'

Joshua looked surprised.

'That's life in the military, Mr Valienté.'

'Call me Joshua.'

'Thank you. But you two are both in the clear. I took some advice on that, my XO did some legal research, and I logged his recommendations and my interpretation. You're simply advisers. Including you, Mac.'

Mac shrugged. 'I'm probably going to quit the service anyhow after this.'

'Sure you are. And you, Joshua – thank you for coming in. I appreciate you putting yourself through this; you didn't have to. By the way, I didn't know you'd met Snowy.'

'He saved my life once. Or at least spared it. I guess that counts as the basis of a friendship.' Joshua grinned. 'Cats and dogs, eh, Captain?'

She glanced at Mac, who was paying no attention. Maggie concluded Joshua knew nothing of the role Mac had played in the subsequent calamity to befall the beagles. 'You said it, Joshua.'

'Look, Captain, I don't fully understand why you chose me for this – what do we call it, a hearing?'

'You could call it that,' Mac growled. 'A group of people are on trial for their lives. Or a whole new species faces extermination. Depending on how you look at it.'

'So why me?'

Maggie thought back over what Shi-mi had advised her, what she knew of this man Valienté. 'Because you too have been an outsider, back in the early days of stepping. You were *different*. You know how that feels. And because, despite all that, you have proved yourself to be a decent human being, with sound instincts. Your public record shows it. Also, records from Pearl show that you befriended one of these Next.' She glanced at her own notes. 'Paul Spencer Wagoner? So you're in a position to understand the issues.'

'I'm not sure I feel like any kind of human being, sitting here in judgement like this.'

Mac grinned, a cold, humourless expression. 'You want to switch seats?'

Maggie said, 'The decision will be mine, not yours, Mac. The responsibility is all mine.'

Joshua nodded, though still clearly unhappy. 'I didn't do any research. I wouldn't know where to start, what to look up.'

'That's fine,' Maggie said. 'Go with your heart. Well. Here we are. I have no fixed agenda in mind, no format, no time limit. Mac, you want to go first?'

'Sure.' Mac glanced at his tablet one last time, then spread his hands on the table. 'To begin with, let's be clear what we're talking about here. We'd be taking a Hiroshima-scale nuclear weapon – more powerful than the one that took out Madison, by the way, Joshua, and I know you saw the consequences of that – and setting said nuke off, *without warning*, in the middle of this township. Of course it has to be without warning if we're to catch 'em all. I might note there will be the usual knock-on collateral consequences. Last weather forecast I saw for the region from the ship's meteorologists said the fallout plume would head south-east of here. Other communities *will* be harmed – many of them having had nothing to do with this business of the Next, as far as we know. That's the nature of the operation. But Happy Landings itself would be obliterated, along with every living creature in the area aside from the cockroaches – human, Next, troll, whatever.'

Maggie nodded. 'The military objective is to eliminate what's considered to be the source of this new phenomenon, the Next.'

'Correct,' Mac said. 'So now we agree what the cost of fulfilling that objective will be, let me give you the single most compelling reason why we should do this now. *Because we can.*

'We may not get another chance like this. We suspect there are other Next centres and we're busy tracking them down, but we're pretty confident from the genetics that this place has been the primary source so far. This surely won't kill all the Next, but it will be a massive blow, and would give us time to hunt down and eliminate the rest at our leisure. But if we hesitate—' He studied Maggie. 'Right now they're super-smart, but they're numerically few, and weak, physically, economically. They don't have any super-weapons or whatnot – in that regard they are no stronger than we are, for now. But that may not last.

'I've seen the linguistics results, the cognitive tests. Our laughable attempts to measure the IQs of these creatures. They are smarter than us. *Qualitatively.* As we are smarter than the chimps. Just as a chimp can't imagine the nature of the airplane flying over his tree top, or even less the global technological civilization of which it's a part, so we won't be able to understand, even imagine what the Next will do, say, or produce. Any more than a Neanderthal could have imagined that nuclear weapon down on the ground there in Happy Landings. We should strike now while we still can – while they can't stop us.'

Maggie said, 'I can imagine that kind of line being rehearsed in the war rooms. We should rise up and hit them the way the Native Americans should have hammered the Conquistadors when they got off their sailing ships.'

Mac smiled grimly. 'Or, a better analogy in this particular case, those Neanderthals I mentioned should have picked up their big ugly clubs and smashed in the flat faces of the first *Homo sapiens* who came wandering into Europe.'

Joshua said, 'Am I allowed to speak here?'

'Whenever you like,' Maggie said. 'No rules.'

'In both those cases you referred to, that kind of resistance would only have bought time against the invaders. More Europeans would have followed Columbus and Cortés and Pizarro.'

'True,' Mac said. 'But we can use that time. We ain't superhuman geniuses like these Next, but we ain't patsies either. We're not as weak as the Indians, or the Neanderthals. And we outnumber them hugely. With more time we can organize, keep hunting, run them down. Their DNA is distinctive, remember; you can't hide that. And there are billions of us, only a handful of them.' He looked uncomfortable. 'Also many of them were chipped, in detention in Hawaii. That would help.'

Maggie said, 'But, Mac, you're arguing for murder. Cold-blooded, calculated murder. Can you justify that?'

To his credit, Mac kept up his momentum. 'Maggie – it's *not murder*. Not if you buy the argument that this is a separate species, that these Next aren't human at all. It may be cruel if I shoot down a horse, but it isn't murder, because the horse isn't a member of my species. All our laws and customs reinforce that view. Throughout history – hell, throughout prehistory probably – we have put human interests before the interests of the animal. We killed the leopard that chased us across the African savannah, we wiped out the wolves that preyed on our children in the forests of Europe. We still inflict extinction if we need to. Viruses, bacteria—'

'The Next are in a different category from viruses,' Joshua said sharply. 'And we don't always eliminate, just because we can. We protected the trolls.' He glanced at Maggie. 'You were involved in that campaign, Captain. Hell, the example of you bringing trolls into your crew—'

Mac shook his head. 'The trolls are protected *as if* they are human, in US law anyhow. They aren't regarded as fully human, or even *equivalent* to human. Anyhow the practicalities are different. A troll has *never* been proved to harm a human save by accident, or under provocation of some kind. It's always been a human's fault. The trolls pose no threat. The Next, so it's feared, may one day pose not just a threat to individual humans, but an existential threat, a threat to us all, just as Cutler says. They may drive *us* to extinction altogether.'

Joshua said, 'That's an extreme position. Even if they were hostile to us, why should it go so far?'

'Fair question,' Mac said. 'But the genetic, linguistic, cognitive evidence all points to one thing – that this is indeed a different species, emerging in the midst of our worlds. And because of that there's going to be conflict between us – that's inevitable. A conflict that must, *must*, end in the elimination of one side or the other. And I'll tell you why.

'The Next aren't human. But the most damning argument I have against them is actually how *close* to human they are. They may be smarter than us, but they're the same physical shape, they eat the same food, they will need to live in the same climates. This is a Darwinian conflict, between two species competing for the same ecological niche. And Darwin himself knew what that meant.' He flipped over his tablet. 'I read all this stuff in med school, back in a different age . . . Never thought it would apply to *me*. Chapter 3, *On the Origin of Species*, 1859: "As species of the same genus have usually, though by no means invariably, some similarity in habits and constitution, and always in structure, the struggle will generally be more severe between species of the same genus, when they come into competition with each other, than between species of distinct genera."' He put down the tablet. 'Darwin knew. He could have predicted this. It won't be war. It won't be *civilized*. It will be much more primitive than that. It will be biological. It's a conflict we can't afford to lose, Maggie. Only one of us can survive – us or them – and if we lose, we lose everything. And the only way we can win is for you to act now.'

Joshua said with some heat, 'We aren't talking about biology here, but about conscious beings. Even if they could destroy us, there's not a shred of evidence that they ever *would*.'

'Actually there is,' Mac said.

'What evidence?'

'The very fact that *we're* willing to sit here debating whether to wipe out an evidently sentient, human-like species. We're setting a kind of precedent just by talking like this, don't you see? And if we can conceive of such an act, why not them in the future?'

'Ridiculous,' Joshua said. 'That's the kind of thinking that could have turned the Cold War hot and killed us all off decades before Step Day. Nuke the other guy *just in case* he ever gets the ability to nuke you.'

'Actually, no,' Maggie intervened. 'The thinking isn't as crude as that, Joshua. Over the last few decades mankind has got better at dealing with existential threats – which are usually low likelihood but with extreme consequences. We didn't see Yellowstone coming particularly well. But we are planning to push rogue asteroids away, for instance – well, we were before

Yellowstone anyhow. I'd say the basic philosophy is that you should act on such threats, ideally with public consent, investing resources at a level you somehow judge to be proportionate to the likelihood of the event and the severity of the outcome.'

'And in this case,' Mac said heavily, 'we're weighing the risk of *annihilation* by these Next – or indeed a range of lesser horrors, such as slavery at their hands – against the cost of a single nuclear weapon, and some kind of campaign of rooting-out and extermination to follow. That, and the deaths of an unknown number of innocents. Regular humans, I mean to say. Although I suppose the Next children are innocent too.' He looked at Maggie, and Joshua. 'I think that's all I have to say.'

For a while there was silence in the sea cabin. Then Maggie said, 'Shit, Mac. You put up a good fight. Joshua, please tell me he's wrong.'

Joshua looked at Mac. He said, 'Well, I can't tell you about Darwin. Never knew the guy. Or Columbus, or Cortés, or the Neanderthals. I don't have any great theories. All I can tell you is about the people I know.

'I guess the first Next I got to know properly, in retrospect, was a kid called Paul Spencer Wagoner. As you know, you have it in your files. I met him here, in fact, in Happy Landings. He was five years old. Now, all these years later, I've brought him back here. He's down there on the ground, sitting on your damn bomb. Nineteen years old . . .'

He spoke about what he'd seen of the growing-up of Paul Spencer Wagoner. The parents who grew uncomfortable in a turbulent Happy Landings. How the emotional stresses caused by the very nature of Next children had shattered the family. How a lost little boy had found sanctuary in the Home where Joshua himself had been brought up. How the traumatized young man he'd become, as institutionalized as any life prisoner, was yet full of life, leadership, compassion when among his own.

'These are our children,' he said sternly. 'All of ours. So they're brighter than us. So what? Would a father kill his son just because the son is smarter than him? You can't eliminate difference, just because you fear it.' He glanced at Maggie. 'I can tell that *you* wouldn't, Captain. Not with trolls and a beagle in your crew, for God's sake.'

Not to mention a robot cat, Maggie thought.

'I mean – tell me *why* you brought these non-humans on board.'

Maggie thought about that. 'To make a point against the small-minded and the naysayers, I guess. And . . .' She remembered what Snowy had said as they had puzzled over a nation of sentient crab-like creatures, a